A Savage Distance

Other Books
by
Thom Reese

The Demon Baqash
The Empty
Dead Man's Fire
Chasing Kelvin
13 Bodies: Seven Tales of Murder & Madness

A Savage Distance

Thom Reese

SPEAKING VOLUMES, LLC
NAPLES, FLORIDA
2015

ISBN 978-1-62815-271-5

For my amazing wife Kathy

Acknowledgements

This is my sixth book. One would think that the process would become easier with each endeavor. Perhaps. Perhaps not. Each tale brings with it its own set of challenges. As always, I must lean on the support of others to give me feedback, to keep me on course, and to allow me to benefit from their knowledge and experience. My wife, Kathy, is my greatest source of advice, encouragement, and, yes, criticism. She tells it like it is. Thank, you, sweetie. I could not do it without you. My girls, Trista, Amy, and Brittany, inspire me daily. You three will never know the remarkable impact you have in my life. A special thank you to my most persistent reader and dear friend, Jeff Granstrom, for his ever useful feedback. Also, great appreciation to Kurt Mueller at Speaking Volumes for his faith in my work and devotion to publishing. Also to Erica at Speaking Volumes for her work on this manuscript. Thanks to Travis Szynski, Sherman and Linda Ray, Linda at Dead Poets, Kym Low, Alissa Rowley (self-proclaimed number one fan), Ken Chapman, Mike Chapman, Topher Barnes, Kirk Bechtold, and all of the others who have stood beside me through the process.

Chapter One

The Republic of Botma Africa
Three Months Ago

Nanji ran as fast as his nine year-old legs would allow. He'd been in the fields, hunting. Well, playing really. But if he'd come across a meerkat or a hare, he would have caught it and brought it home for the family to eat. But it was dusk now. His father might become angry if he arrived much later. But how was Nanji to know the sun would flee with such haste leaving the quarter moon only just peeking over the jutting mountains to the east?

The tall grass slapped against him as he raced toward his village, his feet constantly adjusting to holes and mounds, his raised arms deflecting grass and branches from his face and eyes. Despite the fact that he might receive a reprimand, he felt good, alive, vital. This was his place. His alone place. No parents telling him what to do. No Diallo to pester and cry. He loved his little brother, he supposed, but sometimes he wished the three year-old had been born to another family. He would break Nanji's few precious possessions and then Nanji would get into trouble for not watching closely enough or for getting angry and hitting his younger sibling. Diallo was trouble. Always trouble. Nanji hated being the big brother. It wasn't fair that Diallo could get away with everything and Nanji nothing. Why did his parents even have him if it was Diallo they loved so dearly? Certainly, they wouldn't notice if Nanji never bothered to come home at all. They might even be pleased. More time to spend with their beloved Diallo. More food to feed the plump little ball of blubber.

Nanji came to the crest of a small grassy rise and for the first time noticed the pulsing red glow about his village. The sky was hazy, the image of the rising moon wavering as if submerged in crimson water, the view of the scattered huts and hovels fuzzy and unclear. The vision was nearly dreamlike, or perhaps, nightmare-like. Brutal. Unreal. Deadly.

He tasted smoke as he brushed ash from his eyes.

Pausing at the crest, he felt his stomach drop to his knees as the reality of the scene finally collided with his young mind. The village. There was a fire in the village!

Mother.

Father.

Diallo!

Nanji had thought he'd already been running as fast as he could, but now his legs were like those of a gazelle. Racing down the incline he moved faster and faster and then faster still. His feet, it seemed, were a blur, the tall grass, coarse, rough, sharp, smacking at his exposed skin, sometimes even producing tiny cuts with the blade-like edges, were as nonexistent. How was it that his village seemed to grow further distant instead of closer? He ran harder yet, nearly tripping on several occasions, twisting an ankle, pulling his calf. Still, he sprinted forward, leaning into his stride, his young lungs aching, his legs quivering at the effort. Even so, it was nearly fifteen minutes before he reached his home. Several structures were ablaze, many already burned to the ground. Women were screaming, men shouting and cursing as uniformed men, fierce and grim, marched from point to point, pulling people from their homes, barking orders, and offering strict and severe discipline on those showing even minimal resistance.

Nanji saw a twelve year-old girl grabbed and slapped by a thin and leering soldier, likely only two years her senior. With a wolfish laugh, the boy soldier snatched the front of her faded yellow top and yanked, ripping the fabric and exposing her tiny breasts. The girl screamed as Nanji turned away, embarrassed. He knew the girl—knew everyone in the village—her name was Ekua. He wanted to help her, even as he ran past, even as he ignored her screams and protests. He wanted to help her, but what could he do? He had no gun, not even a machete or a tiny blade. He was small, just a boy. Just a little boy. And so he ran, all the while envisioning how he'd kill that horrible soldier if only…

If only he was someone different. Someone bigger, older, braver.

Bursting into his home, Nanji discovered three such men as he'd witnessed about the village. Soldiers, young, but hard, two of them no more than a few years older than Nanji himself. The scene nearly made him scream. His mother, her clothing ripped, her nose bloodied, kneeled on the floor weeping. His father, a village elder, was in the center of the room, also on his knees, hands tied behind his back, his face bruised and swollen. And Diallo…

Where was Diallo?

"Nanji. Run!" barked his father.

"Where's Diallo?" cried Nanji, somehow oblivious to peril.

"Run!" screamed his father a second time and, for this, earning a smack across the back of the head.

Nanji heard a whimper from across the room, just beyond an overturned table. It was Diallo, huddled behind the rough planked table, tears rolling down his cheeks, eyes wide and pleading. Nanji wanted to go to him, to comfort him, to hold him, protect him, but a uniformed limb shot out, catching his arm just below his left pit. Nanji pulled and kicked and was just about to bite the man's hand when a gun barrel was pressed against his temple. His mother let out a cry and one of the men held her firm, preventing her from aiding Nanji.

"Ah!" smiled the man standing behind father. "So there is another one. A son. Strong. Healthy. You must have forgotten."

Father appeared as if in great pain, and despite his young age, Nanji recognized that the pain was not of the physical kind.

"Little man, it seems you have a choice," said the man subduing his father. He was large. Much larger than any man of the village. Both tall and round, with great muscular arms and legs that surely must have been tree trunks in a former life. "Would you like for your brother to live?" he asked, his large ivory teeth nearly shimmering against his midnight skin, his grin dripping with evil mirth. "Oh, little man. It is not a trick question. Do you want your brother to live?"

Nanji looked first to his mother and then to his father. Of course he wanted Diallo to live, but was he supposed to admit this or was he supposed to play the part of a man and act as if none of this mattered? Could he do that? Could he pretend? Even as he asked this silent question of himself, he knew that he could not. He so wanted to be brave, but the tears streaming across his cheeks made any attempt laughable.

Meeting his father's gaze, his eyes were wide and questioning. He had no voice, not even a squeak. It was as if every emotion he had ever known had rushed to his lips, causing an immovable dam which stemmed the flood of words and cries that so desperately sought to flee.

"Nanji," said his father through torn and bleeding lips. "Do whatever they say. Do not cross them. No matter how horrible the demand."

There was a gasp, a whimper. It almost surprised Nanji when he realized the sound had come from him.

"Nanji," said his father. "Be brave. You are the strong one. You must rise even as I fall."

It was in this moment that Nanji realized that he would no longer be with his parents, that perhaps he would never see either of them again. And with this realization came the burden of responsibility. His father was entrusting Diallo's care and safety to him.

To a little boy.

"Papa, I…"

"Do as they say, Nanji. Please, for all of our sakes."

Nanji nodded the tiniest of nods.

"Good. Good," smiled the big man. "My request is simple and so I will give you very little time to decide."

Nanji said nothing.

"You are very fortunate," said the smiling man. "You are to be offered a great opportunity. You are to become a soldier of the Republic."

Nanji's mind immediately went to the scene on the dusty village road, the young soldier, not even yet a man, ripping the defenseless girl's top, exposing her, lust in his evil eyes. "I don't want to become a soldier," said Nanji, his voice betraying him only slightly with a subtle quiver.

The man patted his glistening forehead with a cloth. "That is your choice, I suppose. But, my young friend, there are consequences to choices. Do you know what consequence means?"

Nanji did not answer.

"Allow me to explain," continued the soldier, now folding his cloth and slipping it into his front pocket. "If you refuse our offer, you, your parents, and your brother will all die. Four deaths. That is quite a few. And quite unnecessary."

The soldier smiled, his head already glistening again. And Nanji had the strange thought that this perspiration was not born of heat, or of fear or concern. This was the product of excitement, of anticipation. "Would you like for your entire family to perish this day?" asked the hulking demon man.

Nanji shook his head slowly right and then left, his fists clenched, his jaw rigid.

"Good. Then I can assume you accept my offer, that from this day forward you will be a soldier of the republic?"

Nanji's mother whimper-squealed, her tear-filled eyes pleading a silent cry. His father then met his gaze. "Whatever they ask, Nanji. It is the only way for you. The only way for Diallo."

It seemed perhaps father already knew what would be required and understood that it would be horrible and that Nanji would refuse to participate. Dozens of horrific scenarios danced across his mind and Nanji felt his innards twist and curl. It was all he could do to keep from wetting himself. What if they asked him to steal something for them, to rob one of his neighbors or to even attack someone he knew? What if they wanted him to embarrass a young girl as he'd seen the young soldier do outside? Could he do these terrible things? What if they asked him for village secrets? He didn't know anything important, not really important at least? He knew where his father hid their money. Would Father forgive him if he told them such a thing?

"Jaafar, bring the boy to me," said the demon man.

Nanji was pushed harshly from behind, a firm grip then clamping his shoulder as he and his young escort moved forward, positioning themselves behind Nanji's father as the larger man stepped to the side.

"I want you to look about the room," said the large man in a conspiratorial whisper. "I want you to understand your circumstance." He paused, and when Nanji remained silent, continued. "Your mother is to our left, a gun to her head. You stand behind your father, a gun to your head. I stand behind you, a gun in my hand. This gun I will give to you and with it you will kill first your father and then your mother."

Nanji released a strangled gasp. Diallo whimpered. His mother whispered frantic prayers.

"I am trusting you to do as instructed," continued the evil man. "You see, you are to become a soldier this day, and soldiers must display acts of loyalty. This is your test. Now, I'm sure you are thinking that you will use my gun to kill me and my companions. I assure you, these are dangerous thoughts. Remember the gun to your head. Remember the gun at your mother's head. Any move on your part will cause both guns to be fired immediately, after which your father as well as your crying pig of a sibling will be executed. The choice, my young friend, is yours. Four deaths or two. A glorious life as a soldier of the republic, or an ugly stain on an even uglier floor."

Perspiration dripped into Nanji's eyes, mixing with the flood of tears. His limbs shuddered. His bowels twisted. Still, Nanji could find no voice. It was his father who spoke next. "Nanji. Do what you must do. There is no disgrace. This is Azibo's way. It is not you that kill me and your mother, but these men and their leader, Azibo. Your role in this is to save your life and the life of your brother. You are not a killer but a savior. Our lives are already lost, but yours and Diallo's are forfeit only if you refuse these men."

"But, papa, I cannot."

"Your father speaks wisely, my young friend," said the large man. "A shame there is no loyalty within him. Perhaps then there could have been another outcome." There was a long pause. So much so that Nanji began to wonder if the man was going to speak at all. When finally he did, it was to change the boy's life forever onward. The handgun was extended in the large paw-like palm. "Take the weapon and accept your role as a loyal soldier of the republic. Refuse it and die. You have five seconds to choose."

Nanji's breath caught in his throat. He could not breathe. The gun, inches before him, black, shiny, hard. Could he do it? Could he kill these evil men before they killed him or his family?

"Four seconds."

How could he do it? He wasn't even sure that he knew how to use the weapon. What if he tried and failed? Then all would die—even little Diallo.

"Three seconds."

But the other way. The man's way. Killing his parents. How could he do that? He didn't think he could force his hand to grasp the weapon, order his finger to squeeze the trigger. His body would betray him regardless of the commands given by his brain.

"Two seconds."

Maybe he should just let the men kill him. Maybe that would be better than living his whole life with the memory of killing his mother, his father. Maybe it would be better to die.

But what about Diallo? He was too little to understand. He was too little to make such a choice for himself.

"One second. You must choose."

No. he couldn't do it. No matter what the consequences, he couldn't kill his own parents. He didn't know if he could kill anyone at all—ever—except perhaps these evil men. But not his parents. Never.

Detached, almost as if watching from a distance, he took the gun.

It was cold, hard, heavier than he'd anticipated. For an instant he thought of pointing it toward the large grinning man, but even at that moment felt the gun at his own head press ever harder against the back of his skull.

"Do not hesitate," said the large man. "Don't give yourself time to think."

"Do as he says, Nanji."

"But, Papa…"

"Now, Nanji. Don't make it worse for any of us."

Nanji moved his quivering hand, placing the barrel of the gun against the back of his father's head. He could barely keep the thing from flying free of his grip; his limb jerked and shuddered so. Somewhere in the background, he heard his mother scream and squeal.

"Do it," said the large man.

Nanji focused, at controlling his own muscles, at the simple task of squeezing the trigger, but not at the larger implication that in doing so he was killing his father. He breathed. Somehow he managed to breathe. Quick hurried breaths. Loud. Harsh.

He squeezed the trigger.

The gun did not respond.

"Ah!" chuckled the large man. "The safety is still set." As Nanji's mother wailed and his father let out a long gasp, the man reached over and released the safety. "Again," said the man. "No more waiting. This time we know you can do it."

But Nanji didn't know if he could do it. Not again. It had taken every bit of control he'd had to force himself to squeeze the trigger that one time. Could he do it again—and then again?

He heard Diallo wailing from across the room, louder even than his mother's frantic screams. The young boy had been strangely quiet throughout, nearly causing Nanji to forget that he was there. He'd wept, yes. Nanji had seen this. But these had been silent tears, the screams buried, waiting to surface some later time when survival was more assured. Strangely, it was Diallo's horrified cry that moved Nanji to act. His one and only mission was to save Diallo. There was nothing else he was capable of doing. Nothing else he could control. But Diallo, he could save.

And as this thought flitted across his mind, before he could assess the situation, before he could hesitate or weep or even speak, he pressed the gun to his father's head and squeezed the trigger.

This time the weapon fired with a blinding flash and a horrifying kick.

Even as his father's blood splattered his face and clothing, even as the near headless corpse tumbled forward onto the dirt floor, Nanji turned as would a robot, stiff, almost sightless, fully automated, and moved toward his screeching mother—"No, Nanji! No! Azibo worships a demon, Nanji! A demon!"—and, gun in hand, without hesitation, without apology or even a tear of sympathy, repeated the process.

The large man clapped and hooted as the soulless killer who had seconds before been a little boy, dropped the weapon, scooped up his frantic sibling, and walked silently out of the room, his face a steel mask, his eyes lifeless and cold.

Chapter Two

Las Vegas, NV
Two Months Ago

The girl was a hussy. They were all hussies. He knew this. How couldn't he? It surprised him that so many didn't understand this. Maybe it was that they didn't want to know. Maybe it was that they knew but didn't want others to know that they knew. Maybe they didn't want anyone to know that they liked—even longed for—the hussies.

This particular girl was truly beautiful. Skinny, but beautiful. At least to his way of thinking. Pale skin. Scattered freckles. Athletic legs. Straight hair, shoulder length, blond. He liked blonds. He liked lips too. Her lips were cute. Maybe it was that lips said something about the girl, communicating emotions: joy, fear, lust. Her clothing looked old, faded, even a little dirty. It was early January and still she wore shorts, exposing her legs, drawing stares from men. But he liked this one, liked the way she shifted as she walked, liked the way she cocked her head just ever so slightly, the way she brushed the hair from before her eyes with a quick whisk of her fingers.

She was moving away now. Frowning. Unhappy with the guy she'd been talking with. Much older than she, paunchy, sweaty. The man had seemed to be a stranger to her, likely someone in search of a hussy. She'd spoken harshly before turning away, likely not believing that she was the hussy he knew her to be. He liked her frown as he did most frowns. A hussy should never be too happy. They had no right.

Squeezing the small cloth bag he carried in his right hand, he waited several seconds and then stepped out from between two tan brick buildings. She hadn't seen him. Good. She shouldn't see him. Not yet at least. He glanced about, nearly a full circle. No one was paying attention to him. Why would they? It was silly to think that they might. He chewed, spit. He could be so stupid sometimes. Stupid! No one knew him here. No one knew the mystic power he held in his palm. No one knew of the sacred cleansing. He paced left and then right, nearly spinning as he pivoted. A short man, Hispanic, thin, middle aged, exited a storefront staring at him as if in confusion or disgust, as if wondering if he was watching someone danger-ous or deranged. Stupid! Why was he so nervous? Why did he spin and stare? He knew this drew attention. She was a hussy. Just a hussy. Nothing more. No need to fret over a hussy. Anything that might be done to her—anything he might do to her—was deserved. He knew this to be true. His priestess had told him so. His magic pouch confirmed it.

His frown slipped into a grin which then descended into a scowl.

If he knew it to be true, why then did it feel so wrong? He knew a wom-an such as this had forfeited her rights, that judgment and punishment were her due, that in choosing such a lifestyle she was now useful for one thing alone. This he had known since he'd had his first sexual encounter at age ten.

And so why did he hesitate?

The priestess—his one true lover—would be displeased if she saw his hands shake so, if she saw him pace this way and that or if the sweat glistening on his brow caught her eye.

The sweat he could explain. It was over seventy degrees. Yes, it was January, but this was the desert. It was warm—hot by some standards. Unseasonable even for this climate, but far from unheard of.

He smiled at the Hispanic, said, "*Hola*," and continued on his way. "*Ho-la*," he laughed. He'd used the man's own language. "*Hola!*" As if he cared what the man thought.

There she was. The hussy. It would be so easy to allow the girl to get away, to let her outpace him or to slip into one of the many ramshackle storefronts. That might be good—might be better.

No.

His priestess might become angry.

He stepped left and then right squeezing his little bag and mumbling a near silent charm.

The bag possessed the power.

The bag possessed the strength.

The girl was almost a quarter of a block ahead of him now. So pretty. So pretty. His priestess would like her. Oh, but would she? He desperately hoped she would approve. This one was so pretty. He was hot. It was warm. It wasn't supposed to be so warm in January. She would approve of this girl. Yes. Of course she would.

Moving the cloth bag from right palm to left and then right again, he quickened his pace. He couldn't let her get away, not too far. No. That would be stupid and he refused to be stupid. So pretty. He liked seeing her from behind, watching the way she walked, the way she swayed. He brought the bag to his lips, kissing it, holding it there for several seconds. She was closer now. She'd slowed down. Or maybe he'd sped up. He wasn't sure.

A young couple across the street glanced his way, the woman saying something to the man. Could they be speaking of him? It almost seemed he had heard her. "That one is dangerous," she'd said, or so he imagined. "Dangerous. Dangerous."

Brushing the mystical bag gently across his cheek, he grinned toward them and then turned. No one knew him here. No one knew. But just as no one knew him, he didn't know the city. People thought that Las Vegas was the Strip and only the Strip. The lights. The casinos. The glitz. But, he had learned that even this strange and foolish place was a city like every other city. And by simply walking two or three blocks east or west of the freeway he could find convenient stores, and bars, and fast food joints, and hussies. No. He didn't know the city. He didn't need to know the city. They were all the same. All of them.

And so were the hussies.

Turning back toward his target, he quickened his pace. She had paused briefly before a small thrift shop, but had moved on again. He would need to be closer than this. Much closer. She could climb into a car or join a friend, maybe she could walk into an office building or a restaurant where others knew her. She might walk into a clinic. His priestess had told him that hussies always needed to go to clinics. If she went to a clinic then she might slip to beyond his reach.

It would be stupid to allow that to happen. And he wasn't stupid.

The narrow city street was dirty. Streets were always dirty. Cigarette butts, smashed Big-Gulp cups, wrappers, newspapers, discarded beer bottles, people didn't care. No one cared. All cities were the same.

He squeezed his bag, brought it to his nose, inhaled the sweet aroma of its mingled contents.

He did not feel right about this but couldn't understand his concern.

His priestess would approve.

There was no reason for her to disapprove.

He was just behind the hussy now.

No one near. Not too near at least. Not too close. Across the street. A few doors forward, a few doors back. It was a commercial neighborhood, but not too busy. Old, worn down, not busy.

The bag shifted from one hand and then to the other.

His lips twisted up and then down.

This was right. Of course this was right.

So pretty.

Blond hair. He liked blond hair.

What did his priestess think of blond hair? Had she ever told him? He wasn't sure she'd ever mentioned it.

She turned. Near the end of the street. Into an alleyway?

No, no, no! She'd turned.

He quickened his step, clutching his bag.

Sweet aroma.

He turned where she had turned.

No.

Don't follow too closely. It was the priestess's voice, a faded memory of only a day past. *Don't appear nervous or anxious.*

Suspicious. He would seem suspicious.

Slow down. Appear casual, uninterested.

His lover, his priestess, had warned him never to appear obvious.

The hussy frowned, glancing over her shoulder.

She'd seen him.

Stupid, stupid, stupid! What was he thinking?

He chewed, spit, clutched his bag.

"Uh, hey!" he said. He didn't know what to say. How could he put the hussy at ease?

She continued forward.

"Hey! Lady! Did you drop this? Is this yours?" He held his precious bag high for her to see. "I... think there's money in it." Yes. Yes. That was good. Clever. His priestess would like that he was clever.

She stopped, turning hesitantly, that beautiful hussy frown frozen on her hussy lips.

"It was on the ground," he said, stepping forward, sweat glistening on his forehead. "I thought maybe... You know, I thought maybe it was yours." He scratched an itch at the back of his head, glancing down to his feet and then again at the girl.

"Who are you? Why are you following me?" She was tense, ready to turn and flee. She'd seen him, known he'd been following her. That was why she'd turned into the alleyway. It had been an attempt to ditch him.

"I'm just a guy. Don't worry. I wasn't following. I... You're really pretty. I couldn't help looking at you, but I wasn't following. I was just going the same way is all." He offered an aw-shucks shrug and extended the bag. "So, is this yours or should I keep the money?"

She stared at the bag, her lips knotting into a twist. Seeing her better now, he realized that not only were her clothes dirty, but her hair had not been shampooed recently and there was dirt on her hands and legs. The woman was on the down and out. It would be hard for her to refuse money. He had been clever—very clever—to tell her that the bag contained money.

"Hey," he said. "If it's not yours, that's ok. I'll just keep it, I guess. I just thought it was yours."

He made as if to turn, although another part of him was terrified that she wouldn't fall for his ploy—and another part was terrified that she would.

He knew what he was doing. He knew the truth as he'd been taught but also knew the other, more conventional, truth of what he was doing. He wasn't stupid after all.

His hands shook. Just slightly. An almost imperceptible quiver.

He spit and then glanced at her before shrugging and taking a step away. "Oh well," he said as if resigned. "Have a good evening." This was good. This was good. He could tell his priestess that he had tried but that the hussy had become too suspicious; she hadn't allowed him to get near to her. He took a step. He wanted to leave, to rush away—so desperately to stay—to be anywhere else.

"Wait," she said, a tremble still tickling her voice. "It's mine."

Suppressing a tortured grin, he turned.

His priestess would be proud.

Chapter Three

Indiana
Present Day

Colonel Lucky Lindell found Marc Huntington at Curly Jake's Tavern, a local watering hole that featured non-stop televised sports, mindless conversation, and a pretty decent burger. "You look horrible, soldier," said Lindell as he seated himself on a squeaky and somewhat loose stool to Hunt's left at the bar.

Recognizing the deep baritone, Hunt didn't bother to turn, but kept his eyes focused on the Chicago Blackhawks game on the fifty-inch flat-screen above the bar. Chicago had just scored, but was still down by one point going into the final three minutes of play. "I'm not a soldier," said Hunt. "My condition is no longer your concern, Colonel."

"You're no longer my soldier, Hunt. Last I'd heard you were still my friend."

Hunt took a slow sip of his Sam Adams and angled his head in the direction of Lindell. The man was in civilian attire, though his military buzz cut and rigid bearing proclaimed his profession to all who would care to see. In truth, Hunt had been uncertain about their friendship. There was a built in social barrier between officers and enlisted men, add to this Hunt's ignoble exit from the military and relationships could be severed. But, to the extent that circumstances allowed, yes, the men were friends. "How did you find me?" asked Hunt.

"Your wife."

"How did she know where to find me?" He paused. "Not here in Ephesus, I mean. That's no secret. But, at the tavern. How did you know to come here?"

Lindell shrugged but offered no reply. Apparently Dana was keeping tabs on Hunt's comings and goings. Interesting.

"I'm guessing this isn't a social call," said Hunt. "You have a reason for finding me." Lindell did nothing without purpose. One didn't rise as high as he had in the military by being whimsical or frivolous. For a moment, Hunt wondered if perhaps this had something to with the charges placed against him seven years ago.

God. Had it been so long already?

"You're right," said Lindell. "This isn't entirely a social visit. Though, in truth, I have been concerned for you and thought this an appropriate opportunity to see you in the flesh."

Hunt stared at the television. Less than two minutes left to play. The Brewers had the puck in Hawks territory. He sipped his Sam Adams and swished it about his mouth before swallowing. "Concerned for me? And why would that be?"

"Well, let's start with the fact that you're drinking again."

"Yeah. And?"

"And after that fiasco in Iraq, you'd sworn never to touch another drop."

"No, Colonel. I did not swear to never touch another drop. I said, 'I'm done with this.' There's a difference."

Lindell nearly grunted his response. "I see you've developed a talent for rationalization."

Hunt met Lindell's gaze. "My drinking was never out of control, Colonel. I am not and never have been an alcoholic. I had binges—occasionally—but that's the extent of it. Trust me. I'm careful to a fault. I nurse one beer through an entire game. Not even enough to get a buzz. Back off."

Hunt neglected to mention his dependence on Oxycontin.

Lindell hesitated for only a moment. Hunt had never before addressed him with venom. And truthfully, he shouldn't have done so now. Lindell had been his commanding officer, but they'd also been friends. And Lindell had been very supportive after Iraq, had quite possibly kept Hunt out of the brig, maybe even short-circuited a Court Marshall. "My point, Hunt, was that considering what happened in Iraq…"

"No one really knows what happened in Iraq."

"Hunt, there were witnesses, testimony."

"Lies," said Hunt.

Lindell's gaze narrowed. His jaw set. "What makes you think there were lies?"

Hunt stared at the screen. Thirty seconds left to play. The Brewers were on a power play, the Hawks had pulled their goalie. The puck was at mid rink, both teams scrambling for control. "Forget it, Lucky. Just sour grapes. Now, what is it you need? Why fly all the way to the Midwest to track me down?"

Lindell angled his head. "Can we talk somewhere more private?"

The Hawks had the puck and were crossing into Brewers territory. Three seconds left. Two. A slap shot. Wide of the net. Game over. Hawks lose. Hunt sighed, upended his bottle for a final swig, and said, "Yeah, Luck. I could use some air."

***

Ephesus Indiana, population 30,000 plus and climbing, had a quirky, urban meets rural flavor to it. There were small cornfields on the southern outskirts of town, bordered by a rich wooded area featuring stately oaks and maples, a meandering creek, and the occasional deer sighting; but the northernmost border was neglected and decaying, populated with bars, strip clubs, and other adult establishments. In this sector, there were gangs and drugs, high crime rates, and domestic violence. But that area was self-contained and off the radar for most of the otherwise healthy municipality. The heart of Ephesus was Andy Griffith's Mayberry meets contemporary suburbia. Modern day strip malls and national retail chains adjacent ma and pa bakeries and diners. Oil and water, yes, but with a warming hometown

18

vibe, a go-figure attitude, and an ample supply of smiles. Hunt liked the place, liked being back in his home state with people who, at least on the surface, were like him. He'd never liked Las Vegas, had only lived there because Dana enjoyed the vibe. But, now… Well, there had been no reason to stay.

Hunt and Lindell made their way up Market Street, passing a nameless thrift store, a soft serve ice cream place called Softy's—where they stopped briefly to partake—and a 1950's era movie theater turned pizza parlor. Hunt had left his vintage Volkswagen Thing parked at Curly Jake's and would retrieve it later. It was a nice night for a stroll, a little chilly, but nice.

"I was sorry to hear about your separation from Dana," said Lindell as he absently licked the rim of his chocolate cone. "Tough break."

"Yeah. Something like that," agreed Hunt. He was sipping from a butterscotch malt and wondering why Lindell was playing this fatherly role. The two had a good relationship, and Hunt had seen the colonel's softer side before, but it still made him antsy, like there was something he was missing. Lucky with an ice cream cone? Hunt wasn't even sure the guy ate at all much less dabbled in defibrillator beacons.

"I've had contact with her," said Lindell. "She still cares for you."

"How nice to know." Hunt paused, angling his head toward his former commanding officer. He'd had enough of the fluff, enough of the gee-wiz-so-sorry-you're-a-loser bit. "Listen, Luck, I get it. You're concerned, blah, blah, blah. Thank you very much for your happy thoughts. But that's not why you made the trip."

They made their way past Market Street Pet Shoppe where an elderly couple was talking to a blue and yellow parrot through the front plate glass window, the woman making cooing and clucking sounds. Lindell sighed. "There's a situation in Botma."

"Botma. Don't think I've heard of it."

"That's no surprise. It's a small African nation that's changed names three times in the last two decades. It's been annexed and released by two of its neighbors. It's currently a sovereign nation, but the land is hotly contested and subject to the whims of tribal leaders and dictators. It's small enough that most people not intimately familiar with the region are unaware of its existence."

"If it's so insignificant, why the concern?"

"I said small and volatile, not insignificant."

A slurp of butterscotch. The cup was nearly empty. "Okay. An even better question. Why are you bringing this to me? I'm no longer military."

Lindell tossed his half-eaten cone into a nearby trash receptacle. His cool gray eyes narrowed on Hunt. "The young son of Botma's leader, a warlord named Nishati Azibo, has been taken hostage by a rival and will be executed if Azibo doesn't cede control to the man."

Hunt slurped off the last of his malt, crushed the cup in his fist, and tossed it into a circular receptacle. He didn't need to be dragged into anything right now. He'd done only sporadic work in the past months, a couple of simple recovery jobs, no rescues. Mostly, he spent his time hiking and fishing, just letting his mind wander.

And then there was the Oxycontin.

He'd determined to take control, to reduce his dependency until he was free of the stuff. But...

He pulled a yo-yo from his pocket, a lime green Duncan he'd purchased just recently. Slipping the string onto his finger, he said. "I still don't see what any of this has to do with me."

"I'll get to that. But let me tell you more about the situation." He paused. Hunt remained silent, his attention focused on his yo-yo, and so Lindell continued. "If Azibo's power is ceded to the rival, things would be much worse for the impoverished people of Botma. What little means they have could be controlled by this man. Any outside aid would likely never reach the people for whom it was intended."

Hunt stared at Lindell. He was a vigorous man of just over fifty. Trim as a man twenty years his junior and twice as fit. His face was unlined and lean, almost youthful, but with the intensity of a food-deprived saber-toothed tiger. His short salt and pepper hair was the only real clue to his age. That and the eyes: clear, intelligent. Eyes that had seen much more than a younger man could have witnessed. "You're a good man, Luck. But you're not a bleeding heart. What's the real angle?"

Lindell contemplated Hunt for a moment, those clear gray eyes glinting with intensity. "Let's just say the interests of the United States would be better served if Azibo remained in power."

Hunt nodded. Of course that would be the answer. That would always be the answer. "I think you've missed a major point, Colonel."

"Really? And what might that be?" Lindell's voice had the twinge of an edge. He wasn't fond of being corrected.

"How about the safety of that kid? Sounds like the boy could end up dead if things go sideways."

Lindell grunted. "That would be unfortunate." He paused, and then added, "Of course, I'm certain a man of your caliber could get the boy to safety."

"Yeah. About that. I'm not going."

"Hunt, I know you're in a difficult place right now."

"Difficult place. Lucky, it doesn't matter what place I'm in, I'm no longer military. I'm out. Why are you bringing this to me? You've got finely honed units that can do a mission like this seamlessly. Why come to a screwed-up has-been?"

"Cut the pity, Sergeant. I came to you because I believe in you. My take is that you can do this thing without complications."

"I.e., you want complete deniability. Nothing that connects this to the U.S. Sorry, Luck, but I'm still red, white, and blue. It wouldn't take much digging to figure out that I'm ex Delta."

"Ex Delta that left under a cloud. Hunt, this is a politically troublesome scenario. You're right. We want deniability. And I think you can give us that. You're a known rescue and recovery specialist. You make your living off of reward money offered for the safe return of persons and property. Nishati Azibo has offered a generous reward for the safe return of the boy. Just do what you do the way you would normally do it and most of the suspicion should fall away."

Hunt nodded. "So, if I get caught, the Pentagon shrugs and says, "Hey, we didn't do anything. He's just a capitalist."

"That's the scenario, yes. And as to the reward, you keep that as your fee."

"How generous of you." Hunt stopped, turning to face Lindell. "I'm not interested."

"Hunt, I'm not at liberty to discuss the ramifications of a poor outcome to this, but they are severe. You'd be doing your country a great service."

"I'm not your guy, Luck. I'm damaged."

Lindell met his gaze. "I know about some of it, Hunt. And have a fairly good idea of the other. How many doctors are currently prescribing Oxycontin for you?" He raised an eyebrow, offering a knowing grin.

Damn! Was his entire life under a microscope? Dana kept tabs on him to the point of knowing his favorite watering hole. Lindell knew of his addiction. "Luck, if you know about that, then why send me? For God sake look at me. You said it yourself. I'm a wreck."

Lindell's eyes lost some of their intensity. His voice softened. "You are a wreck. That's part of the reason I'm here. You need purpose, Hunt. You need something to reignite your fire. This will give you something to concentrate on, something to occupy your mind. I've seen you under combat conditions. You're a strong man. I'm betting you still are and that all you need is the right focus to bring you back into yourself." He reached into his front right jacket pocket, withdrawing a memory stick and placing it in Hunt's hand. "These are the mission basics. You will be responsible for your own travel, lodgings, equipment, the works. Play this like you would any of your freelance rescue jobs."

Hunt studied the tiny blue memory stick. "Luck, I haven't agreed to do the job."

He smiled. "That's what Dana told me you'd say." He then turned and retreated in the direction from which they'd come.

Chapter Four

Las Vegas NV

Dana stared across the table at the young woman: early twenties, thin, straight blond hair reaching to just beyond her shoulders, with the haunted eyes of the nearly dead and a weak and weary grin that desperately desired to be a frown. She cradled a Styrofoam cup of hot cocoa in her slender hands, sipping it gingerly and then licking her lips with a nervous twitch. She avoided eye contact, instead studying the steaming brown liquid. "It's good," she said. "Thank you."

Still no eye contact.

"Cynthia," said Dana. "Drake told me we should speak. That perhaps we could help one another. But he didn't tell me what it was we were to speak about. He said I'd understand once we were face to face."

Drake Collier was the director of the Caring Hearts Homeless Shelter where Dana donated her time. He was a man of about sixty, black, with only a smattering of gray hairs still clinging to his rich chocolate scalp, a healthy waste line, and an infectious smile. He'd always been willing to accommodate Dana's sudden comings and goings as she and Hunt traversed the globe on rescue and recovery jobs. He'd also been happy to give Dana extra shifts on site to occupy her time—and her mind—as she worked through her personal issues of the past several months. Dana wondered why the man had been so keen to have her speak with this young woman, but trusted Collier, and was thus willing to deal with a bit of discovery.

"Cynthia, do you know why Pastor Drake thought we should speak?"

The young woman shrugged, sipped her chocolate, shifted in her seat. Her narrow fingers clutched the Styrofoam like spider legs clinging to a wall. "Kinda. I guess."

Dana waited several more seconds before asking, "Would you care to share?"

The girl shrugged again, her large blue eyes finally meeting Dana's gaze in a silent plea. Her lips twitched at the left corner.

"Cynthia, Pastor Drake asked me to see you for a reason. I'm certain it was a good reason because he's a good man. I trust his judgment."

The young woman exhaled in a derisive chuckle. "Yeah. You think so, huh?"

Dana offered a grin. "I do."

"Where are you from anyway? Australia or something?"

"London."

"How come you look—what is it—Japanese?"

"My mother is Vietnamese, my father British. You're avoiding my question."

Cynthia sipped her cocoa. Dana saw that her fingernails had penetrated the flimsy cup in three visible places. Tiny ribbons of brown liquid seeped stealthily over the girl's fingertips.

"Cynthia, please."

The girl nearly slammed the cup on the wooden tabletop, sloshing the contents onto the coarse worn surface and glaring at Dana. For her part, Dana remained silent, holding a steady gaze. Cynthia glanced up to the tiled ceiling and then to her right toward an age-yellowed print of Jesus as a shepherd. "I think he wants us to talk about me being raped. Okay? God, what am I doing here?"

Dana felt the blood drain from her face. She simultaneously wanted to flee the room and to simply curl into a ball with her hands clamped over her ears. She wanted to lash out and to retreat, to kill someone or allow herself to be killed and end this thing once and for all.

"Aren't you gonna say something? I mean, you forced it outta me. God, this is screwed up."

Dana swallowed, once, twice, attempting to find her voice, to hydrate her suddenly parched throat. "I too was raped," she said, attempting with all of her might to shoo the quiver from her voice.

Cynthia stood abruptly, her chair toppling and clattering on the vinyl floor. "What? Are you supposed to tell me that it's all okay, now? That we can work through this together?"

Dana waited before speaking, allowing the girl to pace off some of her anger. Though the area was small, no more than 15' X 15'. With furniture, the woman was confined to a space of perhaps twenty square feet. "I think nothing of the kind, Cynthia. I think, if anything, Drake is hoping that we can help one another."

Cynthia glared at Dana. Her large blue eyes narrowing. "How am I supposed to help you? God, lady, you got anything to drink?"

Dana offered the hint of a grin. "If you mean alcohol, no. Though I believe I could use one myself about now."

Cynthia continued to pace: right, left, forward, back. No more than three steps in each direction before encountering a barrier. "Damn it! Why do I even try? Why put two screwballs like us in a room together? Does this Drake think we'll just hug and be all better because now we know we're not the only ones to get raped?"

Dana stared at the spilled chocolate, at the damaged Styrofoam cup. "Nothing's going to be all better, Cynthia. Not ever. Drake's a man. A good man, I think. But a man. He'll never understand this. Some things simply never fix."

Cynthia continued to pace, her stringy blond hair spilling before her face as a string of profanities rolled from her lips. Her fists clenched, released, clenched again. Dana remained quiet, allowing the young woman to work off her adrenaline. Finally Cynthia plopped onto a worn leather love seat on the west wall of the room and stared toward the opposite wall, at the cluttered bulletin board filled with schedules, announcements, and job notices, ignoring Dana who was situated slightly right of her.

Leaning forward on her elbows, Dana said, "I considered suicide."

Cynthia bit her lower lip, still avoiding eye contact. She remained silent.

"Listen, Cynthia. Drake meant well by putting us together. But we're under no obligation. If you'd rather not talk, that's acceptable."

Cynthia sucked on her lower lips, shifted on the love seat, and then sprang to her feet. "Hell. I dunno. I mean, what are we supposed to talk about?"

"I would think we could talk about anything. Where are you from, Cynthia?"

"How do you know I'm from anywhere?"

Dana smiled. "No one is from Las Vegas. At least not many. We're all transplants."

Cynthia offered the creeping hint of a chuckle. "Yeah we are." The lanky woman crossed before Dana, paused, apparently considering whether to sit or stand, and then moved toward the wall, staring at the Jesus print. "Missouri. Saint Louis area."

"Ah. And what brought you to Las Vegas?"

"Boyfriend—ex-boyfriend. He had a job opportunity. It didn't work out." She slammed her palm against the wall only inches to the right of Jesus. "Damn it! Why are we talking about this?"

"Alright. What would you like to talk about?"

"Not rape. That's for damn sure."

"I'm fine with that."

Slamming the wall again, this time causing the print to tilt slightly askew, Cynthia turned. Her cheeks were moist; her bottom lip nearly swallowed. "He followed me."

"Who followed you, Cynthia?"

"The guy. The…" She turned, again facing the bulletin board.

"The rapist," offered Dana. Though her throat was tight, her stomach unsettled. She didn't want to broach the subject any more than did Cynthia. Perhaps less. She hadn't fully come to terms with her own rape. How was she supposed to help this woman accept hers? She was furious at Drake Collier. How dare he put her in this situation? How dare he put two rape victims together, neither of which was equipped to aid the other?

"Yeah, the rapist, lady. Who'd you think I meant?"

"I'm sorry," offered Dana. "Please, go on."

Cynthia stomped her foot three times in quick succession. It seemed the jarring might break the fragile-looking woman. "Go on? How do I do that? Huh?"

"Would you rather we stop here?"

Cynthia cursed.

Dana rose, assuming the woman would say no more. In truth, hoping she wouldn't. Dana was barely maintaining composure herself. She'd put so much of this behind her. Or, at least, she'd thought she had. Now, just looking at this broken woman, she wondered if she appeared the same to others: broken, damaged, all but dead.

"Where the hell are you going?" Cynthia's glare was accusatory.

Dana paused. "I was under the impression that you didn't want to discuss this."

"I don't."

Dana nodded, relieved. "Then I'll trouble you no further." Dana moved around the table and then paused, standing only two steps before the woman. "I was raped several months ago. I've made quite a bit of progress, but I'm far from healed. I have no deep all-knowing wisdom to offer other than that it helps to keep occupied... and keep breathing. Don't let this thing ruin you."

Cynthia wiped a tear from her cheek. "Go to hell."

Dana nodded and turned toward the door.

"He had a ritual," said Cynthia, her voice tiny, nearly strangled.

Dana's stomach tweaked. "Pardon?"

"I dunno. It was some crazy mystical deal."

Dana turned. "You said ritual?"

"Yeah. I mean, he had this crazy little bag he kept kissing. I think he was even praying to it. He took me to this… It was a room. Not real big. Not much bigger than this one. Longer, maybe not as wide. I dunno. There were all these weird like statues and candles, a couple of animal skulls. He mumbled some crazy stuff while he was…" She hesitated, shook her head, bit her lip. "While he was doing it. While he was… raping me. I dunno, it was like the whole thing was part of this ritual, like some religious rite or something. Damn weird."

Dana gazed at the woman, at her moist blue eyes, her nearly skeletal form, her quivering lips. "How long did he keep you?"

"I don't know. I think a couple of days. There were no widows in there. He got me high on something. I was pretty out of it most of the time."

Dana's stomach rumbled as she fought the urge to flee the room. She felt for this woman, had compassion for her. She also felt a growing hate for this man, this monster. What he'd done, how he'd done it. She had a feeling, an inkling, as yet indefinable. But it nettled at her, causing the tiny hairs at the base of her neck to crawl up her spine. Not knowing why, cursing herself internally, she faced the woman directly. "Cynthia, do you mind if I ask you some more questions?"

Chapter Five

Botma Africa

Hunt readjusted in his seat while massaging his right thigh. He was cramped, agitated, uncomfortable, suffering from Oxycontin withdrawal as he sat in one of the decade's-old fifteen-seat mini buses used as taxis in the capital city of Mirembe. The name meant peace, but Hunt doubted the city had ever known much tranquility. Right now he simply wanted to make it to his hotel. The temperature was eighty-three degrees Fahrenheit with the humidity attempting to match it at roughly eighty percent. The narrow road was bustling with nearly as many pedestrians darting about the street as with motorized vehicles. Poorly-maintained motorcycles wove through the crawling traffic, mini buses lined the way, their drivers seeking openings where none were to be found. The occasional horse-drawn cart meandered at the shoulder of the road.

Hunt took it all in and yet was simultaneously a world away.

Lucky had manipulated him. Hunt knew this and yet he seemed incapable of walking away. There was a child at the center of this. An innocent. A seven year-old pawn. Lucky knew that Hunt would be incapable of leaving the child at risk.

Lucky knew that Hunt had once killed a child.

Hunt really had no recollection of the event. A bomb blast had occurred nearly simultaneous to the act, obliterating half of his face and nearly all of his memories of the day. There were conflicting reports as to what had occurred, but the end result had been Hunt's exit from the military and a long painful road to recovery.

A road that included Oxycontin as a pain manager.

Sometimes Hunt felt the drug's true use was as a guilt manager.

Hunt opened the file on his lap, staring at the mission specifics. Tahir Azibo. Seven years old. Son of Nishati Azibo, current leader—warlord—of the Democratic Republic of Botma.

Warlord.

Or should the word be war-lady?

Nishati Azibo was a woman, the daughter of Badrani Azibo the former ruler of this tiny troubled land, who had reportedly died during a raid four years prior. Already, Nishati had developed a reputation as a ruthless dictator, enlisting soldiers, many of them still children, by force, often ordering them to kill their own parents as a sign of loyalty. Young girls were sold as sex slaves, dissidents maimed or killed publically.

Having survived a succession of military governments, the land was un-stable, the people poor and largely uneducated, with only forty-one percent adult literacy. The place was like a hot potato, occasionally gaining inde-pendence only to be annexed by a neighbor and then torn free again a few years later. The population hovered somewhere around three million, but no official census had been taken since the nineteen-seventies. AIDS was rampant, there was a high infant mortality rate, and much of the population was transient due to the uncertain political climate. Typhoid fever, hepatitis A, malaria, all played a part in the national landscape. Drug trafficking was a growing problem as was international money laundering due to poorly enforced financial regulations and constant border disputes.

And still these warlords fought over the land like it was some mythical prize.

Flipping a page, Hunt narrowed his gaze. Apparently, the prominent religion had been Catholicism until Nishati Azibo's rise, after which the national religion was declared as the worship of Anascoreth, a scorpion-like god worshiped by remote tribes in northern regions of the continent. Azibo, apparently, was considered a religious leader of sorts, though she bore no official title within the religion. Interesting. And disturbing. Religious leaders, particularly those of the fringe variety, could often be unmovable in conviction. But, Hunt wasn't considering a debate with the woman, but rather the return of her child. With luck, matters of belief wouldn't come into play.

Hunt now studied a photograph of Nishati Azibo. Forty-two years old, her skin was smooth and gleaming, a deep rich black. Her face was narrow, her jaw sharp. Her deep brown eyes, though large and round, seemed cool and hard. This woman was offering one million British pounds for the return of her son. The country's Gross Domestic Product for the year was under ten million U.S. Forty percent of the population was malnourished. How could she offer such a huge sum for the return of one person?

A mother's love he supposed. Of course, if she was truly a terrified mother, why not just give her opponent what he wanted and save her child?

Power. That was the reason. To some, power meant more than even one's own flesh and blood.

Hunt flipped a page, studying the report. English was their primary language. At least that was a plus, but there was a mix of many other tongues as well: Ganda, Luganda, Swahili, Arabic. Hunt spoke Arabic. Between that and English he'd likely get by.

Another page. More depressing statistics.

And another. Now he stared at the image of Zahir Ubora, the rival, the man that held Tahir hostage. He was young. Only twenty-seven according to the intelligence. A native of Uganda, he had emigrated to Botma as a teenager. Ubora had proven to be ruthless and unpredictable, gaining popularity through fiery rhetoric and bloody uprisings. This was the man Lucky Lindell sought to prevent from ascending to true power. In truth, Hunt doubted Ubora could be any worse than Nishati Azibo.

Hunt set the file aside and then picked up a picture of Tahir Azibo. The boy. The hostage. The pawn. He seemed a normal seven year-old: an infectious grin, large expressive eyes. His hair was cropped short, his skin a rich dark chocolate, and his form nearly, but not quite, paunchy.

Why did it have to be a kid?

This was an adult's game, something played on the world stage. Why involve a child?

And why involve Hunt?

Hunt closed the file, massaged his forehead, and then gazed through the bus window. He could see the central portion of the city in the distance with its taller buildings and cleaner façade, but currently he was inching through one of the many surrounding slums. Street vendors lined the road selling dubious-looking tomatoes and cabbages, woven baskets and peculiar idols, livestock and herbs. They chattered and shouted, often hefting their wares above their heads as they called to the passing bus. Potholes were epidemic, most filled with contaminated water and infested with mosquitoes. Hunt had had all of the appropriate inoculations, but still the sight disturbed him. The buildings were decades old, very few in decent repair. Shirtless children darted about the sidewalks and into the slow-moving traffic. Elderly men sat on the curbsides mumbling to themselves. Young men argued and threatened one another on street corners. Though he'd seen similar conditions before, the whole scene had a rather otherworldly flavor to it.

Mirembe offered no skyscrapers, but Hunt's hotel, The Adeola, offered ten stories. The center of this capital city attempted to project a contemporary and stable aura, though the veil was thin, and even at its most luxurious the streets were populated with unfortunates. Hunt entered the vast lobby of the hotel, gazing at the fine setting that so starkly contrasted the sights just beyond the doorway. The floor was of polished white marble. The surrounding walls were of a rich dark wood, the check-in counter black marble with gold trim. Silky golden wallpaper adorned the space behind the counter. All very elegant, all very excessive considering the state of this nation.

A bronze statue, a sphere ensnared in a scorpion's grasp, sat on a pedestal at the center of the room. Hunt could see that the scorpion's tail ended not in a barbed spear, but in a serpent's head, the yawning jaws wide, revealing long dagger-like fangs. The armor-like body glittered a rich rose-brown. The eyes of the scorpion were blank and menacing, while the serpent eyes seemed nearly to glow with some internal flame. Hunt assumed this was the scorpion god, Anascoreth, which Nishati Azibo worshipped and so forced the populace to worship in kind.

Hunt ate dinner in the hotel restaurant. Feeling somewhat daring, he ordered a local dish featuring goat meat, a leafy vegetable called nakati, pineapples, and banana beer. The food was tasty and the atmosphere pleasant enough. The beer was peculiar: thick, yellow/brown, both sweet and sour, and with a very heavy alcoholic flavor. Hunt held himself to one, ordering a Coca-Cola for his second round. Local flavor was fine, but a taste of home was always welcome.

He had an unsettled feeling, a not-quite-right sense that he was being watched. Gazing about the room, he saw nothing to confirm this. The restaurant was sparsely populated, all guests wearing appropriate eveningwear and fully engaged in conversations within their groups. No one sat alone gazing in Hunt's direction. There were no furtive glances or whispered orders. Hunt chided himself for being overly suspicious.

Anxiety was a common symptom of Oxycontin withdrawal. He knew this. It had been nearly four days since his last dosage and he was feeling it. Muscle aches, tearing, sweating, insomnia, and yes, unease. How had he ever allowed himself to become so dependent on a medication? And again he wondered if, in his current state, he was up to the task before him. Could he trust his own judgment or was he so prone to disquiet that he'd jump at every sound and attack every shadow?

***

The front desk manager called to Hunt as he made his way from the restaurant, through the lobby, and toward the elevator that would take him to his room. Hunt tried to ignore him, but the man was insistent. "Mr. Huntington! Mr. Huntington! A word please." He pronounced the name,

"Hoont-ing-tahn." With an irritated grunt, Hunt adjusted his direction, meeting the man at the welcome counter. Reading the man's name tag, Hunt asked, "What do you need, Enrique?"

The desk manager offered an eager smile. His mission was to please. "Did you see your wife, sir? She was looking for you?"

"My wife?"

Enrique nodded and beamed. "Yes, sir. She arrived while you were at dinner. I told her you were not in your room and so she said she'd go upstairs to freshen up and then meet you in the restaurant."

Hunt's heart leaped. Dana, here? That didn't make sense. Yes, he'd emailed her a notification that he was traveling to Botma on an operation— it had been a courtesy, a simple FYI. Had she had a change of heart? Or, with his luck, had she flown all this way just to serve him divorce papers? Or...

Was it really Dana?

Was this what he'd sensed earlier, that seeming paranoia? Had he really been under scrutiny after all?

Hunt returned the man's grin, leaning forward on the counter conspiratorially. "Thank you, Enrique. You're very helpful." *And far too nosy if you know when I am and am not in my room.* "Um... This may sound like an odd question, but did you ask her to show identification?"

"Of course, sir. Standard procedure." Enrique offered a pouty grin accompanied by a clipped tone. Apparently the man didn't appreciate the question.

Hunt could care less about the man's bruised ego and imagined slights. "And the name on her I.D.?"

Enrique glanced at his computer, tapping the keyboard with quick sharp stabs. "Here it is. I added her to your registration. Dana Bell Huntington. Is there a problem, sir?" The question seemed to be more of a challenge than a customer service opportunity.

Hunt raised his hands in mock surrender. "No, no. Not at all. Thank you for your help, Enrique. Thank you." Hunt turned away, marching toward the bank of elevators situated at the back of the lobby. Had Dana followed him to Botma or was this someone else, someone posing as Dana? Hunt was off his game. He knew this. But he wasn't some rooky kid. He knew the score. He'd yet to make waves, had yet to make his presence known. There was no reason for anyone to seek him out. But he couldn't assume that there were no secrets held back from him. Lucky was big on concealment. Hunt certainly didn't know all of the details involving this mission.

Hunt tried to maintain composure as he exited the elevator and approached his room. There was a short pang of panic. He was unarmed. He'd been at dinner, nothing more. He'd yet to initiate the operation. He'd as of yet made no enemies and so had left the room unprepared for confrontation.

He was off his game. He should have prepared for any contingency. Still, no one knew of him here. As of yet, he was a non-entity. A preemptive strike by Ubora's thugs seemed nonsensical and highly unlikely.

Hunt fiddled with the key to his room. His hand was shaking either from nervousness or Oxycontin withdrawal, he couldn't tell which. He shook his arm, loosening his muscles. Again, he inserted the key, this time with a minimum of jitters. Twisting the handle, he took a deep breath, steadied himself, and, opening the door, stepped into the room.

As anticipated, it was not Dana who greeted him.

Chapter Six

Las Vegas NV

Dana couldn't let it go. The woman, Cynthia Marshal. Her story. The particulars of the rape. It burrowed into her, kept her up at night, caused her to pace and shout with images of that disgusting animal rutting and grunting over her, his stale tobacco breath spilling over her face, his fist striking her again and again as his two accomplices held her to the bed, defenseless and broken. She cursed Drake Collier for thrusting her into this position. For causing her to relive her pain as she listened to the horrors forced upon another. She'd wanted desperately to walk away, to simply distance herself from the young woman, to point her in the right direction, recommend a competent counselor and be done with it. She was still dealing with the lingering effects of her own rape, what business did she have concerning herself with that of another? What right did Collier have to expect this of her?

It wasn't just Cynthia though. Dana felt for the woman, wept for her even. But this attack was more than a rape. It was peculiar, ritualized. And this had plagued Dana in a new and curious fashion. What Cynthia had described to her was more than an act of sex, or even of control and dominance. What she related was more of a sacrament, a religious rite. Cynthia had described a dark and musky room with strange icons, animal skins, incense, unfamiliar symbols and peculiar smells. The assailant had cradled a small cloth bag, kissing it and murmuring some sort of chant even as he'd violated the poor girl.

Nothing about this seemed random. Nothing here led Dana to believe this was a single occurrence. Obviously, this man connected the act of rape with some twisted spirituality. And religious experiences were seldom onetime events but rather lifetime devotions. If this was some insane act of worship then this man, this monster, would repeat the event again and again and again.

And he had. Dana was certain of it.

Perhaps for weeks, months, years.

Regardless, Dana had the sense that the rapist would continue, that in likelihood, in the months since Cynthia's rape—yes, months! How was it Drake was only bringing this to her now? —he'd already committed another or even multiple rapes. Other women were suffering as Cynthia suffered. As Dana had for all of these months. This man like all others of his kind, were cancerous to the core, bearing that diabolical seed that sought to rip a woman's very soul from her bosom and bleed it until it shriveled black and dry on the pavement.

Dana cursed. Again and then again. For multiple days. Weeping. Shouting. Walking the Las Vegas Strip for hour upon hour because she simply couldn't stand to be alone. And then she'd march into her office to stab at her computer: searching, seeking, discovering, before once again fleeing into the crowd of tourists for another bout of self-loathing.

Cynthia's tragedy was not her concern, not her responsibility.

Of course it wasn't. How could it be? She was responsible for her own recovery and nothing else. Her duty was to let this go, to move on, begin life anew.

Well, that was a load of codswallop.

She couldn't let it go. Not that easily. But she should. She really should. She wasn't prepared for this. The memory of her own rape was still too fresh.

Half a bleeding year. It was time to move on.

In the days since meeting with Cynthia Marshal, Dana had done research, scanning the internet for similar occurrences, looking for patterns, similarities, sometimes hacking into police department computers when she felt a news story was lacking important details. It had taken all of her will to move forward on this. Every cell in her body squealed in protest. Her rational mind screamed that she should flee, that she should turn away, wish Cynthia the best, and move on; that she should curse Drake Collier to bleeding hell for thrusting her into the midst of this thing. But, if this monster was repeating this act, if another woman and another and another had to suffer what Cynthia had...

What Dana had...

Well, then Dana couldn't simply walk away. She had no intention of pursuing the man. No. She shuddered at the thought of ever again being in the presence of a rapist. But, she'd found nothing to indicate that any law enforcement agency was on the trail of a serial rapist, and so she sought to uncover a pattern, to have something to hand over to the authorities, to give them some basic groundwork that would lead to capture and arrest.

"There's something I don't understand," said Detective Carlos Ruiz as he studied a green grape he'd snatched from a small plastic bowl at the corner of his desk. He was a slight Hispanic man who had far too much gray hair for his thirty some years. His grin was easy and disguised a quick wit and underlying no-nonsense attitude. Ruiz dressed like a Neiman Marcus model: pinstriped Gucci shirt and tie, Hugo Boss slacks and loafers, all immaculate, the clothing pressed to crisp perfection. "Let me get this straight. You suspect we have a serial perpetrator, a rapist."

"Rapist-murderer," said Dana. "It seems he's progressed." She stared at the man—this stranger—hoping against hope that he would believe her, that he would take this burden from her, that he would understand the vital importance and pursue the offered information. It had taken all of the courage she could muster to walk into the Metropolitan Police Department instead of simply forwarding her finding via anonymous email. But this man's victims deserved better than that. Though what Dana had to offer was truly open to speculation.

"Okay," said Ruiz. "Rapist-murderer. So, you've got the same man, raping and murdering in several states?" The man's tone was even, neither threatening nor ingratiating.

"I've identified three thus far, plus an additional woman that escaped before she could be slain."

Ruiz nodded, offering a warm smile. "Alright, four. And no law enforcement agencies have detected the pattern?"

"Apparently not. Until this point, I don't believe the authorities would have known to look for a pattern."

"But, you knew to look."

"I had a sense of it. Perhaps more of a fear. It simply felt like this was not a onetime occurrence."

Another nod. "Alright. Fair enough. And you believe he has a similar lair in all three locals?"

"I suspect this, yes. It would be part of the ritual."

"So, you don't know anything about the other lairs?"

Dana narrowed her eyes. A former British intelligence analyst, she understood the need to clarify specifics and to assess the credibility of a witness. Yet, the process was trying. She was worn weary with worry and insomnia and simply wanted to pass the information on, leave it in the hands of those equipped to deal with it, and forever walk away from the entire mess. "No," she said. "I have nothing on the other lairs. But, he obviously has one here in Las Vegas."

Ruiz slipped another grape between his lips. "Organic," he said. "Would you like some?"

"No thank you."

"I try to eat strictly organic. Preservatives, additives, chemicals, I've learned the body doesn't process them very well."

Dana nodded, but remained silent.

Ruiz smiled. "How do you know he has a lair in Las Vegas?"

"Cynthia Marshal, the rape victim, she described the room to me."

"And again, you know her how?"

"I volunteer at the Caring Hearts Homeless Shelter. The director, Drake Collier, thought the two of us should meet."

Ruiz offered a wry smirk and a muted chuckle. "He put you together because you're both rape victims. Nice guy. I'm sure you appreciated that."

Dana tensed. She hated being referred to as a victim. "Because we had both been raped, yes."

Ruiz slipped a grape into his mouth, sucking on it for several moments before chewing and swallowing. "But you're uncertain of his setup in the other locales? You don't actually know that he has other lairs?"

"I've not interviewed anyone and have yet to confirm their existences."

"But, you suspect he has these kill rooms at each point?"

Dana released a frustrated stream of air. Why the emphasis on the room? "If this is in fact a ritualized act, and if this type of setting is part of the ritual, it would make sense for him to have similar... accoutrements at each site."

"Accoutrements?"

"Pick your term. You know what I mean."

Ruiz angled his swivel chair slightly left, crossed his legs right over left, and leaned on one elbow, his chin cupped between the thumb and index fingers of his right hand. "You seem like a competent person, Dana. Judging from what you've told me of your history, you know the investigative process. Looking at your professional background as well as your lifestyle—high-rise condo on the strip—I have to ask, why donate time at the homeless shelter? It seems incongruous."

Dana angled her head. Perhaps she shouldn't have been so forthcoming concerning her background. But she'd felt her work in intelligence as well as her time spent as a rescue and recovery specialist would grant some credibility. "What does my volunteering at the shelter have to do with anything?"

He shrugged and smiled. "I'm a detective. Curiosity comes with the job. Besides, I find you intriguing."

Dana fiddled with her purse. "I suppose it has to do with my upbringing. My family was rather poor. Perhaps I identify with people in such a situation and want to give something back now that I'm successful." She paused, narrowing her eyes as she leaned toward the man. "Or maybe I want to rub my success in their grubby little faces." She threw up a hand in an exasperated gesture. "Do any of us really know why we do what we do? Should I feel guilty about financial security? Should I have to answer for my every decision? Why do you wear bleeding designer clothing while your coworkers consider Wal-Mart high fashion? Why no Spanish accent with a name like Carlos Ruiz?"

Ruiz laughed. It was genuine and warm. "Alright, alright. The question was out of bounds. I apologize already." He readjusted in his seat, squaring himself with her. "Listen, I need to know what you know. I need to see whatever evidence you might think you have. Otherwise we're just wasting time."

Dana nodded, reaching into her purse and withdrawing a manila file folder. She had to maintain composure. This man was simply doing his job. Even the act of nettling her was likely intended to tell him something of her credibility. In truth, he wasn't a bad sort. "I've identified attacks in Arizona, California, and Texas. The Arizona victim, Monica Granger, escaped. Her description of the act as well as the scene was very similar to that told to me by Cynthia Marshal." Dana opened the folder, sifted through some of the pages, and handed several sheets to Ruiz.

Selecting another grape, he mulled over the pages, his brow furrowing at certain points, his lips curled in concentration. "How did you come to be in possession of this interview?" he asked eventually. His tone wasn't accusatory, but definitely curious.

Dana's lips stretched into the hint of a grin. She'd accessed it by hacking into government computers, but she wasn't about to admit this to a law enforcement official. "I have a confidential source," she said with a bit of a saucy lilt. "Shall we leave it at that?"

Ruiz offered that wry smile again. The man was so unlike Hunt, so much more polished, more professional in demeanor, but at some points she saw subtle similarities. "A confidential source, huh? You're not a journalist and you're not a lawyer. I'm pretty sure you're not clergy. Legally, you have no claim to a confidential source. Unless, maybe, you're still somehow connected to MI-6 or some other intelligence agency."

Now the smile pried its way fully onto Dana's features. What a devious little devil he was. "And you have no need to pursue it further. Let's say we drop it."

He eyed her over the page and chuckled. Again, that hint of Hunt. "Fine, fine. And I was raised in Henderson, by the way. Just ten miles from here."

"Pardon?" Where had that come from?

"You mentioned that I don't speak with an accent. I was raised in Nevada. I never visited Mexico until I was twenty-six. A cruise."

Dana felt chastised like a dog caught rummaging through day-old rubbish, but refused to reveal this in expression or tone. Instead, she nodded, maintaining her grin. "I apologize. That was a boorish comment. I suppose I was becoming a bit agitated. I'm usually not quite so uncouth. Though, I can be a bit of a banshee when provoked."

His smile broadened. "I'm just playing with you. I get that all the time. Just like, I'm guessing, you get asked about the English accent with your Asian features."

Dana returned the smile. Was he flirting with her?

Or, my God, was she flirting with him!

"Yes," she said, now with a dash of unease. "That's pretty well a daily occurrence. All the more reason for me to avoid similar assumptions where others are concerned."

He shrugged, continuing to scan a page. His demeanor was relaxed, as if he was sitting at Starbucks sipping coffee with a coworker. "This interview," he said, holding up the sheet. "Monica Granger in Mesa Arizona. This woman claims the perpetrator held a small idol while assaulting her. Your girl, Cynthia, claims her assailant clung to a small cloth bag."

"There are differences, yes. Aren't there always?"

"I get that, but you're trying to build a case that this is the same man based on similarities."

"And I would still consider this a similarity." Dana leaned forward, placing her forearms on the desk. Her tone became terse, her visage intense. "Think of it in terms of a progression. This maggot began as a rapist. Now, it seems he's become not only a serial rapist, but a serial killer. Serial killers usually have a system, a formula, a way they go about things. That's often how they're identified and eventually caught. But, frequently their system evolves through the first few crimes. It takes some trials to figure out exactly how they want to go about it all. This bleeding piece of filth has made a religion out of rape and murder. At first he prayed to his bag. We have no way of knowing what was in it, but it obviously had a religious significance. Now, he's found his little idol to pray to. If you read further you'll see he's also added small caged animals to the setting. Different, yes. But these make sense in terms of a progression. Animal skins initially, live animals now."

Ruiz rocked casually in his chair. "What significance do you attribute to the animals as part of his progression?"

Dana allowed herself a breath, a moment to calm her nerves. "Animals have been used for sacrifice all throughout human history."

"But, there's nothing here to indicate these animals are to be used that way."

Dana rolled her eyes. "The bleeding plonker has religious objects scattered about the room. He prays to some imagined deity as he attacks these women. Based on what we know of the man and the setting for the crimes, I'd say it's a reasonable theory."

Ruiz set the pages on his desk. "But, that's all it is—a theory. Maybe no more than a guess. We don't know that this is the same man. The physical descriptions are similar but not exact. The rooms could not be the same as they are in different states. You have testimony from two living victims, but you've tied additional murders to the man. I need you to give me something more concrete if I'm to recommend an investigation."

Exhaling a bit more sharply than intended, Dana sifted through her folder, selecting two color 8" X 10" photographs, and laying them before Ruiz.

"What am I looking for?" he asked.

"You tell me."

His eyes narrowed as he leaned close to the photos. He scanned one, then the other, then the first again. Hunt would have picked up on Dana's find in seconds. What was taking this man—this professional—so long?

"I'm sorry," he said with an embarrassed grin. "I don't see it."

"The markings."

"Which markings? These women have scratches and cuts all over their bodies."

"Oh, bullocks." Dana stabbed her index finger onto one of the photographs, indicating what appeared to be two Xs connected with one another and a vertical line drawn between. "The neck. Under the right ear. The marking."

"This?"

"Yes. These photos are from two different victims, yet that particular mark is the same both in description as well as location."

Ruiz studied both images. "Similar. I'll give you that. I wouldn't say, the same."

"Of course it's not exactly the same. The women were probably shaking their heads and screaming their bleeding heads off while he was carving them up."

Ruiz nodded. "Did the Las Vegas woman, Cynthia Marshal, have a similar marking?"

"If she did, I didn't see it. I didn't meet her until months after her attack. Even if I'd known to look for it, the wound would have healed by then."

The detective sifted through the papers again, but he was thinking not viewing. After several moments he raised his eyes to meet Dana's gaze. "I'm not going to tell you that you have nothing here. But I'm not going to tell you that you do either. I see your logic and I won't say that I disagree. But if this is what you think it is, multiple rapes and homicides over at least three states, that's going to fall under the FBI's jurisdiction. And honestly, I just don't believe there's enough here to get them onboard."

Dana stared at him, a flush creeping along her neck and onto her cheeks. Why did she bother? Why did she bloody well think that she could impact a single damn thing? "Have you ever had the feeling that everything is for nothing? That we suffer and live and die and it doesn't mean a bloody thing?"

Ruiz contemplated her for a moment and then handed her the papers. "Yes. I agree. Every last minute of life is for nothing. But only if we allow the opportunities those minutes offer to escape untapped."

Dana met his gaze but remained silent.

"You hold opportunities in your hand, Mrs. Huntington. But right now, until you find something more solid, they're your opportunities, not mine."

Dana contemplated the papers she held. "I can't say you've been overly helpful."

"Really? I thought I'd just handed you a purpose."

Chapter Seven

Botma Africa

"Hello, Hunt."

"Corky? You're not Dana."

Hunt scanned the elegant suite for signs of another occupant. He'd been told by the front desk that his wife had arrived. He hadn't truly believed it, but deep within he'd apparently hoped the improbable—nearly impossible—might be true.

"She's not here, Hunt." Corky Meeks was standing toward the back of the living area, having just risen from a leather love seat. The entire room was bathed in a golden hue, a consequence of the fine silk wallpaper and shear draperies, both of which were of gold.

Hunt stood silent. It was silly, but he was truly disappointed.

Corky smiled. It was a rather subdued smile as were most of Corky's smiles, just a slight twist at the corner of near-puckered lips. "Lucky arranged for me to get a duplicate of your wife's passport with my photograph substituted for hers." Her tone was matter-of-fact. No apology in her manner, no further explanation offered.

Hunt closed the door behind him and twisted the deadbolt before moving through the narrow entrance area and into the room proper. He stared at Corky, his longtime friend and onetime lover. How many years had it been since they'd physically seen one another? Six, he supposed, nearly seven. They'd had phone contact on a couple of occasions, but that wasn't the same. Like Hunt, Corky was now in her mid-thirties. She wore it well: still slight of frame, not curvaceous in any way, but youthful in appearance. Her shoulder-length black hair was pulled tightly into a pony tail which was slipped through the back of a red baseball cap with Spider-Man webbing. She wore a loose-fitting Minnesota Vikings jersey with the image of the

Marvel Comics superhero, Thor, on the chest, tight-fitting blue jeans, and green flip-flops. All very quirky. Nothing to wow or entice. Typical Corky.

But, Hunt knew the true woman beneath the eclectic exterior. There was a fire in there. Maybe not a blaze, but a flame nonetheless. He liked Corky, had a great affection for her as a person but, in this moment, he was mostly confused. For several years during his time in Delta, the woman had been his best friend. For one very short period, they'd been lovers.

"Cork, I need some clarification. What's this about?"

They were still separated by nearly the entire space of the living area as Corky turned, moving to the right. Hunt had always found that she had a peculiar gate. It wasn't that it was masculine—not in the least. But it didn't have that feminine sway to it either. It was more of a quasi-march. All purpose, no anticipation. In truth, Hunt found her movements rather endearing, not sexy, just… Corky. "Lucky told me not to offer you alcohol, so I've asked that the fridge be stocked with soft drinks. They have Coke. Would you like one?"

"Yeah. Sure. Fine. Corky, you didn't answer my question."

She offered a fleeting glance at him from the kitchenette, her deep brown eyes obscured behind narrow tortoiseshell glasses. "Lucky thought you could use a back-up." She tossed ice cubes into a tumbler and then turned to retrieve a cola from the stainless steel refrigerator.

Hunt took another several steps forward. "What happened to no government involvement? Lucky wanted complete deniability in case this thing goes south."

"That's why I'm here as Mrs. Dana Huntington. The two of you work as a mercenary rescue team. If anyone digs into your background it will seem entirely natural that your wife assisted you." Corky poured Coca-Cola into the tumbler and extended it in Hunt's direction.

"Dana and I are separated."

"But, not divorced. The separation isn't even a legal separation. There's no record of it. This is the perfect cover."

"Dana has Asian features."

"And I'm African American. If someone digs deep enough to find actual photographs of your wife then I suppose I've fouled out, ejected from the game. I guess we'd better be careful."

Hunt had to smile. Corky was in business mode. Her speech unemotional, even tomboyish, her tone slightly more nasal than when she was relaxed. This was probably awkward for her considering their past. Hunt stepped closer, taking the drink. "Listen, Cork. It's not that I'm unhappy to see you. I'm just... Surprised, I guess."

Corky poured another glass of Coke and then met Hunt's gaze. Her eyes widened. She maintained enough poise not to say what she was thinking, but he knew she'd just gotten her first good look at his damaged face. She'd visited him in the hospital after the injuries, but he'd been heavily bandaged. Apparently she hadn't looked at him very closely when he'd entered the room. Maybe the minimal lighting had left shadows across his face; perhaps she'd been preoccupied with nervous anticipation.

Hunt stepped to within a couple of feet of her. The woman was usually the poster child for composure and detachment. "Corky, hey, it's okay. I get it. Me and Freddie Krueger hit the bars every Saturday night. He does a lot better with the ladies than I do."

Corky offered a derisive chortle. "It's actually not as bad as you think. Definitely not as bad as it could have been. Just unnecessary roughness. A ten yard penalty."

Hunt chuckled. Corky was a grab-bag of unusual little traits, one of which was her infatuation with sports officiating. He doubted she'd be able to name a single player but she could list every official to have been assigned to the Super Bowl for the past two decades and frequently peppered conversation with whimsical penalty calls as she determined they fit the conversation. She also restored vintage automobiles, flew kites, and played Dungeons and Dragons. Complicated woman.

"Unnecessary roughness? Maybe so, but I'm the one that was expelled from the game." Hunt paused and then added, "Now, are you going to tell me what you're doing here?"

Corky nodded, sipped at her Coke, and said, "Nishati Azibo's seven year-old son, Tahir, was kidnapped by Azibo's rival, Zahir Ubora."

"Nah, nah, nah. I know the mission, Cork. What I want to know is why you're really here."

"I told you that. Lucky sent me."

"Uh-huh. And?"

"And nothing. You and your Missus act as a team. I'm the ninth inning relief pitcher."

"Dana has field experience. Yours is strictly administrative."

"I'm not going in with you, Hunt. I'm your computerized eyes, ears— and much needed common sense. You're Luke Skywalker. I'm the force. Tap into me for guidance, but you're still the one left holding the light saber."

Hunt chuckled. "From relief pitcher to Jedi master in the space of a breath. You're a talented girl, Cork."

After a sip of cola, Corky said, "Should we go over the mission specifics?"

"Yeah," said Hunt with a dubious stare. "The mission. What's the latest?"

Turning, Corky marched toward the brushed leather loveseat and sat on the right cushion. Indicating that Hunt should sit beside her by patting the vacant space to her left, she opened a manila folder situated on a low oval coffee table before her. "How much do you know about Nishati Azibo?"

"I've read the briefing Lucky gave me. She's a warlord. She inherited the regime four years ago after the death of her father, Badrani Azibo."

Corky snorted. "The death of Badrani Azibo. Now, that's a technical foul. There's quite a lot of speculation that Nishati brought about the death of her father."

Hunt nodded, but remained silent. He had not seen this in Lucky's notes, but there had been incomplete data where the father's death was concerned. Knowing what little he did about Nishati, this seemed a possibility.

"The elder Azibo's reign began nearly two decades ago with the goal of overthrowing the rightful Botman government. His raids and the subsequent uprisings helped to destabilize the already fragile state. Twice during Badrani Azibo's drive for power Botma lost its sovereignty, becoming absorbed by neighboring states. But, it was Azibo's tenacity that heralded the revolution that once again set them free as a nation. As a revolutionary, he was ruthless, but as a statesman, he was surprisingly kind and level-headed."

"Yeah. Great. But, the father's no longer alive. The daughter, Nishati, ascended."

"Exactly. Her rule is vicious. Killing and maiming villagers. Abducting children. Thousands of people have been displaced under her rule. We have no death count. But it's in the thousands. Hunt, this is a country of only three million and she's having thousands executed because they might possibly side with the opposition."

"And this is the person we're trying to keep in power?"

Corky nodded. Her narrow, heart-shaped face expressionless as she studied the file before her. "That's our position, yes. Are you aware of the religious dimension?"

"I understand Azibo force fed her religion to the people when she took over. I don't know much else."

Corky nodded. "She's radical in every sense of the word, demanding all other religions be purged from the land, imprisoning those who defy her edicts, desecrating or burning churches. She worships the scorpion god, Anascoreth, but her brand takes a different form than that of other Anascoreth disciples."

"Yeah? How so?"

"There's rumor of human sacrifice. To my knowledge that's not an element of this faith as practiced for centuries. It's not done openly, and there's no verifiable proof or any evidence, but our intelligence suggests that she's performed this rite on at least two separate occasions. Apparently the goal is for her to acquire some sort of enhanced abilities."

"And the U.S. condones this?"

Corky ignored the question, instead saying, "There are rumors of mystical powers. And her opponent, Ubora, refers to her as a sorceress."

"Please don't tell me you buy into this nonsense. I'm not saying she hasn't performed some crazy sacrificial rite, I'm just saying that it is crazy. Azibo has no mystical powers."

Corky hesitated, obviously uncertain as to how to proceed.

"Spill it, Cork. What's the deal here?"

"Hunt, I… Well, you know me. I'm not saying she's stolen the One Ring from Frodo on the road to Mordor, but there are several reports of Azibo having strange control over others. I'm just not sure that…"

"Listen, Corky, you're a rational woman. Well, there's that Dungeons and Dragons thing, but you live in the real world. There are reports that should be believed and there are some that, well, you've got to read between the lines. The lady's a dictator. She's also obviously trying to project some greater-than-human image through all of this mystic nonsense. With her political power and with the threat of death to dissidents hovering in the near distance, she could probably coerce almost anyone in this country to do whatever crazy thing she asked. It might look to some like she's casting some mystic spell. She might even chant some crazy mumbo-jumbo, but I guarantee you there's nothing more to it than that."

Corky stared at Hunt for several moments before speaking. When she did, her voice was firm and even. "I'm a rational person, Hunt. But, don't mistake rational for closed-minded. The two are not one and the same. Sometimes the rational approach is to realize that perhaps there are things in this world that are beyond traditional thinking."

Hunt sighed, snorted, and then said, "I've read the file on Azibo's opponent, Ubora. Word is the guy's ruthless, but I don't see how he could be worse than Azibo. I don't understand why we're in play here."

Corky stared at the files, not meeting Hunt's gaze. Obviously, she was disgruntled at Hunt's quick dismissal of the topic of Azibo's otherworldly traits. So be it. Hunt didn't have time to dwell on nonsense and he found that he was somewhat angered at Corky's apparent willingness to buy into the idea. "There are things that you will never know concerning the U.S. position," she said. "Most of it, I don't know either. My clearance only goes so high."

Hunt studied her. The hair pulled back into a tight pony tail, the singular gaze, the rigid posture. Her skin was smooth and youthful, but in that moment she seemed burdened with the worries of the aged. "Cork, what aren't you telling me?"

She chuckled, but it was forced. "You've had enough dealings with Lucky to know better than to ask that question." There was no condemnation in her tone. Playfulness if anything. She was trying to keep it light. Not very successfully, but she was trying.

"Yeah, I have. And I've been away from the military long enough to know that I should be asking the question."

Corky angled toward him, her deep brown eyes narrow and clear. "Forget the politics, Hunt. They suck. Forget Lucky. Forget everything. The best thing for most of the Botmans would be for them to flee this miserable country and find a new home."

"Why don't they?"

"Some do. But, for many of them, this is their ancestral land. They have roots, family, pride. They want change."

"We're not offering change, Cork. We're trying to keep the same oppressive lunatic in power." He paused, pressing his fingertips into his temples. "No. That's wrong. We, as in you and me, we're trying to save a seven year-old child whose being held hostage. That's all. I'm not here to bolster the U.S. position in Botma or to undermine Azibo's opponent. So, if that's what you and Lucky have in mind, you'd better pull the plug on this thing now." Hunt rose, moving around the loveseat to stare through the glass patio door.

There was a prolonged pause and then an emptiness in the room. A void of silence. When finally Corky continued, she was hesitant, perhaps a bit frightened. Her casual exterior fissured. "Hunt, what's going on with you?"

Hunt was distracted, staring blankly through the window, his mind tumbling through a myriad of thoughts. "Huh? Missed that, Cork."

"You're unwell. You've got goose bumps, your eyes are dilated, you keep rubbing your arms and legs, you're fidgety. This isn't you, Hunt. What's going on?"

Hunt continued to stare at absolutely nothing. "What's wrong with me? Corky, that's on a need to know basis."

Chapter Eight

Mesa AZ

The young woman opened the apartment door only a crack, her brown eyes narrow, as she stared silently between door and frame. "Monica Granger?" asked Dana.

"Who are you?" asked the woman.

"My name's Dana Huntington," Dana offered a smile, hoping to be seen as warm and nonthreatening.

"What do you want?" The girl made no move toward opening the door further.

"I apologize, Miss Granger. I know you probably don't want to discuss this, but I'm here to ask you some questions concerning the rape."

Even through the narrow crack, Dana could sense the young woman tense.

"May I come in?" Dana asked once it was clear that the woman was not going to respond.

"And you are who again?"

"Dana Huntington. An investigator. I'm tracking the man who did this to you." She paused before adding. "I also have been raped."

Monica Granger stared at Dana through the slightly cracked door, her large eyes curious, possibly irritated. "You're the police?"

"No. I work privately. That means I don't have the restraints or encumbrances of those working in an official capacity."

There was a long pause. The woman was obviously sizing Dana up, determining if she was a threat.

"I'm not here to hurt you, Monica. If I was, I could have already done so. But, this monster is raping and killing women throughout the southwest. He must be stopped."

Monica hesitated for another moment and then opened the door, allowing Dana to enter.

She was a small woman, about five foot three inches, which isn't particularly tiny, but the girl was small of frame, very slender. As Hunt would say, no meat on her bones. Her dark brown hair was highlighted with blue strands and her long face was nearly bony yet expressive with large brown eyes and broad tapered lips. Cynthia Marshal, the Las Vegas rape victim, had also been quite thin. Perhaps the rapist was attracted to a particular body type. Or, more likely, he saw these women as frail and therefore unlikely to have the strength to put up much of a fight. For where Cynthia Marshal had been blond and fair, Monica Granger was dark-skinned, of indeterminate heritage, perhaps a mixture of something Middle Eastern with Hispanic or African American. Aside from slight frames, the two women looked nothing alike.

"I understand you're a college student," said Dana as she followed the woman into the tiny one bedroom apartment.

Monica nodded. "Arizona State University. I'm a sophomore."

Dana smiled as she studied the girl. Long dark hair spilling over a red Assassin's Creed T-shirt that featured an image identical to that of one of the many unframed posters littering the walls. "May I sit?" asked Dana, pointing at a rather threadbare couch situated at the eastern wall of the room.

"Sure."

Dana moved a stack of textbooks onto the next cushion over, placing them atop another textbook, and sat down. "What are you studying?"

The girl shrugged. "Right now, I'm still taking general courses. My dad wants me to major in business, but I don't know. Maybe something to help people. You know, like counseling or nursing. I need to decide soon otherwise I'm just wasting time."

Dana smiled and nodded. She could remember her own father trying to steer her toward more practical interests. "I'm sure you'll come to the right decision. My only advice is that you pick something you'll enjoy. You're the one who will spend your life in that field, not your father."

Monica nodded. She stood, studying Dana, her arms crossed before her chest.

"Why don't you sit down, Monica? You'll be more comfortable.

Again, she nodded, and then plopped into a beanbag chair to Dana's right. "I'm not afraid of him, you know?"

"I'm glad to hear that."

"I wish I could see him again. I think I could take him." The young woman's jaw was set, her eyes narrow. Dana had the feeling that under the right circumstances this tiny girl might just have the spunk to surprise and overtake a man. At the very least, she'd make it a quite unpleasant experience for the bloke. This attitude, this verve, might be the reason Monica was alive today where others had perished at this monster's hands.

Withdrawing an electronic notepad from her purse, Dana asked, "Would you please describe the assailant?"

Monica rolled her eyes as if annoyed. She'd certainly already done this for the police, probably assisted in an artist rendition of the man as well as spending an hour or two scanning mug shots. But Dana wanted to personally hear the description. She wanted the opportunity to probe, to ask questions that might jar something in the girl's memory, perhaps something she hadn't thought of in the immediate aftermath of the attack. She also wanted to ask some questions the police had not known to ask.

"I know you've already done this," said Dana. "Please bear with me."

Monica nodded. "He was, you know, scruffy. I don't think he'd shaved for a couple days. He kind of smelled. Not like he didn't shower ever, but like maybe he'd been working all day. That kind of thing. Sweaty not filthy."

Dana nodded. The girl was already better than most witnesses Dana had interviewed. The mention of the odor and offered analysis showed that, even in the midst of it all, she'd been thinking. She'd kept some sense of herself. Bright girl. "That's good, Monica. Please continue."

"Dirty blond hair. Not combed. It was... It looked like hat hair, you know. Like he'd been wearing a hat so the top was all smashed down. The rest kind of sticking out all over."

Dana entered these observations while nodding for Monica to continue.

"He was Caucasian. Still had a little bit of a tan. Just a little. His nose was, you know, just a nose. Nothing special. Just straight, I guess. His mouth didn't look like it knew how to smile." She paused, perhaps pondering this statement. "Does that make any sense? He just looked like his expression was set in kind of an all-the-time frown. He was skinny. And bouncy, you know? Like maybe he was on something. He couldn't stay still."

"How tall?"

"I don't know. Five ten? Not super tall."

"Did he have any tattoos, scars? Anything overtly distinguishable?"

She pondered this for a moment. "Not that I saw. The lighting wasn't very good. Everything is, you know, blurry in my head."

"Eye color?"

"Gray, I think. Or pale blue."

"Age?"

"Maybe a few years older than me. Not much."

"So, mid-twenties?"

Monica nodded.

Dana adjusted, leaning forward, her forearms resting on her thighs. "This is the difficult part, Monica. I need you to describe the rape. Where he took you, what he said, what he did. Anything you can remember about the room or location."

The young woman's eyes diverted to one of the posters on her wall, a full-sized one-sheet from the Scott Pilgrim Versus the World film. "I knew you'd ask that."

Meeting the girl's gaze Dana wondered for what seemed the hundredth time, why she was doing this. Why was she putting this young woman through the trauma associated with these memories, why was she involving herself, prolonging her own recovery by delving into the acts of this horrid rapist? She was being cruel. Both to herself and to Monica Granger. This wasn't her business, not her cross to carry. Clutching her notepad tightly, she said, "It's important, Monica. This man must be stopped or other women will be raped and murdered."

Monica offered a weak smile. "Yeah."

Dana remained silent, allowing Monica to form her thoughts. The young woman glanced to her right and picked up an issue of Gamer Magazine that had been situated on the dirty tan carpeting. Flipping through the periodical, she said, "He caught me off guard. I worked at Louie's on the weekends. I was walking home."

"Louie's?"

Monica flipped a page. "It's a diner just off the interstate. I was a waitress."

"Was?"

"I quit after the… you know."

"I understand," said Dana as she entered a note. "Did you recognize your assailant as a customer from the diner?"

"No. I mean, you know, I don't think so."

"Alright. So you were walking home. What time of day was this?" Dana already knew the answer to this from the police report but she wanted the girl to fully immerse herself in the event, to recall even the smallest detail.

Monica narrowed her eyes, paused, flipped a page. "Five thirty – AM. I worked midnights."

"Had the sun come up?"

"Not yet. Almost. You know, the first rays of light kind of thing."

"How did he come upon you? Was he in a vehicle?"

A flip of a magazine page. "No. I was walking home, you know? Louie's isn't far from here. He just kind of appeared out of nowhere. I didn't see him at all. It was like, I guess I heard a shuffle, but before I could, you know, turn, he'd pushed me to the ground."

"And then?"

Monica flipped several more pages in her magazine. "I was face down. Him on top of me. I think he jabbed me with a needle. It knocked me out pretty fast."

Dana entered some thoughts on this with a few quick taps. How had the man moved an unconscious woman—even in the dark—without being seen? An unconscious body is very cumbersome and difficult to maneuver. "Were you near any building at this point? Did you see any unfamiliar vehicles, or perhaps an accomplice?"

Monica shook her head. "It happened too fast to notice anything. I was just…"

"You don't have to answer those questions again." The voice belonged to a young man just then strolling into the room. Though it was mid-afternoon, it looked as if he'd just crawled out of bed. His light brown hair was a tumbled mess, his blue and gray shirt unbuttoned and wrinkled as if it had spent the night wadded into a ball. He was unshaven. His feet were bare, and his jeans hung at the lower quarter of his buttocks. Plopping into a beanbag chair situated six feet before the television, he grabbed the remote control, clicked the TV to on, and then retrieved a nearby video game controller. "You've answered all those questions already," he added. "Let this thing die already." A combat-oriented video game loaded and the young man began pushing buttons on the controller, never once making eye contact with either Dana or Monica.

Monica turned her attention to the young man while continuing to address Dana. "This is Alex. You know, my boyfriend."

"Nice to meet you, Alex. I'm Dana."

Already engaged in his game, Alex raised his left hand in a halfhearted wave.

Monica returned her attention to Dana. "Sorry. Where were we again?"

"I told you, you don't need to do this," said Alex from across the room.

Ignoring the boy, Dana responded directly to Monica. "You were telling me about that morning. He attacked you from behind and then apparently drugged you."

The girl nodded and then continued, detailing the experience. She'd been shaken into consciousness, finding herself to be in a long narrow room. Animal cages were stacked against the walls. There were raccoons, house cats, rabbits, ferrets. The place had a mingled smell of animal waste and of some sweet and musky incense. She described the many idols and strange bits of paraphernalia littering the space, peculiar wall hangings and candles. Monica was kept drugged throughout her captivity and only had a vague recollection of the passage of time. She detailed the rapes. There were four occurrences that she could recall, but couldn't be certain that others hadn't happened when she was unconscious. Throughout each, the man mumbled in what seemed to Monica to be some strange foreign tongue while clutching a wooden idol.

"Could you describe the idol?" asked Dana.

Monica's eyes rolled up and left as she sought to recall the images seen while in a drugged state. "It was dark wood. Maybe, you know, eight or ten inches tall. With a gold base. Something carved in the gold. Letters, you know? But not English."

"Go on," urged Dana.

"It was of a naked woman. She was African, sitting on a stool, with either some kind of headdress or just big weird hair. I couldn't really tell."

"She had big tits," shouted Alex from his gamming station. "You said she had big pointy tits."

Monica chuckled and nodded. "You're gross, Alex!"

"Maybe. But it doesn't make me wrong." He pressed the controller buttons several times in rapid succession.

Monica shrugged. "He's right. She had, you know, big pointed breasts."

"What did he do with the idol?"

Here, the girl hesitated for a moment, unconsciously rubbing her fore-arms as if cold. "It was creepy. He stroked it like a cat or something and talked to it. I think he was praying to it?"

Dana tapped in a note. "Did you ever see a cloth bag in his possession? It would have been small enough to fit in his palm."

Monica thought for a moment before her eyes widened and she leaned forward in a rush of motion. "Yes. Yes! He kept it in his pocket. But he kept pulling it out and kissing it. Not when he was attacking me, but, you know, like other times. When he was just pacing around acting crazy."

This was it. This was confirmation that this was the same lunatic that had attacked Cynthia Marshal. "Brilliant. That's brilliant, Monica." Dana entered this information onto the tablet. "Now, tell me about your escape."

The girl's large intelligent eyes studied the opposing wall for several seconds. "That's hard to describe. I was, you know, drugged. He'd just fin-ished… Doing it to me. He was all antsy. Pacing around, talking to himself."

"Go on."

"He put the idol on a cupboard. There was all kinds of other stuff like that on there too. He kind of picked through it. So I saw some weird, you know, like voodoo stuff. After that he went to the door and started to open it. It had a weird lock, like a big metal latch kind of lock. I guess it was to help keep me in. But, I think my adrenaline had, you know, kicked in because of what had just happened. I mean, I was still pretty out of it, but I guess not as much as he thought I was. I pretty much knew this might be my only chance. I got up, grabbed the idol. It was heavy, like, solid wood. Maybe it was the gold in it. But real heavy. He heard me move, but I guess I was quick. I smacked him right in the forehead with the thing. Real hard. It didn't knock him out. But he fell. You know, on the floor, and I had a few seconds. I dropped the idol and ran."

"Did he chase you?"

"Yeah. Kind of. I mean, I had a decent head start on him. I must have hit him pretty good, you know? He mostly yelled, I guess. I never looked back at him."

Dana tapped on her pad. "Can you tell me anything about the exterior of the place, where you were, what the building looked like."

Monica shook her head. "No. I mean, the police asked me that a lot of times. But I was scared. My head was foggy from whatever he'd been giving me. I just wanted to run. I did kind of stumble down the stairs, though."

"Stairs? Were these interior stares or exterior, such as porch stares?"

"Exterior."

Dana nodded. "So, the room where you were held had a door leading directly to outside?"

Monica thought for a moment. "Yeah. I guess so. Yeah."

"Were there any windows in the room?"

"No. Not even, you know, shades or curtains. No windows."

"And when you escaped, when you got outside?"

"It was night. Like late night. There were no streetlights or anything. Just dark. I just, you know, stumbled down the stairs and ran."

"How many stairs?"

"Three I think. Maybe four."

"So like a porch, not as if you were coming down from an upper level room?"

"Right. I guess. Yeah. I mean, really I was scared and out of it. I just ran."

Dana nodded. Despite the girl's lapses in detail, this was all very helpful. But, something was nagging at Dana. She couldn't quite place it, couldn't quite formulate the right question to ask. Something about the setting. Cursing her own inability, Dana minimized her notes, tapped an icon, and then scrolled to an image, before handing it to the girl. "Now, let me show you a photograph," she said.

"What's this?" asked Monica as she took the tablet, turning it to gaze at the screen.

"A photograph of scratches on your neck. Do you remember anything about this?"

"He beat me. And there was, I guess, like a lot of thrashing around, you know? I had marks all over my body."

Dana nodded. She understood that this girl had been drugged throughout most of her ordeal, and she didn't want to lead her in any way, but this was an important element. "I'm aware that there was a bit of a ruck. By that I mean, you were fighting, scraping about, but as to these marks on the neck, was that from the ruck or was this something different."

"You don't have to answer this crap, Monica." It was the boyfriend again, apparently in between video battles, and now tuned in again.

"Shut up, Alex." Monica's tone was one of annoyance at the intrusion.

"I'm just saying."

"I know what you're saying. Shut up."

Alex shrugged and returned to his game, muttering something about women under his breath.

Monica rolled her eyes and said, "He thinks he's going into special ops."

Alex turned his head. "I am going into special ops. I report for basic training in June."

"That doesn't mean you'll make the cut for special ops, honey." Monica offered an exaggerated smile, all sweetness, no guile.

Alex snorted as he stabbed at his video control buttons. "Way to support me."

"You're welcome, dear."

Dana smiled at the exchange. She enjoyed Monica's spunk. As for Alex, Hunt had been in special operations and this kid was no Hunt. It wasn't that Alex was small—which he was, perhaps five foot six. But at five foot nine inches, Hunt wasn't a large man either. Still, he had a presence about him, a command. Purpose. Determination. This kid had none of that. Dana seriously doubted if Alex could hold a job much less endure military discipline. She supposed Alex would learn this all, for better or worse, in June.

"About the photograph," prodded Dana.

"Yeah," said Monica. "Yeah…" And here, for the first time, Dana saw the girl break. Her eyes moistened, her lips curled downward, her hands quivered as she held Dana's tablet. It was so sudden. A complete reversal of the joking manner of just moments before. Something about this question had struck this poor girl.

"I'm sorry, Monica. Do you need a moment?"

Monica shook her head and sniffled. "Yeah, um, I remember now. He, um, you know, cut me with a pocket knife. I uh, I thought he was going to slit my throat." She looked away, wiping her moistened cheek with a palm. "I thought I was going to die."

"That's enough," said Alex, now rising to march toward the two women. "Monica's been through all of this crap before. She's had enough. You need to leave." He took the electronic tablet from Monica and handed it to Dana. "You got that? Leave." He was trying to sound much tougher than he was. But at least he was showing some genuine interest in Monica's wellbeing.

Dana nodded, withdrew a business card, and handed it to Monica. "I'm sorry to have disturbed you. You've been very helpful. You're information has helped to confirm that this is indeed the same man attacking women throughout a several state area. Please, call me should you think of anything else." Turning, she glanced at Alex. "Enjoy boot camp." She winked and showed herself to the door.

Chapter Nine

Botma Africa

Only his third full day in Botma, and already Hunt was learning to hate the rain. He understood this was a part of any tropical locale, but in other places, the rain was fresh and clear. Here, in the city of Mirembe, it seemed that even the rain was tainted by the political filth at the seat of power, that the exhausts of one hundred thousand poorly maintained vehicles clung to the atmosphere in a gray haze only to be brought back to earth with the once-pure precipitation. It was hot, muggy, wet, and grimy.

Hunt was in and out of minibuses darting about the city. He was tracking down known Ubora supporters with the hopes of gaining a lead as to the whereabouts of the missing child. This wouldn't be a direct line, Hunt knew. It would be a lead that would follow to another lead, and then with luck to a lead of some substance, and then—maybe—to legitimate intel on the kid.

The problem was that Ubora was a rival leader in a country under martial law. He would make sudden and dramatic public appearances and then disappear into the wind before Azibo's forces could take him out. This meant he went deep underground and that most of his known supporters were not privy to his exact whereabouts and that most of them were very wary of inquiries concerning their hopeful savior. This was a mentality Hunt hoped to exploit.

Exiting a minibus, Hunt strolled through traffic, directly in front of cars, and skirting motorcycles with deft ease—almost like a native—and stepped onto the narrow sidewalk beside a horse drawn cart loaded with goats. "Mine!" shouted a beggar situated at the intersection, his narrow back pressed against a pale concrete storefront, his golf ball eyes and near toothless grin focused upward. "Mine!" he shouted again. He was grabbing a young woman's garment, tugging at it as if expecting her to disrobe and relinquish her clothing. With a hefty yank, the woman disengaged the man and marched into the churning crowd. The beggar, nonplused, immediately turned to a group of three young men as they were the closest prospects. The crowded walkway was rife with pushing and cursing, laughing, and arguing. The rain seemed to bother no one but Hunt. He spotted a military vehicle further up the way—not an unusual site—and another perhaps another half block distant. A man shouted at him from a doorway, offering fresh fruit, another offered to sell him one of three overcoats he had slung over his left arm. Unlike the United States, no one was on a cell phone, no one wore headphones, in fact, there were no electronic devices immediately visible. Several people glanced at Hunt as he went by, noting his skin color and lightly-worn clothing. While he was not the only Caucasian to walk the street, he was definitely in the minority, one of likely no more than five percent.

Turning right, Hunt walked nearly a block, weaving between pedestrians and bicyclists and gazing casually at storefronts. No hurry. No worry. He'd already jangled some chains in the Ubora camp. It was possible that he'd been followed and, if so, he wanted to identify the tail in order to confront him and, with luck, garner his first true lead.

He was approached by several street venders who attempted to sell him local curios, cigars, liquor, and even women. Smiling, he declined each, all the while keeping a watch over his shoulder. He stopped to inspect some pottery sold by a heavily-cloaked woman who may have been nearly a century in age. She spoke no English, but smiled and nodded at his compliments on her wares. He also studied baskets two doors further up the street and rugs woven from a rigid near colorless vine. He noted that many of the shops bore the symbol he'd come to associate with Azibo's god, Anascoreth, the scorpion gripping the globe. He would be curious to learn how many people had truly switched their faith based on Azibo's dictates and how many did so for public consumption only, adhering to their true beliefs in the privacy of their homes.

Locating his destination, Hunt walked into the video rental shop, stomped his rain-drenched feet on the rubber door mat, wiped the moisture from his brow with a sleeve, and glanced about the place. Small. Musty smelling. Maybe five hundred square feet of retail floor space. Wall mounted racks and center displays featuring DVDs and VHS tapes. No sign of Blu-ray. Most of the merchandise appeared to be used, significantly dated, or bootlegged. Many were U.S. films and television shows, others appeared to be from Bollywood, India's film capital based out of Mumbai, and there was a smattering of British and French-made features. Decade-old movie posters clung to the walls, the corners curling, and the colors dull and grimy.

The place was empty except for a young man of about twenty standing behind the counter sifting through stacks of discs. Short, perhaps five-six, black, frighteningly thin, tightly cropped hair, he stood with a bit of a hunch, the defensive posture of someone nervous or fearful. This was not the man Hunt had come to see. Too young. Too small. "Hi," said Hunt. "English?"

"Yes, of course," replied the man with a quick nod and a forced grin.

"Good, 'Cause my Spanish is kinda rusty."

The man narrowed his eyes at Hunt, not getting the joke.

"Sorry. Lame sense of humor. You guys got the most recent season of CSI?"

The man nodded quickly. "CSI. Um, yes. A very good show. Um, most recent? If you mean most recent in the United States, I don't think I could help you. We tend to get things two or three years after their release in the States. I believe I might have season four. It's very popular. They sell quickly. I can check for you."

"Nah. No need. I've actually never seen the show."

The man frowned in confusion, his brow furrowed, his eyes narrow.

Hunt chuckled. "Never mind. I'm being a jerk."

The man nodded, again with a forced smile. He didn't know how to respond to this.

"Is your boss in?"

"My boss?"

"Yeah. Guy named Kofi Ikenna. He here?"

The kid fiddled with a disk. "My employer. Um... He's indisposed at the moment. May I take a message? Perhaps he can contact you later."

"It's okay, Oni. I'll talk to the man."

Ikenna emerged from behind a drawn curtain leading to the rear of the store. He was a large man of maybe forty, six-two, three-fifty, small mouth, narrow eyes gazing through metal-framed glasses. His once-white shirt was the hazy gray of day-old snow on a city street. He walked with a big man's waddle, but carried the girth with confidence and audacity. "Can I help you find a video, sir?"

"Nope." Hunt moved toward the counter.

Ikenna smiled. His teeth were large behind the narrow opening of his lips. "This is a video establishment. If you aren't looking for a video, how can I be of assistance?" His voice was full and rich, a bit playful. There was nothing threatening in his tone or manner. His size took care of that for him.

"A few questions. That's all. Five minutes of your time. But the questions are private in nature."

Ikenna nodded. "Oni, why don't you take a break? Maybe use the toilet."

The younger man nodded, grinned, nodded, and then scurried behind the counter with a hurried, "Thank you."

"I don't know what that lad is so frightened about," smiled Ikenna. "It's not as if we live in a police state." He chuckled at his own remark.

Hunt returned the grin. "My name's Huntington. I'm looking for a missing kid."

Ikenna shrugged. "There's no child here. Of that, I can assure you."

Hunt moved to the counter, leaning both forearms on the smooth surface. "Nishati Azibo's son." He smiled. "Any thoughts?" Hunt wasn't one for subtleties. He found that the simple truth often shocked people into revealing something they may have hidden when playing the cat and mouse nonsense of stealth and guile. Subtly often gave people too much time to think, to prepare misleading responses, to doubt one's sincerity.

Hunt studied Ikenna, looking for hints from his initial reaction. For a little hitch or twist, for an awkward hesitation or averted glances. There were none. Ikenna simply broadened his grin, and opened his arms in a go-figure gesture. "Well, Tahir Azibo is definitely not here."

"Didn't think he was."

"Then how can I help you, Mr. Huntington?"

"Word has it you're a supporter of Zahir Ubora."

There was the reaction Hunt had sought.

Ikenna stiffened, but only just. The man had a certain poise about him. "There are some names that should be kept to private moments, Mr. Huntington. Ubora is one such name."

Huntington glanced about the empty room and shrugged. "Looks pretty private to me. So, you're an Ubora supporter, right?"

Finally, the large man let his grin dip into a straight and even line. "Who gave you this supposed information?"

Hunt shrugged. "Sorry. I never give up my sources. They live longer that way."

"Am I correct in assuming that you're American?"

"Yep. Yankee Doodle to the core."

"What does America care about Azibo and Ubora? What have they ever done for Botma?"

Hunt straightened, now pressing his palms face down on the counter. Ikenna was nearly a half foot taller than him and he wanted to be prepared should the man become agitated. "Listen, I don't know what the U.S. of A.

thinks of Botma. No idea. I'm from America, but I'm not representing America."

"Then who do you represent, Mr. Huntington?" Ikenna now had his arms crossed before his massive chest. His voice was still calm and warm, but the welcome had fled his demeanor.

"Myself. Me. My wallet. Here's the deal. I'm a rescue specialist. I find and rescue missing persons. It's how I make my living. I don't work for any government. I don't work for anyone. I'm my own boss. Truth is, until this kid went missing, I'd never heard of Botma. But, here's something I've figured out already. This place is screwed up and needs an overhaul."

Ikenna narrowed his eyes further. His stern expression now dropped into a full-fledged frown. "You're talking about my homeland, Huntington."

"Yeah, and you wouldn't be supporting the opposition if you thought everything here was pure as a spring rain. You know the problems. You live them every day. Look at that kid you have working for you. He was ready to jump out of his skin just because I walked through the door."

Ikenna remained silent.

Hunt added, "Strange, I don't see an Anascoreth symbol anywhere around here. Where do I report that kind of offence? Is there a Department of Religious Intolerance?"

Still no replay.

"Listen, I'm not an Azibo fan. To me, the lady seems like a fruit loop. But, the kid's an innocent. My intel says Ubora has the kid and is holding him hostage. I know you're an Ubora supporter. Fine. Rah, rah. Go team. But, I'm guessing you can't feel very good about someone grabbing a little kid as a pawn. I'm not interested in the politics. I just want to get the kid to safety."

Ikenna's smile returned. Warm, nonthreatening, perhaps hinting at some internal humor. "Look at me, Mr. Huntington. I own a video store. Half of the people in this city don't even own a video player. I'm just a man struggling to live and eat. I can't get you to Ubora."

Hunt returned the smile. "Listen, Kofi. You seem like a decent guy. Warm, friendly. I'm not here to cause trouble. And, I believe you when you say you don't know where I can find Ubora or where he's hidden the boy. But, I do know you're a supporter. And I know that supporters usually know other supporters, who then know other things. I'm just following bread crumbs. Just like you will never know who gave me your name, the person you give me will never know I got his name from you. Understand? I'm not undermining your cause. I'm not endangering you. I just want to help the kid."

Ikenna stared at Hunt intently for perhaps ten seconds and then broke into a hearty laugh. "Huntington, you do know how to shovel it deep."

Hunt remained silent.

The two men stared, neither breaking the silence, both assessing the other like two predators that had happened upon one another in the jungle. Eventually, the big man shrugged. "Listen, I said I can't help you. Now, how about you buy that season of CSI you were asking about and make this visit worth my time?"

Hunt leaned further forward, his elbows once again on the counter. "I just want to help the kid. I won't put you in danger."

Ikenna leaned in as well, laying his massive forearms only inches from Hunt's. "No. I don't think so. You come in here with your cocky words. You don't care about the politics. You don't care about Botma. You just care about this one single child. I don't know if you're telling the truth. I don't know if you're really some independent guy looking to get rich off of finding Azibo's son or if you're some American spy. But, I do care about the politics. This is my country. These are my people. And there are children killed every day in villages here in my country by this woman and her followers. And you expect me to care about her son?"

"Listen, Kofi, I…"

"I never gave you permission to use my first name."

Hunt exhaled sharply, meeting the man's gaze. "You're right. I was insensitive. I get it. This thing is a lot bigger than the life of one kid. But, tell me, what's going to happen if Ubora executes Azibo's boy?"

The large man stared at Hunt, his eyes mere slits in his charcoal skin.

"Azibo's not going to turn the country over to Ubora. We both know that. So, what happens next? Azibo calls Ubora's bluff. She doesn't cede control. Now, he has this kid that he's promised to execute. He'll look impotent if he doesn't go through with it. So what does he do? The only thing he can do and still save face. He kills the kid. Now, he's given Azibo an excuse to up her insanity. More kids get dragged away. More families are slaughtered as she initiates a mad hunt for Ubora and his followers. She's avenging the death of her son. She's become a living martyr. Hell, she might even gain sympathy from the populace, maybe even from foreign powers. After all, she's a grieving mother."

Ikenna snorted. "I think you'd better leave."

Hunt stood erect, allowing his right hand to linger on the counter top for an extra moment. "Yeah. I probably should. Sorry I wasted your time." He turned toward the door and then paused for just a moment. "And forget the CSI. But you might want to check out a copy of The Walking Dead. For some reason I think it's a fit." Turning, he made his way through the door.

***

"You getting a signal, Cork?"

"Yeah, Hunt. I got him. There's a lot of static, though. Where did you put the transmitter, under a rug in the next store over?"

Hunt turned a corner at the end of the block. He was still only about five storefronts down from the video shop, but was now out of direct line of sight. The rain continued, but was now more of a sprinkle than a downpour. The street was filled with people rushing about, chattering, hustling, and arguing. "On the counter," he said into his Bluetooth. "Between a stack of videos and the register."

"Yeah. It's not a great signal." Corky paused. Hunt could hear her tapping on her keyboard. "Hold on, Hunt. Sounds like he's making a call."

Hunt waited as Corky attempted to better tune the signal. Soon he heard what seemed to be the sound of pen on paper.

"What you got, Cork?"

"Hang on, Hunt. Don't distract me."

Hunt continued walking with no particular destination in mind. The rain damp air was as fresh as he'd breathed since entering the city proper. At some level, he was amazed by the people. The country was in turmoil. Abductions and assassinations were an everyday occurrence, and yet he saw people buying goods, joking, flirting, going about their lives. These people knew the difficulties of the land. Surely some, if not many, had lost loved ones or at least friends and acquaintances due to Azibo's acts. But humans are a resilient breed. It was an encouragement, a reminder that even under the worst circumstances joy could be found. Maybe not much. Maybe not long lasting. But usually enough to move on to the next day.

"Yeah, okay. You there, Hunt."

"Always. What you got?"

"He made two calls. I think you'd better get back here. He's sending someone after you."

But Hunt never heard Corky's final statement for the ambush happened too quickly.

Chapter Ten

Botma Africa

The three men were upon Hunt before he realized he was under attack. They weren't that stealthy and they weren't that skilled. The steady patter of rain could have masked their approach, or perhaps the pressing crowds or the bumper-to-bumper traffic only three feet to his left. But, in truth, there was no reason Hunt should have missed their footfall. Even as he responded to the initial grapple, he cursed himself for lack of focus. Instinctively, Hunt rolled forward, dropping his right shoulder as the first man grabbed him from behind, flipping the assailant onto the rain damp sidewalk where he landed with a sharp crack to the back of the head. Several pedestrians scurried out of the path of conflict. The assailant was young, muscular, but at least temporarily dazed. Hunt nearly ducked a blow from the second man, but, too slow, he was struck in the back of the head. The blow was glancing, and Hunt spun just in time to receive a jab to the solar plexus from the third man. Hunt took an involuntary step back but forced himself to remain upright, not bending at the waist as one might expect from such a blow. He couldn't afford the luxury of responding to his pain just then, not if he wanted to maintain any control of the situation.

A steady rain spattered the sidewalk as the first man, still on his back, was now fishing into his front pocket, most likely for a knife. A gun would have been obvious in the tight jeans. Giving this man only a glance, Hunt kicked backward, connecting with the man's chin, before stomping on his crotch with the entirety of his weight. There was a sharp click, but not a crack at contact to the chin. Likely a dislocation, not a fracture. The process took no more than five seconds, but this was enough time for the two other men to draw knives of their own. The good news, supposed Hunt, was that no one had brought a firearm. Hunt had a pepper spray gun and a Taser, both holstered at the small of his back, but had yet to draw either.

There were shouts and commotion from the periphery as Hunt ducked the first swipe while stabbing his extended fingers into the man's throat with an energy that surprised not only the assailant, but Hunt as well. Apparently he wasn't entirely void of game.

But Hunt had no opportunity to become cocky. For even as this man dropped his knife, clutching his throat, and staggering backward, the remaining man sliced right to left. Hunt was too slow to avoid injury but still deft enough to lessen the damage. The blade caught him on his left side toward the base of his ribcage. He felt the sticky moisture of blood before the pain registered. The crease was not deep. Hunt was certain of this. Yet, there was pain, almost a burning sensation. It inhibited his movement, distracting him.

Still, instinct bred of years of training and experience kicked in. A jab, a flip, an elbow followed by a knee and then a grab and a yank. And that was it. All three men were disabled, two with broken bones: a nose and an arm. Snatching the three fallen blades from the ground, Hunt folded them and slipped each into his pocket. None were switchblades, but simple pocket knives. And the men. They were barely more than kids. Just neighborhood toughs. Hunt was appalled that this had even been a battle. They should never have gotten the drop on him and even if they had, he should have disarmed and disabled them before they'd had a chance to make a move.

The kid with the broken nose had fled, but the other two remained, one still writhing on the concrete clutching his crotch, the other doubled over weeping over his ruined arm. The immediate emergency contained, Hunt now noted that, despite the rain, a crowd had formed. No law enforcement officers yet, but plenty of onlookers. Just regular folks. Curious, frightened, uncertain. One woman crossed herself in the Catholic way. A middle-aged man glared. A small child cried as her father turned to move away. Ignoring these, Hunt snatched the kid with the broken arm by the neck, clutching with the thumb and three fingers, while pressing the knuckle of his index finger up beneath the Adam's apple. "Who sent you?" Hunt's voice was nearly a hiss as he pressed the kid against the pale yellow brick of a storefront. No nonsense. No opportunity for the kid to get cocky or brave.

The kid was tall but thin, lanky. No real muscle on his bone. His wide, terrified eyes gazed down at Hunt, who still held his throat in a tight clutch.

"Speak!" ordered Hunt. He didn't have time for nonsense. Authorities might be on the way, and who knew what kind of kangaroo system he'd fall into. The other concern was that whoever sent these punks had more experienced men on the perimeter of the crowd. Possibly someone with a gun. Hunt had spent the day intentionally rustling feathers, attempting to force a response. Obviously someone had complied. This attack would likely lead to the first true lead. But Hunt needed to make the best use of this moment. "Kid, I will crush your windpipe. You might want to answer my question."

The kid nodded and gasped, "Air. Need air." His English was heavily accented.

It had been less than a minute since the fighting proper had ceased and the crowd was becoming agitated. This was just enough time for some of the local men to gather a dash of confidence and a pound of stupidity. "Back off, people," shouted Hunt. "This is none of your concern. These kids were trying to rob me. That's it. Nothing more. Simple self-defense. Anyone have a problem with that?"

He scanned the crowd, his eyes narrow and jaw set in an intense if unspoken threat. A couple of the men shuffled as if desiring to intercede, but none made the move. This was not their fight and they had no idea what this lunatic—Hunt—might do to them.

Releasing his grip on the kid's throat, Hunt now grabbed the gasping young man's left bicep, just below the shoulder and only inches above the fresh break in his arm. The kid yelped in pain and for a moment Hunt thought he might pass out. "All I need is a name, kid. Just a name and you're free to tend to your wound. Who sent you and where can I find him?"

The kid spewed something in a language Hunt didn't recognize. Still, there was a name in there. It was one Hunt recognized.

Hunt wiped rain water from his brow and shouted into the kid's face. "Kofi Ikenna? You're telling me Kofi Ikenna sent you?"

The kid nodded fervently, still clutching his arm in an anguished wince, his lips pulled back in a pained grimace, his eyes squinting in pain. This kid wasn't even as tough as the average small town gang member much less a combat-trained operative.

"You're telling me this was Ikenna? You'd better not be lying."

"No lies," gasped the kid, his only concern being his own personal agony. Likely he had no true loyalty to Ikenna beyond that bought with a handful of dollars. Hunt nodded. Ikenna. So that was what Corky had been trying to tell him just as the ambush hit—that Ikenna had sent men. Again, off his game. He should have read something in Ikenna's manner, or at least, in Corky's tone. If he didn't tighten up his act he'd likely end up dead before this thing played out.

Releasing the kid, Hunt pivoted with a curse, now facing the crowd. One of the men—mid-thirties, broad shouldered, the beginnings of middle-aged paunch—had somehow produced a three foot length of pipe. Hunt met the man's gaze. "You got a problem?" barked Hunt. "'Cause I'd be happy to give you one."

No response beyond the tightening of lips and an involuntary shudder. To make his point, Hunt marched directly into the crowd and past the man. Even if the guy swung the pipe, Hunt would be prepared.

Leaving the crowd to disperse, Hunt marched in the direction of the video store. He'd been foolish. He should have seen the signs. That kid working the counter had been all nerves. Hunt had written it off to the crazy society he lived in, that, and perhaps an extreme social unease. He should have known there was more to it than that. Thinking back on it,

Hunt now realized that the kid had been forewarned of his coming. Someone that Hunt had questioned earlier had sent word to Ikenna. The store owner himself was confident and self-assured, but his hired help had not been so capable. Idiot! Why hadn't he seen this?

Hunt reached under his water-drenched shirt and tapped his injured side as he walked. Already, the blood flow had ceased. The injury screamed a stinging tenderness but was superficial, likely not even requiring stitches. Though, a couple of butterfly bandages were likely in order. His phone buzzed. "Dana?" he said as he connected.

A pause. "Personal foul, Hunt. It's Corky."

God, he was pathetic. "Sorry, Cork. Force of habit."

"Are you okay? I was getting a little worried here."

Hunt nodded. He'd forgotten that he'd been talking to Corky when attacked. "Yeah. Sorry. Ikenna sent three street toughs to work me over."

"And…?"

"And they'll need more medical attention than me."

"Okay. Good to know." Corky could sound so matter-of-fact, while simultaneously almost cheery and quite sarcastic. It was actually rather cute.

"Listen, I'm heading back to Ikenna's shop right now. You have any need-to-know intel on this guy?"

"Probably nothing you haven't figured out already. He's obviously higher placed in Ubora's organization than we'd thought. The transceiver you left on his countertop is still in place. But they've already left the store. No need for you to go back there.

"Uh-huh. Maybe. Listen, there might be something in that store that could lead us to Ubora."

"Welllll…" Corky let the word stretch into eternity.

"What you thinking, Cork?"

"I think he's smarter than that. I heard part of your conversation with him. He's pretty confident and he didn't do a thing to tip you."

Hunt wiped moisture from his brow. Did it ever stop raining in this godforsaken country? "I only left him fifteen minutes ago. He wouldn't have had much time to clean up."

"Mmm-hmm. Don't forget, someone tipped him. He knew you were coming. He could have taken anything compromising away before you arrived."

Hunt thought about this for a moment. "Nah. Ikenna was cocky. He sent kids after me. Amateurs. He thought that's all it would take. I'm guessing he didn't clear anything out because he didn't think I'd be back."

"Then why did he leave nearly as soon as you left the building?"

"That I don't know, Cork."

Hunt slowed. He was only two storefronts away from Ikenna's video shop now. Turning, he scanned the street for any signs that he'd been followed. Even in the rain, the sidewalks were filled with pedestrians, bicycles and motorbikes wove through near standstill traffic. People criss-crossed the street ignoring motorized traffic. No one seemed to pay him any mind. There were no obvious stakeouts. No one sitting in a car across the street from the shop. No one standing still staring in his direction. No avoided glances. Corky was right. Ikenna had been tipped to Hunt's coming. But, likely he hadn't had much time to prepare. He may have closed up shop and hit the road on the off chance that Hunt would take out his boys, but haste can make a man sloppy. He could have forgotten something.

"I've got a gut on this, Cork. I'm going in."

Hunt could almost hear the roll of her eyes. "I don't know. You could be walking into something."

Hunt smiled. "Cork, you haven't been with me for a few years. I'm always walking into something."

***

Hunt smiled and offered a hushed, "Yes!" It had taken him less than a minute to pick the lock to the rear entrance. A year earlier his headaches and focus had been so poor as to place this task virtually beyond him. The back room to the video store was small and cluttered. Probably little over one hundred square feet in total. There was a desk on one wall, cardboard boxes stacked against another, and teetering towers of DVDs and VHS tapes against every other inch of exposed wall space. There was a toilet in the corner sectioned off by a brick wall and a plastic shower curtain. A similar curtain covered the doorway leading into the retail space. Hunt ignored the store proper, figuring that Ikenna would keep nothing of value where customers roamed and prodded.

A quick scan of the boxes revealed that these were all of two categories: empty and awaiting disposal or filled with commercial videos, many of which seemed to be bootleg in nature. The selection was eclectic: a Japanese release of Mrs. Doubtfire, a copy of Iron Man 2 labeled with a black marker and a rough sketch of Iron Man's helmet, The Beatles Help, Monty Python's The Life of Brian (in French), a few Bollywood releases, a battered copy of Beneath the Planet of the Apes, NCIS Season 2, Cheers Season 6, Barney the Dinosaur, and assorted pornography. No new releases from any country. Nothing to nettle at Hunt's gut or cause suspicion.

The desk was littered with receipts and sticky notes. Hunt collected the notes as many bore phone numbers and/or names. Being as these were in the open, they were likely innocent in nature, but it didn't hurt to be thorough. The desk drawers were all unlocked and filled mostly with invoices and catalogues. One drawer yielded only empty receipt books. A decade-old Dell computer tower sat on the floor beside the desk and was connected to a monitor and keyboard. Hunt was not a computer hacker. That was Dana's gig. Corky was good with online research, but he wasn't sure if she had the skills to breach passwords and protocols. Still, the computer was his best shot at learning anything from this visit. Hunt knelt to disconnect the wires connecting the tower to the keyboard and screen.

It was then that he heard the key inserted into the back door.

Cursing, Hunt yanked the wires free just as the knob turned. He had only seconds before discovery.

Hunt was on his feet, computer tower lodged under his right armpit, and moving through the curtain into the front of the store as the back door opened. There were several voices. Likely more than Hunt could deal with in a cramped space. He couldn't count on Ikenna using unskilled street thugs a second time. Quickly, he moved through the retail space and twisted the lock to the front door, slipped out, computer still clutched under his right pit, and joined the mass of humanity traversing the concrete lane.

***

Hunt sat on the loveseat beside Corky. She'd told him of the more extensive background check she'd done on Kofi Ikenna during Hunt's absence. The man was a closet dissident, never opposing the warlord openly. Likely he voiced opinions only among his neighbors, friends, and fellow revolutionaries. He'd been spotted at two pro Ubora functions but until now had not been suspected of active involvement. He was married with three children and had inherited the video store from his late father. His mother was still living and resided with Ikenna.

Corky told Hunt of Ikenna's actions following Hunt's two trips to the video store. After the first visit he had made two calls: one to an as-of-yet unidentified contact within the Ubora organization, the second to one of the street toughs. After Hunt's second visit, Ikenna had made another call, this one, again to an Ubora contact, whether the same one or not was unknown. "He didn't seem too concerned with the computer," said Corky. "His anger was more directed at you for the intrusion."

Hunt nodded. Though he'd still like to have a look at the computer files, he was mulling over what Corky had heard during the initial recording. There had been a short call ordering the three thugs to rough Hunt up, to scare him away, not to kill or maim. Obviously, that strategy had failed. But the significance here was that Ikenna felt the need to frighten him away. The other call had gone to someone else. Someone higher in the organization. The bug Hunt had placed on the counter was ears only. It had no tracking ability. It simply picked up any conversation within its limited range.

"Play that call for me again, Cork. The first one."

Corky nodded and leaned forward tapping her keyboard, in the process brushing her arm against Hunt's. He felt a tingle traverse his spine at the contact and noted the subtle upturning of Corky's lips. Ignoring the sensation, Hunt leaned forward as well, angling his right ear forward. His left ear—what was left of it—was essentially useless having suffered severe damage in the same explosion that had marred his face. The recording itself was clear and of high quality, but as the tiny transmitter was situated on the countertop it picked up extraneous noise every time someone moved something on the counter or bumped into the structure. As well, Ikenna's voice, though a deep rich baritone, moved in and out as the man paced the floor. When his back was facing the counter, the voice became muffled and small.

Hunt lifted a finger. "Wait, wait... Right there. Did you hear it? I'm pretty sure Ikenna referred to his contact as Kenya. Do we have anything on a guy named Kenya?"

Corky frowned. "No. I'm not aware of anyone named Kenya, but Ubora's right hand man, Ogechi Kirabo, is a native of Kenya."

Hunt snapped his fingers. "Bingo! That's our guy. Right to the top of the organization."

Corky pressed her glasses into place with an index finger and stared at Hunt.

"What?"

She pursed her lips "What about Ikenna?"

"Ikenna?"

"What do we do about him?"

Hunt frowned. "Kofi Ikenna is not an enemy."

Corky shifted to face Hunt more directly. Her gaze was warm yet concerned. "Personal foul, Hunt, he had you attacked. He has your real name. You're registered here under that name."

"Yeah. And?"

Corky widened her eyes as if to say, *"What more do you need?"*

Hunt leaned forward, forearms resting on his thighs. "Listen, Cork. He saw me as a threat. He acted accordingly. Nothing more."

Corky leaned in as well; their faces were now no more than a foot apart. "He's in Ubora's network."

"Again, and?" When Corky didn't respond, Hunt continued. "Ubora has the boy. The kid's our only objective. We're not here to break Ubora's operation. That makes Ubora an opponent but not an enemy. Its poor strategy to have taken the kid and it doesn't say much about the guy's moral character, but it doesn't make him our target. As for Ikenna. At some level he's a patriot."

Shifting, Corky crossed her legs and twisted her lips. "Really?" Her tone said, *"Convince me."*

"Nishati Azibo might as well be Satan incarnate. Butchering families, selling children into the sex trade, burning villages, forcing people to abandon their religions for hers. I don't know why the U.S. wants her to remain in power, but for the residents of this country it's got to suck. Ikenna's one of the guys willing to take risks to make a difference. He's trying to get the wicked witch of the west out of power and start over. Ubora might be a poor choice—maybe there are no other viable choices— but at least he's trying to better his country. You've got to remember, nothing's black and white in this place."

"Except the boy."

Hunt nodded. "Except for the boy."

Corky twisted her lips in contemplation. "So, now what?"

Hunt maintained eye contact but thought through his options before speaking. "Neither of us have the savvy to breech Ikenna's computer, so, at least for now, that's a dead end." He paused, gazing into her brilliant rich brown eyes. "I say we get Ikenna to lead us to Ogechi Kirabo—a.k.a., Kenya—who will then lead us to Zahir Ubora and the kid."

"And how do we accomplish that?"

Hunt shrugged and grinned. "Worst case scenario I talk directly to Ikenna again, maybe convince him to set me up with a meet. But, I have a feeling something else will present itself soon."

Corky placed a palm on Hunt's right knee and squeezed. "Hunt, last time you approached him, he had you attacked. The next time he might order a hit."

Ignoring the physical contact, Hunt said, "We'll see, Cork. I don't think this guy's a killer. Besides, I can be pretty persuasive."

She smiled that cute little smile of hers. "So I've noticed."

***

Two hours later Hunt was staring out through the patio window as Corky entered the room. He felt more than heard her presence. Closing his eyes he attempted to focus on the mission. It was bad enough that he was still suffering the lingering effects of Oxycontin withdrawal, but this close proximity to Corky played with his already conflicted mind. It was a struggle to keep his lingering feelings for Corky below the surface. He still loved Dana dearly and didn't in any way desire to be tempted. But something stirred within him. He remembered how easy and free it had been with Corky, how little drama there had been, how well they'd read one another.

"Hunt?" Her voice was soft, tentative, with a hint of quiver.

"Yeah, Cork?" Hunt didn't turn to face her, but maintained his empty stare. His legs were cramping with withdrawal, but he refused to respond visibly. Better to focus on something other, something exterior and far removed. Beyond the glass pane, the city lights glimmered and shone. They were beautiful really, shimmering reminders of purity piercing the shroud of night that covered the sins of the city.

"I have a confession," said Corky.

"Uh-huh," said Hunt. He'd been wondering how soon she would get around to this.

There were several seconds of silence before Corky continued. "Um, I guess you could call this one a technical foul." Another pause, this one accompanied by the sound of shuffling feet. "Lucky didn't exactly ask me to come here with you." She moved three steps forward. "It was my idea. I talked him into it. I wanted..." She broke off mid-sentence, took another step forward and then stopped. "I came here so that I could be close to you again. I... still have feelings."

"I know," was all he said.

After several agonizing seconds, Hunt heard her move away with quick and hushed apologies and claiming the sudden need to shower. That was for the best. Hunt didn't need to be in the room with her just then. He'd known all along that she was here with hopes of reigniting their relationship. But this knowledge was relatively benign when left unstated. Now it was in the open. The serpent nest had been uncovered, the hidden danger revealed. Now, Hunt would need to deal with it. The thing was, he truly didn't know how he meant to proceed.

Turning, he moved to the loveseat, lowering himself to before the coffee table that bore Corky's computer. Tapping a key, he brought up the recorded conversations from Kofi Ikenna's video store. He could hear the shower in the distance as Corky washed away the dirt of the day while surely questioning her wisdom in baring her soul to Hunt. He would need to talk with her. Somehow make it right. At least to the point where they could work together without obvious tension and unease.

He listened to the recordings two more times, jotting notes and thoughts. Eventually he closed the window and was prepared to exit the computer when he noted a minimized document. Assuming that any open file would be related to their current mission, he maximized it.

Hunt's eyes narrowed as he read the document title and then the first few lines of text. It seemed his heart crept into his throat as he scrolled down, absorbing every word with unnerving dread and anticipation. This could not be. This had to be disinformation. The document was incomplete, a report yet in process: fragments of orders, emails, classified documents. Most names were missing or deleted. Much of the content contained thoughts and suppositions, notes entered parenthetically. By Corky? Was she compiling this? It would seem so.

Hunt squeezed his right temple between two fingers as he exhaled. How? Why? This could not be true. None of this could be true. But it was. He knew it to be so. In some crazy painful way it made sense of all that had made no sense at all. The document was not related to this mission. Not in the least. But rather to something far more terrifying, something far more personal and devastating. The implications were both heartening and unsettling. The gaps, the absence of names, the suppositions, all left him with more questions than answers. But, perhaps now he knew the right questions.

Hunt scanned further down the page, keeping an ear toward the bathroom, taking comfort in the continued sound of the shower. This was a work in progress. This was something Corky was researching, something she'd known of but hadn't really known of—at least not officially. This was something she'd stumbled upon, or perhaps suspected. But, why had she pursued it? Was she compiling it for his benefit? Had Corky meant for him to find this? Was that why it was left open? She was not a careless individual. Hunt reached into his pocket. The one which, until recently, had held his Oxycontin. He found only his yo-yo. Clutching it he cursed. What was he to make of this? And if he could trust what he'd just read, who was behind the charade?

A sharp rapping at the door brought Hunt out of his contemplation. Minimizing the document, he rose, moving quietly toward the door.

Another sharp rap.

Hunt put his eye to the peephole. Kofi Ikenna stood in the dimly lit corridor flanked by three men baring automatic weapons.

Chapter Eleven

Mexico

He lifted the bag to his face and inhaled deeply. The girl was pretty, nearly beautiful. A dark golden brown. All of her. Even in the dim lighting of the cramped and narrow space, he could see that there were no tan lines. No evidence that modesty of any sort had scurried through her cute little head. Her clothing had been tight, revealing, meant to entice, her attitude saucy and flirtatious. Another perfect little hussy. Soft, frightened, convinced of her innocence though her immoral life showed no evidence of any virtue. How deceived. How very deceived. How could someone be so very corrupt and not see it each morning as her hussy face stared back at her in the mirror?

The corner of his lip twitched so very slightly. Nothing he had commanded. Just a twitch of disobedient muscles. Nothing but a twitch. This happened, he knew. Every so often, these twitches. They were nothing. Just... nothing. Again, he kissed his precious bag. And then again. Holding the worn cloth tight to his lips, he inhaled deeply, welcoming the mingled scents from within, embracing them, immersing himself in the familiar aroma. His priestess had told him that the bag would bring clarity. He wasn't sure that he had ever known clarity, not in his own mind. Clarity came from her, from his lover-priestess, his only. But the bag brought comfort and familiarity, especially when he was away from her. Especially when he questioned his purpose. Again, he inhaled. Musky, stale, rich, stark aromas danced about his sinuses. That twitch of his lip, where was it now? Nowhere to be found. He smiled. So simple.

Slipping the bag into his front jeans pocket, he picked up the girl's clothing piece by piece, folding them neatly, and stacking them on a tiny wooden end table. The clothing had scents as well. The sweet flowery perfume, the scents of perspiration, and the scents of lust. He clutched the hussy's black lace undergarments, brought the panties to his face and inhaled. The proof was here. Could there be any doubt that this woman operated in a continual state of lust? He could smell the sin. It nearly danced about the dust-filled air, calling to him, pleading with him to stop her for her own good, before she could spread her disease to others. He folded the soft silky fabric, once, twice, and set it with her other garments.

For several moments, he simply stared at the unconscious form, so still on the coarse brown carpet. He wished for better lighting, that he could see her hussy body all the better. Oh, only so that he could better identify her sin. Only that. But the only option for additional light would be to open the door and he could not do this. Not now. Not when she might wake at some near moment. He leaned forward, gawking, sniffing. Sometimes it seemed she'd ceased to breathe. That would be a shame. It was much too soon for her to die. Much too soon. He was not done. No. Not yet. His priestess had taught him well. He knew how to prolong the discipline. He knew how to absorb every last hint of life energy, to elicit confessions of crimes the girl could not remember ever having committed. Oh, but the crimes were real. Of course they were real. Why else would one confess such wicked acts?

Again, he sniffed the thick and musty air. Many of the animal cages required cleaning. But, he was not in the mood just then. Besides, the animal smells mingled with the incense and herbs, with the perspiration and hormones, to create a wonderful cocktail of truth and death. He liked it this way. It made him feel alive. It made him feel... aroused.

Spinning on one heal, he marched to the end of the narrow space and then back again. No, no, no. This was not about his arousal. No! His arousal was a means to a desired end, nothing more. It was a tool to be wielded, a means of instruction to the many hussies lost in lust and desire.

Still, it persisted. His arousal. The woman was attractive, naked, even in sleep she sought to entice him to her lewd and sinful way. No. It was time. He must act. He must prepare the girl. She must be purified and sealed. She must be made holy so that he could take her sin into him. Yes. Take her sin into himself. And to then later be purged of this same sin by his loving priestess.

Most would not understand this. Most would call him evil and claim that his acts were wicked. But most did not know what he knew. Most did not know of the spiritual reality only a breath's distance beyond their senses, of the forces there, of the needs and desires of the gods. They slipped beneath their comfortable common morality like a frightened child slipped beneath a blanket to hide from the boogie man. They did not understand the greater truths. They did not understand what he knew. They did not understand what the priestess taught. These acts, these deeds he committed, they were not sinful. Not hurtful or repugnant. No. The world did not understand. This was a necessary purging, a freeing of a condemned soul. He was a savior to these women. This was the real truth. This was his role.

There was that twitch again. So annoying.

He turned left and then right, before snatching a Mason jar containing the priestesses' urine from a dresser drawer.

Moving quickly, he marched to the unconscious form, knelt, and kissed her twice on one cheek and then once on the other. He then unscrewed the Mason jar, dipping an index finger into the murky yellow liquid. He pressed this finger against his left temple and drew it across to the right. Dipping his finger a second time, he repeated the process on the unconscious woman, only reversing the direction right to left. He sealed the jar, kissed the lid, and set it aside.

Withdrawing his bag, he passed it over his forehead, again, inhaling the mingled fragrances as he did so. Turning her head, he withdrew a six-inch hunting knife from a sheath on his belt. Muttering several words in an obscure French dialect, he held the head steady with his left hand and carved a small X on the right side of her neck. Though unconscious, she squirmed and moaned. Still, she did not wake. The slumbering potion was strong magic indeed. Smiling, he carved another X next to the first and then a vertical line between the two. Again, he muttered the French words before licking blood from the knife.

Grinning a satisfied grin, he rose and marched purposefully to the animal cages situated to the rear left of the area. He pondered for perhaps thirty seconds and then selected a ferret, long and sleek and gray. Opening the cage, he pulled the animal to him, clutching it to his chest while securing the head position with three fingers as to prevent the frightened animal from biting him. Cooing and mumbling to the creature in an effort to calm it, he moved again toward the young woman and knelt, holding the squirming animal only inches above her. A quick slice of the blade, and the ferret's neck poured bright warm blood onto the still girl. He held the dying animal above her for over a minute, allowing the warm liquid to spill onto her naked form until the flow slowed to an occasional dribble. Tossing the now-useless creature aside, he leaned close, whispering to the woman of love and redemption, of ultimate peace. Then, slowly, purposefully, he dipped a finger into the blood and used it to draw two Xs and a line on her firm luscious belly, the same symbol he'd carved into her neck. Again, he spoke the French words, the powerful words, the unknown words with the unknown meaning, and then kissed her longingly on the lips.

The ritual was complete. The woman was his, her soul bound, her body his to command.

He returned the Mason jar to its proper position and then opened another drawer of the same dresser. From this he withdrew the goddess. She was heavy, the goddess. Only perhaps ten inches in height, dark, gleaming, she was weighty and purposeful, naked, with large pointed breasts. She was a new goddess. Well, new to him, though in truth she was ancient beyond years. And she loved him. He could feel her love, sense her vibration as he held her. He wasn't quite sure where she had come from. She'd simply been there one morning. His priestess told him not to ask about the goddess and so he did as instructed. But the goddess was his. He knew this without ever acknowledging it. He supposed his priestess new this as well, though she never spoke of this sacred and holy relationship. Holding the goddess above his head, he prayed the sacred prayer. How he wished his priestess was here. She was so much better at the prayer. He tended to confuse the words, to stumble through certain phrases. It was a shame the prayer was not in English. Maybe he would remember it better if he understood the words he spoke.

But the goddess didn't mind. She smiled within his head.

He loved her smile.

Now, he closed his eyes, and shook his head in an attempt to rid his mind of this smiling image.

His priestess. It was his priestess that he should imagine.

That was, if these were simply imaginings. In truth, he believed that these were all quite real, that the goddess now possessed his soul, and this made him feel guilty for he missed the priestess. He hated being so far from home. But she said it was for the best, that their mission must take him far and away and that his reward would be all the greater upon return. And he had found this to be true. For every time he returned to her, she rewarded him by purging him of the sins of the hussies. And her methods of purging were a wonderful reward indeed.

The priestess nearly forgotten, his smile grew broad. He would draw much sin from this one, and thus be rewarded greatly for his efforts. Nearly dancing in anticipation, he moved again to the unconscious form, the goddess still cradled under one arm even as he unbuckled his belt and loosened his pants.

Kicking the woman in the side, he said, "Wake up, hussy. It's time for some sin purging." He kicked again. "Wake up. It's time. It's time."

Within his shadowed and fractured mind, the goddess grinned her terrible grin.

Chapter Twelve

Botma Africa

Zahir Ubora marched through the smoldering village, ignoring toppled carts and scattered produce, the numerous corpses and ruined structures. An infant—undoubtedly just orphaned—cried from somewhere off to the right, three vultures circled overhead awaiting opportunity, and several men of his contingent scurried this way and that each dealing with the too-familiar sights in his own manner. Ubora seethed within, opening and then closing his fists repeatedly, resisting the compulsion to strike someone—anyone—simply for having the misfortune of crossing his way. A whimpering pup, mangy and frightened, raced within inches of him and Ubora nearly kicked the flea-infested beast.

The air was yet cool, the sun only just hinting at an early morning appearance. But there was the heat of too many fires, and the revolting stench of human remains. These were fresh, the odor still bearable, but when the midday sun was high, the place would make even the stoutest men retch.

"Where is he?" shouted Ubora as if to the sky. "Where!"

"This way!" The response came from the forward left.

Ubora adjusted his course slightly, eyeing the top of the ridge and the dirt pathway beside it. His man waved. Ubora spit, swatted at a fly, and continued forward. This was not what it was supposed to have been about. None of this was what it was supposed to have been about. But when did anything become what one hoped or dreamed? Better to ask, when did truth or honesty cease to exist? Or, like love, were these simply the comforting lies of childhood that had no hold in the real world?

Making the top of the ridge, Ubora nodded to his man, an overweight near-youngster from one of the country's many tiny and poor towns which, compared to villages such as these, seemed centuries more sophisticated.

Well, sophisticated was a relative term. The towns lacked such rudimentary comforts as plumbing or electricity. Still, structures in the towns did not have thatched roofs, but actual ceramic tiles. Motorized vehicles, though few, were not unheard of. There were markets and vendors. In towns, the people had heard of physicians and medicine. Quite primitive, yes, but better. Everything was better than this.

"He's here, Mr. Ubora." The young man was pointing toward a bound figure on the ground and to his right.

Ubora smiled as he patted his man on the back. Damn. He couldn't remember the fellow's name. "Good work, son. Good work." Son? He'd called the man son. They couldn't be separated in age by more than a decade, likely less. Still, Ubora's position of leadership gave him a certain stature, perhaps a bit of a fatherly air.

"Thank you, Mr. Ubora." The young man nodded fervently. "Thank you." He stood, staring eagerly at the rebel leader as if in anticipation.

Clapping a hand on the man's shoulder, Ubora said, "I need to speak with this man privately. Return to your comrades. Continue with your fine work."

More nods. A half bow. "Yes, Mr. Ubora. Thank you, Mr. Ubora." And he was off. Scurrying away like an overfed schoolgirl. It was upon soft and largely untrained men such as these that the revolutionary army was built. Was there any wonder why they hadn't yet succeeded in unseating Nishati Azibo?

Ubora first gazed into the morning sky before turning his attention to the man at his feet. Cloudless. No hint of the rains of the day before. No help from God or the gods—pick your deity—in dousing the many scattered fires. Returning his gaze to earth, Ubora assessed the man. He was one of Nishati's soldiers. A true adult, not one of her child militia. This one would have no valid excuse for his deeds. Ubora studied him long before speaking. The man appeared to be in his upper thirties and wore the uniform of a sergeant. His deep brown eyes were yellowed as were his few

95

remaining teeth. His skin was of dark leather, sun dried and scared, a face by which a man might read the tale of battles fought and crimes committed. As with most men he encountered, this man was dreadfully thin. He appeared sickly and weak and Ubora wondered if—like so many in this land—he was in some stage of the AIDS. The man was bound by rope, his hands behind his back. His right leg was bent at an unnatural angle and was likely the reason he'd been left behind. It was a wonder his own unit hadn't executed him rather than leaving him to be questioned. Perhaps they hadn't expected Ubora to make his way to this place in any timely fashion.

Less than ten feet to the left was the corpse of a young female, no more than twelve years in age, likely a year or two younger. Her colorful garment was hiked to above her waist, exposing her most private parts. Her face was battered and bloodied, her head angled in a peculiar fashion. Returning his attention to the living soldier, he noted that the man's buckle was undone and his trousers unzipped.

Assessing the situation, Ubora knelt beside the man who, due to the fractured limb, was grimacing and gasping in pain. "It seems you sustained your injury while raping this child. Am I correct?" Ubora angled his head toward the corpse. The soldier only grunted in pain. "Shall I guess then? Let me guess. You were having your way with this baby when her father intervened, or perhaps an older brother. You struggled. Somehow during the process your leg was broken." Ubora paused to smile. "But you are not dead. And this tells me that one of your comrades came to your aid. Perhaps more than one. Your attackers were either slain or taken away to join Azibo's forces. But you were injured and therefore useless. Is this about right?"

The man whimpered, shifting from side-to-side as if attempting to loose his restraints.

Ubora gazed toward the horizon. "Likely your unit was on foot and thus unable to bring you along without great difficulty. I suppose they intended to shoot you, to put you out of your misery, but you pleaded and begged.

You probably sounded quite similar to that dead girl over there. Is that how she sounded as you raped and murdered her? Did she plead for her life? Did she beg you to cease your foul deeds?" Ubora leaned forward, his face now only inches from that of the soldier. "Did she?"

Tears dribbled from the man's eyes, his form shuddered from hics and jerks. "Please," he said. "My leg. Please."

"Please? Did the girl say please? I think she must have."

"Please."

"Yes. Just like that." Ubora slapped him, his palm quick and fierce, connecting with the soldier's left cheek. The man shouted and cried. "Allow me to state the obvious," said Ubora once the cries had subsided. "I own you. I own every breath you have yet to breathe. But how many breaths those might be," he shrugged. "That you might yet influence. Do you understand?"

The soldier nodded fervently.

Ubora smiled. "Good. Now, I find it best to demonstrate that I'm willing to follow through with my promises." Before the man could respond, Ubora stood, and without hesitation stomped on the man's damaged leg with his booted foot. The soldier's howl of pain echoed about the rolling land. As the man writhed and screamed, Ubora calmly walked to the slain girl, gently pulling the fabric of her garment to cover her nakedness. A child. Just a child. He gazed into the blue sky. Not to pray. Ubora did not pray. But simply to contemplate, to calm himself, to find some sense of center.

Returning to the beast of a man, Ubora once again knelt, his expression passive, perhaps even removed. "I will ask you questions," he said. "As long as I continue to get acceptable responses, you will continue to live. It's quite simple. Do you understand?"

Still whimpering and shaking, the man nodded while mumbling something unintelligible.

"Good, good. My questions are simple and painless—provided I remain satisfied."

More nodding.

"Let's begin with a simple yet important question. Why here? Why did the sorceress send you to this place? Was it simply to round up boys and girls, or was there another purpose?"

The man's eyes widened, but he said nothing.

Ubora squeezed the soldier's damaged leg, eliciting agonized screams. "Again, was there another purpose? Were you looking for something beyond human livestock?"

The man shook his head. "No. No."

"No what? Exactly what are you denying?"

The man gasped through his pain, apparently attempting to find voice despite his agony. "I. know. of. nothing."

"Nothing? Are you telling me that you are an imbecile? You know nothing?" Ubora squeezed again, directly on the break in the leg. He could feel the bones shifting as he did so.

A wince of pain. "Our mission was recruitment. I know of nothing more."

With sudden ferocity, Ubora brought his fist down on the break.

The man howled in agony, twisting and shaking.

"The truth. I need the truth." Likely, the man was truthful. He possessed a weak personality and was unlikely to lie through his pain. The very fact that his own unit left him to die indicated that they had nothing to fear from his discovery and subsequent interrogation.

"I am. I am," screamed the soldier. "I am telling the truth."

Ubora cocked his head. "The truth? What truth is it that you claim? Azibo's truth? Do you follow her god? Do you support her sorcery?" The man disgusted Ubora. This was the type that relished in inflicting pain and misery, of savaging those weaker in physical form in the name of Anascoreth, but when challenged cowered and whined like pups beaten in a pen. They were worthless and, as far as Ubora was concerned, subhuman.

"Recruiting," screamed the man. "We were just recruiting!"

"Recruiting?" scoffed Ubora. "And raping. Oh, and murder. Recruiting, raping, and murdering. Does that sound about right?"

The coward nodded amongst tears and whimpers.

"The truth is," said Ubora. "You don't know why you were sent here do you? You're not bright enough or loyal enough to have been given that information. As far as you were concerned it was just another holiday, another opportunity to rape and murder. I suppose you looked forward to this day. Maybe you even got drunk last night in anticipation of raping babies? Does that sound accurate? Or did you pray? Did you pray to your scorpion god as you prepared to defile a child?"

The man shook his head violently from side to side.

There was a sound from Ubora's rear. Footsteps. He rose, turning to face the approaching man.

"Yes?" asked Ubora.

"A vehicle draws near. They arrive with the American."

Ubora nodded and then turned to once again face the soldier. "I will not kill you," he said. "You do not deserve a quick and painless death." Ubora glanced one last time toward the dead girl, withdrew his sidearm, flicked the safety to off, and then fired two shots into the kneecap of the man's previously uninjured leg. Ignoring the man's agonized howls, he holstered his weapon, turned again to his man, and said, "Untie this man. Strip him naked. Leave him for the vultures. Give no aid or comfort. If he attempts to crawl away, let him. He won't get far."

***

Zahir Ubora stared at the man before him. He was Caucasian, not particularly tall, perhaps five foot nine or ten. His dirty blond hair was cut to a short crew, his beard, blond with flecks of red/brown, neatly trimmed. He was fairly fit, bordering on muscular, with the casual stance of someone accustomed to volatile situations. His steel blue eyes were narrow and intelligent. But it was his scared face that drew attention. It spoke of severe trauma, perhaps a fire or even an explosion. Surgeries had been performed, that was evident if one looked closely, but still much of the scaring remained.

As he did with nearly every man he met, Ubora appraised him as an opponent. Should the two engage in hand-to-hand combat, what would be the outcome? It was an egocentric exercise, he knew, but he indulged himself nonetheless. He felt this mental game kept him sharp. Such fights were few, but when they came upon him they were almost always unexpected and short in duration. It was appropriate to be prepared. As with nearly every such evaluation, Ubora projected himself as the victor. But this one would be no simple task. The man was in his mid-thirties and therefore nearly a decade Ubora's senior, but that was his only obvious disadvantage. Yes, he had the beginnings of paunch to the belly, but only just. In general, the man appeared quite fit and agile. Ubora had obtained some basic background information on this Huntington and thus knew that he had a military background and that he had been tasked to a special operations unit. He was therefore a trained killer. Still, it had been several years since his discharge and he'd obviously let himself slip to one degree or another. As well, Ubora had noticed the occasional twitch to the arms and legs. Nothing overwhelming, nothing most people would notice, but it was present, and, regardless its specific origin, it was a symptom of weakness. Perhaps it was neurological in nature, or maybe muscular, or even substance oriented. This was a curious man to be certain.

His gaze still fixed, Ubora stepped forward: deliberate, slow, with purpose and gravity, an entrance designed to project power and confidence.

Seeing him, the man grinned. "Wanna untie my wrists? I've got a heck of an itch on my left nostril and need a finger free to scratch."

Ubora chose not to the grin. Typical American. Everything was a joke. "You have an itch? My men take you from your luxurious hotel, bind you, and transport you several hours to a burned and ravaged village and your biggest concern is an itch?"

The man shrugged. "I'd also like a chance to pee."

Ubora studied the man further. He still had a military bearing, but not entirely. He was too flippant, too casual. Even his investigation into Ubora's whereabouts had been brash and impetuous, with no effort to conceal or evade. It was as if the man sought to be apprehended. "Who are you?" he asked finally. "And I don't mean your name, Mr. Huntington. That, you've broadcasted throughout Mirembe City."

Again, the man shrugged. It was astonishing how at ease he seemed. "I'm pretty much exactly what you see. My gig is rescue and recovery. My purpose in tracking you is to locate and rescue Tahir Azibo. Give me the boy and you and I have no issue with one another."

Ubora smiled. "Your purpose in tracking me? It seems my men did the tracking. You are the one bound, or hadn't you noticed?"

"Yeah, there's that. But I'm here—in front of you. That was pretty much what I was going for."

Ubora nodded. This one was quite unconventional. Instead of stealth and guile, he'd sought to make a clamor among Ubora's followers, thus causing Ubora to bring him in to learn of his true purpose. "How did you know I wouldn't simply have you killed?"

"You could have. But it would have been a stupid move. And from what I've read of you, you're not entirely stupid." He paused, grinned, licked the dust from his lips. "The way I see it is that you probably did a background check on me as soon as I started making waves. But background checks don't tell the whole story. There was no way for you to be sure that I was operating alone or what my true purpose might be unless you questioned me. Bingo. Here I am."

At this Ubora allowed a laugh. He couldn't help but enjoy the man's brash style. His apparently lackluster approach to locating Ubora had, in actuality, been designed to bring him to this moment. Maybe not brilliant, but clever at least. Ballsy.

"Who do you work for?"

"Freelance. Me, myself, I. If you've done your homework, you already know I'm ex-military and that I didn't leave under sunny skies. Besides, see my face, my ear?" Here he offered a left-facing profile displaying an almost nonexistent ear. "Technically I'm disabled. There's no way that I'd still be active. I work for reward money. Nishati Azibo's offering a hefty sum for the return of her child. I intend to collect that reward."

Huntington was right. Ubora had investigated his background. Everything the man said was true—as far as that went. But that still didn't mean Ubora believed him. There was more to this man than what was available in public files. "What has brought you to believe that I have the boy?"

"That's the hot word on the street."

Ubora chuckled. "As in, this is what Nishati Azibo has broadcast."

Huntington narrowed his gaze. When he spoke, his tone remained light, but his focus had intensified. "You telling me that's not the case?"

"What would you say, should you venture a guess?"

"I'd say that, like most things, there's more to the story than I can read in the Sunday funnies."

Ubora nodded. "I would like for you to see something." Motioning for Huntington to follow, he turned, walking toward a series of burned out huts. Their thatch roofs were gone, but much of the mud brick structures remained. The grim image of Azibo's god, Anascoreth, was spray painted on some of the remaining buildings. Marching past the still-smoldering structures, Ubora led the American to a gnarled tree. Silhouetted in the early morning sun, three limp forms hung suspended on coarse Manila ropes, their necks broken. "Do you see any children playing?" he asked. "Any boys and girls carrying water from a well? Any women weaving mats or washing plates and bowls? Do you see any villagers tending their gardens, perhaps sitting on tree stumps and eating their morning meal as the sun rises to greet them? Do you see any villagers at all?" Here he paused, glancing about in an exaggerated act, pretending to search out life. "Ah! There's one," he said pointing to the corpse of an elderly man laying face down before a smoldering hut. "Ah. And another, and another. There they are. If you would walk the village as I have, you would find all of the adults, not one among the living. Where are the children, I ask you?"

Huntington simply stared at him.

"They're gone, Mr. Huntington. They're gone. All of them. The girls and perhaps some of the softer boys to be sold to rich perverts as sex toys and the more formidable males into Nishati's brat army." He marched to within a foot of Huntington, gazing down on him. "This village was small. No more than a few dozen residents. And so it was decimated. Other, larger villages are allowed continued existence, but their most able bodied children are stolen day and night. The adults are either cowed into submission or slain for their petulance. This is the reign of the sorceress Nishati Azibo. Is this the person you seek to aid?"

Huntington remained silent for several moments, his face a stern mask, noncommittal, unreadable. He surveyed the fresh and pointless devastation. Ubora saw his gaze linger on the corpse of a young woman of perhaps thirty years in age. She was rather frumpy in appearance, plain to the eye and therefore not desirable for Nishati's purposes. Still, her clothing had been ripped free. Likely she'd been raped, each man taking a turn, before these animals slit her throat ear-to-ear. The American then settled his gaze on the remains of an elderly couple. Two bullet holes in each of their backs. They'd likely been gunned down as they fled the horrors of the night. Still, Huntington showed no emotion. But it was this stoicism that told the tale. Ubora was a student of men. And here he saw a man moved by that which was before him. But he also saw a man of discipline and control. Despite his flippant exterior, this was a man who felt the pain of another, who had a moral compass. Ubora could not be certain if that compass pointed true north. Perhaps, it skewed slightly east or west. But the man had a code by which to live, of this, Ubora was certain. And he was certain as well that this scene affected this military man, this retired soldier who had likely witnessed his share of atrocities.

"You have nothing to say, Mr. Huntington?"

The American waited several more seconds before replying. Perhaps he was suppressing his emotions before risking a response for fear of displaying weakness. "I'm not here to aid Azibo," he said at last. "I'm her to retrieve her son."

"To what end? For the sake of monetary reward? Do you really believe that a person capable of this," here he swept his arm slowly across the scene, "will honor her debt to you?"

"The boy deserves to be with his mother."

"His mother is a monster."

Huntington turned to face Ubora directly. "Listen. I don't disagree with you. But the child's an innocent. He doesn't deserve to be used as some crazy bargaining chip while you two squabble over power." A pause. "Will you please get me out of these damn ropes?"

Ubora grinned and nodded, indicating to one of his men to release the American. "This is not a mere power squabble, Mr. Huntington. This battle is for the survival of our nation. Nishati Azibo is draining this land of its people, of its resources. She's turned our banking system into a clearing house for criminal enterprise. Drug dealers, arms dealers, terrorists, they all send their cash through our system to be washed. And who profits? Azibo of course. Our children are sent to foreign lands to service grown men. What will happen when there is no new generation to take hold when my generation becomes old and decrepit?"

Rubbing his now-free wrists, Huntington stepped forward. "Let's be sure you're telling the whole story. You're not even a native to this country. You emigrated from Uganda, what, ten years ago? Much of your rise in popularity has come through bloody uprisings. Yeah, you decry Azibo. Who wouldn't? Obviously, she needs to be taken out of power. But are you any better?"

Ubora nearly slapped the man. How could a man seasoned by battle be so naïve? "I won't sell our children."

"You took Azibo's child."

Ubora turned away, composing himself. It would do no good to display his true hatred and anger. "You do not understand," was all he said.

Huntington marched forward, moving so that they were once again face-to-face. "I understand you've threatened the child's life should Azibo not meet your demands. The way I see it, she's too power hungry to acquiesce and the only way for you to save face when she snubs you will be to follow through with your threat and kill the boy."

The man was a fool. How had Ubora thought him anything but? "You idiot! That is exactly what she wishes you to believe."

"Meaning what exactly?"

Ubora squared himself with the man and contemplated how much of the true nature of things to reveal. Already he could see that Huntington was both rash and contemplative, that he had a worthy soul, but an impulsive spirit. In truth, neither were entirely horrible traits. But, how could Ubora use this man to his advantage? Would the truth set him on the desired course, or would he require some additional manipulation? Or, perhaps, would it be best to simply execute the man rather than to deal with his unpredictability in an already volatile situation? "Listen to me, you American fool. I do not have Tahir. I wish with all of my heart that I did. For then I would know that he is safe."

"I'm not convinced, but go on," said Huntington.

Ubora glared at Huntington. "While I know Nishati Azibo intimately, there is much you do not know of me. For example, did you know that I once served beside the sorceress? Do you know that I rebelled because I witnessed her dark magic first hand and could not live with myself as a man if I remained? Do you know that I made a failed attempt on her life and barely escaped with my own?" He paused, studying the American, wondering if he should risk exposing the truth. "When I say dark magic," he said after several moments. "I say that in the most literal sense. Mr. Huntington, you are an American. You believe the supernatural to dwell only in the fantasies of children and the follies of the weak-minded. Even your churches are filled with people who believe in their deity with their mouths but not with their souls, not with their day to day actions. I tell you now, that when I refer to Nishati Azibo as a sorceress I do so in the most accurate sense. There are things I have seen, things I have been party to that your western mind will forever seek to dismiss as fiction and fancy. I tell you that if you are to live through an encounter with Nishati, you'd best find it in your being to look past your pathetic modern worldview and into that which is beyond the veil."

Huntington stared at Ubora, obviously contemplating these revelations, assessing their truthfulness, likely scoffing at his primitive third world superstitions.

"The scenario that you have just painted," continued Ubora. "That I would slay Tahir once it became clear that his mother refused my demands. That is exactly the lie that Nishati promotes." Stepping forward, he placed his palms on Huntington's shoulders. "Nishati still has her son. She hid him away and then claimed that I had taken him. My fear is that she will execute him and then blame me with hopes that this will undermine my integrity and deplete my support. I don't have the forces to stage a frontal assault on her, I have no means to defeat her sorcery, and I fear for the boy's life. Her intent, Huntington, has always been to sacrifice the boy. The only difference now is that she seeks to blame me for the death."

Huntington cocked his head. "Sorry, Ubora. All of the spiritual lingo aside, I just don't see you as giving a damn about one kid. Especially, not Azibo's child."

Ubora shook his head. Huntington was bright, but his perception had been skewed by false information. The American had no reason to believe

Ubora. They'd met only minutes before. Still, perhaps the man could be used. "I am going to ask you a question, Mr. Huntington. I would appreciate a forthright response."

Huntington nodded.

"Whether you trust my claims or no, I believe we would both agree that Nishati Azibo is an unfit mother."

Another nod, accompanied by a shrug.

"Wouldn't you agree that the boy would fare much better with his father than with his sociopathic mother?"

Ubora recognized the dawning of realization in Huntington's eyes. They met one another's gaze, Ubora assessing the man yet again, what he'd already known, and what he'd learned—what he'd sensed—from this brief exchange. "Yes, Mr. Huntington. Tahir is my boy. And I believe you might aid me in rescuing my son before his mother follows through with her plan to sacrifice him to her cruel and merciless god."

Chapter Thirteen

Austin Texas

The past three days had been a whirlwind of travel and investigation for Dana. But she was getting close now, she could feel it. The scene was a roadside bar in Austin Texas, the site, six weeks earlier, of an abduction leading to a rape and murder. The victim had been taken upon leaving the bar after midnight on a Friday night. She'd been alone, as her companion for the evening, a young woman named Gloria Snell, had left with a young man she'd met the hour before. The victim, Samantha Liss, had not been so fortunate—or so adventurous; apparently she'd also had some offers—and so, slightly intoxicated and feeling mildly abandoned, she'd left alone intending to catch a few hours of sleep before returning to her job at a car rental agency the next morning. Dana had interviewed the bartender, the kitchen help, and scattered patrons, some of whom had been present on the eve in question. None had seen the incident; none remembered much of what Samantha Liss had done before leaving. One woman had commented that her boyfriend's cousin, Percy Harris, had chatted up the girl but had been rejected. Harris was back in his home state of Idaho and, when reached by Dana via telephone, had hung up almost immediately. Apparently the man was married and wanted no connection to any of it. This made him a prat, but not a suspect. Harris had spent the entire evening in the company of his cousin, who was a regular at the bar. Their testimonies had the air of truth and there was no reason to suspect the man of having been within hundreds of miles of any of the other attacks. The man was a lowlife, but of the non-violent variety.

Dana's break came from the security footage. After becoming a bit of a purposeful nuisance, the barkeep/proprietor, Eric Hayes, allowed Dana to view the security footage from the time in question. It was digitally recorded, but grainy, dark, and of poor quality. Not asking permission, Dana copied the file onto a flash drive and then spent much of the following day cleaning up the images. The attack itself was quite obvious. Samantha Liss could be seen leaving the bar. She'd paused only steps from the door to search her purse for keys. Something dropped from her purse; it appeared to be a cell phone. Apparently cursing—Dana could see the lips moving but there was no audio—the young woman bent to retrieve the phone. She then dropped her keys, cursed again, bent again, and, snatching these from the concrete surface, marched angrily toward her vehicle, a brown late model Chevrolet sedan. Occupying the forth space distant, the car was near to the building. Still, Liss showed difficulty in navigating the gravel lot in stiletto shoes. The woman was obviously uncomfortable with this style of footwear. Dana could always spot a novice at wearing heels. They clomped about like a plow horse with hemorrhoids, obliterating any style or finesse the usually-overpriced footwear might have offered.

The man was waiting behind her car, crouched in the shadows. Obviously, he'd already selected her as his target and had lain in wait. Dana could only speculate that had Liss succumbed to Harris's advances she might well still be alive. For surely, the attack would have been aborted if she'd not exited alone.

The man had hesitated, begun to move, paused, readjusted himself, and then, just as she'd opened the driver side door and slipped her right leg into the vehicle, he'd pounced, pushing her further onto the seat and then climbing in after her and slamming the door shut. Her screams would have been muffled now and likely not heard from within the bar. No one else was in the small gravel lot and only two vehicles passed on the dimly lit road during the encounter.

Dana could not tell from the image how the man subdued her. Even after enhancing the image, it was still simply a mass of shadows moving this way and that until the man sat upright, inserted the key into the ignition, and drove away, turning south onto the boulevard. The woman, likely unconscious at this point, was no longer visible. Dana could see clearly that the man had worn gloves. But this she'd already assumed. No unknown finger-prints had been found when the car was recovered three days later.

The best image of the assailant had been as he stepped from the shad-ows and before he made contact with the victim. The dual floodlight mounted toward the roof of the bar and aimed at the small gravel lot splashed light across his face for only three seconds, but this was enough for Dana to select a single frame on which to work her digital magic. It had taken a good deal of finesse, but Dana now had an image of the man.

His hair was a bit darker than that described by Monica Granger, but that could simply be due to the fact that it was nighttime. As well, based on the earlier description, Dana had pictured him as a bit wirier, less substan-tial, but otherwise this man fit the general profile. These minor variances were commonplace. Eyewitness testimony always varied from person to person, even when each had stood side by side throughout an incident. Adrenaline, fear, one's own biases and perceptions all colored the memory. And so Dana studied the image, memorizing the features, the narrow eyes and bushy brows, the lower lip, slightly thicker toward the lower right. The nose was straight, the cheek bones subtle, though the face was nearly gaunt.

Accessing—hacking—the FBI facial recognition database, Dana had scoured hundreds of images without finding a match. This did not mean the man was not wanted, it simply meant that as of yet there was no verifiable image of the man on file. Setting her tea aside and nibbling on a cracker, she printed several copies of the image. She would need to return to the bar and hope against logic that someone recognized the man.

Bar owner, Eric Hayes, caught Dana's eye as soon as she entered the square dimly-lit space. It was still early evening and the bar was populated by only about a half dozen tired business people, likely catching a quick drink before heading home to eat steaks and watch television. The place smelled of beer and tobacco as was typical of most bars. A middle-aged couple played darts toward the left rear, a youngish red haired waitress meandered from patron to patron, chewing gum and yammering nonsense as she dispensed libation. The slate floor was freshly mopped and not yet as sticky as it would surely be some hours hence. A man in his late fifties, Hayes wore a walrus mustache which extended to below his lower lip meeting his salt and ginger goatee. His colorless gray eyes peeked out over the top of wire rimmed glasses. He walked with a bamboo cane and smacked his lips between every sentence. Apparently intrigued by her presence, he offered a twist of a grin and a shallow chuckle as she approached the bar. "I'm gonna guess you're not here for the beer," he said, gazing over the top of the gold-colored rims.

"If it would please you, I'd be happy to purchase a beverage."

Hayes smacked his lips three times. "Nah. One Michelob ain't gonna make or break my day. Whatcha got this time?" His drawl was subtle, yet present, adding just a touch of flavor to his otherwise nondescript voice.

Dana slipped the photograph from a manila folder held in her left hand and placed it on the bar facing Hayes.

The bartender cocked his head back and stared down through his lenses. "Huh! That's my lot. I wonder how you put your hands on this photo." He winked and grinned. "I suppose you're hoping I know this fellow."

Dana returned the grin. "That certainly would simplify matters."

He nodded. "Well, why would we want to go and do a thing like that?"

Dana angled her head toward the photograph. "And do you know him?"

"Nah. Well, I couldn't promise that I'd never met the man, but I don't think so." Placing his cane on the bar, he snatched the photo and held it up. "Horace, you seen this bozo before?"

Horace, a young business type seated at the bar and about ten feet to Dana's left, shrugged. "Not that I remember."

Hayes shouted to a young couple seated at a table just behind Dana. "Hey! Hey, you people ever see this man?" Winking at Dana, he added, "Show them the picture, miss." He handed the page to Dana who dutifully turned, handing it to the young woman. She couldn't help but smile. Hayes was a bit of a card. He was also disturbed at what had happened. Just the day prior, Dana had spoken with him at length and he considered his establishment to be a respectable place and seemed genuinely troubled by the attack.

The young couple studied the photograph, but already Dana could see that there was no recognition in their eyes, no sudden hesitation or intake of breath. Neither tensed nor glanced at the other in silent communication. Neither bit a lip or sucked on a knuckle. "No," they both said nearly simultaneously. "We don't know him," added the female with an apologetic shrug.

"Can I see?" It was the lone waitress working this earlier shift. Dana had questioned the girl the night before and had been less than impressed. The woman was in her mid-twenties going on early forties, with the beginnings of crow's feet already creasing her post-adolescent face. She wore too much makeup, too-tight clothing, and spent more time twirling her bright red hair and smacking waded chewing gum than she did attending to her duties. She was a dramatic personality, seemingly intent on impressing everyone with the rigors of her existence and Dana had to consciously restrain from rolling her eyes at the girl's approach.

"Hello, Scarlett," said Dana. Certainly this could not be her real name. It was probably a nickname given her due to her hair color. Or, likely, the girl had given herself the nickname attaching some farfetched tale to its origin.

"Can I see the picture?"

Dana handed it to her. She could hear Hayes chuckle as she did so. Certainly the bartender had similar feelings about the girl. He seemed a level-headed man. He'd know her for what she was.

Scarlett chewed her cud as she studied the image, her jaw working, the gum smacking. She seemed in deep contemplation. "That's Greg Walters," she said at last.

"You know him?" asked Dana. Her tone was wary. Scarlett was not likely to be a reliable witness. More likely, this was simply another grab for attention.

"Yeah. I used to know him."

Dana heard Hayes smack his lips from behind. "You sure you're seeing that right, Scarlett? Sometimes you jump to things."

"Don't lay an egg, Eric. Yeah. I'm sure of it. That's Greg Walters."

Dana met the young woman's gaze, still unsure of her claim. "How do you know Mr. Walters, Scarlett?"

She chewed and smacked. "Church. He's a little older than me. But we used to…" Here she paused, possibly for dramatic effect.

"Go on," prodded Dana, dutifully playing her part.

Scarlett twirled her hair and giggled like a schoolgirl. "Well, we used to hook up out back of the sanctuary."

"Him too, Scarlett? I thought it was only me!" shouted a young man from the far end of the bar.

The girl flushed. "Put a sock in it, Simon. Like I'd ever." She grunted, twirled, smacked her gum. "Simon has his dreams," she said, flipping bright orange strands from her face.

Dana eyed Hayes who shrugged . "Really, Scarlett?" she asked pouring as much doubt into the four syllables as possible. "Are you positive this is Walters?"

"Well, don't tell anybody. No one knows. I was, you know, a minor."

"You ain't been a minor since you were twelve," shouted Simon.

Dana nodded. "Go on, Scarlett."

Scarlett looked right and then left as if ensuring that no one else was listening and then proceeded in a near-holler. "Well, he wanted to keep doing it, but I had half the football team chasing me. What did I want with that old fart?"

"How much older is he then you?" asked Dana

"Five or six years, I guess."

"Old fart?"

Scarlett shrugged and chewed. "Yeah. I mean, I was what, fifteen?" Here, she glanced about, just checking to make sure everyone was listening. Dana wondered how Hayes put up with this bimbo. Probably comic relief, she decided.

"When was the last time you saw him?"

She cocked her head and twirled her hair. "Years, I guess. Maybe five of them."

"And you're sure this is him? People change with time."

"I'm sure. What? Do you think I'm lying?"

Well, yes, actually. "No, not at all, Scarlett. I'm just trying to be certain. Tell me, what do you know of Greg Walters?"

"You mean now? Nothing. Jeez, I haven't seen him since we were kids. I mean, since I was a kid."

Dana nodded. "What was he like then? Aside from the age difference, why did you break it off?"

A few chews, several twirls, and then she leaned forward as if with great purpose. "He scared me."

"Scared you?"

"Scarlett, you'd better not be pulling a yarn." This from Hayes.

"Yeah," said Scarlett. "He was getting into weird stuff. Creepy evil stuff."

"Define creepy evil stuff."

"Voodoo," said the girl in a dramatic hush.

And the bimbo wins the booby prize, thought Dana.

***

It took nearly thirty minutes of questioning before Dana was satisfied that she had a fairly accurate accounting of Scarlett's knowledge concerning Greg Walters. Scarlett was hardly a reliable witness, but with each additional question and subsequent follow-up Dana came to realize that the air-headed waitress did indeed know the man, hadn't seen him for years, but wasn't entirely oblivious to his current state either. In this age of social networking, people often keep some minimal contact even if they haven't been in the same room together for a decade or better. Such was the case here. Scarlett and Walters were Facebook friends. They'd rarely interacted but she at least had kept tabs by following his posts. To hear her tell it, he had stalked her online and insisted they renew their romance. Dana later confirmed this aspect as fiction by searching Walters' Facebook history.

The man was a lifelong resident of Austin, with only a one year stint in Oklahoma as an aberration. This due to a year-long marriage to an Oklahoma girl. At thirty-one years of age he'd spent the previous decade floating from job-to-job, mostly in retail sales with a two year stint at a family-owned restaurant as the only detour. Here he'd worked as a busboy.

Following his online trail from Facebook to email accounts to websites visited, Dana found that Walters frequented numerous pornographic sites including many that promoted violence against women and yes, voodoo-themed sites as well. The fertility idol did not specifically fit the voodoo profile, its origins appeared to lie elsewhere, but despite this minor aberration, this voodoo obsession seemed a good fit to what Dana had learned. The man obviously intermingled rough sex and spirituality at some bizarre level.

Dana found that her hand quivered as she clicked the mouse from one disgusting image to another and she cursed herself for being here. Why was she putting herself in a position to relive the horror of rape again and again?

The answer was as simple as it was frightening.

Because she could do nothing but.

Something within her screamed at the injustice, at the horrors visited upon these women. She couldn't go back and prevent her own rape from having happened, but maybe, if she stopped this man, if perhaps she brought an end to this reign of terror, maybe she would have regained some measure of control in her life, of power and security, of self-respect.

Walter's address was unlisted but this was no problem for Dana as this was an easy hack and the man had done nothing else to hide himself. In addition to locating his residence, she wriggled into his bank accounts—one checking, one savings, both meager—and emptied each. She told herself that this was meant to prevent access to funds should he attempt to flee, but she knew it was simply a means of sticking it to the piece of slime. She also suspended his driver's license and plates, and entered several unresolved traffic tickets to his record including three DUIs. Walters would have a very difficult time of it should he slip free.

Dana had never before abused her computer prowess to such an extent. Normally her hacking was entirely benign, and—in her eyes if not the law's—justified. She wasn't in the habit of altering records or of draining funds. Normally, she utilized her skills simply for research purposes, locating addresses, discovering where credit and debit cards had last been used and for what. She was in the business of tracking people not destroying them.

This was different.

And so when Greg Walters arrived home to his rented two bedroom ranch at ten-seventeen PM, he soon found that he was not alone.

Dana didn't attempt to conceal herself, but rather met Walters just inside the door. But though Dana stood only a few feet before him, it was his living room that first caught his attention. Dana had littered the walls with images from pornographic sites visited by Walters. These photographs were horrific and disturbing at a primal level. Dana had found it difficult to keep the contents of her dinner down as she'd taped pictures of rape and torture, of naked, terrified girls in the midst of abuse, of women bloodied and chained, of gang rapes and sadistic violations.

At the center of the wall was a poster-sized image of Walters, the still shot from the security camera at the roadside bar. The damning evidence.

The proof. Dana knew she had the right man. She'd compared this image to that of his driver's license photo. This had been her first move. Confirmation.

Walter's hair had been trimmed since the security photo, and he wore a white business shirt and a tie, loosened, around his neck instead of a black pull-over sweatshirt. But this was the man. This was the scum.

"Whoa, whoa, whoa. What's going on here?" stammered the pig.

Dana smacked him across the face with a wooden bludgeon, eighteen inches in length, weighted with lead.

***

Greg Walters awoke to the splash of cold water over his aching head. He was bound to a wooden kitchen chair now situated in the center of his living area. Allowing the plastic water pitcher to drop to the dirt-stained carpet, Dana studied the mongrel. There was a golf ball-sized lump just below the left eye where Dana had bludgeoned him. His greasy brown hair was now wet and dripping over his gaunt and pale face. He spat and sputtered unintelligible curses from his uneven lips. "What in the hell?" he finally managed as he lifted his head to meet his assailant's gaze.

"I'm sure that's the same question asked by your victims."

"What?" He drew out the word into a three second drawl. "Whaaaaat?"

Bludgeon in hand, Dana bent at the waist, meeting Walters eye-to-eye, her gaze intense with simmering hatred. "Oh, bollocks, you little rodent. Don't dare play innocent with me." Too quick for Walters to react, Dana slammed the bludgeon into his left side, eliciting a loud *Crack!* from his ribcage.

Walters screamed and jerked, nearly toppling the chair. His breath came in harsh gasps. "God, woman!" he hissed. "Damn it, who are you?"

"That," said Dana. "Doesn't matter." The bludgeon felt good in her hand. She liked the weight of it, the sleek perfect brutality of it. Lovingly sliding her left hand across the smooth surface, Dana allowed a snickering grin.

Walters panted, attempting to gain breath. "Damn it. I think you cracked a rib."

"Only one?" quipped Dana. "I suppose that means there's more work to be done."

Dana was on autopilot now, her true self—or, at least, what she considered to be her true self—buried somewhere underneath, observing, listening, feeling, but not taking the lead. It was a frightening yet exhilarating experience. Total abandon. This pig thought he could dominate women, that he could rob them of their dignity, of their very core, the essence of who they were. He was wrong. Deadly wrong.

Walters took several deep breaths, apparently attempting to gain voice through the pain. "Listen, I don't know what this is about, but…"

Crack!

Dana slammed the bludgeon onto his left collarbone, the force of the blow sending Walters tipping backward his head striking the carpeted floor with an audible *thunk!*

"I'm not interested in lies," said Dana as she bent, grabbed Walters by the hair, and hoisted him, chair and all, back to an upright position. "So, why don't we try the truth? I guarantee it will be less painful for you."

Aside from a groan of pain, Walters remained silent.

"Let's begin with Monica Granger."

"Who?" Walters only barely angled his head toward Dana, apparently avoiding direct eye contact.

"Oh? You don't even know her name? Not even her bloody name?" Dana stalked slowly, circling the man, keeping him off balance, sliding the bludgeon about the circumference of his skull as if tracing a circle. "Mesa Arizona. Does that clear your noggin, you skanky little prat?"

"Damn it. I've never been to Arizona."

Twirling to face him, Dana jabbed the bludgeon into his gut. Walters jerked forward, but the restraints prevented him from doubling over. "How about Las Vegas? Are you going to tell me you've never been to Las Vegas either?"

Several huffs as Walters sought breath. His brown eyes seethed with hatred. The man couldn't fathom that he'd been bested by a woman. "God, woman, no. I've barely been anywhere." He coughed and hacked.

Dana's eyes narrowed as she studied the man. "Let's say that again, only this time subtract the lying bits and add a dash of truth and a dollop of sincerity." Dana swung. The bludgeon connected with Walters' left bicep.

"Damn it, woman, I'm telling the truth." tears dribbled from his eyes as he gritted his teeth, inhaling deeply in an effort to control the pain.

Dana snatched him by the hair, jerking his head up to meet her gaze. "Tell me about Samantha Liss."

At this name, she saw his Adam's apple bobble, his eyes widen, and his lips move silently.

She repeated the name. "Samantha Liss."

"Oh, God. Oh, God."

"I am not God, but I'm bloody well ready to hear your confession." Something was not right. Walters' reaction to this name was strikingly different from the effect she'd witnessed at the sound of the others.

"Oh, God."

"Tell me!" Dana slammed the bludgeon onto his right kneecap.

"Damn it!" he screamed.

"I'm in desperate need of sincerity. And you have a desperate need to continue breathing. Talk."

"Oh, God, that hurts."

"Walters!"

"Okay, God, yes. Okay!"

"Samantha Liss?"

He shook his head, now weeping openly. "I didn't know he'd kill her."

Dana's stomach dropped to her knees. "He?"

"Yeah, damn it. Yeah. I didn't think it would go that far. How could I?"

Dana glared at the broken man, her stomach churning, her hands twitching with suppressed frustration. "Are you telling me there's another man involved?"

"Damn it, woman, I'm telling you he's the only one involved. Or almost. I guess. I don't know. God!"

The man was in pain. He was desperate. She'd broken at least one of his bones and beaten him to mush besides. Still, this couldn't be true. She had the right man. She had his photograph. She'd done her research. It all added together.

But it didn't.

She'd known it but had refused to know it. There were anomalies, questions unanswered. The man's banking activity showed no evidence of Walters having traveled. There were no hotel charges, no out of state debit or credit transactions. Unless the man had money hidden under another name or in cash, he lived check-to-check. His job didn't require travel, which, in truth, had been one of Dana's primary assumptions, that the perpetrator either traveled professionally or was independently wealthy and therefore not bound to a specific locale by his employer.

"Tell me about the other man," said Dana, her voice nearly cracking. At her core, she still wanted it to be Walters—needed it to be him—but she had to follow this line of questioning. "Answer me, pig! You're still involved in at least one murder and you've yet to convince me that you're not my man."

Walters inhaled and exhaled several times before speaking. He was in obvious pain, each injury screaming for attention and primacy. "God, I don't know what to say."

Dana slammed the bludgeon against the nearest wall, leaving a jagged hole in the drywall. "Well, you'd bloody well better think of something!" she screamed.

"Alright, alright." Walters was cowering, injured and terrified. "I met him online. Damn. Okay, y'all got to understand, I didn't know it was going to go this way. I was just looking for some thrills. That's all."

"Thrills! Just thrills—that's all! A woman died." Dana swung the bludgeon like a baseball bat, connecting mid chest.

Walters coughed and hacked, tears poured from his eyes as he articulated meaningless sound.

"Talk to me, Walters. I'm a bit hinky on the details. I need them all."

Walters spit and coughed. It took nearly another two minutes before he again spoke.

***

Dana sat in her hotel room, on the king-sized bed, laptop resting on her thighs, gazing stupidly at the opposite wall, a pile of tear-damp tissues beside her. She could have killed the man. The wrong man. Well, not the primary perpetrator, at least. And at the time, in that frenzied moment, she would have had no regrets. In her mind, it would have been justified. Some others might even claim it was the right thing to do. Not again, she thought. Please, not again. There had been an incident, after her rape, a matter of revenge dealt to those she believed to be associated with her rapist. Dana shook her head, driving the horrid image from her psyche. This wasn't her. It wasn't who she was. Yet still, it was Dana that bore the guilt. She bore the pain, the doubts, the memories.

And now she'd nearly done it again.

And wasn't this one of the reasons she'd pushed Hunt away? Wasn't this it at the core? The rape was part of it, yes. She hadn't yet been comfortable in such close proximity to a man—a husband who would have needs and desires that she wasn't yet ready to fulfill. But the killing. That was different. The rape had been an evil perpetrated on her. The killing had been done by her. Dana had killed and she'd yet to come to terms with who that made her as a person. And now the realization that she could so easily slip back into a lethal frenzy with little more than a thought.

Chilling.

Sniffling, Dana returned her gaze to the computer screen where she'd summarized Walters' confession. Should she continue with the investigation? Would she lose her mind again? Would she kill someone—possibly an innocent?

No.

Too soon.

Much too soon to make such a decision. She was still emotional. Adrenaline still flowed in the aftermath of the encounter. Better now to focus on the facts. Better to review her notes, too make sure that all was accurate. If then she decided it best to walk away, at least she'd have something of substance to pass on to the authorities. Perhaps now they would take this case seriously.

Perhaps.

Dabbing her eyes with tissue, Dana scanned the screen. Walters had met the man online and knew him only as Bill. It was unlikely this was his true name, but it was all she had for the moment. The website had been one dedicated to sexual spirituality. Dana had surfed several of these sites and most were rather harmless with catch phrases such as "primal creative energy" and "sexual divinity." It was all rubbish as far as Dana was concerned. But the site these two men frequented took it to a different level in that it tied spiritual sexuality with domination over women. The men met in a chat room and when it was discovered that, in addition to weird kink, both also shared an interest in alternative religions such as voodoo, they began corresponding more directly. Bill had revealed little to Walters, but said that he was an anointed missionary sent to purge wayward women of their carnal sins. It had all sounded exciting to Walters and he'd agreed to aid Bill when he came to Austin.

The mysterious Bill was not from Texas, of that Walters was fairly certain. He'd explained that he was just passing through and would leave in less than twenty-four hours after arrival. Bill also explained to Walters that he normally worked alone, but felt that Walters might be a kindred spirit, that perhaps they would eventually join on a more long-term basis.

Walters had apparently been quite excited about the meeting, but only for a time. Bill had hardly been what he'd expected. The man was jittery. He spoke in fragmented sentences, his clothing was dirty, his hair greasy. He was not near as articulate as he'd been online. In truth, he wondered if the man had had another's help in the correspondence. The real-life man's vernacular was less sophisticated, his understanding of the spiritual world more simplistic than that of his chat room alter ego. Still, Walters was a randy sort and followed his hormones more than his brain. He'd decided to see it through, at least to the point where things became too weird.

The two men had sat in Walters' Ford for three hours, binoculars in hand, watching the roadside bar. Bill insisted on selecting the target. And when finally he'd found a young woman that fit his criteria, Walters thought her too puny to be truly attractive. But this was Bill's rodeo. Walters was simply along for the ride.

Following the sexual missionaries' instructions, Walters had subdued the woman as she'd entered her vehicle. He'd then driven her to a flea-bag motel where he was to meet Bill for the purging. Bill had followed in Walters' car and Walters never once saw Bill's own vehicle.

But upon arrival, Bill had become agitated. Pacing back and forth, talking to himself, continually rubbing a small cloth sack that Walters recognized as a hoodoo bag. According to Walters, these bags normally contained assorted spices, chicken bones, a rabbit's foot, ashes, possibly broken pieces of razor. It was supposed to possess some power, but it sounded mostly daft to Dana.

Bill had become irrational, shouting at Walters, saying that he'd defiled the woman by touching her. Eventually Walters feared the man might become violent and fled the scene. Being a truly caring individual, he'd left the unconscious girl with the loony. Walters swore he had no idea that Bill had meant to kill her. His impression was that they would simply drug her, strip her, tie her up, maybe chant some spiritual nonsense, and scare her a bit. Dana wasn't sure what any of this had to do with purging the girl of her supposed sins, but this was Walters' tale. Dana took it as mostly accurate. No, she didn't believe that he'd intended to stop at simply stripping the girl. Likely his intent was to force her into sexual acts. But, after spending two hours with the man, Dana didn't feel that Walters had murder on the brain.

One other point of interest was the fertility idol. Walters had seen this and was able to give Dana a more accurate description of the piece. Monica Granger had described it as a deep dark wood, but Walters claimed that, though it looked like polished wood, it was actually a jet black stone, likely obsidian. The base was indeed gold as described by Granger, but, in addition, this base also contained strange markings, possibly hieroglyphics. His impression was that the piece was very old and likely very valuable. The goddess it portrayed had African features and the headdress seemed vaguely Egyptian.

Peculiar.

This sounded like a most unusual specimen. How had this lowlife, Bill, come to be in possession of such a piece? And would it be possible to trace him by tracking the obviously unique, and likely valuable icon?

Dana allowed the whisper of a smile to crease her lips. She knew someone who always had his finger on the pulse of obscure and valuable pieces. Someone who would be more than eager to offer assistance. Dana lifted her phone, punched in an international number, and then waited as it connected. "Jonathan? Yes, it's the ex. I'm wondering if you could lend a hand."

Chapter Fourteen

Botma Africa

The forest green uniform was too big for Nanji. The cuffs of the sleeves were rolled back twice in order to uncover his hands, the pants continually slid to mid buttocks, even the hat shifted about on his nearly-shaved head. But ill-fitting clothing was nothing new to the nine year-old soldier. In his home village, with his parents and baby brother, articles of clothing floated from family to family as need arose. A child from one home would outgrow a shirt and a boy—or girl—from the next hut over would then possess it until he or she outgrew it and passed it on again. This was the way life was, the way it had always been.

But nothing of Nanji's new life was as it should be, not since the day he'd been forced to kill his own parents and become a foot soldier for Nishati Azibo. He'd learned much in the months since that tragic day. Learned much and refused to forget anything. Mostly he remembered his three year-old brother, Diallo. He was held somewhere within the ranks, though Nanji had seen him only once since that day. He'd been told that he was too young to care for the boy, that Diallo needed a female to tend to his needs. Diallo had had a perfectly capable female—his own mother—until Azibo's soldiers had come to the village.

Nanji clutched his too-large weapon firmly in both hands, a fully-automatic machine gun. He had learned how to use it, he supposed. But not well. It was large and awkward, far too heavy and long for his frame. It was quite a process for him to heft the thing, aim, and eventually fire. Nanji was certain he would die in the early moments of his first true battle. He was simply too small for the role he was forced to play.

He stood guard outside of the small plywood building used as a head-quarters for the camp, shooing flies away by blowing on them. His hands, after all, were occupied with the weapon. He could flee his post—and often times he thought of fleeing—but knew the consequences of desertion. Certain death for himself, likely death for his younger brother. In truth, he wasn't sure anyone remembered that the two boys were connected, it was a nameless existence mostly, but Diallo was the only family he had left. He wasn't about to risk him.

But even if he was to find Diallo and flee—where too? Could he return to his home village? Even if he could locate it, would the people have him? He'd killed his own parents, joined the army, allowed them to cart Diallo away. Likely everyone he'd ever known and loved now hated him as they would a devil. Would they mob him, hurl stones at him, cry insults and vulgarities when finally he returned?

If he was one of them, he would certainly treat such a person in this manner.

Nanji was a coward. He knew it as a certainty as did any witness to the events of that day. Why couldn't he have stood up to those men? Why couldn't he have refused them, killed them even? They'd put a gun in his hand. A loaded weapon! All he'd needed to do was to use it. Something deep inside of him knew it hadn't been that simple, that in that moment the options had been few, possibly even nonexistent. But Nanji couldn't help but believe that if he had been braver and maybe a bit smarter or even bigger or quicker, if he'd been anyone other than a scared little boy, that things would have turned out differently.

"Hey, Weasel. Pay attention."

Nanji blinked.

"Idiot, Weasel—look!"

Nanji had been daydreaming again, lost in his sorrow and doubts, a bottomless pool in which he drowned daily. "What is it?" he asked Rafiki, the eleven year-old stationed just to his right.

"Look. Listen." Rafiki angled his head to the left. "You hear?"

Nanji nodded. Motorized vehicles coming up the road. He could now see the swells of billowing sand kicked up by their progress. The camp captain, a tall angry man in his mid-twenties, had just exited his tent, still buttoning his shirt, shouting orders, and doing his best to appear impressive as the small convoy arrived.

"Who do you think it is?" asked Nanji.

Rafiki snorted. "How am I supposed to know?" He was a hefty kid. Not fat, no one here ate enough to become fat, but Rafiki had a full look about him. Maybe it was muscle, maybe just a natural bulk, but he seemed substantial. If Rafiki lived long enough, he would one day become fat, he just seemed that way.

"I don't know," said Nanji in a tiny voice. "I just thought you might know."

Rafiki glared at him. "Shut up, Weasel. Here comes Senwe."

"Don't call me that."

"Quiet. The captain's coming."

Nanji hated the nickname and still wasn't sure how it had settled on him. Perhaps because he was so skinny. Or his ears, he supposed: big. And they stuck out—like a weasel's. Maybe.

"You two, stand tall," said Captain Senwe as he marched between them and into the tiny structure they guarded, slamming the door behind him and barking orders at someone within.

"Who do you think it is?" asked Nanji in a near whisper. Whoever was coming, they must be important to get Senwe hopping about like that. Nanji had seen him take a young girl, a captive from a recent raid, into his tent only twenty minutes before. Under normal circumstances he would have been occupied for at least an hour, possibly two.

"Shut up, Weasel. I don't know," hissed the larger boy as he glanced over his shoulder in fear of being heard by Senwe. Rafiki could be mean, even hateful, but not always. When they were alone he could joke and laugh, sometimes sharing food and gossip, but whenever a superior officer appeared he changed, attempting to impress, demeaning his companions and playing the know-it-all. Still, he was the closest thing Nanji had to a friend, but that was as far as it went: close, almost, not quite.

Nanji gripped his weapon tighter yet, pulling it close to his chest and attempting to stand perfectly still and straight as the vehicles approached. He could now tell that there were three of them, all military, each with armed soldiers standing in the beds, weapons at the ready.

A fly buzzed about Nanji's head. He blew at it while attempting to appear still. He stared forward, out into the grasslands, forcing himself not to gawk at the new arrivals. Again, the fly pestered. Nanji blew at it but it didn't care and perhaps even intensified its attack on the young boy's face. They were close now. He'd need to suffer the fly.

The lead vehicle came to a stop only ten feet shy of Nanji. The driver-side door opened, a man emerged, glancing first north and then south before barking orders to his men in the trailing vehicles. Nanji fought the urge to spit as stirred up dust from the motorcade settled on his tongue. But he dare not tend to the matter for fear of appearing disrespectful. Momentarily distracted by the dust conundrum, Nanji had not noticed the passenger-side door open, or the tall slender figure emerge. When again he focused on the scene, he felt a cold quiver skitter across his form as his hands became as stone, clutching the deadly metal of the weapon in a granite grip.

She was here.

Nishati Azibo was little over ten feet in front of him and turning to walk in his direction. She was tall for a woman, not freakishly so, but five foot nine or ten. Her skin was a gleaming black, nearly polished in appearance; her eyes were wide and knowing, her mouth slightly peculiar, with a pronounced upper lip and rather large obvious teeth. This did not make her unattractive. Quite the opposite. If anything it added to her mystique. She wore military garb, including a dull green cap that covered her close-cropped hair.

From the left, there was a rustle, a romp, and three woofs. Crook, a stray mutt that had become the unofficial camp mascot and so named do to a broken tail, bounded toward the warlord. Nanji tensed, not knowing what to expect. Likewise did Azibo's men, each drawing a weapon, but none firing without her command. The dog was not attacking; this was obvious by the lulling tongue and wagging tail which shook the entire rear portion of the ugly, matted beast. Noting the dog, Azibo smiled and knelt, greeting the gray and white dog with coos and hugs. Nanji couldn't help but gasp as she allowed the animal to lick her face and did so with a laugh and a grin as if enjoying the experience. How could this be? The devil herself acted as if human.

Offering the cur a final ruffle, Azibo rose, smacked her hands together as if cleaning them, and conferred with the man to her immediate right.

"Weasel! Quit gawking," warned Rafiki in a quick whisper, but it was too late. The warlord had already met his gaze.

Strolling casually toward Nanji, she stopped before him, appraising the two young guards with dark intelligent eyes. She didn't speak for what felt like an hour, but rather gazed curiously, first at Nanji then at Rafiki, and then back to Nanji. Her rich brown eyes gleamed in the midday sun and when finally she spoke, it was with an easy smile. "Your name, soldier?" Her voice was warm, husky, almost masculine yet unmistakably feminine.

Those eyes. Deep, rich, with tiny flecks of green. It almost seemed she could hypnotize him with nothing more than a casual glance. So compelling. So warm. So very intense. Was there any wonder men followed this woman even unto death? Nanji swallowed. "Weasel… Um… Nanji, sir, uh, ma'am. My name is Nanji." He was an idiot. A coward and an idiot. How was it he found this woman compelling, enticing even, when revulsion was all she'd earned?

Azibo angled her head toward the other boy. "And yours?"

"Rafiki. I'm Rafiki." The eleven year-old's voice seemed to have raised nearly an octave.

Azibo nodded, and then returned her gaze to Nanji. "How old are you, Nanji?"

Regaining his perspective, Nanji stared into those deep brown eyes, his sweat-damp hands clutching his weapon. All he needed to do was to shoot and the horrors would end. Just a single quick move, swift, sure, confident. He'd been instructed on how to use the weapon. He knew the mechanics of it. Here she was, not three feet in front of him. Just one sweep of the gun, a single squeeze of the trigger, and Nanji would be the savior of Botma. Just one move—that was all.

If only he was something other than a coward.

Anything or anyone else. Someone like his father, or the other elders of the village. His father had ordered Nanji to kill him in order that his children might live. He had been brave, willing to die in order to save his family. He'd been frightened, yes. Of course he'd been frightened. It showed by the strain on his face, by the moisture under his arms. It showed by the quiver to his normally strong and commanding voice. But despite his fear, he had sacrificed himself.

A strange thought wriggled into Nanji's mind. Had this been why Nanji had been spared? Was this what his father had in mind, that one day Nanji might stand before Azibo herself and do what his father had not had the opportunity to do? Had that been the plan all along, to sacrifice himself and his wife, the mother of his children, that Nanji would one day have this opportunity?

No. Certainly not. Father had not had the chance to make such far-reaching plans. The soldiers had come upon the village suddenly. No one had had the opportunity to prepare, to conceive grand schemes and devilish tricks. And likewise, Nanji had no chance to plan. But despite the lack of preparation, this was an opportunity and Nanji was certain that he would remain as cowardly as he'd proven to be on that horrific day.

"Nanji, I asked how old you are. I'd appreciate a response." Azibo's gaze was stern, but not unkind.

"Oh… Um, I'm sorry. I… am frightened by you." He paused, gasped, and quickly added, "I'm nine. Nine years-old."

Azibo's face broke into a broad grin. It almost seemed she might have laughed. "You're frightened by me. Yes. Of course you are. How refreshing to find someone brave enough to tell me this to my face."

Nanji didn't know how to respond. The woman was mistaken. He was not brave. Not at all. He was just too stupid to keep his mouth shut when it was better off closed.

"I'm frightened of you too," offered Rafiki, apparently feeling left out.

The smile was gone, the warm rich voice now frigid. Her gaze became stone-like as she studied the husky lad, her eyes unblinking, her form as rigid as the unfeeling stones on which she stood. "As well you should be, child."

Nanji saw Rafiki's Adam's apple bob as he looked to his feet. A dark spot appeared at the front of his pants and then continued down his leg. "Yes, ma'am. I'm frightened, ma'am."

Azibo nodded and redirected her attention once again to Nanji. Idiot! She'd been distracted. Why hadn't he made his move? Why hadn't he leveled his weapon at her, squeezed the trigger, and ended her deadly reign?

"You are frightened. This is understandable. You've likely heard many strange tales. You believe me to be some strange demon. Understand, what I do, I do for Botma. Do you believe me, Nanji?"

Nanji held her gaze. This woman ordered the execution of his parents. How could he believe her words?

Azibo's eyes narrowed. A slippery grin slithered across her lips. "No answer. Interesting. This time it is not fear which holds your tongue; that much is obvious. You don't believe me but have too much integrity to lie and so you remain silent." She nodded in approval. "Is Captain Senwe in this building, Nanji?"

The boy nodded, meeting her gaze, memorizing her features, her vocal tones, even her rich musky smell. One day. One day, maybe a distant day, but one day Nanji would not be a coward. "Yes, ma'am. He's in. Would you like me to announce your arrival?"

"No need. I'm certain he's aware."

With that, she turned, now approaching the trembling Rafiki. Gazing at him with those probing eyes, she cocked her head, studying him as one might a curious specimen. It seemed almost she was probing the depths of his soul, that somehow she was connecting with his inner being. "You are too stupid to be of use," she said at long last. "Remove yourself."

Rafiki stared at her, eyes wide as his jaw jittered. It was the first time Nanji had known the boy to be speechless.

Azibo reached for the boy, almost lovingly cradling his jaw in both palms as she continued to gaze intently. Those eyes, though not directed at Nanji, it seemed he could still feel their power, their will. It was nearly palpable. Nanji could swear he felt a rise in temperature about the two as Rafiki's eyes became wide, seemingly glazing over to a near white. It had to be some sort of optical illusion, some trick of the sun, but it did seem the boy's eyes had lost all pigment. How could that be?

"Rafiki," cooed Azibo. And then she added words in a low, nearly inaudible tone. It seemed another tongue.

No. Not another tongue. Not exactly.

She spoke syllables: strange, melodic, harsh. But syllables only. These were not words, not at least, in the traditional sense; somehow Nanji was certain of this. But, Rafiki apparently understood. For at this utterance his back stiffened, his jaw went slack. And though her hands dropped away from his face, still Azibo and the boy maintained that complete and unaltered eye contact, that oneness of mind and thought. Azibo smiled that peculiar yet compelling smile, and offered a near imperceptible nod. At this, Rafiki adjusted his weapon, turning it so that the end of the barrel pressed against the underside of his chin. Holding the stock with his left hand, he placed his right thumb above the trigger. Before Nanji could utter a word in protest, the older boy used his index finger to flip the safety to "off" and discharged the weapon, effectively obliterating his own head in an echoing stutter of automatic gunfire.

As the twittering corpse fell to the dusty earth, Azibo, spattered with blood and brain matter, glanced at Nanji, grinned, and marched casually through the entrance to the small wooden building.

Nanji continued to clutch his weapon, his teeth gritted, his knees wobbling and threatening to buckle. But, he maintained his stance and restrained the tears. After all, he was too cowardly too cry.

Chapter Fifteen

Botma Africa

Corky moved toward the doorway as Hunt entered, her eyes wide behind the tortoiseshell glasses. "Hunt!" she nearly shouted. Her dark eyes were moist, this visible even beyond the lenses. Her lips were tight and hopeful, her arms crossed protectively across her chest. Again, she wore a football jersey, this time the Denver Broncos with a unicorn image on the chest. But even in this seemingly whimsical attire, she seemed somehow vulnerable, frightened even, and not at all at ease. Hunt could only imagine what she was feeling in this moment. Likely, she'd feared him killed. Likely she wanted to embrace him, possibly even smother him in kisses. Instead, she stood, arms crossed, awaiting Hunt's cue.

Offering no hint to his thoughts or feelings, Hunt nodded, suppressing the confusing rush of emotion he felt for the woman, and strode into the living space, passing Corky with hardly a glance. "Hey, Cork. We've got work to do."

The next half hour was spent briefing her on his experience. He told her of his encounter with Zahir Ubora, of the man's claims concerning the child, and of his proposition to Hunt. She chastised him for not contacting her, but what could he have done really? Even from the moment Ubora's men had shown up at the door, Hunt hadn't had a moment to notify Corky, who had been in the shower at the time. In truth, his hope had been that they'd leave without ever having known that she'd been present. It was alright, thought Hunt, that she was put out. She'd deal with it. She had no other choice. And in truth, it was better she focus on petty anger and disappointments rather than any of the more real and more personal matters creeping about the shadows in each of their hearts.

"You don't actually trust him, do you?" she asked, her tone dubious if not outright condescending.

"Trust? Nah." Hunt set his juice on the low-sitting coffee table and took a bite of meat. They'd ordered room service knowing they'd likely work straight through the meal.

"But, you plan to go along with his plan."

Hunt shrugged and chewed. "Yeah, well, Cork, here's the deal. As an independent foreign operative, I'm off the radar. Ubora's dead center of the bull's-eye. If Tahir Azibo really is his child, then yes, I think he's probably giving me accurate intel." Hunt took another bite of the salty, lightly-spiced beef. "That doesn't mean I trust his intentions. He's clearly trying to use me to his own ends, but that's okay. I plan on using him for mine." He paused, studying her for a moment, attempting to read her mood. She sat cross-legged, picking at her meal and looking at her computer screen far more often than she did at Hunt. He'd noticed crumpled tissues in the wastebasket beside the couch. She'd been crying during his absence, but for the moment she was business and nothing but. "For now," he continued, "you're up to bat. I need you to get on that computer, utilize the Pentagon's resources, investigate the boy's parentage. Is there anything at all that points toward Ubora as the father?"

Corky met Hunt's gaze. "In a moment. I still have questions. Ubora gave you the locale, the place he believes the child is held."

"He did."

She offered a contemplative pout. "Okay. So, what exactly does he expect you to do with this information?"

Hunt waited a moment before answering and then decided to tell Corky the truth. It would be interesting to see her response. "His stated reason is that he wants me to rescue his son. His movements and those of his upper men are subject to scrutiny. Me? No one knows or cares about me. So, yeah, he'd like me to rescue the boy. Oh, and bomb Azibo's compound while I'm at it."

Hunt smiled.

Corky did not.

"Really, Hunt? You can't be serious."

"Oh, I'm serious that he wants me to do it. No, I don't have any intention of getting involved in the politics of the thing—and that means no bomb."

"But what about Tahir Azibo?"

"What about him?"

Corky relaxed her posture a bit, uncrossing her legs and reaching for a piece of boiled chicken. Angling her head toward him, she said, "You were sent here to rescue Tahir from Ubora and return him to his mother. Now, you're planning the opposite. If I was officiating the game, I'd call an illegal return. Are you really thinking of giving him to Ubora?"

Hunt shrugged. "Not sure, Cork. My take on Ubora is that he believes in what he's doing—but Azibo probably believes in her crackpot scheme too. Right now I just want to keep the kid from being dead. Beyond that…" Another shrug. "Here's the deal. Ubora claims Azibo had another kid. A girl. He says she killed her in some crazy sacrifice to her god. Corky, if that's true, if she's already killed one of her own kids, how do I not go after this boy?"

Corky placed a palm on Hunt's thigh in a comforting gesture. Just friends. Just reassurance. Yeah, right.

"Hunt, Nishati Azibo has ordered the deaths of innumerable people. There's nothing you can do for them. It's not like saving this boy is going to change anything. You were sent here for a specific purpose, to find Tahir Azibo and return him to his mother. If he's already with her, there is no mission."

Hunt shook his head. "Yeah, you see, Cork, in Lucky's eyes, the goal was always to appease Azibo and to prevent her from using the child's death as a lightning rod. But, to me—the reason I accepted this gig—it's always been about saving the kid. And it sounds like that still needs to be done."

Corky allowed an exasperated sigh. "Abduct the boy and you could up-set the balance. If word gets out that she held her own son hostage, that might be the trigger that bolsters Ubora's uprising. And that is what we were sent here to prevent."

"I was sent here to rescue a boy."

"For the purpose of maintaining the status quo." Corky stared at Hunt, her dark features stern and unreadable. "Right now, all we have is Ubora's claims concerning Tahir Azibo. If you go in there and take him from his mother, it will prove Ubora's allegations."

Hunt leaned forward, glaring at Corky. Didn't she see what this was all about? "Cork, I realize you work for Lucky. I get it, for whatever crazy reason the U.S. wants Azibo in power. Now get this, I don't give a damn about that. I don't know who's in bed with who that makes Azibo the shining star over here, but we both know what's really going on. And if getting Tahir out from under her control brings some instability and causes Azibo to lose whatever credibility she has, so be it. As far as I'm concerned that will probably lead to more lives saved. Now, are you with me or not?"

She remained still for a moment, arms crossed, eyes locked on Hunt. He knew her professional self, the part of her loyal to Lucky Lindell and all that he stood for was wrestling with her feelings for Hunt, and possibly with the morals of the situation. It couldn't be an easy call for her. She'd been working for Lucky for the better part of a decade.

"Yeah, Hunt," she said finally. "I'm with you."

Chapter Sixteen

Mexico

Dana's Spanish was weak at best and so it was fortunate that most residents of this small border town spoke at least passable English. The sheriff was a man of about fifty, dark hair, wavy and full, speckled with emerging gray. He was forty pounds overweight, about Dana's height, and was seemingly obsessed with American football, a passion he'd apparently acquired while attending a Texas university some thirty years prior.

The sheriff, Hector Lopez by name, had at first been dubious of Dana's credentials—such as they were. But once she explained the situation, the lack of interest displayed by American law enforcement—a fact she overplayed to her advantage—not to mention a couple of passing comments concerning her husband's football career at Indiana University, Lopez warmed to her. "Our town is respectable," he said in heavily-accented English. "We are not like Tijuana or some of these other place. We don' have a big drug problem here. Trafficking, eh, not so much. Organize crime, not so much. Border crossings…" He shrugged and rocked his hand in a so-so fashion. "This is a town of the family. Not the tourist. Not for, eh, the troublemaker." He reached across his desk and picked up a glass bottle of Pepsi-Cola and took a generous swig.

Adjusting in the rigid wooden chair on which she sat, Dana pressed him concerning the rape victim. "Now, about the young woman, she was a local?"

Lopez screwed his face into a twist as he traced figure eights on the Pepsi bottle with his finger. "Eh, well, sí. Yes. But new to here. She was…" He hesitated, perhaps attempting to determine how best to say something delicately. Glancing through the small rectangular window to his right,

Lopez stared out onto the sparsely-populated main street of this tiny little spot of a town.

Dana folded her hands as she placed them on the small wooden desk. Smiling, she said, "Hector, please be forthright. I'm not here to judge. My only goal is to identify this perpetrator and to assist in his capture before more women are assaulted."

The portly sheriff shifted and sighed. "Yes, you see…" He nearly swallowed his lips, his cheeks swelled, and then he released his breath in a slow steady stream. "Listen, this girl. I don' want to cause any more, eh, grief for the family. You understand?"

Dana nodded and remained silent. There was something the man desperately wanted to say, but feared revealing, possibly due to potential embarrassment for the town. Dana glanced to the crucifix on the wall behind Lopez. Beside it was a photograph of a much younger Lopez with a young wife and two grade school-aged children, a boy and a girl. Beside that hung his degree in marketing from Texas A & M. There was also a photograph of Lopez receiving an award from several men in business suits, possibly a town council or some such. This was a good man, a family man, likely a religious man. He was a part of this community and obviously loved his home. This crime had hurt him personally. An attack by an outsider on one of those under his protection probably angered him, likely even hurt him on a personal level. This was his place, his home. These people were under his protection.

"I understand your concern," said Dana at last. "I understand how this attack affected this community, how it affects you. I want only to help."

Lopez offered a tight grin and then took a sip of Pepsi, smacking his lips as he drew the bottle away. "The girl," he said. "She was a relative, a niece, of a good family. She came to us only three month ago. Her family send her here because, eh, she need a better, what, environment. She was an adventurous girl—comprende? She had a wild side."

Dana nodded. A wild side. She remembered the scum Walters's comment that the rapist's ritual was designed to purge these women of their sins. This seemed to fit the profile. "I understand," said Dana. "My purpose is not to embarrass the family or disgrace your town further—it seems a lovely place. My only goal is to learn all that I can concerning the attack as a means of tracking the perpetrator."

Lopez offered a relieved nod. "Sí, senorita. Gracias."

"Now. The police report, the autopsy photographs, may I see these?"

The man studied her for a moment, his eyes dark beyond hooded lids. It seemed he came to a decision. "Yes. Of course. But, first this." Lopez bent, reaching into his lowest desk drawer to withdraw a clear plastic bag. "These were found scatter about the body," he said, handing her the bag.

It seemed to be an assortment of roots and powders.

"So far we indentify five root. Two are tea root. One called Dragon blood. One, rattlesnake root. One, Valerian root. These name, they are no' the normal name. They are hoodoo name."

"Hoodoo?"

"Sí. The placement, it seem like ritual. I ask a woman, an expert, a mystic, from another town, to give opinion." He angled his head, offering an embarrassed grin. "I don' believe in these thing. I bring the woman for the case only."

Dana returned the grin. "I understand, Hector. That was good police work. This definitely ties this crime to the man I'm after." And again Dana wondered why it was that she pursued this personally. Certainly she'd now collected enough evidence that the FBI would latch onto the case, finally seeing it for what it was. But then, why hadn't she made the call? Why hadn't she contacted any authorities since Las Vegas? True, she was speaking to Lopez, but he was a small town official on the wrong side of the border. There was little risk of federal agents learning of her investigation through him.

"I need you understand something," he said. "I attend a Texas University, but this is my home. I left almost thirty year ago. And when I leave, I think I will never come back. Bye-bye forever. I'm too good. After university, I take job in Houston. three year, maybe four. Then I get a call. My mother, she is dying. My father, he is senile. They need me home. At first, I am angry. I have life here. I make good money to send to them at home. Cannot my sister take care, or my little brother?" Lopez paused, shaking his head. "No. Not my sister. Not my brother. Not my cousin. Not my aunt or uncle. Are they able? Sí. But this is my responsibility. My family." He reached across the desk for the Pepsi and finished it off in three long gulps. "You know what I find when I get home? I find me. Yes, me. All this time I am gone, I play the big shot. I make money. I date many pretty girl. I drive new car. But I don' realize I leave me here in this little speck. This place, this is me. Someone hurt this town they hurt me. When I come home, I realize I am part of this. So this man, this, eh, stranger, he come here, he kill the girl, he kill part of me. This I will not let happen."

Dana smiled and nodded. "I respect you, Hector. I respect what you stand for and what you believe. I'm only here to help."

He smiled as he fiddled with the now-empty Pepsi bottle. "And you. I don' know why you care. You are not police. You are not…" He shrugged. "You are not official. But I think you have reason. I think I might trust you." With that he nodded and rose silently to retrieve the files.

Five minutes later he returned, a new Pepsi bottle in hand and two manila folders. "You may keep those for the night," he said. "But one thing you must notice."

Accepting the folders, Dana said, "Yes?"

"In the autopsy, there is a substance they find." He took one of the folders back from Dana, and sitting, flipped through several pages before stopping. "Here," he said. "Tetrodotoxin. This is a neurotoxin, very potent." Here, he paused.

"Go on," said Dana. There was obviously more he wanted to say.

Lopez nodded, flushed a bit, took a swig of Pepsi. "The woman, the mystic I consult. The witch." He said the word with distaste if not outright venom. "She bring it to my attention and so I bring it to you."

"I'm not familiar with it," said Dana.

"Tetrodotoxin is ten thousand time more lethal than cyanide. It come from the blowfish."

"You're saying she was poisoned? That this is what killed her and not the knife?"

Lopez shook his head. "No, no, no. The witch lady, she say this use in Haiti to make zombie."

"Zombies? I don't follow."

"In Haiti, a priest, he called a bokor, he mix this poison with other powder. In small dose, this cause paralysis. It look like death. People bury but still alive, they still awake but cannot move, sí?"

"Yes, I understand. It sounds horrid."

"The bokor then dig them up. Pretend to raise them from dead. The zombie, they can now move, but have very little self-will. Very confuse. Disoriented. Many believe they really die and come back undead. The bokor use zombie as slave."

"And you're saying this substance showed up in the report. That it was this zombie powder he used to drug the victims?"

"Yes. Sí. It fit, does it not?"

Dana nodded. It fit. Every aspect of this had some mystical component. Lopez stared at her, a peculiar expression etching lines in his genial face. Twice, it seemed he might speak, but remained silent. "What?" asked Dana. Obviously, there was something he was afraid to say.

Lopez remained silent for nearly another ten seconds, sighed, indicated for Dana to wait by holding up one finger, and then swiveled to face his nearby filing cabinet. Withdrawing a key from his right front pocket, he bent, unlocking a padlock on the bottom drawer. Shuffling several folders out of the way, he withdrew a dark wooden box of about ten inches in length, six in depth, and four in height. The heavily knotted wood was polished to a fine gloss. Placing this on his desk, he unfastened the golden latch and turned the now open box to face Dana.

The box was etched with a peculiar script. Dana's impression was that it was some form of hieroglyphic, but she was far from being a linguistic expert. There was but a single item contained within the felt-lined case, a necklace of sorts. The fine golden chain was attached to four prongs which wrapped cage-like about what appeared to be an oblong chunk of amber, brilliant in clarity, but unformed. No jeweler had cut this to perfection or even polished away scuffs or scratches. Dana narrowed her eyes, studying the curious piece. Suspended within the rich butterscotch colored amber was an insect. Large, gangly, winged. "What is this?" she asked in revulsion.

"It…" he hesitated, not meeting her gaze. "I don' believe, but… The witch lady, she give this to me. It has power, she say. Much power."

Dana stared at the uneven golden blob. "I don't understand. What do you mean by power? What is this?"

A shrug, a nervous grin. "Again, I don' believe. But, maybe." Here he paused. "The witch lady, she say this is locust from Egypt plague."

"Egyptian plague? Mister Lopez, You can't mean the Biblical plagues. Moses, the exodus, that plague?"

"Sí."

Dana stared at Lopez as if he'd just told her that he was an alien from beyond the stars. "You're telling me this is an actual locust from the Biblical plagues?"

"Do I believe? Eh? Who is to say? I no like the magic, but if this from plague of God then maybe it of God." Another shrug.

"Why are you showing me this?"

"Not show, give."

"You're going to need to explain. None of this makes sense."

Lopez nodded in agreement. "The witch lady, she say one day a woman from afar would visit me and that I am to give her the locust. This is strange, yes. But, somehow, I don' know how, but it is right. Loco, but right."

Lopez reached into the box, lifting the chain gingerly and extending it toward Dana. "Please," he said. "Please."

When Dana received the amber necklace she immediately noticed two things. So startling were these that she nearly dropped the necklace. The first, and most obvious, was that the amber was warm, not hot, but well above room temperature. But, this wasn't the thing that disturbed her so. Temperature variation could be explained away. Perhaps the safe had contained some sort of heat source. Dana could think of no reason why this might be the case, but it was a plausible explanation nonetheless. But the thing vibrated, and this she could not explain. It was very subtle, almost nonexistent, but it was there. She could see no movement, and the crystal clear amber hid no wires or mechanisms. The vibration was like that of insect wings, accelerating, pausing, adjusting. The locust was still and unmoving within its golden prison, but still somehow its wings sang their song.

***

That evening, Dana sat studying the reports in her small motel room on the outskirts of town. The girl's body had been found in the rocky desert area just to the south of town, the various hoodoo roots placed about her in similar configuration to the mark on her neck. This mark was consistent with those of the other victims and was obviously a deliberate part of the man's methodology. There had been no attempt made to hide the body. The girl had been naked but for a red silk scarf covering her face. The man apparently wanted to display her shame, but was uncomfortable being face-to-face with his dead victim. This was a common trait among killers that felt some level at shame in what they'd done, or perhaps felt some connection—real or imagined—to the victim. It showed some twisted form of conscience. The man, this Bill as the creep Walters had named him, could not bear to gaze into his victim's dead eyes.

The Tetrodotoxin had been found in the girl's system along with several other substances including toxins made from the marine toad and hyla tree frog, both of which were part of the Haitian zombie formula. Researching the compound, Dana learned that the powder was often applied topically, which would make it quite easy to use on an unsuspecting victim. It caused paralysis and confusion, though the subject was often fully conscious throughout. Though a victim's vital statistics might slow to the point where the person would appear dead, full recovery was also possible, provided the dose had not been fatal. There was some debate as to the effectiveness of the substance, but it seemed to have worked for Bill the rapist. Though, at least two victims had obviously come out of the stupor in time to escape, Dana guessed that the man might still be perfecting his dosage. He wanted the woman compliant, but not comatose, and certainly not dead until he decided it time. But the man was likely not a physician, and it was highly unlikely that he was a Haitian bokor. Likely he was someone with bizarre tastes and misguided beliefs and simply used these methods for his own twisted ends.

Dana was beginning to build an image of this Bill. He held mystical ideas, or at least used them as part of his method, but they stemmed from more than one source. Much of it centered on hoodoo and voodoo, but there was the African fertility idol as well. There were also Catholic images displayed, but these were often used in hoodoo and so not entirely inconsistent. Monica Granger had also seen a Buddha idol and a Star of David in the kill room. It seemed the man merged a cacophony of belief systems, likely pulling favored teachings from each, creating a hybrid mythology to justify the acts of rape and murder. Perhaps the only way he could live with himself was if he could convince himself that he was somehow doing good through these evil works. Again, the victim's covered face. The man felt shame at what he'd done.

One of the other great perplexities was the kill room. He apparently had one in each locale. Or, likely not one in each, but the same paraphernalia in each. Did he rent a room, or perhaps a storage space, and set it up in near identical fashion prior to each attack? Both living victims had described similar rooms: dark, windowless, similar bits and pieces of mystic props. It was unlikely he had several sets of these, particularly if he was only attacking in a given locale once.

And why these locales?

Why these particular women?

The accomplice, Walters, had verified much of the man's hoodoo leanings and indicated that he and this Bill had staked out the Texas roadside bar for quite some time before Bill had indicated his choice of victim. Had he already done preliminary work of which Walters was unaware? Had this girl already been preselected or was it perhaps body type and clothing alone that qualified a victim? All were thin, nearly frail. It seemed most may have dressed provocatively, though Dana was uncertain if this was universal. Most victims were found naked. Dana would need to go back and research any clothing found. Another conundrum. Was the location of the attack based on these specific targets, or were the targets selected because they were at these locations?

Dana believed it to be the latter. Something brought this Bill, this hoodoo maniac, to these locales, where he then selected victims from the available pool. This again led Dana to the question of Bill's occupation. At first she had thought he might be in sales or marketing, something that required travel, but descriptions of the man didn't match with a polished professional appearance. Likely he was a trucker, someone who could wear T-shirt and jeans, have a bit of a scruffy look and still be accepted on the job. True, most truckers looked better than the description of this Bill, but as a rule they had quite a bit of leeway as to appearance and attire.

Dana was about to search trucking routes that matched the attack sites when she was drawn to gaze at the necklace now worn about her neck. Why had she allowed Lopez to force this hideous thing on her? And why had she allowed him to drape it around her neck? Why was she still wearing the bleeding thing? Admittedly, the warmth and subtle vibrations had a soothing effect. The locust—if that was what it truly was—was ugly, the amber gangly and uneven. But, it bore a sort of rustic beauty as well. It was compelling in some incomprehensible way. Dana refused to believe Lopez's supernatural claims about the thing—it seemed Lopez himself only vaguely believed—but she had to admit the thing had acquired a strange kind of hold over her and for perhaps the dozenth time she wondered if all would be better if she were to simply toss the thing away with the rubbish and be rid of it.

There was a sharp rap on the door. Rising, she considered who it might be. The sheriff, most likely. She'd told him where she was staying—the only motel in town, no big secret there—and invited him to contact her with any additional information. Still, a phone call would have been sufficient. Peeking through the curtains, her heart jumped. No. Not the Sheriff. Not the Sheriff at all. Though she wasn't sure whether to be joyful or put out.

Opening the door, she said, "Jonathan, what in God's name are you doing here?"

"Lovely to see you as well, my dear. May I come in?" Not waiting for a response, Dana's ex-husband, Jonathan Thorpe, strode into the room. "I've dug up some information on that idol of yours. I thought I'd bring it by."

"From the UK? You just thought you'd bring it by."

He offered a broad endearing grin, his lady killer grin, as Dana called it. And yes, it was striking. "Yes, well, you see, it's been several months, hasn't it? It seems, well, in truth, I've been worried about you. All alone. Confused. Forlorn. I thought it as good an excuse as any to visit." He glanced about the tiny sparsely-furnished room. "Hmm, yes. Quaint, I suppose. Not exactly the Four Seasons, is it, dear?" He crossed to the desk, glanced at Dana's notes and then turned. "Ah! Mustn't forget. Bad news, I suppose. It appears there's been another victim, just this past evening. Louisiana this time. Our flight leaves in three hours."

Chapter Seventeen

Botma Africa

Hunt peered through his night vision binoculars from his hiding place some three hundred yards distant from the compound. The camp was located in an isolated area surrounded by grasslands and outlying forests. Corky had gotten him satellite images of the place—a difficult task even with the aid of Colonel Lucky Lindell—but even these sophisticated images could not tell him the location of the child and even if he was present. As of the last satellite pass, Corky had determined the number of personnel—forty-seven—and their positions within the compound, but this only served to tell him the size of the force he'd be facing, not the location of Tahir Azibo.

Corky had verified that Nishati Azibo did indeed have another child, a daughter, aged ten. She'd also found no mention of or known location for the girl within the past three years. This didn't mean that Ubora had been truthful concerning the girl's fate at the hands of her mother but it certainly didn't disprove it. As to Ubora's paternal claims, this seemed a possibility. Corky had been able to verify that, prior to rebelling, Ubora had been a member of Azibo's inner circle. There were photographs of the two together. The timeframe fit the conception of the boy, but still, this proved nothing. There were many other young males in her company during the same period. If Hunt succeeded in securing the child, he would insist on a DNA test before turning him over to Ubora—if DNA testing was even available in Botma. The capital city of Mirembe was the only truly modernized municipality in the country, but in many ways even this seemed twenty years behind the United States.

Corky had argued that she should accompany Hunt, but both knew this to be unwise. She was not and had never been a field operative. Corky rode a desk, she did it well, and could be a font of information as well as the source of occasional strategy, but she was no Dana.

Dana.

That was a person Hunt couldn't afford to dwell on at this moment. No more than he could allow thoughts of Corky to muddle his head.

His departure had been difficult. Corky had been...

Persistent.

Pressing her palms against his chest in intimate fashion, she'd said that after this was over they needed to talk—about feelings, about the future. Hunt had tried to dismiss her. He was still married, he'd said. He still loved Dana.

"Hunt," said Corky. "I'm not a home wrecker and I'm not going to be 'the other woman.' If there's still something salvageable between you and your wife, I'll respect that. But be realistic. It's been over six months and she's not given you even a hint toward reconciliation." Here, she'd paused, meeting his gaze with earnest liquid eyes. "We had something, Marc. Something based on a lot more than sex. We were friends first. Very close friends. In my opinion, the only reason we didn't make it as a couple was that you weren't done sowing your wild oats. Now, obviously, you're settled down. Once you know for sure that Dana is out of the picture, I'd like you to give us another chance. I know you still feel our connection. I can see it in the way you look at me. I can tell by the easy way we've fallen back into our old groove." Here, she smiled and patted him playfully on the chest. "I bet I could even coax you into a game of Dungeons and Dragons if I smiled just right." She winked. It was cute.

He shook his head. These thoughts were counterproductive. He was headed into an operation. The lingering kiss on the cheek, so innocent yet so very intimate, had no business in his thoughts just then.

Neither did thoughts of what Hunt had found on Corky's computer. Was it true, what she had found? And if so, how long had she known—and why hadn't she told Hunt?

Too many questions. No clear answers. Again, nothing that should be on his radar going into an operation.

Spitting sand from his mouth, Hunt refocused on the scene. The compound consisted of four sand-colored block-style buildings each situated two to three hundred yards from the next. Corky's intel had not given him specifics as to the nature of each. Which was the command center? Which would likely hold a prisoner? And would Tahir Azibo be held as a prisoner? Yes, Nishati Azibo might use the boy as a tool, she might even execute him if it suited her goals, but in the interim, would he even know that he was being used as such or would he still roam about, oblivious to it all, sleeping in the same room he would sleep in on any other occasion?

Hunt needed better intel and it wasn't going to come from a satellite and Zahir Ubora had given little more than educated guesses. That meant human intel. That meant Hunt had to get face-to-face and down and dirty with someone. Two guards were stationed at each entrance. It was questionable how much they knew. Likely not much in terms of the boy, but a guard might at least reveal how each building was tasked. From there Hunt would surmise the most likely option.

If Hunt had still been in Delta Force, leading his unit into this situation, he'd have likely aborted. The intel was simply too sketchy. He wouldn't have put his men at such a risk. If he at least knew which building to breach, if he knew the location of the boy within the building, anything! But here he was, a lone man with only an open line to Corky and whatever minimal insights she could offer as his support.

He had a good vantage, hidden amidst the low brush on a rise near the eastern side of the compound, but he couldn't wait indefinitely. During daylight hours, he'd likely become visible, and there was simply no chance of breaching the facility once the sun was up. So, whatever move he was to make, he'd need to do so soon.

"Cork," he whispered into his headset. "You there?"

"Nope. On a ski trip. Want to join me?"

"Your jokes are almost as bad as mine, you know that?"

"That's all I've ever aspired to. What do you need?"

"Any updates from the eye in the sky?"

"Twelve of the men are on guard duty outside of the buildings. Four are in building two, six in building three. Eighteen are in building four. That leaves seven in building one. Eleven of the eighteen in building four appear to be motionless so my guess is that's the barracks. The most activity is in building one. All seven have been in motion."

"Okay. Let's assume building one is the command center and building four, the barracks. I'm guessing the kid isn't going to be in the general barracks and it doesn't make sense that he'd be in the command center, especially in the middle of the night. How much activity are you seeing in buildings two and three?"

"At last pass, minimal. But, Hunt, this intel is twenty minutes old. It'll be another hour before I can give you an update."

That was the problem with satellite surveillance. The things only passed over the desired target about once every ninety minutes. True, they were near miraculous during their active window, but then they were useless until they completed another orbit.

"Fair enough, Cork. I'm going to guess the kid is in either building two or three. That makes sense. Little activity, small contingent. Sounds like the right setup to guard a sleeping child."

"I suppose…" Corky drew out the word as if to say, "I don't know about this."

"Why the hesitance, Cork?"

"It's nothing more than an educated guess. And even if you're right, you've only narrowed it down to two buildings. That still leaves you a fifty percent chance of entering the wrong structure."

"Are you a glass-half-empty kinda girl, Cork?"

There was a pause. "Hunt, I think you should abort. You just don't have enough information."

Hunt gripped the binoculars tighter. By all logic, Corky was right. The problem was, he didn't see a way to get any better intel the following night, or the one after that, or ever. Azibo didn't stay in one location for more than a week—usually less. The fact that Ubora knew of this location likely meant she was close to moving on. And then to where? Likely he'd lose her, and Ubora would lose her as well. If Hunt was to make an attempt at rescuing the boy, it would need to be now. There was simply no other way around it.

***

Hunt's goal was to avoid lethal force whenever possible. He was no longer military and thus subject to civilian laws. But aside from the legality of it, Hunt had long since come to the conclusion that simply because someone wore a different uniform didn't make him worthy of death. Hunt's goal was to strike quickly and silently, taking out the guards, and evacuating before they regained consciousness.

Tazing both men guarding Building Two, Hunt pulled each into the shadows, quickly zip cuffing and gagging them before they could so much as moan. He'd have liked to question one of them concerning the boy's locale, but not out of doors. There was too much risk of being seen. Possibly, he'd question someone inside.

Gazing at the unconscious faces, Hunt was disgusted to discover that one of the two was a youngster no older than thirteen. The kid reminded Hunt of the boy that shoveled his snow back in Indiana. He'd known of Azibo's child soldiers, but it was disconcerting to come across one. The boy had been paired with an actual adult—maybe nineteen years-old—and Hunt wondered if this was common procedure, partnering an experienced man with a youth. Hunt pressed two fingers against the kid's neck. Yes. His pulse was strong. He'd be fine, if not a bit disoriented.

It had been a tossup as to which building to penetrate first, number two or three. He'd chosen two simply for the fact that, as of the most recent satellite pass, there were only four known occupants.

The building had a small entry area of perhaps seven feet by seven feet, which led into a narrow, dimly-lit hallway which had two doors on each wall. Strange symbols were painted on each of the hallway walls: long swooping lines, angular curves, nearly identifiable images but not quite. Hunt couldn't make it out as language characters, but sensed that they definitely had some meaning—likely in relation to Azibo's god. Though he took no stock in such things, the look of them caused him pause. It almost seemed they sensed him—or perhaps he sensed them, some malignant intelligence, some force or presence.

Ridiculous!

Get your head in the game, Hunt.

There was a bathroom at the far end of the hall, door open and unoccupied. Hunt moved slowly. According to the near hour-old intel, the first door on the left should be unoccupied. Gently, Hunt tested the doorknob. It was unlocked. In a flourish, he pushed the door open, entering the room, pepper spray gun drawn.

Empty.

It was a small kitchen area. A table, four chairs, a decades-old refrigerator, a microwave, and cabinets. No stove, not even a coffee maker. The lights were out, but Hunt's eyes had long before adjusted to the dark. The room had one window, and so Hunt moved along the parimeter, not wanting to be seen from the exterior. He peeked through the glass, which afforded him a view of building one. The guards remained at their posts, unmoving, bored, unaware.

Moving again toward the door, Hunt peeked into the hallway. Still empty, only one bare bulb illuminating the corridor from halfway up the way. The room directly across from Hunt had had one occupant at the previous satellite pass. The room next to that, three. Assuming the intel remained intact, he would subdue the lone man and hope that the boy was in the next room over, likely guarded by two. If Tahir Azibo was not present, that likely meant three men to subdue in the next room. After which he would move on to building three in search of the kid.

Hunt moved stealthily across the narrow hall, slowly testing the door handle as he had at the previous room. He felt his pulse race, his limbs tense, and his mind focus. It was likely he'd face resistance here. Unlike the guards, whom he'd seen clearly, unlike the previous room which he'd assumed to be unoccupied—intelligence aside, it was unlikely anyone would be using the kitchen in the middle of the night—the probability was that there was an unfriendly immediately beyond the thin wooden barrier. In one fluid motion, he twisted, pushed the door open, and rolled into a shooter's stance.

The room was empty, nothing but boxed supplies lining the walls.

Hunt was quite skilled. He'd been quiet. But there was always the chance someone had heard movement through the thin common wall to the adjacent room. In less than three heartbeats Hunt was into the corridor, moving toward the next room. The door did not fly open; he could hear no frantic discussion from beyond. In some ways it might have been better had they heard him. It might be preferable to stun the first man through the door and then deal with the others before they had a chance to organize. This way, assuming all three men were in this room, he'd have to deal with them each simultaneously, and likely tend to the child's safety as well.

Less than five seconds since exiting the previous room, Hunt pushed the door open, rolling into a crouch.

Two unfriendlies, no boy.

The men were on cots, unarmed, just gaining consciousness. One was up and moving almost as Hunt entered the small space, the other moaned and rustled.

Sweeping his right leg, left to right, Hunt tripped the more alert of the two and slammed his left elbow into the back of his head, knocking him unconscious. The second hollered less than a second before Hunt's fist connected with his jaw. Two more quick jabs and the man was out.

But, Hunt hadn't dropped him before he'd hollered. By all logic there was at least one combatant now aware that there was trouble. Hunt would have preferred to zip cuff these two, but had to assume he was now the hunted. What he would prefer no longer came into the equation.

Hunt burst into the corridor just as three more men—young teens, really—emerged from the room across the hall. Three, not two. Were there more yet?

Hunt dove into the three like an NFL tackle, bringing two to the ground with him while knocking the third back into the room from which he'd come. The kid wobbled, but maintained his balance. The fallen kids were scrappy and Hunt had no desire to inflict significant injury. It was too close to use the pepper gun and his Taser was currently pocketed. Hunt gave the first kid a jab to the solar plexus. The third was moving forward, armed with an automatic weapon. Good, thought Hunt. The gun would keep him out of the battle—for a time.

"Stop! Or I'll shoot!" he yelled.

No. He most definitely would not. Hunt was rolling about wrestling with the man's companions. Even at such close range there was no way the guy could risk a shot. There was simply too great a possibility that he'd hit one of his own.

Hunt elbowed the larger of the two combatants. The young soldier had attempted to squirm from underneath and trap Hunt in a bear hug. Hunt rolled, once again jabbing this larger man. Simultaneously, he pulled the other man with him, grabbing him by the shirt collar, and thus ensuring that the gunman would not risk a shot.

"I'll shoot!" barked the gunman, his voice nearing a panicked falsetto. Fortunately, it had not yet occurred to the man to call for reinforcements.

Hunt jabbed the man to his back again, and kneed the forward man in the groin. One of them got a decent blow to his left cheek, but Hunt was in motion, the punch was mostly glancing.

Without warning, Hunt jerked forward, thrusting the smaller man directly into the gunman's legs. Hunt kicked, hacked, and sliced, freeing himself in the confusion, and jabbing the now-off-balanced gunman in the neck before he could whip the gun around. The gun was in Hunt's possession before its former owner had reached up to his bruised neck.

Hunt swung the gun like a bat, clipping the largest man, who had untangled himself and was charging. A kick and a chop took care of the second man, and a jab to the gut with the gun barrel and a twist and a blow to the left temple finished off the former gunman.

Moving quickly, Hunt zip cuffed and gagged the three and collected his fallen pepper gun from the floor. He needed to be on the move. Someone may have heard the commotion.

As of the last satellite pass, building three had six occupants. But that same intel had been incorrect by one occupant in regards to building two. Obviously, some shifting had occurred. Slipping around the back of the building, Hunt approached the guarded door from the left. Unlike the previous building, there was no easy means of sneaking up from behind. The long wall of the structure necessitated him being in plain view for at least three to five seconds before engaging the men. Hunt felt it better to lure them to him.

"Shhh, don't let them hear you," said Hunt in a loud whisper to nonexistent companions. "Paul, you and Gene go around the back. Ace, Peter, and I will take this side."

Immediately, he heard movement and whispers from the men. One at least moved in his direction. Now, he needed to engage before a call went out. Stepping out from the shadows, Hunt fired pepper spray into the face of the nearest guard. This was a new mixture. Developed in Switzerland, it was more of a gel than a spray and exited the spray gun at just over 400 miles-per-hour knocking the target from his feet and incapacitating him for up to forty-five minutes. The downside was that each gun held only two cartridges. Hunt carried two of these guns.

The second guard darted clear of the spray, stuttering to the right and then left. Hunt dropped the empty gun to the ground as he leaped, tackling the man and rendering him unconscious in three staccato jabs. Moving quickly to the writhing and moaning first guard, Hunt slapped thick adhesive tape across his face. This diminished, but did not eliminate his moaning.

This entire encounter took less than a minute, but had been anything but stealthy. Hunt didn't have time to hide these two. He needed to enter the building, find the boy, and get out. At this moment, he considered his chance of success at less than ten percent. Still, he felt a thrill of exhilaration. He was in this thing. He was performing with a high level of efficiency. For the first time in months he felt like himself again.

Hunt's approach was audacious as he burst through the door in a full trot. Three men were already moving up the corridor. All three were adults in their twenties or thirties. No boy soldiers this time. They looked as if they'd been sleeping, but the adrenaline rush would make them alert. Two carried weapons.

The layout was similar to that of building Two, and Hunt paused short of the first two doorways off the hallway. He didn't want anyone coming from those rooms to attack from the rear.

"Hi, ya," he said as he hit the first, unarmed, man with pepper spray and the second—armed—with the Taser. The first was thrown back by the fearsome pepper blast, falling to his back and tumbling about clawing at his eyes in pain. The second dropped his weapon, collapsing to the floor, unconscious and twitching. The third man was drawing his weapon as Hunt plowed into him at full force.

But, the man held tight to his weapon, shouting a warning as he did so. Hunt slammed the guy into the corridor wall, once, twice. Grabbing the brawny man behind the neck with his right hand, Hunt jabbed his fingers in and down at the base of the man's neck at the jugular notch, causing the opponent to cough and sputter.

But he was not incapacitated, and, in a surprisingly quick move for a large man, twisted, slipping around to behind Hunt. The guy was good. Maybe the other guys had been as well, but Hunt had gotten to them before they'd cleared their heads from the mists of sleep. This man had had those few precious extra seconds to assess the situation. But he still held the rifle and in close hand-to-hand combat, the lengthy and suddenly awkward responsibility was a hindrance.

As the man reached around Hunt's neck from behind, Hunt drove backward, now slamming his assailant against the opposite wall and causing the man's weapon, held only in his left hand, to jam into his own gut. Hunt elbowed once, stomped on his opponent's foot, and then spun, grabbing him by the one-inch hairs at the back of his skull, pulling the man into himself, and jamming his knee into the soldier's hefty yet solid gut in four rapid-fire blows. Hunt then jammed the heal of his right hand up into the man's jaw. The heal is one of the body's strongest natural weapons, but Hunt had a poor angle and the move proved useless.

The weapon fell to the floor as the man attempted to drive forward, using his head as a battering ram. Allowing his opponent's momentum to carry him backward, Hunt dropped into a controlled roll, curled, and flipped his opponent over his head and against the opposite wall. Here, Hunt applied a chop to the neck, finally rendering the man unconscious.

There was a sound from behind the nearest door.

Crying.

A child's cry!

Hunt now realized that it had been there throughout most of the engagement. He'd simply been too focused on survival to allow the sound to truly register.

Snatching the fallen man's weapon as to make it unavailable to him, Hunt tested the door handle. Locked. But it was a standard interior wooden door, hollow, and insubstantial. It could be breached. Hunt stepped back and, with the heal of his booted foot, kicked about ten inches below the handle. Once. Twice. Thrice. He then pushed it open with the simple press of his hand.

The boy was alone in the room. There were two beds, and the other had obviously been occupied as the sheets were in disarray and tossed to the floor. Likely this bedmate was one of the three men incapacitated in the hallway.

Tahir Azibo was small but paunchy. His cheeks were near as round as his eyes. The boy was sitting on a cot, rivers of tears running over his round cheeks, his stubby fingers clutching the rim of the cot. The boy wore a red T-shirt and black baggy pants. His hair was shaved nearly too bald and he screamed a high-pitched wail at the sight of Hunt.

Marching forward, Hunt knelt before the boy. "Tahir?" he asked "Are you Tahir?"

The boy continued to scream.

Hunt suddenly became self-conscious of his face. The scars tended to frighten children until they got used to him, and in this setting, this kid would have been frightened if Hunt had been as handsome as Pitt or Cruise.

"Tahir, my name is Marc. I'm here to help you. Is that okay?"

The boy stared. His cries softened some.

"I won't hurt you. I'm here to help." Hunt paused, a thought striking him. "Tahir, do you speak English?"

The boy nodded amongst hics of fear.

"Good. Good."

There were dozens of questions Hunt had for the boy, but there wasn't time now. Hunt had to get him away and then sort things out once they were in the clear.

There was a sound in Hunt's ear. "Cork, is that you?"

"Who else? The Bluetooth fairy?"

"Cute."

"The satellite's on another pass. Looks like you're in Building Three."

"You're good, Cork."

"You and one other in a room, several unconscious in the corridor. Am I reading that correctly?"

"Yep."

"Is that Tahir with you?"

"Nope. A voluptuous blond. You jealous?"

"I could only wish that you'd care if I'm jealous."

Ouch! Dumb joke. "Yeah. It's Tahir." Hunt smiled at the now-silent child, who was looking at him as if Hunt was insane. Pointing to the earpiece, Hunt said, "I'm talking to a friend. It's like a phone."

"What was that, Hunt?"

"Just talking to the kid, Cork."

"That would have been my second guess. Right after multiple personality syndrome." A pause. "Hunt, wait a second." Another pause. "Uh, Hunt, you might want to put some wings on your feet."

"What you got?"

"Looks like mobilization from buildings one and four. Move!" The last word, she nearly shouted.

"Got it, Cork. Guide me through this." To the child, he said, "Tahir, we've got to go. I'm going to carry you. Don't be frightened."

Scooting back on the cot, Tahir uttered his first sentence to Hunt. "Please, don't kill me, Mister."

Hunt extended his arm, placing his palm gently on the kid's shoulder. "Kid, I promise I will never hurt you."

"Hunt! You've got maybe thirty seconds before six hostiles hit your door. Exit the room; turn right till the end of the corridor. Four of the six are entering through the front. If you hurry, you might get out through the back just before the other two arrive."

"Got it," said Hunt as he scooped the kid up and immediately moved into the corridor. He could hear footfall from behind, though it was difficult to hear anything above the boy's renewed screams. Glancing back, he saw the front door swing open just as he reached the end of the corridor and turned right, nearly shattering the rear door as he slammed into it.

Tahir screamed even more. He kicked and squirmed nearly causing Hunt to drop him.

"Kid. Please. I'm really going to need you to be quiet." Hunt had hoped to gain access to the boy through stealth and to establish at least some minimal report before secreting him away. There was nothing secret happening now.

"Hunt! To your right rear!"

"Got it, Cork!"

One of Tahir's frantic kicks connected with Hunt's side.

Two men were shouting after him, pointing their weapons, but not firing. They wouldn't risk hitting the child.

"What's my best option, Cork?"

Hunt came to the edge of the building and stuttered left, narrowly avoiding the first of the two men.

"Cork!"

Hunt spun, jabbing the heal of his hand into the chin of the closest man.

"Corky! Do I have any options!"

Where was she? Had they lost the connection?

The first man, the one Hunt had avoided, was upon him again. Hunt slowed him with quick crescent kick, nearly losing his balance in the process due to the weight of the boy. Turning, Hunt found that he was facing four more men to his left, two from ahead, and three, the rear. Even if he'd had full use of his limbs, his options would still have been nonexistent.

Chapter Eighteen

Botma Africa

Hunt's eyes had grown accustomed to the midnight dark. His lungs grew weary of his own recycled breath as he sought to breathe from within the musty canvas hood. His wrists burned where they were bound, rubbed raw from his attempts to free himself from his coarse bindings. His back ached from being strapped to the seat for so many hours. He shivered as the brisk breeze poured over him from the vent above. Two hours earlier it had rained unbearable heat, before that, cold.

There had been others in the room from time to time, voices that came and went, sometimes only footfall with no conversation. Hunt had not cried out. He had not begged for water, though his thirst was intense. He had not questioned anyone, nor asked where he was or what they planned on doing to him. This, he already knew. He had tried to kidnap Azibo's son. He would be put to death. Likely, the only reason this hadn't already occurred was that they planned to interrogate him first. They wanted to know who he worked for, perhaps pry some secrets from him. His only possible hope for continued survival was if they deemed him valuable enough to be used as a negotiating tool. But, he held no hope in this. The U.S. would deny any knowledge of his mission. He would be denounced as a rogue operative, his well-documented debacle in Iraq and subsequent departure from the armed forces would serve as proof that he was no longer active and never again would be activated.

Hunt was on his own.

He was going to die.

He'd spent the past several hours mentally preparing for this eventuality.

Hunt squinted at the light as the coarse hood was ripped from his head. He'd not heard anyone approach. Maybe he'd dozed, or perhaps he'd simply been too deep into his own mind to have noticed. Gasping, he drank in the fresh air, filling his lungs repeatedly. His eyes finally beginning to adjust, he took in his setting. The room was of decent size, perhaps two hundred fifty square feet. A bedroom by the look of it. Most of the furniture had been removed, but Hunt could see the paint discoloration where wall hangings such as photographs and paintings had been removed. There were divots in the carpet from a dresser, a bed, and other smaller furnishings. The single window was boarded over and the closet door was open revealing only empty space. There was a faint smell of perfume and powder. Likely this had been a woman's bedchamber, now tasked for a different purpose. Based on this space alone, Hunt speculated that he was either in or near Mirembe. The room was simply too nice, too modern, to be located in any of the outlying towns or villages which were near primitive.

The most striking aspect of the room, though, was Nishati Azibo.

She sat before him on a wooden chair, likely the twin of the one to which he was tied. The laddered seat back turned to face him, she leaned on the chair frame, legs spread about the framework. She wore an olive drab military uniform with no insignia or sign of rank. Her eyes, set wide, were of a clear rich brown and flecked with near-iridescent green, her teeth, quite pronounced and gleaming white, seemed pure ivory against her musky charcoal skin. Her prominent upper lip was curled ever so slightly at the left, offering the near hint of a saucy, possibly even seductive, grin. Hunt knew her to be forty-two years of age but she could have passed for someone in her late twenties. The mannish uniform, though bland and unadorned, did not subtract from, but somehow accentuated, her femininity.

Even before she spoke, Hunt could sense her charisma, her ability to command people by her mere presence. It was no wonder that she was able to convince those of a supernatural mindset that she was some sort of mystic, some sorceress who communed with the gods. In some ways, her appearance was nearly peculiar: narrow, almost skeletal face, sharp jaw, subtle overbite. Irregular, yes. Unusual, maybe even a bit off-putting, but only if one looked at these characteristics individually. For as a whole they conspired to make her stunning, not conventional, not a classic beauty, but stunning nonetheless.

She studied him, the canvas sack that had covered his head held loosely in her right hand. She appeared relaxed, casual, in no hurry to speak. Perhaps she was attempting to build tension, or maybe simply observing his reactions both to her and to the surroundings. Whatever the case, Hunt was fine with it. He was in no hurry to proceed. He could play the waiting game as well as she.

Finally, she dropped the sack to the floor and said, "Have you nothing to say?"

"Hi, I'm Marc. Got any gum?" The comment didn't come off quite as whimsical as he would have liked. This was his first attempt at speech since his capture. His throat was raw and dry. Speech was painful at best.

She smiled. "Marc? Hmm. To me, it seems water might be the more appropriate request." Her voice was husky, rich, full.

Hunt shrugged. "If you want me to participate in a conversation, yeah, not a bad idea." God, did that hurt.

She stared at him for several moments before nodding. "Bello! A glass of water!" She'd raised her voice to utter the command, but only just. It was less than thirty seconds before a soldier entered carrying a wooden cup. Wood, not glass. Nothing Hunt could easily break and then use as a weapon.

The soldier, a man of perhaps thirty-five, well-built, and expressionless, marched to Hunt and tipped the cup in order for him to drink. Hunt noted the man's ring, a golden representation of Anascoreth, Azibo's scorpion god. Lukewarm water dribbled over Hunt's cheeks and onto his neck and then chest. It was brackish-tasting and stale, but still welcome. He doubted he could have gone much longer without liquid and still maintained his semblance of calm. When the cup was nearly empty, the man called Bello withdrew it, stepped to Azibo, and placed the cup on the floor beside her. It seemed a ritual that had occurred many times before. The servant left and Azibo stared at Hunt, her rich intelligent eyes contemplating him, her peculiar lips hinting at contemplation by the merest of twist at the left corner.

"You attempted to kidnap my son," she said at last. Her tone was casual, not accusatory, not outraged as one might expect from a mother under such circumstances.

"Well, he hadn't seen Disneyland yet. I felt it was overdue." Hunt had been trained to remain silent when interrogated. In most cases this was a sound premise. The more a man talked, the more likely something classified would slip out. Speaking gave the enemy a chance to get into one's head, to play with the prisoner, manipulate him. But Hunt was no longer military. Any classified information he had was three quarters of a decade old. Beside, Hunt had determined to be the interrogator instead of the interrogated. Through his brash responses and careless attitude, he hoped to draw Azibo into conversation. Perhaps his only hope at survival was to get her and/or any subsequent interrogators talking. The more he learned, the better his chances.

"Disneyland, hmm. Yes, I suppose he might enjoy that. But, perhaps it is his mother that should make that decision."

"Or maybe his father. Tell you what, let's call Zahir Ubora and see if he's up for the outing."

Azibo laughed a hearty laugh. "My God, you're flippant. I am truly going to enjoy breaking you."

Hunt smiled. "Too late. Already broken. Damaged goods. Blue light special. Three for a dollar. But thanks for your interest." Hunt felt somehow freer than he had in years. Maybe it was that he knew he was to die. When nothing is left to hope for there's very little left to fear. Whatever he said here could not worsen his situation.

Or so he thought.

Azibo returned the grin. "So, you know Zahir. Did he send you?"

Hunt shrugged. "Nah. Well, kinda. See, here's the thing. You made it known that your son had been kidnapped by Ubora. You offered a reward. I'm big on rewards so I went after Ubora. But guess what? He didn't have the kid. In fact, he said you had him."

"And so he sent you."

"No one sent me. He did, though, tell me where to find you. He was hoping I could get in, get the kid, and get out. His reward offer wasn't quite as generous as yours, but seeing as you already had the boy my options were limited."

She nodded, contemplating this, her stunning eyes never straying right or left. It seemed she attempted to read the core of his person. "And you want me to believe that you are here alone, simply in pursuit of a reward."

"Nah, lady, I don't care what you believe. But here's the deal, I work for no one. You'll check me out, I'm sure. Go ahead. You'll find that I'm former U.S. Army, Delta Force, that I left under a cloud, and have had no involvement since. I make my living rescuing missing persons and reacquiring stolen items of significant value. I live off of reward money."

Azibo stared, emotionless, unhurried, unperturbed, her eyes clear and unblinking, her lips subtle yet motionless, an obsidian statue, beautiful, mysterious, cold. Perhaps she was formulating a response, but more likely she was simply studying Hunt, perhaps attempting to sort truth from lie, or, more likely, contemplating how best to break this audacious man. After perhaps a minute, she rose, slowly, purposely, smooth and subtle as a sleek jungle cat. Her gaze did not waver as she approached Hunt. A grin crept through her lips, but only just. She allowed her fingers to trail over his shoulders as she circumvented him. She bent, her lips now less than an inch from Hunt's right ear. When finally she spoke, her husky voice was low and sensuous.

"Perhaps we can speak of options—later. Once I've consulted the great god Aniscorath and determined what use to make of you. You do like options, don't you?" A hand crept under his shirt and caressingly down his chest, fingernails brushing lightly against flesh, teasing, taunting. "You've been injured. Your face has been damaged. But a woman would be a fool to miss that you had once been a handsome man. In many ways you still are. Firm, fit, brave. And the residue of former agonies can be quite stirring, can even be, for a person with the proper knowledge and skill, a window—or perhaps a door—into a man's soul." She blew in his ear. "Tell me, Marc, do you enjoy pain?"

Hunt glanced up at her. His body tingled in response to her seduction, but he knew better than to trust a lioness in her lair. "Nah, Nishati. I'm not a Fifty Shades of Grey kinda guy."

"Oh," she cooed, her fingertips dancing teasingly about his right nipple. "That really is too bad. I enjoy the sensation of pain, the raw exhilaration, the honesty of agony, the freedom of ultimate abandon." She smiled, tickling him with her nails, sliding her left hand across his scared face. "I find pain most intimate and telling. One can learn so much about a person through their relationship with pain." Again, she blew in his ear. "And you, Marc, are about to embark on a meaningful relationship with Lady Pain. She sings such a sweet song and soon you will be humming her melody even in your deepest sleep." Teasingly, she nibbled at his right ear. "I will be most curious to see just how you handle such an intimacy." And she bit down on Hunt's ear, her prominent teeth sinking into the flesh, her hot breath mingling with blood as it spat across his face.

Chapter Nineteen

Louisiana

Dana was different. Thorpe could tell this nearly from the onset. And now, three days later, his assessment had not changed. Dana had become more rigid, seemingly never at ease even at the end of the day when she sought to unwind. Her blue-violet eyes, so beautiful and filled with life, now seemed cool and cautious. Her lips, which so often bore a saucy smirk and a luscious hue, were expressionless, hinting at nothing, but, in doing so, revealing much. She had trouble remaining still for all but a few moments, seeking to be in near constant motion. Her clothing had become as conservative as an eighty year-old preacher's wife and her make-up was apparently hermetically sealed within a vault somewhere atop a mountain peak. She'd even cut her long silky hair to an efficient bob. Her over-the-top humor had fled into the night and her warmth had left no forwarding address. And that necklace, an amulet really, some form of talisman. It was ancient; he could tell this by the style of the thing. Amber secured by golden prongs, unformed, containing the carcass of an insect. Thorpe was a thief by trade, dealing in rare art and ancient artifacts. He'd seen such things before and it troubled him that Dana rubbed it constantly as if it was some strange charm, as if she believed it to contain some power or mystery. She told him nothing of it except that it had been a gift from a friend. It was a little thing, he knew, a nonissue, really. But, it was peculiar, and so, troubling, nonetheless.

Thorpe missed the woman he had loved. He even missed the woman who had deceived him and eventually married another. He missed Dana and hoped—prayed, though he was not a religious man—that she was not eternally absent. Better even that she return to Huntington, to the way things had been for the past few years, than for her to continue as the cool, emotionless automaton standing beside him.

"Mr. Thorpe?"

Thorpe blinked, focusing again on Mrs. Calloway, the boxlike woman in the doorway. "Umm, yes? I apologize; it seems I'd lost focus for a moment. What was it you said?"

"I said, what business is it of yours where my Jimmy is now or whenever?" She stood, fists on her heavily-padded hips, narrow gray eyes peering through wire-rimmed lenses beneath salt and pepper bangs.

"Yes, well, indeed. I thought we'd been clear on that topic. We're investigators. We know nothing of Jimmy, per se, but are doing background research on a number of owner/operators from this region."

"Is he off playing poky-poky with some bimbo?"

"Well, that I couldn't say, but, as I said previously…"

It was here that Dana broke in. "Mrs. Calloway, at the present time, we have no reason to suspect your husband of anything. But, as is the circumstance in most cases, investigators must eliminate dozens of innocents before uncovering the guilty."

"Uh-huh. Who are you with again?"

"We're investigators."

"That tells me diddlysquat."

Dana offered a tight smile and withdrew her wallet from her jacket pocket, extracting a card and handing it to the perturbed woman. "I'm a private investigator, ma'am. This is my license. To clarify, there have been a series of instances throughout the southern portion of the country. I'm not at liberty to discuss specifics, but the locations of the crimes have led us to believe that a long-haul driver might be the perpetrator. It seems these might correspond with delivery routes. That said, nothing specifically points to your husband. We're simply in the process of eliminating innocents in order to narrow our search."

"Poppycock. You're beating the bushes hoping you'll stumble across your man. If this is such a big deal, why aren't the real cops involved?"

"That," said Thorpe, "is a question we all should ask. Why indeed are the real cops not involved?" Here, he eyed Dana. They'd had this discussion. Thorpe had insisted that there was now enough evidence to tie the crimes together, that the FBI should be informed, but Dana had held tight to this like a sandbox toddler with a prized Tonka Truck. Something within Dana needed this. Thorpe didn't fully understand it, but essentially Dana felt a drive for revenge. The man that had violated her was beyond her reach, but this man was not.

No. That wasn't entirely correct. Revenge, yes. That was certainly a part of it, but it went deeper than that. Dana obviously needed to feel control in her life. She needed to prove to herself that she was still the capable woman she had always believed herself to be. She needed to confront a man—a rapist—face-to-face and prove that she could overcome. Thorpe prayed she'd survive the encounter when finally she was upon it. He also knew that it would likely fall on him to ensure that she didn't kill the beast and spend the rest of her productive years staring at concrete walls and iron bars.

The Calloway lead proved fruitless, as had seven prior interviews. They were nearly halfway through Dana's list of potential suspects and no closer than when they'd begun. But Dana was determined that she was on the one true course. Her research all pointed to a truck driver. Louisiana and Texas were the only two states with multiple assaults. Dana had now identified fourteen potentially connected attacks and, using these, had plotted the assailant's course. The grid she'd developed clearly implicated this area as the most likely base locale with California being the furthest most point. This assumption could be reversed, with California as the point of origin, should Louisiana prove unfounded, but both believed Dana's conclusion to be the correct one. It seemed abundantly clear that the man traveled to and from Louisiana and California with regular stops between, Highway 10 West being the primary conduit, with minor deviations for cities in Arizona, Texas, Nevada, as well as dips into Mexico.

Evening was upon them and Thorpe was hoping for a warm meal and perhaps a dash of relaxation. He was still feeling a bit of jet lag and knew Dana would keep him moving throughout the next several days. But, Dana wasn't yet prepared to retire the day. One more interview, she'd insisted, for the third time consecutively. Thorpe sighed and nodded. She was in the driver's seat literally and figuratively. He was a tag-along and as such stifled his many objections. He gazed at her from the passenger seat of the plain vanilla rental. Her clear blue-violet eyes were focused on the road, her jaw set, her fists clenching the steering wheel. She was beautiful, fragile, strong, and courageous. Damn, he missed her. And for what had to be the thousandth time, he wondered if maybe there might still be a chance for them.

But even should Dana resolve her issues and once again regain her vitality, she was married to another man. Despite the nature of his occupation, Thorpe wasn't the type of man to steal another man's woman. It was one thing to appropriate an over-priced trinket from the filthy rich and sell it to someone richer yet, but it was another to sweep away a man's wife, his soul mate, the person he cherished most in the world. Then again, Dana wasn't presently another man's woman, was she? True, the Huntingtons were still legally married, but they'd been separated for over six months, living on opposite ends of the continent. In such a situation, would he truly be taking another man's wife? The question bore further scrutiny.

Dana pulled the car to a stop in front of a small ranch-style home in an older neighborhood situated about thirty minutes distant from Shreveport. Most homes dated from the nineteen forties and fifties, had small yards with plenty of mature trees: magnolias, small pines, and impressive oaks. The Pohl residence was a modest white brick home situated three lots from the end of a block, a late nineties model Chevrolet parked in the driveway. The lawn looked as if it might be in need of love. Crabgrass dominated, the hedge of shrubbery beside the drive pleaded for a trim. There was a dead bush below a bedroom window. Some sort of vine ruled a small flower garden.

Dana studied her electronic tablet. "William Pohl, twenty-eight," she said. "Owner-operator for nine years now. He apparently inherited the truck from his deceased father. Delivers seafood throughout the south as far west as California."

"Well, yes, I suppose it would be difficult to deliver much further west than that," smiled Thorpe. Dana apparently didn't appreciate the humor and simply stared at her screen. "Of course, yes, so, ah, criminal record, I don't suppose he has a history of violence against women?"

"If he had, I would have come here straightaway."

"Right. Whatever could I have been thinking?"

Dana studied the home. "His name is William, though."

Thorpe nodded. "Ah! And this is significant, why?"

She turned to him, her mouth curled down at the corners, her head cocked. And then her expression softened. "I'm sorry, Jonathan. I hadn't told you. I hadn't really thought it through—rather scattered, actually. A witness claimed the man went by the name of Bill."

"Yes, well, that would be significant, wouldn't it? Any other useful tidbits you'd care to share?"

She contemplated for a moment. "No. I suppose not." And with this she exited the car.

***

Celeste Pohl was of indeterminate age, somewhere between mid-thirties and late forties. She wore a long flowing gown that Thorpe could only think of as a moo-moo, though he was certain there was another more accurate description floating about the ether. She was one notch over slender, big-bosomed, and a devoted fan of facial make-up and gaudy costume jewelry. Her smile resided elsewhere and her pale green eyes were apparently stored in an ice tray when not in use. Her words drawled while simultaneously registering as clipped. "Don't know exactly what business you have with my Willy, but I can tell you your tree is darn barked up wrong."

Curious. "Yes," said Thorpe. "Presumably, you are correct in all you say, but, may I ask, your Willy, does anyone refer to him as Bill?"

"Why would any blamed fool call Willy Bill?"

Her words were casual and nearly ludicrous, but her eyes were intelligent, possibly even calculating. Thorpe had a peculiar sense about this woman. "Oh, no particular reason. Simply a follow-up question," he said.

Dana snorted, obviously irritated at the course of the interview. "When might we speak with Willy, ma'am?"

Celeste tilted her head, gazing at them askance. Thorpe was certain he detected a lingering grin creeping about the shadows of her lips. "Well, I don't know that you'll ever speak to him. He ain't here now and he won't be soon. Now, are you going to tell me what this is about or do I toss the door in your faces?"

Well, Thorpe had no desire to experience any door toss facing, but Dana was determined to press onward. "When was Willy last here?"

"Right before he left." She paused, studying them, before adding, "Now, why are you two after Willy?" Her voice was smooth, nearly a coo. It seemed some of the twang had fled with its companion, southern hospitality. Thorpe noticed movement somewhere up the hall behind her. Could that have been William?

"As stated," said Dana through the narrow line of an emerging scowl. "We are not police, but only investigators. We simply need to ask Willy a few questions."

"Ask me instead." Before Dana could respond, the woman's head whipped around. "You two! Your room—now! Or consequences." Thorpe heard the rush of feet receding into the home and what might have been a child's whimper. Not William after all, he supposed.

Dana's scowl dropped into a full-fledged glower and Thorpe spoke before Dana could spin her head and vomit pea soup all over an already dicey situation. "Mrs. Pohl," he said through a hastily manufactured grin. "William is suspected of nothing. But there have been some irregularities with shipments from other truckers making similar runs. As such, we'd like to ask him if he's been approached, and by whom, concerning carrying illicit materials—or persons." Thorpe's smile broadened, his puppy dog eyes joining in.

Celeste Pohl's eyes narrowed as if in suspicion. "You're talking about transporting illegals."

"Of course we are," smiled Thorpe. "What else could you suspect?"

Celeste grinned with all of the warmth of an iguana. "You're a little weasel, ain't ya, mister?" Before Thorpe could respond, she added. "I don't take kindly to weasels."

***

"That woman knows something," said Dana as she paced the small motel room, slipping between the bed and television and then past Thorpe who sat at the tiny writing desk adjacent the television.

"More than likely, yes," agreed Thorpe. "I would be surprised if darling Willy isn't involved in something dodgy. The question, as I see it, is whether his particular crime is your particular crime. Perhaps he is shipping illegal immigrants. It certainly wouldn't be out of the question."

Dana scoffed, obviously believing Thorpe's conjecture to be ludicrous. Stroking her amulet, she said, "It seems the obvious guilt would be the one we're pursuing."

"Yes, of course, well, from our perspective it would seem that way wouldn't it? And you might very well be right. You likely are, in fact. But it doesn't, in my opinion, behoove us to disregard other possibilities. His known route, for instance. The logs you've so cleverly accessed indicate

175

that, as a rule, Route 10 serves as his primary conduit. But, we also know he sometimes delivers south of the border as well as in several southwestern locales connected by tributaries to his primary route. These deviations, of course, suggest he might have been present for some of the assaults."

"Some?"

Thorpe shrugged. "Most, perhaps all—likely all—but your research is inconclusive. There are missing log entries, at least three during the days women were attacked."

Dana whirred, glaring at Thorpe with a venom normally reserved for cheating husbands, child molesters, and those who harm small animals. "He was covering his bleeding tracks. That's why the entries were incomplete."

"Agreed. That would be the logical assumption," said Thorpe with a patience developed over a lifetime of stealth and deceit. "But those dips into Mexico may suggest something entirely different."

"He raped and murdered a young woman in Mexico."

"Someone—possibly William Pohl—raped a young woman in Mexico."

Dana nearly growled. "Jonathan, why are you opposing me on this?"

Because I'm afraid you'll run off and murder the man or be murdered yourself in the process of trying.

"Dana, dear, you must know that I'm your staunchest supporter. And truly, you are likely correct in this matter, but why not be certain? You now have a suspect. Investigate him further. Be sure of his guilt before you do anything rash. Perhaps now would be a good time to notify the authorities."

Dana exhaled what surely would have been white hot flames had she only been a dragon, rolled her eyes, and stomped through the doorway to her adjoining room.

Chapter Twenty

Louisiana

Dana's eyes fluttered open. There was light within the room. It was minimal, granting the space a hazy yellow/red glow and splashing great distorted shadows across the walls and floor. It was coming from the far end of the long narrow space. She could make out animal cages lined against one wall and a rustic chest of drawers against the opposite, unidentifiable objects sitting atop. The walls were lined with large rugs of random design. The type one might find at a flea market.

She was not alone.

A scarecrow was with her. Somewhere deep in her mind she knew that this was ridiculous. A scarecrow was not a living entity.

The scarecrow had hair of straw. Light of color. Straight. Protruding in multiple directions. The scarecrow was thin to the point of emaciation. But, of course it was thin. Scarecrows have no need of food and are thus skinny. Everyone knew this. Most scarecrows weren't naked though. Nor did they dance about in skitters and hops as this one did.

And this one chattered. Dana couldn't make out the words and wasn't certain if the constant flow of syllables was directed at her or if the scarecrow was talking to himself. She supposed a scarecrow might talk to himself. To whom else would a scarecrow talk? She'd never known one to be sociable. Except in The Wizard of Oz. But that was fiction. In fiction a scarecrow could be sociable.

The scarecrow spun as if in surprise. It glanced in her direction and then in another. It clutched something in its right hand and brought this up to its face. The scarecrow hopped and giggled, its long gaunt face stretched into a jack-o-lantern grin. Again it spun and muttered. The scarecrow was funny.

At some level Dana knew this wasn't true, that the scarecrow was anything but funny, that it—he—was dangerous and unstable, but Dana wasn't fully herself just then and so attempted an unsuccessful giggle.

The scarecrow turned, frowned, stared. And then the grin returned accompanied by a chattering snigger. It marched toward her, skinny and naked and white, and knelt, leaning over her, one knee on either side of her. It spoke. Not English. Something else. French perhaps, but no French she'd ever known. The pronunciations were all wrong, as was the conjugation. The words had a cadence to them and seemed almost a chant, but not quite. Perhaps a prayer. That was funny, a scarecrow praying in broken, poorly articulated French. Silly scarecrow.

Now it leaned closer, sniffing at her, inhaling her scent. It came to Dana that she was naked. Had she known this before? Was it something she'd forgotten? She was naked and so was the scarecrow. He sniffed again, at her neck, and giggled, and then licked. He was licking her neck and babbling French nonsense. And he was erect. The scarecrow was aroused. Dana could feel this as the scarecrow rubbed against her.

And now the scarecrow didn't seem very funny. In fact, she began to wonder if it was a scarecrow at all. Who'd ever heard of a French speaking scarecrow with an erection? The scarecrow licked again, prayed again, giggled again. It slid across her body like a pale white snake, writhing and giggling and moaning. Dana attempted to move, to throw the scarecrow off of her, but her arms would not obey and her legs were as concrete, hard, cold, immovable. She sought to speak but could not summon the skill. Perhaps she uttered some faint syllable, perhaps nothing at all. There was nothing Dana could do. Not a thing. Reality came in a wave of understanding and then fled as an outgoing tide. She understood all one moment and then nothing but flights of fancy the next. The only consistent was dread. Deep, into the marrow, dread. And Dana so wanted to scream if only her voice would comply.

***

The scarecrow licked the woman one last time and then rose. But, he did not think of himself as a scarecrow. The thought that Dana saw him as such would likely make Willy Pohl laugh and giggle. Though, in truth, these he already did. He gazed down at the woman. Asian. Chinese? Japanese? He couldn't tell the difference. In truth he could care less. All the same, he supposed. Still, he'd never purged an Asian before and he wondered if there were any special rules. Did they have unusual sins known only to them, strange indulgences that might require particular ways of purging? He didn't know, and couldn't know. Not yet at least. But, this one was different in more ways than race alone. This one had chosen him, where he was usually the one to seek and find. She had sought him out, tracked him, apparently from a great distance. This concerned him. How had she known that there was someone to track? How had she known that there was one purging sinners at the priestess' behest?

His priestess. She wasn't aware that he had come out to visit the girl and he hoped she would not be upset when she found him missing from his place beside her in their bed. But, he hadn't been able to sleep. His mind kept turning to the strange Asian woman with the British accent. She was a curiosity and she was a concern.

She was a hussy.

His priestess had said she was just another hussy like all of the other hussies.

But, she hadn't dressed like the other hussies. She hadn't flaunted her flesh. She didn't wear too-tight clothing or skimpy little skirts and tops. She wasn't drenched in perfume. He hadn't found her in a bar, or waiting tables with winks and flirts, or walking a street in search of men. Instead, she had come to his home in the middle of the night—alone. His priestess said a decent woman never came to a man's home alone, especially in the dead of night. His priestess said the Asian woman was obviously there seeking the opportunity to sin. Willy wasn't sure this was why the woman had come. She'd picked the lock to their home and sneaked around with a pen-sized flashlight. She'd not been flaunting herself as if on display. If not for the home's silent alarm they'd never have known of the intrusion. But his priestess knew about these things. If she said the woman was a hussy, then certainly she was a hussy.

***

Concentration was becoming more difficult for Dana. Certainly, she'd been drugged, and whatever the substance, it was dragging her further and further into the hell of oblivion. She couldn't quite grasp a line of thought. It was the scarecrow's fault, she supposed. The naked dancing scarecrow was distracting.

Dana closed her eyes. "Jonathan," she tried to say, but the syllables wouldn't quite form. But that was silly to call for him. Why would Jonathan be here? Jonathan was not a scarecrow. She'd left him alone and unknowing in his motel room. Jonathan. She'd never asked him to come with her on this investigation; he'd simply reinserted himself into her life under the guise of concern. As such, she simultaneously appreciated and resented his presence. She wondered if Jonathan had yet discovered her missing. How long had it been since she was taken? An hour? Several hours? A day? More? In truth, she couldn't say. Her mind was muddled, her thoughts scattered. But regardless of the current time, Jonathan would eventually discover her missing. She hated relying on another for her rescue, but had to figure he'd make some sort of attempt, whether successful or not, he'd likely cause a stir. In which case, she needed to prepare herself. She needed to be ready when opportunity arrived.

The scarecrow hopped and skittered, breaking Dana's brief affair with linear thought. Strange scarecrow. Strange naked scarecrow.

***

Willy longed to proceed with the sacrament, but hesitated. Would his priestess agree with the timing? He turned, marching toward the caged animals. He liked having the animals here. He liked the smells. He liked the way they scurried about in their cages. He particularly liked the way they squirmed when sacrificed. It was so much better now that he had live animals to sacrifice. It made the sacrament complete. The addition of fresh warm blood upon the flesh enlivened the spirits and consecrated the purging.

Willy locked eyes with a ferret. It was a sleek creature, but deceptive. The teeth were long and sharp, the eyes small and dark, the snout long and twitchy. The creature danced one way and then the opposite. Willy matched the movement, giggling hysterically. In a quick reversal, he leaped forward, hissing at the little creature and causing it to scurry to a far corner of its cage. Willy could see its breathing quicken, its feet twitch. The animal knew who to fear. Its blood would be warm and slick and sticky. Its blood would help to consecrate the purging.

Turning, Willy again marched toward the woman, dropping to his knees, leaning into her, inhaling her scent. Her eyes followed him, but she was powerless to move. He wondered if she even truly saw. The priestess practiced powerful magic. And she had prepared this one herself. It wasn't like those times when Willy was away from her and left to perform the sacrament alone. His priestess was here, available to him, able to prepare the woman as only she could do. She'd tried to find him helpers for when he was far and away, assistants who could help in preparation, helpers who could aid him in capturing the hussies. She'd found one such helper on the internet, but he was not strong like Willy, he was not brave like Willy, and so he'd fled before the sacrament could truly begin. Willy didn't know why the priestess thought he needed help when traveling. Willy was fine. He had the goddess to guide him. Willy knew just what to do.

Willy sniffed the woman again, trailing his face down her form. Certainly she was ready. Certainly, his priestess would want him to proceed. The woman had obvious sin. One could tell simply by the supple texture of her golden skin. A righteous woman would never allow her skin to be so enticing. A righteous woman would never allow her form to ensnare innocent men.

He inhaled again, this time tasting the skin with the tip of his tongue. Immediately, he felt the urge to purge grip him from within. Yes. This one was in great need of salvation. He could see it in her eyes, the pleading eyes, crying for release from the burden of her many sins. This woman was lost to hell without the purging that he alone could offer. It was his duty, his right, his mission. He was helpless to delay. There were no other options but to proceed in haste.

He nearly leaped to his feet. His bag. His precious bag. He'd dropped it, cast off like his useless clothing. Marching to where it had fallen, he bent, scooping it up in one fluid motion and bringing it to his lips. How could he have forgotten his bag? Without it, his act would be nothing but fleshly lust, just like that of the woman he sought to save. How could he have been so foolish? How could he have forgotten it?

Willy inhaled, losing himself in the pungent aroma. How close he'd come to lowering the sacrament to a simple act of animal lust. Pressing the bag against his forehead, Willy turned to contemplate the obsidian goddess. Dark, shining, cold as winter sleet. She was here, atop the dresser, overseeing his actions. She was still relatively new to him and he was not yet accomplished in reading her direction. It was his priestess who interpreted the goddess's desires. They'd only been in possession of the idol for a few months and sometimes Willy was still frightened of her.

Willy cocked his head. Had the goddess just spoken to him? Had he heard some inner voice? He met the eyes of the goddess. Contemplating.

Listening. Absorbing. Was it true? Was she telling him to purge the woman now?

Willy shook his head and then gazed again at the goddess. Had she really just spoken directly into his mind?

A flitting shudder and a giggle. Yes. Yes, she spoke. The goddess spoke. He was sure of it.

With a nervous twitter and hop, Willy turned, once again facing the golden woman. Yes. Yes! The goddess spoke to her true servant. Look at that skin so full of sin. Surely the hussy's soul was in distress. Surely she needed the salvation that only he could offer. Willy dropped to his knees, still clutching the precious bag in his hand. His priestess would be angry. Certainly she'd be angry. She'd not given him permission to proceed. But the goddess had granted the permission. Surely the goddess outranked the priestess.

Willy crawled forward on hands and knees praying in a language he did not know, reciting words he would never understand. His arms shook in anticipation. He felt lightheaded and giddy. He would purge this woman. He would take on all of the sin she had to offer, bringing it onto himself to then be purged by his priestess. What a glorious experience. What a dreadful experience. Willy whimpered in glee and attempted again to recite the meaningless words.

There was a sound. Loud. Almost thunderous.

And then there was light. Bright and damning.

"Willy!" shouted the priestess as she climbed into the temple. "Willy, what are you up to?"

She turned, closing the door with an echoing crash as she awaited his response.

"Willy! I asked you a question."

He was on his feet now, bag clutched in hand, pacing two steps one direction and then two steps in another. "I was going to purge her sins, Mommy. I was going to set her free."

Chapter Twenty-One

Louisiana

Dana was gone. Thorpe had felt it in the night. Some intuition, perhaps, or maybe his subconscious mind had somehow heard her slip away, perhaps the sound of her door closing, or the rental car engine coming to life. Perhaps the simple truth that he'd once shared a life with this woman and had fallen victim to her stealthy ways had sent his internal alarms ablaze. But he'd disregarded his instinct. And, as always, he regretted such a decision. His instinct was solid; it had saved his life on multiple occasions. But, Thorpe had been tired, jetlagged, his mind cloudy and unwilling to wake.

He'd knocked on the connecting door to Dana's room early in the morning. It was possible, he'd supposed, that she was still sleeping, or perhaps in the shower, but his instinct knew better. Quickly picking the nearly useless lock, Thorpe entered the small motel room to find it empty save for Dana's luggage and few travel belongings. He knew where she'd gone. He had no doubt. She'd returned to the Pohl residence. That had been the one. The guilty party. They'd both known it, though there was little more than a feeling that led them to the conclusion.

An instinct.

Ignored.

At least on Thorpe's part.

Dana had likely slipped off into the night because she didn't want him pressuring her to take her information to the police. She'd been single-mindedly bullheaded on the issue and was likely to get killed as a result. Pulling his phone from his pocket, Thorpe dialed Dana's number. No answer. This was not surprising. She was either avoiding his call because she didn't want him talking sense into her or, more likely, she'd encountered some sort of hitch.

Just like it had been during their marriage. Thorpe's instincts had told him something was wrong then too. But, he'd been in love. He'd been a fool. And still was one, he supposed. Nothing brings stupidity forward in a man like a woman. He knew this intellectually—he'd lived it too many times to deny it—but still Thorpe found himself enthralled by Dana's womanly spell.

And so Thorpe called a cab, instructing the driver to drop him two blocks distant from the Pohl residence. He needed every advantage and didn't want to be seen. Even as he made his way toward the small home near the end of the cul-de-sac, Thorpe had yet to determine a firm course of action. It was now daylight, residents were entering their vehicles, driving off to work, some even watering their lawns. Stealth was not a viable option. Thorpe couldn't approach the home with claims of being a repairman, sales person, or even a Jehovah's Witness because Celeste Pohl had seen him the day before. They'd spoken. She knew him on sight. And, even as much as he'd nettled Dana to involve the authorities, calling the police now would be of no use. Dana was an adult, missing for only, what, an hour, two, three? They wouldn't file a missing person report for at least another day, perhaps longer.

No, Thorpe was left with only one option. The direct approach. He'd knock on the door, claiming he had a few more questions for Mrs. Pohl, and, depending on her response and demeanor, determine an action plan from there. Quite possibly this would involve breaking and entering and likely even assault. It was such a lovely way to start a day.

As it turned out, Thorpe needed no plan. The Pohl's had anticipated his return and were waiting. The ambush was swift and stealthy. Thorpe was subdued before he'd had time to react. Damn his stupidity, he hadn't expected them to use a child as a distraction.

***

Thorpe woke to discover that he was bound within the narrow confines of what Dana, in her drugged state, had not recognized as the trailer to an eighteen-wheel big rig. The mingled smell of animal excrement and incense was heavy in the air and caused Thorpe's nose to itch in retaliation. Dana was present as well, also bound, and apparently in a state of drug-induced hallucination, mumbling about a dancing scarecrow and its mother. They were both sitting on the carpeted floor, backs against one of the long walls, but Dana appeared to have difficulty remaining upright as she continually dipped to the left before righting herself just at the point where she might topple.

The single lamp, situated at the far end of the space, cast a golden hew, spilling elongated shadows about the narrow area. Occultic paraphernalia littered the floors and walls, strange symbols that Thorpe recognized as coming from varied origins. As someone who'd spent his life acquiring various pieces of art and antiquity for clients, many with varied and eclectic tastes, he'd become familiar with religious art of numerous flavors. Many of the samples were of African source while some South American, and still others of Native American. Hanging on the far wall was a cluster of shrunk-en skulls of the type one saw in documentaries featuring witch doctors and the like. The features were distorted, the hair stringy and thin, but to Thorpe they all seemed feminine and he wondered with a sudden emptiness at the pit of his belly if these were the partial remains of some of Pohl's previously unknown victims. He also spotted the animal cages on the opposite wall and to the far right. There were ferrets and rabbits, a house cat, a raccoon, a couple of squirrels, and several guinea pigs. He assumed these were to be used as sacrifices.

The children, two of them, a boy and a girl, each of preschool age, were caged beside the animals. It had been the girl, feigning a twisted ankle and calling to Thorpe, that had distracted him resulting in his capture. The boy, at perhaps four years of age, was the older of the two, but not by more than a year. They sat cross-legged in their cages atop sofa cushions, the girl playing with a tattered doll that seemed old enough to have belonged to the child's mother and the boy picking his nose and studying his findings with the curious eye of an archeologist examining a newly acquired relic. Neither appeared injured or drugged. If anything they seemed content with, or, at least, accustomed to their circumstances.

The Pohls were present as well, both Celeste and William. Celeste wore a colorful flowing robe adorned with numerous pieces of gaudy jewelry, most of which displayed a hodgepodge of occultic designs: a plastic Star of David, a silver cross, an iron goat's head, a Buddha of plastic, and several other random symbols of various origins. Her frizzy hair nearly flapped as wings when she moved about the trailer, chanting random prayers in heavily-accented French and alternately barking commands to William.

The young man, for his part, resembled Celeste in a way that caused Thorpe discomfort. The woman was likely in her forties, the man in his twenties. The familial resemblance suggested mother and son, but the relationship between them seemed more that of lovers. No. Lover was the wrong term. Thorpe saw no affection where Celeste was concerned. But the relationship did imply a sexual intimacy. There was touching, even casual fondling, a stray kiss here and there, and lusty leers from both participants. But, love? No. Thorpe was already coming to believe Celeste incapable of such.

William, clothed in an olive T-shirt and ill-fitting jeans, danced around the small space as if hopped up on the latest street drug, his bare feet barely striking the carpeted surface before rising in subtle rabbit-like hops. His eyes, small and deep set, darted one way and then the other. His thin rubber-band lips twittered and trembled as he glanced from Celeste to Dana and to Celeste again, lust for both women evident. "She needs to be purged," whimpered William. "The goddess told me she needs to be purged." His Louisiana drawl was pronounced and forlorn.

Celeste turned, causing William to scuttle backward in a hurried stutter. "The goddess does not talk to you, Willy. You know that."

187

"I know. I know. You say that. But how do you know she doesn't? Did she tell you?"

Celeste's green eyes blazed with frigid fire. "Are you questioning me, Willy? You know you'd best not be questioning me."

William's shoulders rolled forward, his head dropped. "No, Mommy. I just. I mean, I could a sworn she talked to me. It is possible, isn't it, that she could talk to me too?"

Mommy! He called her mommy. Thorpe had been correct in his assessment of this twisted relationship. It was all Thorpe could do to remain still and silent, feigning unconsciousness as he continued to snatch glances at the scene in hopes of developing an escape plan.

"Willy," said Celeste, in a tone that suggested she was regarding a young child. "I know you think you hear things, spiritual things, deep and important things. But that don't make them so. You ain't quick enough to understand something even if you heard it. And you ain't gifted like me. And so you don't hear none of it right. You just think you do. But you get it all muddled up. You need your priestess to interpret for you."

"But, Mommy, the goddess, she said…"

"The goddess said nothing. That was your little pecker talking and you know I speak the truth on that. It seems you might be due for a little purging yourself, isn't that right?" This, she said with a wry grin and a near wink. Thorpe prayed they didn't decide to "purge" right there in front of everyone—in particular the children.

"That woman is not like the others," Celeste continued. "Now, I'm certain her sin is as bad as any other hussy you've healed on your sojourns, but this one is different. Ain't that right?"

William glanced at Dana, a lost puppy expression in his tiny green eyes, and then turned back to Celeste. He said nothing.

"She has attachments, Willy. Connections. Look at this right here." She angled her head toward Thorpe who kept his eyes all but closed entirely, his head angled gently toward his left shoulder, his mouth slack. "Already she's up and sent another problem to our doorstep. Not to mention that she tracked you here. Are you too thick to realize she found you, not the other way around? Are you so thick?"

"No, Mommy, I was just thinking that she's gonna die, and she's a hussy, and she needs to be purged before she dies, and... I don't know exactly. It seemed, like I said, the goddess, she said to purge her."

"What'd I tell you about the goddess? She don't speak to you."

William twitched his head sharply to the left as if cracking a kink from his neck. "I know. And I didn't mean no problem for you. I just thought she spoke to me."

Celeste smiled. "We both know what spoke to you and it wasn't no goddess. Now, how do you suppose we deal with your little problem here?"

William gazed at her, a vacant look in his pale green eyes. He hadn't understood the question.

"The man and the woman, dumb-head. We can't just keep them for pets, now can we?"

William stared at his feet as intently as if they were the most interesting things in the world. "No, Mommy. They need to die, I suppose. Purge them first, maybe. And kill 'em."

"You may not be as stupid as your late father, yet. You know that?" And she moved forward, kissing him passionately on the lips. His arms came up, first embracing her in a firm bear hug, and then sliding south. At this point, Thorpe did close his eyes.

Chapter Twenty-Two

Botma Africa

Sweat dripped from the tip of Hunt's nose onto the interior of the canvass hood. Or was it ice water—or urine? He'd experienced each and was at a point where he could barely distinguish the difference. And he was long beyond the point where he cared. He'd been beaten, drugged, starved, frozen, baked, all designed to encourage him to break. What his interrogators didn't realize was that he was already broken and had been so well before entering this country. Maybe he hadn't realized just how broken he'd been, probably he had, but had simply buried it beneath the haze of Oxycontin. But regardless the specifics, his spirit had been rent, his core crushed.

Part of it had been Dana, yes, but the fissures had been in place well before they'd met. Hunt simply hadn't yet realized what the events in Iraq had done to him. It wasn't the bomb blast that had destroyed the left side of his face. It wasn't his dishonorable discharge, though this had hurt him at a level he could never have expressed. At his core it had been the thought that his actions had led to the deaths of two of his team members and an innocent child.

But, even this he could have weathered.

The crucial element had been that his own men had turned on him. All of them. Each surviving member of the team. Not one had come forward in his defense. Not one had maintained contact after his discharge. These men had been as family to him. He would have died for each a thousand times over if such a thing was possible. Hadn't they felt the same of him? Why hadn't a single member of his team confronted him face-to-face about the events of that day? That he could have handled. Anger. Confrontation. Even a sense that they'd somehow been betrayed. This he could understand.

This he could process. Why hadn't they dragged him out back and beaten him to a bloody pulp or cursed him into his grave? Anything but silence and disregard. Had they not felt anything? Was he not even worthy of scorn?

Apparently not.

Hunt was as nothing to the people who had meant the most to him. Whatever he had done that day, whatever the specifics of those forgotten hours had been so horrible as to forever turn these men from him. And he would never know why. Those memories were forever gone to him, locked away in some dusty corner of his mind where he was forbidden entrance.

"Dog!" screamed the voice. It registered near simultaneously with the blow to the back of the head. Hunt's chair toppled. He let out a grunt as his left shoulder hit the unforgiving floor. Almost before he could gasp a breath, he was righted with two swift jerks. The hood over his head made it impossible to anticipate his attacker's movements and so Hunt's neck jerked harshly to one side at the sudden jolt. Another blow, this one to the balls. Hunt gasped as his form sought to double over but the restraints forbad even this small comfort and so he simply shuddered and wheezed.

Another blow.

Another.

Three more and then a kick and a shove.

Again, Hunt toppled and was immediately righted.

Next came a sharp rap against his shins, the instrument of his pain, likely a baseball bat or metal pipe. It didn't matter which. The pain was the same.

Footsteps to his rear. Hunt tensed, even though they were moving further away. The steps ceased. He heard the clank of metal. In a moment he would realize that the sound was of a bucket handle. The footsteps resumed, coming from behind. There was the rustle of movement and then scalding liquid poured over his head.

Hunt screamed and writhed tipping his own chair this time.

No one bothered to right him.

"Who sent you?" asked a man.

"Lucky!" screamed Hunt. The word was out before he'd fully processed that he'd said it.

A chuckle. "Oh, no," said the man. "You are not at all lucky."

A swift kick to the gut.

"Who sent you?"

"Lucky," whimpered Hunt through tears and gasps. "Lucky. It was Lucky."

"Foolish man," hissed Hunt's tormentor as he offered another kick before pulling Hunt upright.

Even this rather benign jostling sent waves of pain through Hunt's form and he prayed that nothing had been ruptured by the kicks. His mind swam. His thoughts danced about never landing. Had he just given up Lucky Lindell? Had this man just broken him? He thought that he might have but couldn't quite remember.

There was a shuffle of movement from behind and then a firm grip on Hunt's left bicep followed by the prick of a hypodermic needle. "There," said the man. "We'll see how lucky you feel after this settles in."

As the hot liquid raced through Hunt's veins, as Hunt drifted into the haze, he thought of Dana and was glad she'd not accompanied him on this mission. At least she was safe. At least Dana was safe.

Chapter Twenty-Three

Louisiana

Dana was uncertain how Jonathan Thorpe had come to be her fellow captive. Her last relatively coherent thought had been of Willy Pohl—or had it been a scarecrow?—preparing to rape her only to be stopped by the woman, Celeste. Pohl had drugged her. That was certain. Even now her mind was fuzzy. Had it been the zombie drug? Most likely. That was what Pohl used on his victims, that frightful, lethal, mixture based on a toxin harvested from blowfish. She supposed she should be thankful that the woman had stopped the man, berating him like a child. It even sounded as if she forbad him to rape her. Forbad him! Her admonitions had not excluded any possibility, but only caution and watchfulness. As in, she was in favor of rape but only on her own terms.

Dana seethed at the thought of the woman. How could any woman take part in, or encourage, the rape of another? How could she be party to such a thing? How could a woman become so twisted as to go against nature itself? Woman didn't rape. Woman wanted no party to rape. It was an affront to their freedom, to their worth, to their personhood. But there was more to this than rape alone. Dana's mind was still fuzzy, but already she recognized the religious symbolism about the place. She'd heard the talk of purging and sacrifice. These people had somehow turned rape into a religious sacrament. This didn't in any way lessen the crime, but merely added another dimension to the perversion.

And no matter the reason, no matter the rationalizations, it all came down to one truth. Dana was to be raped. She was certain of it. This was one thing she could never—NEVER—allow to happen again, even if it meant dying to prevent it.

Attempting to appear incoherent and stupefied, Dana wriggled her hands. They were bound behind her back by what felt to be a thin rope or cord, perhaps clothesline or something similar. She was seated on the carpeted floor beside Jonathan. He appeared listless, but perhaps, like her, feigned unconsciousness. She wriggled again. The binds were tight, nearly tight enough to cut circulation, but still maybe with some work she could loosen them enough to free a hand. It would be a slow process, especially since her captures were present and she couldn't risk their noticing her efforts.

Her mind becoming clearer by the moment, Dana was more aware of her surroundings. It was obvious now that she was in a trailer, the type pulled by big rigs. This explained the presence of the kill room in multiple cities. It wasn't various rooms containing the same paraphernalia, it was the same space moved from city to city. The other women had simply been too deep into their drug stupors to recognize it for what it was. Likely, when on runs, Pohl pulled two trailers simultaneously, one containing legitimate cargo, and the other, this diabolical space. Dana had been in the same foggy state as the others only an hour before and was still shaking off the remnants of the cloud. She saw the animals in their cages and also the children. She assumed they were the same children she'd heard scampering about the Pohl residence on their first visit. Why were the children caged, and why were they so complacent? Shouldn't they have been screaming to get out? Shouldn't they be clamoring for release? Their actions seemed uninhibited. There was no visible evidence that they'd been drugged.

And then the thought settled on Dana.

The reason these children weren't frightened or angry was because this was all they'd ever known. They were accustomed to these cages because to them the cages were a normal part of life.

Dana risked a quick glance at Willy Pohl who paced about clutching his dark and angular fertility idol. Had a cage such as this been a normal part of his upbringing as well? Celeste was his mother; that much Dana had deduced. And the woman was obviously unstable and controlling. Willy was her son and Dana would lay odds that these young children were also Celeste's and fathered by her own son Willy. It was no wonder that Willy was off his onion. Had he ever had even a remote shot at normalcy? Had he ever attended school or had a playmate—or an actual girlfriend? The man continued to pace, chanting unintelligible drivel. He cradled the idol, petting it as one might a kitten. His eyes darted about the room, never resting on anything or anyone for more than a moment and absolutely never meeting his mother's gaze.

"I know you're awake," said Celeste, shocking Dana from her contemplations. "I know you are. Little Willy, he didn't give you more than an initial dose of our magic powder. We give it slow. We're careful. That stuff, it's got magic, like stupefied dynamite. Give too much and your brain is blown to Hiroshima and back. Not much use in that. Not yet anyway." She moved toward Dana, giving her a sharp kick on the foot. "I said I know you're awake. You want to have a honest to goodness conversation or should I just let Willy have his little ol' way with you?"

At the threat of rape, Dana's belly tightened. Her limbs went rigid. She met Celeste's gaze. It was as cold as an arctic night. "I'm awake," she said through a molasses tongue.

"Well, good to hear." She cocked her head gazing at Dana who suddenly remembered that she was naked. How could she have forgotten that she was naked? Her hands were still bound behind her back, but she attempted to hunch forward in an effort to hide her breasts.

This futile effort elicited a strangled chortle from Celeste. "Well, ain't that precious. The hussy's shy. But you're not one of Willy's regular ol' hussies are you? You're a different critter altogether."

Dana remained quiet, merely returning the gaze. She was naked, fully exposed, but now realized that one item had not been removed from her form. The necklace, the one Lopez had given her. It nearly burned against her bare skin and vibrated so that it seemed it might leap free of its chain.

Why had it not been taken? Perhaps it did have some strange power. Perhaps the amulet had forbidden the Pohls from removing it. Perhaps...

"Not the talkative type, are you?" asked Celeste. "At least not now you ain't. You seemed plenty willing to yack at me last evening when you came pounding on our door with all your crazy stories about Willy transporting illegals. Does Willy strike you as the type to transport illegals?"

Dana simply stared at her. The amber hunk burned. How did it do this? Was it truly possible that there was something to Lopez's strange claims concerning its origin?

"I think this one's some kind a half breed, Willy. You think she's a half breed?"

Willy paused, still clutching his idol, and glanced from Dana to Celeste and then back to Dana. "Guess so," he said. "I didn't think too much about it." He then resumed his pacing.

"And that's why I'm the priestess and you ain't," said Celeste.

"Why are the children caged?" asked Dana. She wasn't sure that it was a good idea to engage this woman directly while her mind was still mush, but sensed that she'd best seek some advantage before she lost what small opportunity she might find.

"They're children," smiled Celeste with a quick over the shoulder glance at the cages. "A good parent can't leave the little rug muffins unsupervised now can she?"

"Ah! Parenting one-oh-one," quipped Jonathan from Dana's right. "No home is complete without a childproof cage."

Celeste smiled and gazed at Jonathan with Harlequin eyes. "Oh, the cute one is awake. You just wait, honey pie. I might just have something special for you." She winked.

"Yes, well, otherwise engaged and all that. Perhaps in another lifetime."

"You said I'm not like Willy's other women," said Dana in an effort to keep Celeste occupied. "In what way, exactly?" She'd continued to work on her binds. They'd loosened some, but not near enough. She needed more time. Maybe if she and Jonathan tossed her to and fro conversationally, she could complete the task unnoticed. Thorpe seemed to understand this instinctively.

"I thought that was clear," said Celeste. "Willy, you want to tell this nice lady why she's different than the other hussies?"

"She's a half breed," offered Willy with hardly a glance.

"No, doofus, she tracked you here instead a you tracking her. Ain't you listened to nothing?"

Chastised, Willy nodded and stroked his idol; his eyes narrow as they avoided his mother's gaze.

"So, you're a priestess?" asked Jonathan. "A priestess of what exactly? I see religious symbols from numerous sects. In truth, there's very little consistency. It seems rather a hodgepodge."

"I am the priestess," said Celeste. She offered nothing more.

"That is, I suppose, impressive," said Jonathan. "But, again, are you connected with a particular belief system?"

"I'm connected to the universe."

"Well, obviously. It baffles me that I could have missed that." He offered an apologetic grin.

"I'm a priestess of universal truth," continued Celeste either oblivious to, or purposefully ignoring the sarcasm.

"Of course."

"We practice sacred sexuality and purge the sin from those who debase the purity of divine physical communion."

"I'm stupefied. Truly."

"She doesn't have an answer," said Dana with obvious venom. "She picks and chooses whatever mystic nonsense will justify her perversions."

Celeste shifted, now contemplating Dana with a slippery grin. "Take this one for example," she said, ignoring Dana's comment. "She ain't a common trollop, that's for damn sure. But, she has a sensuous air about her. Which inner drive commands her desires? Does she acknowledge her pure innocent sexuality or does she allow other forces to pervert her wholesome drive?"

"Rubbish," said Dana.

"You see?" offered Celeste. "She ain't open to the truth of it. She's allowed societal norms and expectations to color her perceptions to the point where she don't even recognize the divinity within."

"Divinity?" shouted Dana. "How about rape? How about murder? Preach all of the bleeding touchy feely nonsense you want, but at least be honest about it. You've trained your boy to be a rapist and a murderer. There is no purification. There is no redemption in what you do. You're just a twisted monster who gets her jollies off by ordering her son to attack unsuspecting women."

Celeste paused and then stepped toward Dana.

"Now, now," said Jonathan. "Perhaps that was a bit harsh. My dear woman, would you care to explain further, the details of your belief?"

"Let it go, Jonathan," snapped Dana. "This nutter already knows what she's going to do to us."

"Brilliant," quipped Jonathan. "And so let's accelerate the process."

But Dana wasn't focused on her ex-husband, but rather on the room, its layout, its inhabitants. The sliding door was to her left, latched, but possibly not locked. On this she was uncertain. There were two antagonists to consider, mother and son, but there were others present as well. Jonathan, obviously. Likely, he'd not yet freed himself, and the two children, each in a separate cage, and therefore, each a separate rescue. Could she even worry about them at this point? But then again, how could she not? They were children.

Dana wriggled her wrist. Almost there. "How can you do it?" she asked. "How can you encourage the rape of other women?"

Celeste appeared nearly confused. "Rape? You consider this rape?"

"I've yet to hear a more accurate term."

"Why, salvation, of course. We offer these women—we offer you—salvation."

"That's rubbish and you know it. Perhaps your son is too thick to distinguish the difference, but I recognize you for the twisted pervert you are. Priestess! What a load of hogwash!"

Dana noted Willy as he paced behind his mother. His eyes were wide as in horror. Certainly he was unaccustomed to someone speaking to his mother/priestess in such a fashion. He clutched his idol closer, pivoted, glanced from Dana to Celeste.

The priestess smiled at Dana. Her teeth were yellow and uneven. Her dirty blond hair habitually spilled over the left side of her face. This woman had the unrealized potential to be attractive. Not beautiful, never that, but appealing still in a rather roughhewn fashion. Likely in her younger years she had been somewhat fetching, at least enough so as to warrant attention from the local boys. Dana wondered if Celeste had always been sexually perverse or if some traumatic incident had brought this behavior about.

Again, Dana noted the amulet around her neck, the heat, the sensation. Nonsense. It was nonsense, all of it. The bleeding rock had done nothing to help her in any way.

Celeste turned, strolling to a walnut dresser situated to Dana and Jonathan's right, her colorful wrap billowing behind her as she moved, giving her a somewhat surreal air. Certainly this was the intent. Dana noted that the furniture was bolted to the floor in order to prevent movement when the trailer was en route. Celeste withdrew two glass containers from the second drawer and moved again toward Dana, kneeling before her and placing each container on the floor.

Dana could hear Jonathan jabbering protests beside her, but was focused on the woman. Unless Jonathan was near to freeing himself, he was not currently a part of the equation. Behind Celeste, Willy continued to pace, his speed increasing as did the intensity of his strokes on the obsidian idol. He mumbled something repeatedly. Dana thought she recognized it as

French, but the pronunciation was so poor as to make the words unintelligible.

She heard the whimper of children from across the room. Each of Celeste's children, both young and grown knew what was about to happen and was reacting to the coming event with fear.

"What is that?" asked Dana. "More of the drug? It's tetrodotoxin, am I right? Extracted from blowfish, it causes paralysis, though the subject remains conscious." Dana paused, eyeing her adversary, watching for a reaction to Dana's knowledge of her method. "Oh, surprised that I know the science behind your voodoo? There's nothing mystical here, priestess. Just flash and perversion."

Celeste grinned as she unscrewed the lid to one of the containers. "Oh, I'm sure you think you have it all figured out. But, you don't see through the spirit's eye the way I do." She dipped two fingers into the mouth of the container and then withdrew them dripping with an olive green paste. "This ain't my zombie powder. You see, your type needs a particularly powerful type of exorcism."

"Exorcism? Really, I do believe that is a bit much." This from Jonathan who was obviously struggling with his binds.

Celeste leaned forward, smearing the paste across Dana's forehead. It was cold to the touch and smelled rancid like old meat. Though Dana writhed and protested, still Celeste continued. Chanting prayers in broken French, she painted patterns about Dana's naked form, strange swirls and weaves, skipping over the amber necklace but paying it no particular heed. Her eyes rolled up, revealing only the whites. Willy placed the idol on the dresser and then continued in his pacing, now pressing each of his palms against his forehead while he jabbered in an eclectic mixture of French and English. The younger children wept openly.

"Prepare yourself, Willy," said Celeste, this in a dreamy tone.

"But, Mommy…"

"Prepare yourself, William. We must draw the demon forth."

Willy shook his head violently and then began to shed his clothing, dropping each item randomly about the space.

Celeste chanted something and then reached to her right, snatching the second container. A moment later, she withdrew the serpent. "You can call this rape if you like, but this ain't like nothing you ever seen."

Chapter Twenty-Four

Louisiana

Willy Pohl was confused. This woman was different. As much as he desired to purge her of her sins—as much he would have done so had the priestess not arrived when she had—he couldn't quite see this woman as a hussy. Not, at least, as a normal hussy. She was very pretty, older than he was, but not by too many years. She dressed pretty, but not sexy like a hussy. She showed no cleavage or mid-section but had rather worn a simple silk top and gray cotton pants, not a short skirt, ripped and revealing jeans, or short shorts. The pants were relatively form-fitting, but not tight, not sleazy. Professional had been the word his priestess had used. Her make-up was almost no make-up at all, her hair shoulder length and basic in style. To Willy, she'd appeared more as a business person than a hussy. She could have worked at a bank or at a real estate office.

But, hussies could have jobs. He knew this. He was a missionary of sorts and yet he still drove a truck to pay the bills. Hussies had bills too.

But, his priestess had said this one was different, hadn't she? Different, but in what way? His priestess still labeled her a hussy, just a different breed of hussy. A more dangerous breed. Sneaky. No, a different word. Stealthy! That was it. Stealthy. She didn't dress like a hussy because she wanted to hide her sin and lust. She didn't want anyone to know what she was. This one was sneaky sleazy.

"Willy! You undressed yet?"

It was his priestess. She'd already painted the sacred symbols onto the hussy's flesh and was now removing the serpent from its jar. Willy felt a throb of excitement as he unbuckled his belt and allowed his jeans to slide to the floor. This would be a good purging. Very, very good. And then, afterward, his priestess would purge him of the filthy sins he'd taken from the strange and exotic hussy. It would be a wonderful, exciting purging.

He watched the hussy intently as he slipped from his boxers. The serpent coiled about his priestess's forearm, writhing and hissing, its tongue darting, its black soulless eyes cold and glimmering in the dim light. The hussy squirmed as the priestess reached forward allowing the serpent to slip from her clutches and onto the woman's bare flesh. The man to her right hollered as he struggled with his binds. The man was a distraction. Why did he have to be here? How was Willy supposed to purge the hussy with this man sitting only three feet away screaming and squirming?

"Shut up!" screamed Willy as with three quick steps he marched to the man and kicked him in the gut. The man doubled over with a cough and a groan and Willy kicked again, this time connecting with the man's jaw. It hurt Willy's bare toes and he hopped away with a yelp of his own.

"Willy!" the priestess shouted. "We are in the midst of ritual, you doofus. Ain't you aware of nothing?"

"Yes, mommy. Yes." He hated it when she called him doofus. It made him feel small and stupid. He was neither. True, the priestess was the smart one. There was no question of that. She knew things he could never know. She heard from the spirits and the gods. They told her things—secret things—that normal people could never know. But he was smart too. And he heard things as well. Maybe not as many things as the priestess did, but he was sure the new goddess had told him to purge this hussy, and even though the priestess said she hadn't, he knew better. The priestess was proving it right now. She was preparing the woman for purging. True, she was performing a different ritual than the one Willy had intended, but the result was the same. Purging. Sweet, sweet, purging.

But then why was he so nervous? The goddess had spoken to him, urging him to purge this woman. And so he must purge. But none of this seemed quite right. Not entirely wrong, but not right either. He couldn't place the thought. The other hussies had needed Willy, needed the release he offered, the freedom from future sin, the absolution of past wrongs. This one, certainly she sinned. Of course she sinned. Of course there were sins to release. So why did he feel that this was somehow wrong? Willy moaned, long and mournful as he pressed his palms against his temples.

The hussy screamed as the serpent slid up her thigh and onto her belly. She squirmed and kicked and the priestess smiled and prayed. She asked the hussy questions: how had she learned of them, who else had she told. She whispered of the serpent's venom, of the slow painful death it would bring. But, the woman said nothing of import, deciding rather to insult the priestess, charging her with disgusting crimes. Willy couldn't listen to such blasphemy and so he turned away only to stare into the face of the woman's companion.

Despite Willy's efforts, the man was still conscious and continued to shout and thrash. He would be a problem. Willy could not hope to purge the hussy with the man present. He couldn't. Things simply wouldn't work—his body wouldn't work—not when he had an audience. Willy looked to the far wall, to the cluster of shrunken skulls, to the ones who had come before, and sought their advice. Should he kill the man now? Willy had never killed a man. His only acts of violence had come in the purgings and those were for the remission of sins. He didn't have the ability to purge a male and so had no right to kill the man. But if he didn't kill him, how could he hope to purge the hussy? He couldn't possibly do that with such an audience.

Palms pressed against his forehead, Willy marched forward and then back, praying the unknown words in the unknown tongue. Could the new goddess guide him? Could those that had come before offer wisdom? Or perhaps his priestess. Why hadn't he thought of his priestess? "Mommy!" he yelled, though he hadn't intended to yell. "Mommy, I need you."

"Not now, Willy. Can't you see I'm in the midst of magic?"

"But, mommy. The man. What do we do about the man, Mommy?"

"Shut up, Willy. All in good time. Right now, we're going to tend to this sweet little hussy, aren't we?"

"Yes, Mommy. I want to purge her."

The priestess leered at the woman and then at Willy. "And I desire that you purge her, Willy. So, you'd best be about the purging."

"But, Mommy, the snake."

The priestess giggled. "The serpent will do as the gods demand, ain't that right, Willy? You ain't got nothing to fear from the serpent unless you ain't in the right place spiritually. You are in the right place, ain't you, Willy?" She giggled again. Happy. Goading.

Willy spun, marching away. The hussy's eyes. Her eyes! So wide. So fearful. Like the others, but so different. It was a different kind of fear than he'd seen before. A knowing fear. A fear that touched the soul. He wasn't sure exactly what that meant, but it felt right. There was something in this woman. Something dark and secret. Maybe some past sin. Some huge sin. He'd been wrong. This woman needed purging, perhaps like none he'd purged before. She had secrets. Dark, filthy, hussy secrets. He turned again, facing her, and moved slowly forward. It seemed impossible, but the hussy's eyes became wider yet, tears streaked her face. The man beside her continued to shout and thrash, but was still bound.

He wanted her now, the hussy. Whatever doubts he'd had, those wide tearful eyes had told him the truth. The woman had much to purge. But, the man. The man refused to quiet, refused to still. In one fluid move, Willy stepped past the man to his left, grabbed the goddess from her perch atop the dresser, and shuffling right, slammed her against the side of the man's head, knocking him sideways and leaving a jagged gap in his temple. The goddess was of stone and quite hefty. The man was stunned and would likely cause no trouble. He was not unconscious, but he was nearly still, and quiet except for low moans of pain.

Willy stepped to before the hussy and dropped to his knees as the priestess shuffled to the side. The hussy had been quiet for a minute or so, perhaps mute with fear, perhaps praying to some false hussy god. But she remained silent no longer. The words tumbled from her mouth in a gush of fear and pleading. "Willy, you don't need to do this. Your mother's insane; she's manipulating you into doing these things. You don't need to do this!" The last sentence was nearly a scream. "Locust, help me!" she bellowed now. "Locust, please!"

What a strange woman. Did she say locust? Wasn't that some sort of bug? Willy studied her as he lowered himself over her, the serpent curled on her flesh, the only barrier between them. Those eyes. Something in those eyes.

And then it came to him.

He didn't know how, perhaps the goddess revealed it to him, he couldn't be sure, but he knew her secret. She had been purged before. This was not her first experience of this kind. He could see her concentration; he could nearly feel the memories electrifying the air between them. She had been purged and she was readying herself for a repeat performance. Willy smiled and giggled as he inched forward. "I know," he said. "I know what you're hiding."

And perhaps he did know something. Perhaps she had been purged before, but what he hadn't known was that the woman had managed to free her hands. The hussy's right arm came up in a flash, the cord that had bound her clutched in her fists. The cord whipped across his face, snapping against his left eye. Willy tumbled to his right with a yelp as he pressed his palm against his damaged eye.

Grabbing the serpent by the tail and hurling it to her left, the hussy scrambled to her feet, but her stance was unsure, still wobbly from the drug. She glanced about the room, to her male companion, to the caged children, even to the tiny heads of those who had gone before, seemingly unsure as to what to do next.

The priestess moved toward her, pulling a ritual dagger from within the folds of her gown. She meant to kill the hussy.

"No, Mommy! Not without the purging!" screamed Willy. He knew that killing someone without first the purging of sin was an unforgivable crime.

But the priestess raised the blade, bringing it down in a swift arc. "No!" screamed Willy again, but the priestess wasn't listening to him.

The hussy dodged to her right, but there was blood. A great splat of it landed on the serpent which then slithered under the dresser and out of sight.

Willy blinked tears from his injured eye.

The priestess raised the bloodied blade, preparing to strike again.

The hussy, now cradling her wounded side, shuffled sideways, but her footing was unsure.

Her companion, the man, was still bound, and writhing about the floor, his injured forehead spilling blood across his face. He was obviously attempting to aid the hussy, but in her confused state she didn't see that he had moved, and so tripped over him, falling clumsily to the floor.

The priestess cackled in glee, lifting the knife again.

Somewhere in the background, Willy heard the youngsters screaming.

"No, Mommy!" screamed Willy. He couldn't let her do it, not without the purging. Didn't she realize she was endangering not only the hussy's soul, but her own as well? "No, Mommy," he screamed again as the blade descended.

The hussy screamed.

The children cried.

Willy leaped, tackling the priestess like a football linebacker.

"Willy, you doofus! What are you doing?"

Everyone was scrambling now. The knife had fallen. The hussy was closest to it, but she was dazed and injured, now bleeding from at least two points. Still, she made a grab for it. But the priestess had fallen near the blade and she snatched the weapon.

The man, still bound and injured, managed to kick her in the gut.

The priestess dropped the blade.

Recovering it, she twisted, stabbing the troublesome man in the upper chest.

His eyes went wide as he fell backward with a gasp and a gurgle.

Willy grabbed the priestess from behind as she sought to turn and finish killing the hussy. "Willy, you idiot, let me go!"

The hussy twisted from beneath them, her arm shooting up, knocking the blade from the priestess's hand.

"See what you've done, doofus!"

The hussy scrambled for the blade, but Willy was quicker, he snatched the weapon, but in doing so released the priestess.

"Kill her, you idiot! Kill her!" screamed his mother.

"Don't call me that!" Tears raced across Willy's cheeks. His head hurt. He couldn't think. "Stop this, Mommy! Stop this!"

"Kill her!" bellowed the priestess.

Willy's arm shot forward. He hadn't given it a moment's thought. Certainly the arm acted without his consent. Later, he would ponder why. Had the goddess directed his hand, or perhaps those who had gone before? Had it been the will of the serpent or perhaps some other trickster of a spirit that moved him? Certainly, it had been one of these—or even all. But, the one certainty was that something had directed Willy's hand. For it was beyond possibility that he had killed the priestess of his own free will.

She fell, eyes wide, mouth agape, hands at her chest where the dagger protruded. Willy slumped to beside her, his entire form quivering. "Mommy, I didn't mean to. Mommy, please. Mommy." But, she would not answer and so, slipping to behind the fallen form, he cradled her, his arms reaching around her belly, his head resting against hers, squeezing, weeping, apologizing. He barely noticed the hussy as she picked up the goddess from her resting place and brought the stone idol down onto the back of his head.

Chapter Twenty-Five

Botma Africa

Time had ceased to be linier. Hunt could not distinguish day from night or one hour from three or even ten. His meals, such as they were, came at erratic times, sometimes, it would seem, with more than twenty-four hours between. The interrogations were sometimes spread apart by days and other times grouped in close clusters. Everything was designed to confuse him, to break him, to force him to retreat into a semi-madness driven by fear and overwhelming need.

The drugs, though, were the worst, for with them came memories. Fragmented, distorted, dislodged from dark shadowy corners of his mind not trodden for years and lifetimes. Hunt couldn't be sure that these scenes were true. Or, perhaps, better, he didn't want to believe them to be true. Sometimes the sweet fragrance of a tender lie is much more appealing than the stench of rancid truth. Though, in this case, the lie was only moderately less vile than the reality.

Hunt was still cognizant enough to know that he was in Botma, strapped to a table—hadn't he been strapped to a chair? When had it become a table? He couldn't quite remember. Nothing was linier. The memories cascaded past, slipped in and out in no particular order. They faded and blended, twisting and writhing like phantom serpents in an endless pit.

Hunt shivered, goose bumps scampering across his flesh, seeding the landscape of his form. He fought the compulsion to chatter his teeth but failed even in this. His captures used temperature as a torture devise. Extreme heat followed by extreme cold. Never anything but the extreme. Hunt fought the quivers, but it was a useless exercise. His body was attempting to generate heat when there was none to be had.

Hunt was not alone.

Someone had entered the room. How long had this person been here? Hunt hadn't been aware of the approach. He'd been somewhere else, drifting about his past, floating above it like a vulture circling carrion, observing only, not participating.

"Huntington, did you hear me?"

He did not respond.

"Huntington!"

Hunt allowed his hooded head to roll toward the voice.

"Are you listening, Huntington?"

It was warm in the room—comfortable even. Hadn't it been bitter cold only moments before? Or had that been hours ago? Maybe days. It didn't matter, he supposed. Nothing mattered really. There was nothing left of his life and therefore no need to concern himself with anything past or present. Strange, the obstinate comfort one can find in the thought of his own demise.

There was a sharp tug at the head as the hood was removed. Hunt blinked, his eyes adjusting to light for the first time in what may have been weeks. The experience, like every other experience, was painful. Always, his eyes were covered. He never saw his interrogators. He never saw his meals, never gazed upon the fetid water he consumed. Always, the hood was in place. Food was slipped beneath, the same with liquid. Often, much of what he was meant to consume spilled across his naked chest. Rarely was the mess wiped away and so Hunt smelled of putrid meat.

Shaking his head, Hunt blinked multiple times, cracking his eyes just a bit, allowing a sliver of light to reach his pupils, and then a bit more, and a little more yet. When finally he raised his head he was surprised to see that Nishati Azibo stood before him. To the best of his knowledge this was only the second time she'd visited this room, the first being immediately following his capture.

But, it wasn't the same room was it? The other had been plain, all furnishings removed, the walls bare. This room was, well, he wasn't quite sure. The walls were draped with black curtains. Candles stood on tall golden stands in each corner, the gold formed into the image of fierce open-jawed serpents. Glittering diamonds littered a table to Hunt's right. Azibo's god, the scorpion ensnaring a globe with its bone-like legs and snake's-head tail poised to strike, peered down on him from one corner. The idol was nearly eight feet high and made entirely of jade. Bizarre symbols were etched in exposed areas of the coarse stone walls. A strangely reptilian odor assaulted Hunt's nostrils. Tilting his head, he realized he wasn't on a table at all, at least not a traditional table, but a raised slab of granite. It seemed a perfect setting for some weird fantastical sacrifice. If Azibo had been wearing a black hooded cloak instead of army fatigues he would have probably kept an eye out for Bella Lugosi.

"Well, hello there," cooed the self-proclaimed sorceress. "I was beginning to wonder if we'd lost you altogether."

Hunt remained silent. Rarely does a corpse bother with responding to the living.

"Most likely, you wonder why you are allowed to live." Here, she smiled, displaying her prominent teeth and peculiar overbite. "There is a reason. Perhaps you should ask your friend Colonel Lucky Lindell."

At this, Hunt's eyes widened, just a fraction, but obviously noticeable to Azibo.

"Ah! You don't remember, do you? You've been broken, Huntington. You told us of Lindell and of how he recruited you for this mission because of your deniability. Your military intelligence is dated and all but useless, but that's of no concern. We have an agreement with The United States and so have no fear of military action against us from that quarter. Even your foolish mission was meant to help maintain my hold on the country. It's truly unfortunate that you chose to work opposite your directives and side with Ubora. Perhaps if you'd simply followed orders things could have been different."

To this, Hunt offered no response, but instead allowed his head to drop back onto the slab. He had no need of this. Better that she simply allow him to die. Physically, he felt he'd hit a threshold. There was nothing more that they could do to him of consequence. He lived in a swirling cloud of near oblivion and desired only to cross that final bridge.

"Oh!" said Azibo, as though a thought had just struck her. "Aren't you curious about Corina Meeks, your friend? Or is she a lover? She is pretty enough, I suppose. Were you two intimate?"

At the revelation that Azibo was aware of Corky, Hunt couldn't help but raise his head.

"Ah! That got your attention." Azibo stood, arms crossed at the chest, her head cocked at a saucy angle, a woman in complete control of the situation.

"Corky?" he croaked.

Azibo smiled. "Yes. We are aware of her. She is monitored closely."

"Corky," hissed Hunt as he strained feebly against his bonds. Why had he allowed her to be drawn into this? What had he told them of her?

A throaty chuckle and a dismissive gesture. "Don't fret, Huntington. She is unharmed and will remain unharmed as long as you cooperate."

Hunt glared at the woman. When he spoke, his words were husky and halting. "It seems... you've already gained what little information... I have... to offer. What cooperation are you... talking about?"

"This photograph," said Azibo as she withdrew something from her pocket and lifted a picture to where he could see it. The shot had apparently been taken soon after his capture as he was being led through the compound at gunpoint, the boy, Tahir Azibo, carried two steps behind by a young soldier.

"What about the picture?" asked Hunt.

"It has been broadcast over our national television network with a story claiming that you, a foreign insurgent working for Ubora, was captured as you sought to move my kidnapped child from one locale to another."

Hunt managed to croak, "Yeah, and?"

"You will make a public statement declaring Ubora the culprit behind the abduction."

"There was no abduction."

"We have security footage of you carrying Tahir. The boy was screaming. You were actually quite rough with him. That wasn't very noble, really."

"I can see you're shedding a motherly tear."

Azibo smiled, broad and seductive. "Ah! Sarcasm. Perhaps you are not so far gone as I'd been led to believe. Well, I have means of tickling a man's soul that go far deeper than pharmaceuticals."

Hunt considered his situation. Perhaps she was right. Maybe he wasn't as far gone as he'd thought. Or maybe he simply had nothing left to lose and so sought to get his parting shots in while the opportunity was at hand. "Lady, you can kill me if you like. I'm beyond caring. But, I'm not towing your line in front of a camera."

"Really? And what of Corky?"

"What about her? You said you're watching her, as in, you don't actually have her. And what about your boy? You going to make him stand before the entire country and lie? What'll he think of dear Mommy then?"

Azibo shook her head slowly as she paced before Hunt. "The boy will do as I instruct or suffer for disobedience. He's of little concern. As to Corina Meeks, would you like me to bring her to you? Would you like me to offer her an extended stay in this room? Perhaps she'd make a worthy sacrifice."

Hunt blinked, straining to maintain focus. "What's the deal, Azibo?" he asked as a means of gaining some minimal control of the conversation. He wasn't going to allow her to frighten him with threats against someone she'd yet to capture.

"The deal?" She sounded amused.

"Yeah. The deal. Why is the U.S. backing you? Why do they care at all about this backward hellhole of a country?"

At this, Azibo allowed a true and full laugh. "Huntington, you are a prize. I don't think you realize just how much so. I'd have thought you'd be babbling like an infant and here you are pushing me for answers."

"I'm glad I amuse you. So, again, what's the deal?" Hunt was manufacturing a strong front, but he knew his resolve was nearing an end. Likely he'd pass out from pain and fatigue within minutes.

"The deal," chuckled Azibo. "The deal, Huntington is diamonds. Hundreds of thousands of diamonds. Billions of dollars into American pockets should the U.S. government provide us the proper support."

Diamonds. Hunt recalled reference to some diamond mines in the research provided him, but the gemstones weren't considered a major natural resource. Perhaps there'd been a recent discovery, maybe a major cache had been found. A game changer. An abundant resource. A store large enough to be used to bribe the U.S. into turning a blind eye to Azibo's many crimes against humanity. "None of that surprises me, Azibo. And, to be honest, I don't give a damn about any of it. You have me. I don't expect to leave here alive, so why don't we just finish this thing and be done with it?"

Azibo smiled, strolling toward him seductively. "Oh, we are far from finished, Huntington. You will be of great use, both to me and to Anascoreth. You see, soon you'll go before the cameras and tell the world exactly what I've instructed you to say. And with that, Botma will find itself at the center of the world stage."

Hunt met her gaze. "Not while I've got free will, I won't. And if you drug me, it'll be evident that I'm not in my right mind. The world would know I'd been coerced. Any claims made will be met with skepticism."

Caressing his forehead with her fingertips, Azibo uttered a rich chuckle. "Drugged? No, Huntington. Something much better. You forget who I am—what I am." She paused, gently tracing the contour of his face with a fingernail. "What does my opponent, Ubora, call me? I'm a sure you know."

"Sorceress."

"Mmmmm," purred Azibo. "Yes, Huntington, sorceress." With this, she allowed her fingertips to trail down his form until she reached his left wrist. Here, she lifted his hand, turning it palm up and studying it for several moments. Hunt was weak and listless. He had no strength to fight. In truth, it was only now that he realized that he was no longer bound to the slab.

Gently, Azibo kissed his wrist, allowing her full lips to linger on the flesh for several seconds, for her moist warm breath to roll across his skin. Gently, she stroked his flesh before, with one quick movement, slashing his wrist with the long sharp nail of her index finger. Blood oozed out as Azibo lowered her head, a saucy grin dancing across her lips as she extended her tongue, sampling Hunt's blood as one might a lollypop or a sucker. She then blew softly on the cut, causing a peculiar tickling sensation that supplanted even the pain. Again, she brought her head down, this time allowing a slender thread of spittle to drop onto the wound. She teased this with her tongue, simultaneously chanting in some unknown tongue. The sensations were peculiar, both cool and hot. It tickled and stung. Hunt watched as what appeared to be a faint gray shadow scampered down Azibo's tongue and into the open wound. Azibo smiled, again kissing the wound with the tenderness of a satisfied lover.

Straightening, Azibo strolled to the head of the table, staring down on Hunt for several seconds before leaning and gently brushing her lips against his. "When the scorpion reaches your brain," she whispered. "You will belong to Anascoreth, and so, to me as well." Another quick peck on the lips, and then she turned, leaving the room without another sound.

Hunt remained still for several seconds, his mind racing as he attempted to understand what had just occurred. At last, he dared a glance at his wrist. Lifting it before his eyes, he saw blood, tacky and drying, but no evidence of the wound so deep and obvious only moments before. About an inch up from the wrist, he saw what appeared to be a faint blue tattoo. A scorpion with the head of a serpent as the end of its tale.

Chapter Twenty-Six

Las Vegas Nevada

Dana was conscious and at some level Thorpe was wondering if perhaps it had been better when she'd been nonresponsive. His own wounds had been less severe than Dana's. The knife wound to the chest had at first seemed something that could be life threatening, but the blade had not penetrated deeply, had missed all internal organs, and had instead penetrated musculature alone. It was painful to lift his right arm and he would face many hours of physical therapy. This aside, he'd not even been held over-night. Quite fortunate, that.

Dana's injuries had been more worrisome. Two stab wounds, both to the belly. The first had done no substantial damage, but the second had penetrated her gallbladder. The surgeon had saved the organ, there were hopes of a full recovery, she'd been sent home after only a week, albeit under strict instructions detailing follow-up care. But apparently this wasn't enough for Dana. Her moods were arbitrary, her temper volatile. She worried about her husband, who had recently made the news as being captured during an apparent kidnapping attempt in Africa. Beyond this, she fixated on peculiar little things that, in Thorpe's mind, were of no conse-quence. She ate little, conversed less, and stared through the window toward the surrounding mountain range for hours at a time.

Thorpe met her hazy gaze as he settled on the corner of her king-sized bed. "Dana, dear, you do understand, this is all quite beyond our control."

Dana offered a low growl. "What duffer is running Child Protective Services in that bleeding town? They can't possibly consider returning those children to Willy Pohl."

Thorpe sighed, placing a hand on Dana's shoulder. "I said it's possible, I said nothing—even slightly—indicating that it is in process."

"Still, the thought that it could be considered—the bleeding plonkers!"

"Yes, well, the mother, Celeste, she's deceased. William, as suspected, is the biological father. He's of course incarcerated, but his attorney will plead insanity. Even if he's found not guilty by means of insanity, he'll likely do a lengthy stint in a mental institution. It's only after he's found mentally competent that he could petition for the children. Dana, that's likely years away, if ever at all. I do believe you're worrying yourself over nothing."

Dana sighed, closing her eyes, and allowing her head to sink back into the pillow. She remained so for several moments and Thorpe had begun to think she'd drifted off again. But then he noticed the way she worked her lips, that curious scrunch of hers, a sure sign of intense contemplation. Thorpe knew the look well. "What is it, dear? What's really bothering you so?"

Dana harrumphed but didn't respond.

"Is it Marc? I'm sure he's, well, fine. Certainly nothing but a misunderstanding. The U.S. embassy will be involved."

She remained silent, staring into nothingness. It wasn't Huntington this time.

"Dana, this is quite unproductive. You know I can be a persistent little gnat."

At this, Dana offered the hint of a grin.

"That's a girl. Now, tell me what's troubling that wonderfully complicated mind of yours."

"It didn't work." The words were barely a whisper, nearly inaudible.

"That's interesting, dear. Care to enlighten me further? What, exactly, didn't work?"

"I don't want to talk about it."

"Yes, well, me, persistent, all of that. Care to rethink this, or should I proceed to nettle you to the point of insanity?"

A sharp exhalation of breath. "The bleeding locust. It didn't work."

The locust? It took Thorpe a moment to connect Dana's statement to the necklace she bore around her neck. He'd thought the thing peculiar. It was nothing like Dana had ever worn previously, at least not to his knowledge. But he'd never attributed any true significance to it. Apparently, he should have asked. "You'll need to explain, dear. I assume you refer to the necklace, the one containing the insect."

"It's silly."

"Yes, and some would argue that it was silly of me to race halfway across the globe to aid my married ex-wife in an investigation. Let's say we call it equal."

A sigh. "It was given to me by a sheriff in Mexico. It had been given to him by some sort of witch."

"Witch. Yes. Interesting, that. Continue, please."

"She instructed him to give it to woman who came from afar. He took that to mean me."

"Fascinating. And what, in particular, is so special about this particular piece?"

"The locust. He claimed it was from the biblical plague. Moses and the exodus, the swarms of locusts. It's supposed to have power. I thought…" Here she trailed off, cursing under her breath. "I was a bleeding fool. I didn't believe it—of course I didn't believe it!—but, I suppose at some level I thought it might protect me. I was foolish to have entertained the thought. May we move on now?"

Thorpe nodded. "Of course, dear. Just, may I see it? The locust."

Dana glared at him for a moment, nodded, and then leaned forward, allowing him to reach around her neck to remove it. As he lifted it over her head, she released an almost stifled gasp almost as if the air had been forcibly drawn from her lungs.

"Are you alright, dear."

Dana nodded, her eyes narrow as she glared at the trinket in Thorpe's hand. It seemed she was still catching her breath.

Thorpe held the necklace before him, his fingers spreading the thin golden chain, allowing the stone to dangle, his milk chocolate eyes examining the amber specimen as it glinted in the subtle light of the room. The nugget had weight, and, he supposed, something he'd call substance, though this was an ambiguous thought. It was a formidable piece, though subtly so.

"You don't actually believe it has some sort of power, do you?" she asked, an almost hopeful look creasing her face, especially, thought Thorpe, considering her attitude toward the thing.

He decided it best to be honest with her. "Power? No. Of course not. But, value, well, let's suppose for a moment that it is a piece of antiquity. I'm not saying the locust actually originated in the biblical plague—how could one prove such a thing even if it were true?—but let's, for a moment, consider that it has been passed down through centuries with that tale ascribed to it. Let's consider that perhaps a bit of legend has been built. In that instance, I might, perhaps, be able to find a buyer that would pay a handsome sum for a trinket with that brand of history."

"And what does your practiced eye tell you? Is it an antique?"

"Antique? Well, yes, most certainly. The rich hue, the cut of the chain, the high collar design, this is not of recent time. But, is it ancient? Well, here, I suppose a more knowledgeable man than I must be engaged. The amber, with its enclosed occupant, is naturally much older than the golden setting. But, even this is likely from centuries past."

Dana harrumphed. "Do what you will with the bleeding thing. Consider it payment for your troubles. I, for one, never want to set eyes on it again." She rolled over, clutched her pillow, and closed her eyes. Thorpe was left staring at the peculiar piece dangling from his fingers.

Chapter Twenty-Seven

Botma Africa

The footsteps were clumsy, hesitant. Even secured safely beneath his hood, Hunt could sense the tentativeness of the approaching form. Though his body ached a thousand separate agonies, his mind had cleared some. Azibo had backed off on the drugs. She planned for him to make a statement before the world. There was nothing she could do to hide the fact that he'd been abused, but likely she wanted him to at least appear somewhat coherent.

Of course, there was the other thing. That crazy thing in his arm. He'd felt sensations since his encounter with Azibo. They were strange, indefinable. She'd obviously somehow injected him with something. Another drug? Perhaps. But, he'd seen something peculiar flow from her mouth. There had been no injection, no application of any kind. Had it been a hallucination? He supposed it could have been, but what about the tattoo? How had that come about?

Another stutter of footsteps. A pause. A sniffle. Four more steps. Two days earlier he'd likely not have even noticed these. Now, just a day without the medication, each step echoed like cathedral bells in his one good ear.

"I hear you," said Hunt. "Care to tell me who you are and what you're up to?"

Near silence. Only the sound of quick shallow breathing. Hunt's head was still cloudy with pain and fatigue, but he felt like himself again for the first time in several miserable lifetimes. He might not be at the top of his game, but at least he was once again aware that there was a game.

"Listen, I don't know who you are, but I know you're not one of Azibo's goons. So, cut with the silent treatment and get on with it."

Four more footsteps, this time retreating.

"Hey! Where are you going? Who are you already?"

A sigh, almost a squeal, and the footfall resumed, this time in a deliberate march toward Hunt. He prepared himself to be struck, but instead the hood was pulled hesitantly from his head. The face before him was that of a child, nearly round, with large brown eyes and a build that bordered on pudgy.

"Tahir?"

The boy simply stared, the hood still clutched in his trembling right hand.

"Tahir, what are you doing? Does your mother know you're here?"

Tahir Azibo shook his head slowly, still remaining silent.

"Hey, kid, I appreciate the company, but if your mom catches you in here, I'm guessing you won't like the punishment." Tahir stared at Hunt as if he was some sort of alien just freed from Area 51 and out on the prowl. Hunt couldn't imagine that his mother had anything to do with this encounter and it certainly didn't make sense that any of her men would have utilized the boy. "Tahir, somebody may come in here any time now. I need you to tell me why you're here."

Those eyes, so wide and seemingly innocent. What atrocities had they witnessed?

"They hurt you," said Tahir, his voice registering something akin to wonder.

Hunt couldn't help but smile, though it pained his dry and split lips to do so. "Yeah, kid. I guess they did."

"They hurt you because of me."

"Nah. Not because of you. Because I tried to take you away from here. Dumb move on my part."

The boy leaned closer, staring directly into Hunt's eyes. It seemed he might have taken one of Hunt's hands had they not been tied to the granite slab on which he lay. The restraints had been reapplied only minutes after his encounter with Azibo. "Why did you try to take me?"

Hunt hesitated. What could he say in response? *Well, kid, you're mother's a psychopath and was using you as a pawn in her lunatic fight against your father—who by the way, may or may not be as bad as dear old ma. Oh, and your mom, yeah, she planned on killing you and pinning it on your dad.*

"Listen, kid. I don't know what you've heard, but I wasn't here to hurt you. I promise you that. I was just trying to get you away from danger, that's all. I just didn't want you to be hurt."

Tahir stared at Hunt for a long time before saying, "My mommy hates me."

"Nah, kid. No. Your mom, she just, I dunno, she's got a lot going on. I'm sure she loves you."

"She sacrificed my sister to Anascoreth."

"My God, you know about that?"

Tahir nodded, tears now appearing in the corners of his eyes.

"Tahir, I'm sorry. I'd heard rumors, but I didn't know for sure." Hunt wanted to say more, but there were no words. What could he say that could make this kid's existence any better? According to Ubora, Azibo had sacrificed the girl as a means of enhancing mystical power. Apparently the act of killing one's own child is considered high art in wacko sorceress circles.

"She thinks I'm fat," continued Tahir. "She calls me useless."

Oh, God, this kid knows he's going to be next.

"Tahir, I don't know what happened with your sister, but I can tell you're a good kid. I'm sure your mom sees that too."

Tahir gazed at his feet and shook his head, freeing the tears to dribble down his cheeks. The poor kid was terrified. And who could blame him? His mother had murdered his sibling in the name of her crazy sect; Tahir probably lived each day wondering if his time would come any minute. They remained this way for several moments, neither knowing what to say. Finally, the boy raised his gaze to study Hunt. "Will you take me someplace happy?"

***

It had taken Tahir Azibo nearly a half hour to untie Hunt's binds and Hunt had been certain that at some point a guard would enter, catch the boy in the process of his mutiny, and haul him off to his mother. But, no guards had come.

Upon gaining freedom, Hunt's first move had been to inspect his left wrist. He needed to see if what he recalled from his bizarre encounter with Azibo was true or if he'd simply been hallucinating as a result of the drugs.

It was there.

The faint blue scorpion.

But it had moved.

It had moved!

Where initially the form had resided no more than an inch up from his wrist, now it was halfway to the elbow joint. How could that be?

And worse yet, he could feel it within, tingling in frigid fire. It was almost as if he could feel each tiny yet deliberate step the thing took up his arm. Slow, very slow, like the hour hand on a clock, invisible movement but movement nonetheless: creeping, steady progress, a silent death march toward Hunt's brain. Hunt was a rational man. He had no room in his life for superstition or mystical mumbo-jumbo, but he could find no rational explanation for this. He could conjure no logical rationalization. Hunt touched the thing, tentatively, with two fingers of his right hand. He could feel no lump. There was no rise in his skin. Pressing against it he could find no ball of matter, no hard substance beneath as there might be with a tumor or even an ingrown hair. But though there was no noticeable substance, the skin at that point on his arm was cold. Bitter cold. Hunt could have been pressing his fingers against an ice cube, or maybe even dry ice, and experienced a similar sensation.

The matter troubled Hunt deeply, but he knew there was no time to dwell on the problem. If he and Tahir were to escape, they had to move quickly. Upon exiting the room, Hunt found the adjacent corridor to be devoid of personnel. At some level this made sense. Hunt was often left for long stretches—sometimes for more than a full day—with no human contact. Isolation was part of the interrogation process. If there had been activity in the hallways and adjacent rooms, Hunt may have been able to hold onto snatches of conversation and foot traffic patterns as a means of orienting himself to reality. Better to minimize the sensory input, keep him in a state of confusion and listlessness.

Hunt had no watch—in fact he was naked—and so had no basis for knowing the time of day, but it was obviously nighttime, likely late, perhaps after midnight. This was advantages as Tahir would likely not be missed until morning. Still, Hunt was certain there would be patrols. As such, they needed to flee the building as soon as possible or risk recapture. Hunt determined almost immediately that he was no longer in the building where he'd been held when first captured. That building, he was nearly certain, had been a city dwelling, as modern as one might find in Botma. This sprawling edifice had a feeling of the ages about it. The walls were of an irregular stone of tan and rust, and sporting occasional cracks. The floor, a different breed of stone, was rough, uneven, but strangely attractive to the eye. In the corridors, the ceilings were high, perhaps fifteen feet or better. The furnishings had a slightly Asian appearance. Oil lanterns lit the space from high above. Fantastic depictions of serpents and scorpions littered the way, on canvass, marble, even in elaborate golden statues. About one corner sat a large jade carving of Anascoreth, its bone-like legs wrapped about a screaming child, its snake's-head tail poised for the kill. What sick minds conceived these things?

Peering through a narrow arched window, Hunt saw a large barren yard surrounded by a tall chain link fence topped with barbed wire. He'd be surprised if it wasn't electrified as well. In this initial reconnaissance, Hunt identified one guard walking the grounds and two German shepherds milling about. He was certain there were other guards not immediately visible. As well, Hunt was certain that the further they explored the residence, the more likely they would come across a security patrol. Whatever move he was going to make, he would need to do so quickly.

"Tahir," said Hunt as he knelt to speak with the boy eye-to-eye. "I'm going to ask you this one time and I need you to give me an answer, okay?"

Tahir nodded.

"If you stay with me now, you could be hurt very badly. Men with guns are going to be chasing me. I could be killed. I'll understand if you want to go back to your bed and pretend like you never saw me tonight. I think that might be safer for you."

A sharp shake of the head.

"You know that it will be very hard for us to escape. You could be in big trouble."

Tahir nodded. "I go with you."

"Why, Tahir? Why with me? I'm a stranger."

The boy leaned forward, laying his head on Hunt's shoulder and squeezing. "No one else loves me."

Hesitantly, Hunt returned the hug, but could think of nothing to say. How could it be that the only person in this child's life from whom he perceived affection was a complete stranger? How horrible. How unfair. Despicable. Hunt found a new level of loathing for Nishati Azibo and felt a flaming rage settle in his gut. Pulling back only enough to make eye contact, Hunt said, "Listen, I don't know how this is going to play out and I really don't want you to get hurt."

"I know the grounds," said Tahir. "I know the good hide places."

Hunt nodded. "I'm sure you do, kid. Tell me about them."

Tahir had trouble explaining much of what he knew. His seven year-old's vocabulary was limited and there were certain portions of the property he'd never seen. Apparently this was one of several secure residences Azibo kept. She rarely stayed at any locale for more than a week, but Tahir spent most of his time here. The boy did not know the locale of the estate, but was able to tell Hunt that it was not near a major city. Azibo was here now and had been for the past three days.

Tahir led Hunt to a small alcove on the second floor. The spot was fairly remote, but far from secure. Hunt needed to find some clothing, a weapon, and get a better idea as to the layout of the place in order to facilitate an escape. Tahir was able to confirm that guards patrolled the facility, but he was unclear as to the number. Hunt got the impression that depending on the needs of the day the contingent could range anywhere from three or four up to a couple dozen. Perhaps the most heartening discovery was that Tahir carried a cell phone. Hunt had no way of knowing if the calls were monitored, but felt he'd have to risk a call, possibly two. Besides, what use would there be in tapping a seven year-old's phone? Likely the thing was used simply to keep tabs on his location. Hunt had to force himself to remember Corky's number as his mind was still not entirely free of the multiple drugs used in interrogation, but he eventually came up with what he believed to be the right number, and prayed the phone would allow a connection to an international number. It did. He got her voice mail and decided against leaving a message. If she'd been caught and he indicated that he was free and with Tahir, it would send Azibo's hounds on the hunt all the sooner. Hunt pulled another number from his mud-caked memory, this time receiving an answer on the second ring.

"Who is this and how did you get this number?"

"Lucky, have you heard anything from Corky?"

"Hunt?"

"Yeah. Listen, this line is anything but secure. No idea if we're monitored. My situation's dicey. Not much time. What about Corky? Is she safe?"

"Yes, Hunt. She's fled Botma and is currently in Uganda and awaiting orders. She's available should you need assistance."

Hunt closed his eyes. Thank God. It had been a bluff then. Azibo didn't have access to her.

"Hunt, where are you? What's your status?"

"Like I said, not a secure line. Let's put it this way, I'm in the lion's lair and am with the package. I need an evac."

Lucky Lindell paused before speaking. "No can do, Hunt. You understood the mission parameters."

"Yeah, deniability, but that ship's already sailed. Apparently my tongue got a little slippery as a result of drugs and torture. Listen, I'm pretty well exposed here. What can you do for me?"

A muttered curse and then, "Am I to assume you've escaped?"

"Still on the grounds, but free at the moment."

"And the child is with you?"

"Affirmative."

"Turn yourself in. The mission was to give the child to Azibo."

"Luck, I don't know how much you know of what's happened, but there was no kidnapping. Azibo had the kid all along."

"That's not how it's playing in the media, soldier."

"I'm not your soldier and since when does the media ever know the whole story?"

"Turn yourself in, Hunt. That's my best advice."

"Luck, this woman performed a human sacrifice on her own daughter. I've got her terrified son with me. Get us out!"

A sigh. "We've got a fairly good relationship with her regime. I'll make some calls. We can probably short circuit an execution should you turn yourself in. Executing an American citizen, especially without due process, would be a diplomatic disaster for Azibo."

"Probably short circuit my execution? I wouldn't take those odds to Vegas, Luck. I don't know if you've met the wicked witch of the west, but she's not rowing with two oars. Forget about me, this kid's in danger here."

"It's all I can do, Hunt. But I'm confident we can delay any action until we come up with a more sustainable solution."

"That is as long as Azibo doesn't threaten to withhold the diamonds, right?"

"What are you talking about?"

"Don't play the game with me, Colonial. Sometimes information flows both ways during an interrogation."

There was a pause on the line as Lindell absorbed this revelation. By the time he responded, Hunt was no longer able to hear him.

The guard came around the corner as Hunt finished his final sentence. Tahir screamed a warning and Hunt dove and rolled. His reflexes were off and his body was stiff and abused. What had been intended to be a smooth roll into a fighting stance, careened into a stumble and then an awkward fall. The guard, a lanky soldier of about eighteen, turned, raising his weapon as Tahir's scream turned into a sob.

Hunt managed to flip and then rake his leg left to right, catching the solder on the right shin. It wasn't enough to topple him, but it did interrupt his rhythm. Still on the floor, Hunt dove forward, now hugging the man's lower legs and pulling him to the coarse surface. Scrambling up the guy's torso, Hunt landed four solid blows, rendering the man unconscious. It was an ugly win, but he and the kid were still living and free. Sometimes a win was a win.

It took Hunt less than three minutes to strip the soldier, don his ill-fitting uniform—too long and too tight—and deposit the unconscious form in an unused closet. The door didn't lock, the man was not bound. But at least he'd likely not be discovered until he regained consciousness.

Peering around the corner to ensure that they were alone, Hunt said, "Tahir, does your phone have video and email capabilities?"

The boy looked at him as if he'd been speaking Hungarian.

"Here, let me see your phone." Hunt snatched it from the boy's up-raised hand. Yes. Both video and internet. The country was rife with poverty, but apparently the Azibos had every modern convenience. He wondered if they'd had cell towers installed in strategic locales simply to ensure that she would have constant communication access. Kneeling, Hunt said, "Listen, Tahir. I need you to do something for me, okay?"

The boy nodded.

"I'm going to make a video of you telling what happened. I need you to tell everyone that your daddy didn't kidnap you, that you had never been taken away from your mommy, and that I was not trying to hurt you. If you want, you can say more. Maybe about your sister or anything else about your mommy that you think people should know. Do you understand?"

Again, the boy nodded.

"Alright. Let's do this then. Speak clearly. We're going to let the world see this video."

Chapter Twenty-Eight

Botma Africa

Tahir had only just finished his video testimony when Hunt heard the footsteps. The boy's statements had been incomplete, sometimes meandering, but Hunt felt he'd hit the high points. Regardless, the statement, as it was, would need to do. There would likely not be an opportunity to do a second take. Hurriedly, Hunt emailed it to three separate numbers with instructions to get it to the media. He hoped that within the hour Tahir's face would be plastered on television and computer screens across the globe. With that kind of scrutiny, Azibo would have little choice but to allow Hunt and Tahir to leave. Or, at the very least, to provide a fair and public hearing.

At least that's what he tried to tell himself.

Hunt and Tahir were in an alcove with no escape route other than from the direction of the approaching footsteps. They moved quickly toward the approaching footfall hoping to reach an intersection before encountering resistance. Staying close to the uneven wall, they managed to slip unseen around a corner and down a winding staircase. No more than a minute later Hunt heard footsteps descending behind them. It seemed two perhaps three sets of feet, no hurry, no urgency. Casual conversation. Apparently neither Hunt nor the boy had yet been missed, but they were in danger of imminent discovery.

The stairway descended into a large oval room, illuminated only by torchlight. The walls were of jagged and irregular stone: red and tan, unadorned, cold, unforgiving. A musty smell pervaded the area and Hunt could hear water dripping in uneven plops and splats from somewhere off to the right. There were two corridors, one to the right, the other to the left, leading from the room, and an iron gate directly across from them. "The gate," whispered Tahir.

This choice seemed the least advantageous, but there were people coming from behind and Hunt had no time to question Tahir's suggestion and so moved quickly across the space. The boy claimed to know the best hiding places. Hunt was now locked into staking his life on this declaration. The gate, a large wrought iron thing, brown and green, with bars more than an inch in diameter, was locked. The voices were getting closer and Hunt felt a surge of adrenaline rush through his limbs. He was still very weak following his weeks of captivity and torture and not likely fit for hand-to-hand combat against multiple persons. But, in truth, there would be no fight. The men were likely armed. Hunt and Tahir would be trapped with no place to flee.

"There is a key," whispered Tahir as he bent to the ground, feeling along the stone floor where it met the wall. He smiled as he found a stone that wobbled just slightly when touched. It took him a moment to get a good grip on the corners of the rough-hewn stone, but once this was accomplished, the floor stone slid easily from its resting place. A moment later, Tahir produced a long iron key from within the gap. "I told you I know the good hide places," he smiled, replacing the stone before rising. Tahir inserted the key into the lock but struggled to turn it. The boy quickly became frustrated and Hunt moved in, twisting the key, pulling it just slightly back, jiggling, getting a feel for the mechanism. Finally, he angled it slightly left and then turned. The lock disengaged.

The gate offered a hideous creek as Tahir pulled it open only wide enough for them to slip through. Reaching back through the bars, Hunt twisted the key once again, this time locking the gate. He then withdrew the key and slinked into the darkness beyond as he listened for footfall. He couldn't make out the approaching steps as well from within the darkened space, but took this as a good sign. If others had heard the creak of the gate the footsteps would have become rushed, voices would have become urgent.

Turning, Hunt squinted into the darkness. "How are we supposed to see in here?"

"There will be a torch. Further in. Deeper. Not here."

Hunt nodded. "And where exactly is here?" he asked, still in a whisper.

"Dungeon," answered the boy matter-of-factly. Tahir took Hunt's hand and began moving further into the darkness. "Put your other hand against the wall," he said. "Just follow the wall."

Hunt's eyes still hadn't adjusted to the complete darkness. It was as if his head was covered by the canvass hood again. "Is there another way out of here, Tahir? Or will we need to go back the way we came?"

"We go out through the sewers."

Hunt allowed a brief chuckle. "You really do know all the little tricks, don't you?"

Tahir giggled.

The floor sloped slightly downward and Hunt heard the skittering footsteps of rodents from somewhere above. "Didn't you say there'd be a torch somewhere down here?"

"Not yet. Soon. Around a corner."

"Why torches? Why not electric lights or flashlights at least?"

"It's old down here." Tahir said this as if Hunt was the silliest person on the plant to have asked such an absurd question.

"Yeah, I guess it is, kid." Hunt glanced back over his shoulder and could no longer see even the flickering illumination from the room they'd exited. Complete, utter darkness and yet the kid continued forward at a steady pace. "Do you come here to hide, Tahir? Is this one of your secret places?"

"Yes."

"Why? What are you hiding from?" It was probably a stupid question, but Hunt was curious nonetheless. He'd love to hear that the boy hid from some fictitious bogeyman and not his much-too-real psychopathic mother. Slim chance there.

"Shhhh. They'll hear you."

"Who will hear me?"

"The slaves. If they hear you they make noise. If they make noise, the guards come."

"Slaves? There are slaves down here?"

"For the mines, yes. Now, shhh!"

The boy sounded matter-of-fact, as if the concept of slavery meant nothing to him. Just another facet of life. Nothing to create an uproar. Hunt supposed this was exactly the case. Tahir's mother had likely kept slaves throughout the boy's short life. How could he feel moral revulsion over something that had been a part of his day-to-day existence? Hunt wondered if Lucky Lindell—if the U.S. government—knew of this. He wondered if it would matter if they did.

Hunt paused, listening. He heard no footsteps from behind. Likely whoever had come down the stairway had been unaware of the two fugitives and had turned right or left down one of the corridors to go about their business. He did, though, hear continued skittering from above. He wondered if the rats were within the wall or if perhaps there was a ledge they traversed, thus making it possible for them to leap down upon Hunt and Tahir at any time.

Tahir tugged on Hunt's hand, pulling him forward and around a subtle bend. Now, Hunt could see a faint light flickering in the distance. His heart quickened. Even this minimal illumination was a strangely comforting thing. He'd spent most of the last several weeks in total darkness. The midnight black unnerved him.

Hunt now heard voices. Muffled. Not urgent. It wasn't guards. Tahir would have reacted if there had been danger, Hunt was certain of this. No these would be the slaves. Slaves! Right here. Right now, in the twenty-first century. Though the dungeon was damp and cold, Hunt still felt the flush of heat race through his form fueled by anger and revulsion.

There was an odor as well. More prominent than the voices. Feces mingled with sweat and urine. Hunt had encountered similar odors coming from some of the people Dana helped at the homeless shelter. He moved toward the wavering light. He'd faced gunfire, bombs—he'd had half of his face blown off—but he couldn't think of a time he'd been more nervous than at the prospect of encountering these poor souls enslaved by a madwoman. It was a peculiar emotion: a dash of shame, two dollops dread, a pinch of fury.

There were not so many as he'd feared, perhaps two dozen. Most were middle aged or better. Few were young. All but one was black. There were both males and females, all in the same cramped cell. They stared at Hunt through the bars, twenty-something living skeletons, eyes wide and vacant, sunken cheeks, teeth overly exposed behind withered lips. Each wore identical clothing: a pullover black shirt and black pants, each garment of a coarse fabric, perhaps burlap, but it was difficult to tell in the dim flickering light. Almost all of the clothing was torn, often in multiple places. They were barefoot. Nearly each showed obvious signs of physical abuse. One man sat in a dank corner moaning, his leg jutting at a peculiar angle, obviously broken and unattended. A woman stood nearby cradling her blood-stained side. Every eye met his, each pleading in personal agony.

Hunt stood immobile. He could think of nothing to say. Nothing to do.

"Come!" urged Tahir. "We have only small time."

Go?

Hunt couldn't go. He couldn't flee this place without making an attempt to free these poor souls. How could he even contemplate such a thing?

"Tahir, give me your key to the dungeon."

"We have to go."

"The key, Tahir."

"Why?"

Why!

How could the boy ask why?

"I'm going to free the slaves."

Tahir's eyes became wide in the wavering light of the torch.

"Tahir, please."

The boy dropped his gaze. "She will kill us all."

"Then give me the key and leave. But I can't ignore these people."

"The key won't work. It's a different key. Not the same one."

Hunt nodded. Of course it was a different key. How could he have expected it to be the same one as the outer gate? He began going through the pockets of the stolen uniform. Was there anything he could use as a lock pick? It appeared to be an ancient gate. The locking mechanism couldn't be too complex.

There was a shuffle of movement, a vague murmur from within the cell. Glancing up, Hunt noticed that one of the prisoners had moved to directly before him. The man seemed almost familiar, as if Hunt had seen him at some other time and place, in other circumstances. He was likely seventy years old or better. His hair was all salt with just a sprinkle of pepper, his beard mottled and uneven. His heavily-lined face was the deepest ebony and his full lips, despite the deplorable circumstance, seemed capable of a rich and endearing grin. His eyes were weary and worn, and yet there was a spark, some internal fire still lit, some glimmering passion pressing through from within the confines of his soul.

"Do I know you?" asked Hunt.

A gradual turning of the head from left to right. "I highly doubt it," said the man. His voice was warm, revealing that inner strength. "Not personally, I'm sure."

Hunt studied him. There was definitely something familiar. "You're a politician, or a diplomat, an ambassador. Something like that. From Nairobi, or maybe Kenya. I know I saw your picture in the news. It's been months now, maybe more. I think you'd gone missing."

The man nodded, offering a weary grin. "Missing. I suppose that would suffice."

Hunt scanned the small group, meeting the many pleading eyes. "Are you all political prisoners?"

The man shrugged. "Political, religious, one flavor or another."

Hunt met the man's gaze. What could he say to these people? His inclination was to promise to free them, but his own liberty was far from a given, he couldn't make guarantees to anyone—not even to Tahir, who he saw as his personal responsibility. "Listen," he said. "I've just escaped myself. I didn't even know about you until a couple of minutes ago. I want to get you out of here. Any thoughts? Do you know where a key is kept? Where's the guard? Maybe I can subdue him and use his key."

Another slow shake of the head. "No regular guard. No key. They only come if we make a fuss. And then it's most unpleasant. Nishati Azibo is secure in her power over us. She doesn't feel the need to waste manpower on a sentinel."

Tahir tugged on Hunt's arm. "Come! We need go. We need go."

"Hang on, Tahir. Just give me a minute."

The boy harrumphed, quieted, but didn't release Hunt's arm. It was then that the prisoner's eyes narrowed and his expressive lips twisted into a grimacing pout. "Your arm, son. Let me see your arm."

Tahir released his grip and Hunt lifted the arm for the man to see. The uniform was of the short sleeve variety and the mark of Anascoreth was clearly visible. Hunt's eyes widened with terror when he realized it had now moved to above the elbow and was on his lower bicep.

"How long?" asked the prisoner.

"Huh?"

"How long since she initiated the possession process?"

Possession? "Um, a couple of days, I guess. Time's still a little fluid for me. I'd been drugged."

"And tortured. That much is obvious by the look of you." The man reached through the bars, taking Hunt's arm and inspecting the tattoo-like scorpion. "Two days, you say? I assume this started at the wrist."

Hunt nodded.

"That is what I feared." The man paused, gently squeezing Hunt's forearm in fatherly kindness. "You don't have time to worry about us. And even if you did, you don't have the means to facilitate our escape. Take the boy. Run. Flee this place if you can." Here he paused, his grip becoming firm, his eyes liquid. "Listen to me, understand, accept my words as truth, and act on this advice. If you escape, if you get free of Nishati Azibo, you must lose the arm. Do you understand, son? You must lose the arm."

"What?"

"Amputate the arm above that image before the spirit of Anascoreth reaches your brain. I know it sounds ludicrous, but it's your only hope. If that thing reaches your brain it will consume your soul and take control of your form."

Hunt pulled his arm free of the man's grip in a violent jerk. Glaring into the pleading eyes, heedless of who might hear, he shouted, "Listen, I don't know what this crazy thing is, but it's not some mumbo-jumbo horror movie possession. I don't believe in that nonsense."

The man nodded slowly. There was no anger or insult in his voice as he said, "No? Then offer a more rational alternative. I tried when first I encountered this. Oh, she didn't do it to me, the mark was on another, but I witnessed the process. And I offered every excuse I could imagine and still I was hard pressed to concoct one that I believed in the depths of my being. And that's because it's true, son. It's insane, it's uncanny, and it's real. Do not doubt me in this."

Hunt was preparing to offer some feeble response when he heard a subtle movement from behind. He turned to see Nishati Azibo as she emerged from the darkness flanked by two large lions, each male, each likely weighing nearly eight hundred pounds, each of which bore the pulsating image the Anascoreth scorpion centered between their eyes.

"That's good advice, he gives you, Huntington. Though, it's unlikely you'll have opportunity to act on it."

***

Hunt was once again strapped to the coarse stone slab in the same chamber-like room he'd occupied when young Tahir attempted the ill-fated rescue. He still wore the uniform he'd stolen from the unfortunate guard and he hadn't seen Tahir since the time of their capture. He worried for the boy's safety. Nishati Azibo paced before him, sometimes circling the stone slab, other times simply strolling back and forth, her lithe form catlike and brisk in movement, her dark green-flecked eyes dancing with some internal mirth. The two lions were present, each seated statue-like before the entrance to the room. Their behavior was peculiar in that they spent no time licking themselves, scratching itches, yawning, fidgeting, or in any way acknowledging the presence of the humans. They stared ahead as silent sentinels awaiting a command. Even well-trained guard dogs followed movements with their eyes, but these savage beasts might as well have been blind and deaf for their lack of interest in their surroundings. Hunt focused on their foreheads where the same symbol that was currently making its way up Hunt's arm was clearly visible.

Under his skin, creeping centimeter by centimeter, freezing the blood in his veins, desiring his mind, his will, his very being.

The concept of possession was absurd. No modern-day person would believe such a thing, and yet, as predicted by the caged diplomat, Hunt could find no alternate explanation that he could believe in the core of his being. No rationalization held up under scrutiny. Hunt was not a religious man, though neither was he an atheist, nor even an agnostic. He supposed, if anything, the subject was simply on hold. He'd not allowed himself to delve too deeply into such things. There would be time for that later. And if he didn't happen to survive until such a time as to contemplate things ethereal and eternal, well, he supposed he'd find out the hard way. Short-sighted thinking perhaps, but it had been his thought process nonetheless.

239

And so the concept of possession, of an ancient scorpion-like spirit active and influential in the modern world, seemed the stuff of fantasy, of pulp fiction and late-night horror films. Was this thing truly a god—more likely a demon or some other sinister haunt—or was Hunt simply mentally imbalanced after weeks of drugs and torture? As much as he preferred to believe the latter, he couldn't find it in himself to take that ever so comforting rationalistic step. Deep within, he knew that something beyond the scope of his imaginings was in play and it terrified him more than any mortar round or frontal assault he'd yet encountered.

"You are very resourceful," said Azibo, wrenching Hunt from his contemplations. "I'd love to hear the details of your escape attempt."

Hunt wasn't sure if she knew that her son had facilitated the escape and wasn't about to tell her this particular truth. Though, he did believe that knowledge of Tahir's video testimony might protect the boy in that she would then know that she would soon be under close scrutiny. "I dematerialized and meant to reappear in Paris," said Hunt in response to her question. "Guess I took a wrong turn."

Azibo offered that rich sultry laugh of hers. "I do believe I will miss your sarcasm once your mind is taken. Though, I suppose it would become annoying after a time."

"Yeah, about that demonic mind control possession thing, you might want to reconsider. This scheme of yours is about to come crashing down around you and you'll have no choice but to release me and to surrender to the international community. I'm guessing you'll be charged with crimes against humanity."

She smiled, strolling to him and gazing down on him with those wide-set eyes. "And what thing is that, Huntington? What thing is going to come down upon me?"

"Your scheme to make it appear as if Ubora kidnapped Tahir. Your false claims that I took him under Ubora's orders." Hunt paused, meeting her gaze. "Here's the thing. There's a video. Not Hollywood quality, more of a B movie grade, but it'll be effective."

"A video? How clever."

"Yeah, well, I try. It's of Tahir explaining what really happened. You know, that whole pesky truth thing. He states that he was never kidnapped, that you kept him hidden away, that you murdered his sister and that he lives in fear that he'll be next. The video has been sent outside of the country. Even now the U.S. government has it in hand. I've sent it to others too with instructions to forward it to the media."

Azibo laughed. "The U.S. government is too greedy and cautious to move on such flimsy evidence. And the media? Only a soft, spoiled American would believe I'd fear the media. The only media within Botma operates under my command and I'm unconcerned about the international press except where it aids my cause." Here, she moved closer, only two inches from Hunt's face, a broad grin stretching across her strangely attractive features. "And soon it will do exactly as I please, exposing Tahir's claims as nothing more than a child's fantasy."

"I dunno. The kid was pretty convincing. He's not exactly Pacino, but there was genuine emotion."

"Yes. I'm sure he was, but not as convincing as the footage of you murdering my son in cold blood. That, Huntington, will cause a news sensation. That will cause an uproar which will ignite the world behind me."

Hunt angled his head at her. "You know I'd never harm the kid and my picture is on file in the Pentagon, a stand-in wouldn't hold up under scrutiny. You'll never get a convincing video involving me."

Azibo stroked Hunt's head, and then ran her fingers teasingly down the damaged side of his face. "Oh, I do believe you'll feel differently when Anascoreth burrows into your brain and you lose all freewill. That will change your view, I think."

"You're a monster."

Azibo pouted as if hurt by the comment. "I'm sure from your standpoint that seems true. But, what I do is not for my own gain, but for the betterment of Botma."

"Give it a rest, Azibo. You've slaughtered thousands of your own people, you keep slaves, you force your religion on the populace. You sacrificed your own daughter to your crazy god. Don't try to pass it all off as noble."

Again, she stroked his face, gently, her eyes were moist, her voice soft and tender when she spoke. "You are a brave man, Huntington. And under other circumstances I might have tried to keep you near to me, perhaps very near. But, you are wrong about me." He moved to speak, but she placed a single finger over his lips to silence him. "No, no. Allow me to tell my tale before you set about disassembling it. I love my country, Huntington. But it is a small country and is subject to the whims of other nations. We have lost our sovereignty twice in recent history. We are absorbed by one nation, struggle to become again free, only to be annexed into another. Our people are poor. They live primitive lives without the benefits you take for granted in the United States. My father was our leader before me. He was a good man, but he was not strong. I knew, as a youth, that should I ever helm the nation, if I hoped to bring our tiny country into a state of peace and prosperity, I would need a power greater than my own."

"A power greater than your own, I'm guessing you're talking about your crazy scorpion god."

"Anascoreth, yes. And if you are willing to set aside your western thinking for only a minute, you'll realize there's nothing crazy about it. Picture, Huntington, seeing your birth land batted about like a tennis ball, always subject to the fancies of other nations. Picture your children starving, disease running rampant. Picture being one of the poorest nations on the earth with no natural means of turning the tide. Now imagine what you would do if you were offered the opportunity to change it all. What sacrifices would you be willing to make? What terrible deeds would you perform in order to give your beloved land a chance at true freedom and prosperity?"

"Well, to begin with, I wouldn't kill my own children."

Here, she clenched his hair. It was still short, but now grown out just enough for her to clasp. She yanked his head back, moving so near that her nose met his. "Do you think that I go into this lightly? Do you think I feel nothing? Huntington, I wept each night as I sought to become pregnant for I knew what would be asked of me. I conceived with full knowledge that I would be required to relinquish my children to Anascoreth. Whatever you might think of me, I am still a woman, and I grieve for my children as all mothers grieve. But, the power to save my country was given to me through my willingness to sacrifice my own blood. And already Anascoreth has blessed the land with a resource plentiful enough to grant us wealth and influence on the international stage."

"The diamonds?"

She released her grip on him, moving back only inches. "Yes, Huntington. Diamonds. An incalculable amount."

"And you're telling me the diamonds didn't exist before you made your pact with the devil."

"The devil? No, Anascoreth is not a devil. But neither is he a merciful god. There are many great sacrifices to be made if he is to grant us long-lasting strength. But yes, Anascoreth bequeathed us the gemstones. Diamonds are abundant in several areas of this continent, but never before here. And yes, geologists drilled and studied, they took their surveys, examined the soil, the bedrock. As recent as a decade past, there were none to be found."

"So, now what?"

"Now?" she asked. "Now, Huntington, we wait for Anascoreth to complete his work in you." She paused, inhaled deeply, and then added, "And then, I suppose I will be required to part with yet another child." Blinking, she wiped a single tear from an eye, bent, and kissed Hunt gently on the lips. "Forgive me for what I do and for what I would have you do."

Chapter Twenty-Nine

Uganda Africa

Dana had never met Corky Meeks face-to-face, never seen a picture of her, never given her more than a passing thought. She knew very little of the woman save for the fact that Hunt had once considered her a dear friend and that they'd, for a brief time, been lovers. As such, Dana was determined that she would dislike the woman. Corky had not been Dana's first choice as a contact person. When she'd received the video recording from Hunt, she'd sought the council of Hunt's former commander and mentor, Colonel Lucky Lindell, but Lindell had proved decidedly unhelpful.

Dana was furious with the man.

Lindell had received the same video as had Dana. It showed a young boy, Nishati Azibo's son, frightened and anxious as he told of how his mother had put him into hiding, claiming to the world that he'd been kidnapped by her rival who, apparently, was the boy's father. He stated clearly that Hunt—whose name and image had been splashed across the world news in connection with the kidnapping—had had nothing to do with any of it, that, in truth, Hunt had intended to remove him from danger. The boy also claimed that his mother had killed his older sister and that he was terrified that he would suffer a similar fate.

Lindell had buried the video claiming that the boy's testimony could not be verified, that as much as he liked and admired Hunt, he couldn't vouch for his motives. Hunt had gone to Botma on his own volition. Besides, he said, Hunt had been dishonorably discharged from the military some years earlier, and had Lindell himself not intervened, Hunt might likely have been court-martialed. Perhaps this was a similar lapse in judgment.

It was all poppycock.

Hunt had emailed Dana before leaving for Africa. He'd stated clearly that Lindell had asked him to take this assignment. It was covert, the U.S. would deny their involvement if he was caught, but he was acting on their behalf. Well, Lindell certainly held to his deniability. The thing that nettled Dana was that he and Hunt were supposed to be friends. This video implicated the U.S. in no way. The country wasn't even mentioned.

Lindell urged Dana to keep the video private until such time as its authenticity could be verified. When she'd shown hesitation, he'd become gruff, nearly ordering her to keep it out of the media, claiming national security interests as the issue at hand.

Dana had released it anyway. Hunt was obviously in danger. This was clearly his desperate attempt to draw attention to the situation and perhaps gain some much needed time. The very fact that he'd once again become unreachable following the transmission of the email testified to this. She wasn't about to play politics with his life. She'd forwarded the clip to several major news outlets both in the U.S. and abroad where the story gained some attention. But the true clamor came from the thousands that saw it on You Tube. Less than twenty-four hours after posting, she'd received the call from Corky Meeks.

Jonathan had warned Dana against making the trip. The doctor didn't believe she was yet ready for exertion, much less a potentially volatile situation, but Dana would not be detoured. Hunt had been off grid for weeks, footage of him apparently kidnapping the Azibo child had surfaced nearly a month ago, and, at that time, this Azibo woman claimed him to be imprisoned. It was bad enough thinking of Hunt locked away, and, in truth, at that point she'd been hospitalized and unable to contemplate intervention. But things had changed. Hunt had escaped. Or, at least, he had been free long enough to record and then send the video testimony. But now his status was unknown.

Corky Meeks had called with additional information and, regardless of Jonathan's yammering objections, Dana needed to act. Of course, Jonathan had insisted on accompanying her. As much as she pretended otherwise, this was for the best. She was only a week free of the hospital and far from healed. Jonathan wasn't much better, having only stopped utilizing a sling ten days prior.

***

Corky Meeks did not stand out in the small crowd at the airline terminal and it took Dana several moments to make eye contact and to then determine that this was the woman she sought. Corky was pretty enough, but not beautiful. Rather, she was more cute, in a bookish sense. She was African American, a little too thin by Dana's standards. Her hair was pulled back into a tight ponytail. Her face was heart-shaped, her lips, a bit of a twist. She wore tortoiseshell glasses, a red football jersey with the symbol for pi on the chest where a numeral should be, faded blue jeans, and sandals.

Hunt had once been attracted to this woman!

Possibly, he still was.

The thought gave Dana's belly a rile. It wasn't fair to be jealous, she supposed. She had, after all, been separated from Hunt for the better part of a year. But, she hadn't expected him to rush out and find a replacement. She'd just needed time. She'd just… Well, she wasn't quite sure.

"You must be Dana," said Corky as she stepped forward, extending a hand and adding, "And this must be Jonathan Thorpe. Pleased to meet you as well." Her voice was nasal. How annoying! Whatever could Hunt see in this woman?

"Yes. Corina, is it?" asked Jonathan. "Pleased to meet you." He offered his hand, shaking hers, firm but with grace and deference.

"Corky. I go by Corky." A quirky little twist of a grin, how salacious!

"Of course," smiled Jonathan. "Corky."

Corky again addressed Dana. "I understand you've both recently been hospitalized. I'm sorry to drag you into this mess, but the situation is beyond my capabilities."

"Of course it is," snapped Dana. "I'm astonished you thought yourself able to contribute at all."

Why did she feel so threatened by this woman?

Jonathan cleared his throat. "Yes, well. Tense situations all around, or so it would seem. May I suggest we retire to someplace less public in order to strategize?"

"Yeah. Good idea," nodded Corky as she offered Dana an awkward glance. "I've got a rental car and there's a small restaurant about a mile from here. It's pretty private."

"Perfect!" chimed Jonathan with a clap of the hands. "I can already feel the sense of comradery in the air."

***

In lieu of local flavor, Corky Meeks selected an Irish pub. The place was not overly large, but offered three small, rather private, dining areas in addition to the long u-shaped bar which was the nucleus of the establishment. The floor was of tiny black and white mosaic tiles, the rafters were Kelly green, and there was a small stage set-up on the eastern wall where, apparently, a band performed in the evenings. The lighting was rather bright as pubs go, the atmosphere cheery, and the patronage sparse at this midday hour.

Corky asked that they be seated in a tiny dining alcove containing only three tables. The other two tables were unoccupied. The woman then ordered pizza. At an Irish pub. Pizza! Dana and Jonathan withheld from the food, each ordering only Guinness.

"The pizza will take a while," smiled Corky. "The waiter won't have a reason to pester us."

"Oh. Brilliant, that," quipped Dana. "Now I understand how you attained your position at the Pentagon. You developed the pizza stratagem."

Here, the two women locked eyes for several seconds, after which Corky offered a prolonged sigh. "Enough, Dana. You're jealous that I was with Hunt on this mission. Oh well, too bad. Guess you'll have to deal. You could have been here but you weren't. I was. And for the record, nothing happened between us. Not a single personal foul. And to be clear on the matter, I wish something had. You let him go, Dana. You sent him away and now here you sit with your previous husband in tow, glaring daggers at me while a man we both care about is in danger of losing his life. Now, can we put the high school drama behind us until this is over, or should I bring in someone else to extract Hunt?"

Silence.

Utter, center-of-a-black-hole silence.

And then Jonathan erupted in raucous laughter.

As surprisingly, did Dana, to the point where she sprayed beer from her nose. She simply couldn't contain herself.

Corky, for her part, stared befuddled at the two. "Um, okay. Not sure I meant that to be funny."

"I'm sorry," giggled Dana as she wiped suds from her chin. "Too much strain on the noggin lately. I've been a bit of a prat. You're right. There will be time enough to gouge each other's eyes later. Share your data. What do you know?"

Corky blinked twice, twisted her lips, nodded, and then withdrew her laptop computer, angling it so that each could see the screen.

They spent the next hour sifting through intel, batting about ideas, and forming the basis of a plan. Though Dana was loath to admit it, Corky had done a first-rate job at assembling relevant information. Apparently, she'd made contact with Azibo's rival, Zahir Ubora, and between his insights and her Pentagon connections had been able to determine Hunt's likely whereabouts. The difficulty was now in concocting a plan that would result in the safe evacuation of all involved.

"Look," said Corky at one point. "We have up-to-date intel—for now. I work in the Pentagon, I've got friends there. But, you've got to know, Colonial Lindell has ordered me back to the States and I've yet to comply. I'm A.W.O.L. That means I'm officially locked out. I can't offer any satellite surveillance or more current intelligence. Once you go in, there won't be much I can do to help."

"A.W.O.L.," said Jonathan. "That means, I suppose, you could be imprisoned upon return. Certainly, well, at the very least, you've put your position at risk."

Corky leveled her eyes at him. "I probably should have taken some risks long before this, but yeah, I've committed a technical foul." She paused, glanced down at her pizza, and then added, "I'm not walking away from Hunt again."

Dana eyed the woman. It was clear that the statement was meant romantically as well as strategically. This mousy little woman was a bit of a tiger incognito. At some level, Dana admired her rather introverted brand of spunk, but she also understood that she was in an unmistakably declared battle for Hunt's affections. Dana still wasn't quite certain that she'd adequately worked through her personal issues where romance was concerned, but was bright enough to realize that the choice to prolong a decision had been taken from her. If she wanted Hunt back, the time was now.

"So," said Jonathan after allowing each woman to toss one last glare at the other. "The operation, shall we review the plan again?"

Dana and Corky each nodded, neither taking their eyes from the other.

"Yes, lovely," sighed Jonathan. "Have I mentioned that every moment is a joy?"

The plan was for Dana and Jonathan to enter Botma with falsified press credentials from the BBC and to then utilize the ruse as reporters to get close to Azibo, learn of Hunt's exact location, and then extract him. Corky would monitor communications from within Azibo's suspected compound utilizing a device carried by Jonathan. With luck, she'd then be able to gather useful real-time information and feed it back to the two operatives.

Dana had contributed what she felt was a fair dash of brilliance in that she'd hacked into the BBC server and installed a program which would redirect any web or telephone activity originating in Botma to a duplicate site she'd established. This site was a replica of the original with a few slight enhancements. Dana and Jonathan were both credited as employees, she as a reporter, he as a cameraperson. Any attempt at communication, either by phone or email, would be directed to Corky Meeks who would verify Dana and Jonathan's story. The woman could actually pull off a passable accent. Not brilliant, but passable. They'd equipped Jonathan with a camera. Encased within this, the monitoring device and a sophisticated piece of software designed by Dana. It also contained one weapon. There simply wasn't space enough to hide two without increasing risk of detection. As it was, Jonathan's pistol had had to be disassembled in order to alleviate suspicion.

***

Botma Africa

The compound was in a secluded valley located nearly two hours from the nearest village, had only one dirt access road, and looked to have come from centuries past. It was surrounded by a twelve foot high chain link fence topped with barbed wire. The grounds were large but not rambling. The structure, though, was a near castle. The edifice was of a rich almost golden stone, uneven in size and texture. It looked to be five stories in height, but there were few windows delineating one level from another. Three cone-shaped peeks, likely used as lookout posts, were spaced atop the roof. These were set back from the face of the building. The main entrance was an arched doorway to the right front of the facility, large enough in both height and width to allow a relatively large truck to pass within. The grounds were patrolled by a small contingent of armed soldiers, many of whom were accompanied by German shepherds.

Dana and Jonathan arrived in a rental car leased, ostensibly, by the BBC. They set up the camera on a grassy bluff located perhaps a quarter of a mile from the gate. Dana held a microphone and a notepad. The dog-eared pad contained handwritten notes containing the copy she was to read during her faux broadcast as well as numerous notes on previous reports, many written with different pens in order to give the appearance of age and use. Their hope was to be seen by the sentries and then confronted as they shot their report. They would then ask for an interview with Nishati Azibo, which would, of course, be denied. This was fine. The true plan was to create enough of a ruckus that the guard would feel compelled to bring them within the compound until someone in authority decided just exactly what to do with them. Once inside, Jonathan would activate the transmitting device and the two would improvise from there. In addition to transmitting audio and video, Dana's software would collect data based on sonar-like signals. These would help to build a blueprint in process. Once enough data was collected, assumptions could be made considering the rest of the layout. It wouldn't be perfect, but it could conceivably point them in the direction of the prison cells and then, with luck, escape routes.

They made a bit of a scene about camera angle, always with Dana in the foreground and the facility over one shoulder or the other. They were recording and Corky received the live feed as did the blueprint-in-a-box software within the camera casing. Already, the apparatus would be estimating the dimensions of the exterior, thus formulating the foundational parameters on which to base the interior layout. Dana also wore an earring set that sent and received signals, allowing her an additional means to remain in constant contact with Corky, the assumption being that she would not always be in immediate proximity to the heavily-modified video camera.

Phase one of the plan went as anticipated.

Within fifteen minutes of their arrival, four young guards appeared, two on foot and another two in an off-road vehicle. The vehicle came from further up the road, blocking a retreat until the intruder's identities and potential threat could be established. The officer in charge was likely no more than twenty-five years old and senior his men by half of a decade or better. Once Dana and Jonathan had shown their credentials and insisted on seeing Azibo, the man became nervous, denying that the dictator was at this facility and threatening them with bodily harm should they not leave.

"Yes, well, brilliant that," said Jonathan. "But, one must consider that we are here on assignment. The BBC is expecting a report. They know our exact locale, they set our itinerary. Should we suddenly evaporate, well, I'm sure you can imagine the international uproar. Two British journalists slain by an outlaw regime. It would be quite ugly, I'm sure. Allow me to be frank. We found this hideaway. I would think that means others can find it as well. This particular secret is out, chum. Now, about that interview with Nishati Azibo?" Here, he winked and grinned, though the young officer didn't find the situation humorous in the least.

They were frisked and then ordered into the vehicle.

Jonathan was not allowed to take the camera.

Dana still had the earring communicator/transmitter, but the signal booster was hidden within the camera. It was uncertain how far into the compound she would be able to maintain contact. The range was some-where just over five-hundred yards—just slightly over the distance to the door of the place. With the camera left on the rise, they were likely on their own.

***

The building had an unhealthy musty smell about it. Old. It smelled old. Ancient, even. The heavy scent of mildew and mold, of rotting wood and possibly fleshly decay, wafted through the air. There was a peculiar mix of modern and antique. Spider webs crisscrossed rafters and Dana spotted a large deep blue scorpion moving along the upper wall. It almost seemed the thing was pacing them. The guard station, situated in a small tan brick shed in front of the main building, was equipped with video monitors and computers. Obviously, the place had electrical generators. But the corridors of the primary structure were illuminated by torches and gas lamps with no sign of any fixture from this century or even the previous. There were no security cameras here as there had been on the exterior. There was no hint of modernization of any kind. Though it was midday, the interior corridors had no windows and thus no exterior light. The wavering flames cast dancing shadows and to Dana it felt as if phantom creatures, maybe trolls or goblins or even dragons from some medieval fantasy, were hiding about every corner. Dana could make no sense of it. If electrical power was available, why not power the entire building? It was large, true. But far shy of monstrous. Surely, generators could be brought in. Perhaps, she supposed, that since this was only one of many short-term hideaways and located near no power lines, it was impractical to modernize the entire structure. In any event, the setting gave Dana a bit of a quiver. This was silly, she knew. It was just an old building. Nothing to fear. But Dana recognized that due to recent experiences she'd become more emotional than in previous times. She was now subject to whims of fancy and superstition, where before she had been levelheaded and quite rational. She hid this well from others, or so she supposed. But, within her placid façade she was a hotbed of turmoil and illogic. She despised her current lack of rationale, but at least maintained enough of her facilities to recognize it for what it was.

They were taken to a small windowless room situated perhaps two hundred feet into the structure and slightly to the north of the narrow door by which they'd entered. There were no chairs, no furnishings at all. The uneven stone walls were bare except for a web of cracks on the surface just right of the door.

Left alone with Jonathan, Dana immediately tested her contact to Corky Meeks.

Yes. The transmitters were still sending and receiving. The signal was weak, but functional. Dana proceeded to relay all she had seen. To Dana's delight, Corky informed her that the camera had been retrieved and brought into the compound through a separate entrance and was still gathering data. Already, between the camera's sensors and Dana's earring transmitter, Corky was seeing the beginnings of a floor plan, though it would be far from complete unless either the camera or Dana was moved again, allowing for additional information to be collected.

Dana's elation at the continued contact was cut short when a monster of a man entered the room. At least six foot three inches in height, he was as broad as two average-sized men, had tree trunk legs, and biceps to make the Incredible Hulk weep. His eyes were narrow slits, revealing nothing of the man's temperament. His nose lulled to the right, and had obviously been broken on more than one occasion. A thick mustache partially hid what appeared to be a jagged scar on his upper lip. The behemoth took a smart phone photograph of Dana and then Jonathan before handing the devise to a young soldier waiting just outside the room. He then closed the door.

"Reporters, huh?" said the man. His voice was not rough or booming as one might assume from someone of his girth. If anything, it hinted at a weary amusement.

"Yes, BBC," said Dana. "I do hope you're taking care with our equipment. We're really not supposed to leave it unattended. Company policy and whatnot."

The man chuckled. He was standing, arms crossed at his massive chest, looking down on them both as would an adult assessing small children. "Your equipment. That's what you're worried about?"

The man was attempting to frighten them by his size, posture, and innuendo. Dana played dumb. "Of course we're concerned about the equipment. I for one certainly do not want damaged equipment charges deducted from my pay. And that aside, we'll need our camera if we're to interview Nishati Azibo."

Here, he offered a bear-like grin. "You really think we're going to let you interview Nishati?"

Dana feigned indignation. "I don't see why not. I understand she's under duress and governing while in seclusion, but a public interview could assist in rebuilding her image in the public eye."

"Yes," added Jonathan. "A chance, perhaps, to enlighten the masses, to give her side of the story."

"And you feel you're the ones to give her that opportunity." Here, he stepped forward, glaring down on Jonathan. "Has anyone ever told you that you're a weasel?"

"Um… In so many words, well…"

"I have a good sense of people," said the giant, cutting Jonathan off mid-sentence. "And I'm pretty certain I'm not going to believe a single word that comes out of that little weasel mouth of yours. What do you think of that, weasel?"

"Well, I would say that you are, well, that you have misjudged me. In truth, I'm rather brilliant. Not weasel-like in the least."

"Are you telling us we're not to be allowed an audience with President Azibo?" asked Dana in an effort to distract the man. She had a sense that he was edging toward violence, and it was much too early into the operation to get cornered into a futile fight with no hope of a positive outcome.

The man angled his head toward her. "Are you stupid?" he grinned.

"Certainly not and I resent your implication. I'm simply stating that if we are not to be allowed access to Nishati Azibo then perhaps we can speak with some other high ranking representative. We've a deadline to meet."

"Oh, that's right—you're reporters." His sarcasm was palpable.

"Of course we're reporters," snapped Dana. "If we were anything but, we wouldn't have been so obvious about our approach, now would we?"

Another grin. "Ah, well, you did get to within the walls. I've seen worse strategy."

Before Dana could respond, the door opened. In walked Nishati Azibo. "Dana Huntington," she said. "I've been expecting you."

Chapter Thirty

Botma Africa

Nanji hated that Nishati Azibo treated him with kindness. She would laugh at things he'd said and sometimes stroke his hair before pulling him closely to her breast. She'd often offer him snacks or allow him small freedoms forbidden to other soldiers. He'd found the courage to ask her once, why she treated him with such tenderness but ignored her own son as if he was diseased.

She'd smiled, pulling him close and kissing him on the forehead. "Nanji, if one knows that she must soon lose something precious it is much better to remain distant. Then the loss is not so great, the soul is so less burdened. But, with you, I have no reason to believe that you will soon be forever gone and so there is no fear in keeping you close."

Nanji did not understand the statement. He'd come to know her son, Tahir. The boy was not sick or diseased. Why did she think that he would soon be gone? And why had she picked Nanji as some sort of replacement? This woman's men had forced him to murder his own parents. Couldn't she see that he despised her with every thread of his being? Couldn't she feel his skin squirm and crawl when she pulled him into a hug, could she not feel his stomach turn when she offered the occasional kiss? She was the devil. The very devil in flesh. He'd known it from the moment Rafiki had blown his own head into a thousand pieces at her whispered instruction. How could anyone but the devil have such control over another person?

And why had she then selected Nanji to become part of her personal guard? Why had she taken him away from his post and brought him with her? She said that he was brave because he had told her the truth concerning his fear of her. But he was not brave. He was simply too stupid to keep his mouth shut when it was better off shut.

He thought that maybe she kept him near so that he could be a some-times companion to Tahir. Due to their transitory lifestyle, the boy had no ongoing friends and she often posted Nanji as Tahir's guard, knowing that they were close in age, perhaps hoping that they would bond and that Tahir would be less lonely. Though, Nanji somehow felt many more years older than their true age gap. Tahir was prone to bouts of moodiness and tears. He often seemed weak and childish while Nanji had been forced by life circumstance to become hard and uncaring. Still, as much as Nanji could think of nothing good or pure ever coming from Azibo, he had found a certain fondness for Tahir. It wasn't his fault that his mother was the devil. In many ways he seemed to hate her as much as did Nanji.

Nanji feared that he may have contributed to Tahir's current troubles, that he may be at fault for Azibo's heightened contempt of her own son. Nanji had been on guard duty the night Tahir had decided to slip out, free the prisoner, and attempt escape. Tahir had not confided in Nanji concern-ing his plans, but had only whispered, "Don't tell anyone," when he'd exited his room that night.

Nanji hadn't told anyone. After Tahir's capture, Nanji had planned on lying, he'd planned to claim he'd gone to the bathroom and had not noticed that Tahir was gone after his return. But no one had questioned him. Nishati Azibo had seen him the next day, their eyes had met, he was certain she'd somehow seen the truth within his coward's soul and knew that if she asked him how the boy had been able to flee that he would be too fearful to lie.

Perhaps she had sensed this. Perhaps she had known that to confront Nanji on this would mean that she would learn a truth which would then prevent her from keeping him near. Because Nishati Azibo could never have someone near to her that was untrustworthy. And for whatever reason, the devil enjoyed his presence.

And so Nanji had retained his post.

And thus Nanji was in a position where one day he might slay the devil responsible for his parent's deaths.

And still Nanji was too cowardly to act on this opportunity.

Chapter Thirty-One

Botma Africa

It felt to Hunt as if the right side of his body from wrist to neck was frozen. He couldn't see the scorpion under his skin because he was tied to the rock slab, his arms and legs bound, his head resting on cold hard stone. And, no, he couldn't specifically feel it making its way toward his brain; he couldn't feel the crawling steps or feel the bite of the serpent's-head tail. But, he could feel the chill.

No. Not just a chill, but a burning cold.

True, the words burning and cold don't normally go together except as opposites, but this was exactly what he sensed. It felt as if ice was burning through his veins. Creeping closer, closer to its goal.

And what then?

What happened when the thing reached his brain?

Would it be as Nishati Azibo claimed? Would some insane scorpion spirit seize his soul, possess his body? Would Hunt's consciousness be buried beneath?

Or worse.

Would he fail to exist altogether?

Would his body live on without Hunt's own consciousness to guide it?

The rational aspects of his mind sought to reject these thoughts outright. He didn't believe in this nonsense. But, people's belief that men could never fly didn't prevent the first airplanes from being built. And rational or not, Hunt had to come to grips with the idea that something beyond the scope of his learning and belief was happening. And at least for the moment, there was nothing he could do about it.

The words of the political prisoner—the slave—came back to him. The man had instructed him to amputate the arm above the scorpion, that this was the only means of preventing the possession. Well, by all indication, it was now above the arm. It was on his neck. Too late for drastic measures now. Unless Hunt could find some way to halt its progress, he likely had only hours of sanity left to him.

Already he could feel the things tendrils tickling at the perimeter of his mind, tossing random thoughts and images his way, whispering in some long forgotten tongue. They were shadowy thoughts, misshapen and incomplete. Images of strange forms dancing through the darkness, dripping venom and devouring people young and old. He could nearly hear the screams of sacrificial children as flames licked at their limbs before reaching up to consume them in entirety. Hunt could feel the revolting glee the scorpion took in these heinous thoughts, he could sense the near erotic surge of passion for destruction and death.

This was the thing Nishati Azibo hoped to use to bolster her homeland. This beast. This demon thing.

Hunt wondered if the woman had ever truly tasted of the thoughts now creeping through his skull or if the scorpion had seduced her with lies and promises, painting for her a scene more placid and inviting. If she did know, if she had seen this reality, how could she be so deluded as to think she could harness this thing for anything but its own dark desires? Was she truly blind to the truth of it? Hunt had no answer. The only thing he did know was terror like he'd never known before.

Terror, and a certainty that this was the end, that whatever happened next, he would no longer be present in his own mind to participate in his life. Hunt would perish as a man with these foul imagines plodding about his brain.

Chapter Thirty-Two

Botma Africa

Nishati Azibo smiled. It seemed, to Dana, an atypical smile. There was the overbite, of course, which added a dash of eccentricity, but there was something more disturbing as well. Something in the wide-set deep brown eyes, perhaps the near iridescent flecks of green. Yet, something even more haunting than this. The eyes were nearly hypnotic. Though, wide and beautiful, they appeared precise and targeted at Dana in a narrow focus. And that grin, that ruthless grin had grown out of those mesmerizing eyes, each a part of the other, one entity in two components.

"It was sweet of you to come to your husband's rescue," she said. Still the gaze never wavered, her expression remained the same. "You are too late, of course."

Dana allowed a quick gasp to escape before regaining composure. Was Azibo saying that Hunt was already dead? Was that the implication?

Azibo's smile widened, a throaty chuckle spilled over her lips. "Oh, he's still alive. But, he'll never again be the man you remember." Here she stepped closer, and as she did, the massive guard standing just behind and to her right, tensed as if in anticipation of something dreadful. Now nearly upon her, Azibo's stare burrowed deeper into Dana's being. It seemed Dana had no means to avert the gaze. "Ah, but do I see ambiguity? Dana, you are not sure of your relationship. Something is between you and Huntington, some savage distance, some great gulf you've yet to navigate. Is it this man, this Thorpe who obviously worships you? Is the other man the cause or is he simply a diversion?"

"I don't know what you're talking about." The words were thick in Dana's mouth. It was an effort even to speak. Why? She'd been in tight situations before. She was not easily frightened or intimidated. Why was her mind suddenly so muddled?

"No," grinned Azibo. "Not Thorpe. Not entirely, at least. He's simply another distraction, am I right?"

Dana opened her mouth to speak but found no words.

"Oh, there's all manner of turmoil within you, isn't there?" Azibo was now no more than an inch before Dana, their eyes locked, neither blinking, neither even aware of the two men in the room. "Yes. So much turmoil. You fear losing him and yet you're not sure that you will ever truly desire him." A pause. "Ah, and there is a rival for his affections as well, a former lover perhaps. Tell me, Dana, if not for this other, would you even consider returning to your mate, or would you simply allow him to dangle in listless anticipation until all hope dissipated like a summer breeze?"

Dana could feel Azibo's breath upon her. And the woman's eyes, so wide, so deep, they seemed nearly eternal at this close proximity. How did the woman know any of this? How could she discern Dana's inner turmoil? It seemed she sifted through the tangled web of Dana's fears and desires, giving voice to thoughts Dana had only half conceived and scarcely identified.

***

Thorpe wasn't sure exactly what he was witnessing. Nishati Azibo had moved to within inches of Dana, whispering in deep throaty tones as her shoulders and hips undulated in a sensuous serpentine rhythm. Dana appeared spellbound, mesmerized. Her speech was slow and dreamy as if she was lost in some nightmarish reality and only tenuously present in this room.

Dana had not been drugged, Thorpe was fairly certain of this. They'd been in each other's presence throughout the encounter. He'd witnessed no injection; Dana had been given no pills or serums. It was possible, he supposed, that Azibo had breathed some sort of hallucinogenic on her when she moved to within an intimate distance, but this theory made little sense. Azibo would likely be affected by the drug as well if she's held it in her mouth.

"This is all very interesting," said Thorpe in an effort to break the strange hold the woman seemed to have over Dana. "But, I suppose the question at hand is where is Marc Huntington and what would persuade you to release him into our care?" He then offered his most charming grin. "I'm sure reasonable people can come to some suitable agreement, hmm?"

Azibo ignored him.

"Yes, well, I see you're preoccupied, but don't you have a country to defile, some dissidents to stifle? Certainly, there is some better use of your time." Thorpe was forever aware of the looming guard, but the massive man gave Thorpe no more notice than did Azibo.

Nishati Azibo moved closer yet, her forehead now resting against Dana's. "Such anguish in your soul," she whispered in a throaty hush. "Dana, why do you even go on living when your spirit is racked with pain?" Here, she added several syllables that seemed nonsensical to Thorpe. He could identify no language group; the sounds didn't have the cadence of speech, but seemed something more sinister. Not speech exactly, but communication nonetheless.

Whatever Azibo had done, it seemed she had Dana entirely spellbound. Something was wrong with the woman he loved. Something very wrong. Her baring, her very being had changed. She appeared as lifeless as a department store mannequin.

"Dana!" hollered Thorpe. "Ignore her. She's doing something to you. Dana, break her gaze!"

Thorpe expected the guard to silence him, but still the man paid him no mind.

Nor did Dana seem to hear him, though he was no more than six feet distant. Her eyes had become wide, her jaw slack, it seemed the color had fled her face. Azibo took one step back, still not breaking eye contact for even a hint of an instant. Again, she whispered those strangely melodic syllables.

Dana's arms rose slowly, bending at the elbows. Her hands opened, fingers spread like spider legs before closing about her own neck. She began to squeeze.

Chapter Thirty-Three

Botma Africa

Hunt knew that scorpions had no tentacles. But this fact didn't stop this particular specimen from using them to creep methodically through his brain. It seemed a thousand different feelers slithered about his consciousness, inspecting every nook and cranny, delving into every shadow and crevasse, removing little pieces of Hunt and depositing in return dark thoughts and darker images, sick twisted things that could make even a devil squirm and retch.

He wasn't sure how much longer he could hold onto any sense of self. Already, it seemed another presence held the keys to his most intimate thoughts. His senses had all but evaporated: his vision now only spiraling wisps of light and color, his ears perceived only chattering demons, taste ceased to be, as did most physical sensations. But his olfactory sense was intact. And this to his dismay. For he was aware of a deep, dreadful odor of decay and defecation and feared it might originate in his own body.

And for what must have been the dozenth time in as many minutes he wondered if perhaps he was already dead, that the decay he sensed was his own flesh breaking apart, cracking, maybe even melting away from his bones into pools of festering muck. That perhaps, already worms slithered through his nostrils and eye sockets, that there was nothing recognizable as Hunt to be found or seen. He wondered if his body existed at all in any tangible state or if perhaps he'd entered some previously unknown hellish realm.

He saw things now.

Not with his eyes.

Or, at least, not with physical eyes.

And the things he saw—hideous things. Creeping, drooling, malevolent things. They wanted him, these nightmares. They wanted all that he was, all that he ever had been. They wanted his very sense of self, his knowledge that he existed as a distinct individual. They sought to dismember his soul as one carves a Thanksgiving turkey, piece by fleshy piece, slicing, separating, setting aside little delicacies to then devour. Though, sanity would dictate that the sensation could only originate in his head, still he could feel these foul things rending his flesh, biting deep into his being, pulling, ripping, shredding, consuming in a lusty frenzy.

And the shadow things, they grew. Oh, did they grow. And as they did, they became more grotesque. Where once there had been four limbs, now there were six. Two eyes became a dozen. Eight tails. Sixteen darting drooling tongues. Some even had two and three heads.

And every one of them in some twisted fashion resembled Hunt.

It dawned on him that as these things ate away at him, that they absorbed his characteristics, his DNA, his essence, whatever word a philosopher or theologian would ascribe to the consciousness that had once been Hunt, these beasts now owned the broken and shredded pieces.

Pain.

More pain.

Searing.

Blinding eruptions of sensation.

What sanity Hunt held in his feeble grasp scattered into the ether.

And though at some level, there was still some sense of thought and existence, nothing that could be called Hunt remained.

Chapter Thirty-Four

Botma Africa

It seemed to Jonathan Thorpe that he was the only person not mesmerized. Dana and Nishati Azibo were locked in their death gaze, Dana squeezing her own throat with amazing vigor, her fingers digging into flesh, droplets of blood oozing between fingers. Even the massive guard, standing before the door, seemed lulled into inactivity. Whether by the bizarre scene before him or by some peripheral effect of Azibo's seductive trance, Thorpe couldn't say. And as he couldn't explain how the guard was affected, neither could he explain why he was not. There was a strange vibration traveling up and down his form, centered at his right thigh. This had commenced about the same time Azibo had entranced Dana. He didn't know what the connection might be—if indeed there was a connection—but whatever the cause, Thorpe was still free in mind and body.

He had been led to understand that persons could never successfully strangle themselves to death because at the point of lost consciousness, their grip would release. But in this instance it was apparent that whatever spell this mad sorceress had cast on Dana had overridden this contingency. To all appearances she was already unconscious. In truth, he was fairly certain that though she still stood, she had stopped breathing. Her body was on some strange deadly autopilot and Azibo was at the helm.

Thorpe moved quickly, screaming Dana's name as he sent a heal jabbing upward into the guard's unprotected groin. This Goliath must be subdued or any other action was futile. The man curled in upon himself with an agonized howl as Thorpe charged into Azibo knocking her against the nearest wall as would a hockey player checking an opponent. The woman's eyes went wide in surprise as she stumbled to the floor.

Pulling Dana's hands free of her neck with a fierce yank, Thorpe yelled at full volume. "Dana! Dana dear, wake up!"

Already, Azibo was scrambling to her feet. "I don't know how you were unaffected, but you…"

"Not interested!" hollered Thorpe as he smacked her across the face, again sending her against the wall. One thing was certain; he did not intend to make eye contact with the woman.

He didn't know what had happened here. There was no time to sort out his belief in and/or alternate explanations to what he'd just witnessed. He had only seconds to get Dana free of this room before Azibo's forces stampeded through the door.

Even as Azibo shouted and cursed, regaining her footing and taking chase, Thorpe pulled Dana by one arm, leading her around the moaning giant and toward the exit. Not desiring to risk the man regaining mobility, he gave the guard a quick kick to the chin causing the giant to bellow as he tumbled sideways still cradling his crotch.

Immediately upon exiting the room, Thorpe slammed the door, then leaning against it with his full weight as Azibo flung her slender form against the barrier.

"Dana," he said. "Dana, snap out of it, dear. I'd appreciate an extra set of hands if you don't mind."

She was coming back into herself. He could see this. From the moment eye contact had been lost with Azibo, she'd begun to come around. First with several loud gasps and then in her willingness to stumble along behind Thorpe as they'd fled the room.

"Dana, are you uninjured? Are you thinking clearly?"

Azibo was pounding on the door, creating quite an uproar. Soon her pet giant would regain his footing. They would need to be well clear of this space by then.

"Dana!"

A shake of the head, a strangled cough. "Yes. Jonathan. I hear you." Another cough.

"To my left, Dana, do you see it? The statue?"

It was a large marble piece, vaguely resembling an upright lizard in the way a Picasso might resemble an actual human face. It looked to be quite heavy and was located just beyond his reach.

"The lizard?" croaked Dana, still gasping air in long raspy gulps.

"Yes. We need to bar the door."

Dana nodded. She was regaining her capacities. Her eyes were clear and focused, she'd recovered her bearing.

Moving to the sculpture, Dana leaned into it, attempting to topple the thing across the doorway. "It's too heavy," she gasped as she pressed against it. "The bloody thing must weigh three hundred pounds."

"Just scoot it a bit. That's all. Just enough so that I can reach it."

Azibo was repeatedly running at the door, attempting to shoulder it open. Even though Thorpe outweighed her by a hundred pounds or so, still it was an effort to maintain his position. She was screaming at the guard. Certainly, he would soon be on his feet and adding his massive weight to the effort. Thorpe waited for Azibo to step away again, preparing for another charge, and leaned to his left, grabbing the thing by its gapping jaw. As Dana pushed, he pulled it toward himself, jumping out of the way, just as the piece crashed to the floor and thus blocking the door. Several pieces of the thing broke away skittering across the stone surface in multiple directions, but the core of the sculpture was intact. It wouldn't lock Azibo away indefinitely, but it would allow them a window of opportunity for escape.

Chapter Thirty-Five

Botma Africa

Dana was still a bit fuzzy and so not entirely sure what had just transpired. She'd been in the small holding room with Jonathan and their gorilla-like escort, Nishati Azibo had entered the room, and then...

Nothing.

It was almost as if some strange vapor had sifted through the air, wrapping itself about her, entering her through eyes and nostrils, ears and mouth, and then tickling her brain, teasing, exploring. It hadn't been an unpleasant experience in the least. But, she'd somehow become lost in it as if the only thing that mattered in the world was this strange dancing mist flitting about in her head.

She vaguely remembered Jonathan shouting at her, pulling her through the room and into the adjoining corridor, causing the mist to become angry and then to dissipate with a primal scream. It seemed her first competent thought had been the realization that Jonathan had trapped Azibo and the guard behind the door and that he wouldn't be able to hold them at bay much longer without her assistance.

"Dana dear, do you still have contact with Corina? Does she have any input into the layout of the facility?"

They were racing down a long torch-lit corridor, their footfall echoing against the stone walls, their shadows stretching into the darkness beyond. They'd yet to encounter resistance, but certainly this would soon change. Azibo would be free and immediately deploy her troops with orders to kill on sight. Dana blinked several times. She was still not entirely cognizant. "Right. Corky. I'm sorry. I hadn't thought of that."

"I'm here," came a soft voice in Dana's right ear. The signal was weak, the voice a bit garbled but understandable. "What happened back there?"

"No time for an explanation, Corky. We're in a bit of a bind. Can you pinpoint our location?"

There was a slight pause, the sound of fingers tapping on a keyboard. "Yes. Your signal is weak, but you're still transmitting."

Dana nodded to Jonathan, who could not hear the conversation.

"Good, good. Ask her about the floor plan. Has the device given her an adequate layout of the facility?"

Dana relayed the question.

"Partial," said Corky. "You're not located near the camera and so I have a much more complete layout on the east side of the building where it's located than on the west, but the program is imputing your tracking signal as we speak and extrapolating projections from the new data."

"So, we're currently running blind." Dana was exasperated. The building was quite large, it was ancient, corridors would weave and turn; nothing seemed at right angles or to follow any logical floor plan. She glanced through a narrow doorway, arched, with many of the surrounding stones loose or cracked. There was another, nearly identical opening, just twenty feet beyond, the space between the two being nothing more than a small alcove, the stone floor crushed to near gravel in some spots.

"Blind? Not entirely. Your program is using data collected in the east wing to make assumptions concerning the west."

"Yes, I understand that. I did right the program after all. But, it's not accurate. At this point it's all a bit of guesswork. If the two wings don't have similar floor plans, you could lead us directly back to Azibo."

Jonathan was eyeing her, listening to her side of the conversation. "Dana, well, I understand you may not have an ironclad blueprint. Even under ideal circumstances, the program is unlikely to provide that. But the computerized model might still give us a better guess than we would have running blindly through these corridors. Can she give us any advice at all?"

They rounded a corner and the lighting was dimmer yet. The nearest torch was mounted some hundred feet forward and seemed no more than a dim flickering light. The floor was uneven and angling further down. Many of the footstones were loose or missing. They would need to be careful not to trip as they raced through the near-black space. There were occasional pillars of yellow and red stone, narrow toward the squared base but fanning out toward the high ceiling as would water shooting up from a fountain. Strange swirling carvings of scorpions and serpents were etched into these and Dana was forced to suppress a shudder as she passed near to these as it seemed the eyes of these stone engravings followed her as she passed by.

"Corky, we're lost and literally in the dark. There's no electric lighting to be found in these bleeding corridors. We need a bit of targeted speculation in order to find the most logical place they might keep Hunt and then the quickest way out from there."

"Okay. Understood. The further you go the better I can guide you. If you come across any offshoots to that corridor, move down them just a little bit so that the program can get a reading. For the time being, you are still moving away from the room where I'm guessing you were locked up. Some of the passages would have taken you back in that direction but you've been lucky so far."

The next quarter hour was spent traipsing through the darkness. Twice, they heard footsteps in the distance, but on both occasions the footfall moved off in another direction. Many of the corridors were entirely devoid of light, but there was always a torch mounted high on the wall around the next turn. They considered carrying one of the torches, but these were just above their reach. As well, it seemed better that they remain as invisible as possible. No need to carry a beacon that would direct troops right to them.

Each stumbled several times. The floor was of varied stones and in no way level. As well, they were trying to keep an aggressive pace and this led to potential stumbles. There were sounds. Echoing sounds. Skittering sounds. It almost seemed the moldy stone walls were alive. Perhaps it was rats that they heard, or maybe some other rodent or even insects. But whatever the source, it had the effect of keeping them on the move. Neither wanted to pause long enough to be located by either human or creature of the night. Twice they found windows. These were narrow arches, the sills being tunnel-like at five to six feet deep. On both occasions, Dana crawled through the sill to discover that the windows opened onto a small courtyard, apparently situated in the center of the place and thus of no use in terms of escape.

Throughout it all, the transmitter in Dana's earring continued to send its signal and eventually Corky announced the first bit of good news. "I've got a fairly complete blueprint now. If this is correct, you're at the northeast corner of the facility. There appears to be a basement area to your left and down a flight of stairs."

Chapter Thirty-Six

Botma Africa

The odor was familiar. The being that had once been Marc Huntington couldn't identify it specifically, but he knew it from somewhere in his past.

He was free now. He'd been released. The mistress had instructed him to follow his nose, to obey his senses. He was on a hunt and though he had no single mind, no master intellect, all of the numerous presences within chattered and gabbed in delight at the prospect of a hunt and even more so at the prospect of a kill. To slay was the ultimate freedom. To do so in service to the mistress was the definitive joy.

The thing that had been Marc Huntington smiled. The scent grew stronger with every step. The kill was upon him.

Chapter Thirty-Seven

Botma Africa

The prisoners were emaciated, all of them. Their skin clung to their skeletons like cellophane wrapped about a chicken bone. Their eyes were wide and sunken, their hair thin and uneven. The stench of the overcrowded cell was overwhelming and Dana immediately set about the business of lock picking as Jonathan poked about the greater space looking for signs of Hunt.

Through hurried questions and sometimes rambling responses, she soon established that the prisoners had seen Hunt. It had been a few days prior, and he had been in the company of Azibo's child. Dana deduced that this had likely been during the same period that he'd sent the recorded video of the boy. Obviously, he'd been recaptured since then.

One prisoner, an elderly man with rich brown eyes and broad expressive mouth approached Dana as she studied the lock. He was a bit of a presence, displaying a regal bearing and clear mind that transcended his current circumstance. She was nearly certain she she'd seen him somewhere before. "Miss," he said in a rich warm tone. "I take it this man is important to you, may I assume he's a husband or lover?"

"Husband," said Dana as she worked on the lock. "Well… Yes, husband. A bit complicated now but, yes."

The man nodded slowly. "May I assume also that you've had no contact with him in recent days?"

"No contact. This is a rescue mission."

The man contemplated her with those rich brown eyes. "Miss, you don't know me, and you'll likely dismiss me as some crackpot from a third world country, but there's something you'll need to know before locating him."

Dana met his gaze as her stomach dropped. Was he about to tell her that Hunt was dead, or perhaps severely injured? Was she about to learn that they'd spent the last several months of his life apart and that there would now be no chance of reconciliation? "Go on," she said, though her voice was tiny and tight.

"Your husband has been infected, not with some terrible disease, but with something much more terrifying, a demonic spirit." Dana began to speak, but the man held up a hand to stop her. "No, no, no. Allow me to finish. I understand this is hard to accept, and you can believe me when I say I struggle with the concept myself. I'm a man of reason, a man of the twenty-first century; I'm not prone to flights of fancy. But, I've seen things. Nishati Azibo claims to be a sorceress, and, like you, I initially thought it was a load of bunk. I'm telling you it's not. There are some things in this world better left undisturbed and that maniac has stirred the kettle."

"Sir, I'm sure you believe what you're saying, but..."

"I don't just believe it, Miss. I know it. I've seen it." He paused, his gaze both sorrowful and intense. "I see that you'll resist me in this. I understand. That's only natural. But, be cautious. When next you see him, your husband will not be the man you know." He held her gaze for a long moment and then nodded. "Now, I suppose you'd best tend to that lock."

Dana nodded, rejecting the comments as superstitious nonsense and tended to the locked gate, now ignoring the man in awkward silence. Despite her feigned indifference, the news was disturbing. She'd thought of otherworldly concepts more in the past several weeks than she had in years. As a rule she was a pragmatist and prided herself on living by rationale and logic, but as she'd tracked William Pohl with all of his occultic rituals and mystic chants she was forced to consider the validity of such things. She dismissed them outright, of course, or at least until she'd been given the amber-encased locust. Supposedly an actual locust from a biblical plague. The bearer of this strange gift had been instructed to give it to a woman who came from afar. Dana had not realized it at the time, but this had caused her pause. The story was too fantastic to be true, and yet, too fantastic not to be true. Without even realizing it, she'd come to believe in the thing as some sort of magic token that would protect her in times of crisis.

Well, that had turned out to be a load of bollocks.

And so now, despite the fact that she'd recently been primed in spiritual thinking, she did her best to maintain her rational senses.

Except, she could not explain what had just happened to her in Nishati Azibo's presence. Some sort of hypnotism, she suspected. Nothing supernatural, just a parlor trick really. Hypnotism was used in actual science. Obviously the supernatural claims were nothing but a charade meant to frighten the small minded. Dana was not so easily fooled.

So, why then did her stomach creep and twist at this man's words concerning Hunt? Why then did she consider, even in a passing thought, that the claim might be true? The locust had been a hoax, and it had been given to her by a well-meaning individual, what stock could she put in the words of this stranger of whom she knew nothing?

Dana felt a minor resistance within the gate's locking mechanism, adjusted her pick slightly, and twisted. The ancient lock released with a clank and a groan. The prisoners were free.

Dana opened the gate, stepping back, allowing the prisoners to file into the open area. The elderly man approached her yet again, clasping her hands in both of his. "Be careful, Miss. I understand your disbelief, but please, proceed with caution."

Dana nodded as they shared a squeeze of the hands. He turned away, now addressing the other freed prisoners. Obviously, they looked to him in some leadership capacity. Again, Dana considered that she'd seen the man before, but still failed to place him.

It was at this moment that Hunt entered the room.

He was wearing an ill-fitting military uniform. His feet were bare. He was thin, nearly as emaciated in appearance as the prisoners that had just exited the cell. He'd been tortured. His face was bruised and swollen; there were gashes and streams of dried blood on his arms. His eyes were wide, staring. The word vacant came to mind. It seemed at once he saw, but saw nothing at all. There was what appeared to be a tattoo of a blue scorpion at the center of his forehead. Deep blue, nearly purple, it seemed to throb and pulse.

Dana's heart quickened at the sight of him. Though her internal alarms blared some indistinct warning, she started forward to meet him. "Hunt, my God, what have they done to you?"

Hunt grinned a twisted grin and released an inhuman screech unlike any Dana had ever heard.

Chapter Thirty-Eight

Botma Africa

Jonathan Thorpe was unsure of what exactly he was seeing. And as such, he was late in acting. Obviously, something was very wrong with Huntington. The man's appearance was more that of a creature from a low budget horror film than of a human being. His eyes were glazed-over, wide and vacant. Hunched forward, he moved with a peculiar gait, legs spread uncomfortably wide, knees bent severely, feet angled so that only the ball and toes met the uneven stone surface. The movement was simultaneously fluid and halting, very insect-like in manner. He offered a skeletal grin that nearly split his tortured features and emitted a piercing shriek the kind of which might possibly shatter crystal. But, despite all that had happened Thorpe couldn't find it in himself to believe the man would attack Dana. Huntington was his competition, true, but Thorpe had a grudging respect for the man. In truth, he wasn't a bad bloke.

And so Thorpe hesitated when he should have acted. Huntington moved toward Dana with a terrifying screech. Several of the just-freed prisoners recognized the danger before Thorpe understood Huntington's intent and rushed him as he moved toward Dana. But despite their numbers, they were weak from captivity, and, worse yet, terrified of the form they sought to intercept. Their movements were tempered by fear and uncertainty. They rushed, but then hesitated, slapped instead of grappled. They were like flies to the man, nothing more.

Huntington moved much more quickly than Thorpe would have believed possible, tossing Dana's terrified defenders aside with hardly an effort and, in at least two instances, breaking bones with his bare hands. How could this emaciated man possess such strength and speed?

Just as Huntington reached for Dana, one of the freed prisoners, the elderly gentleman with whom Dana had conversed, launched himself at the crazed man catching Huntington off guard and causing him to stumble. By the time Huntington had tossed the man aside and begun to rise, Dana had discerned the truth of the situation and met her husband's jaw with a fierce roundhouse kick.

"Hunt!" screamed Dana as she crouched in preparation for another strike. "Hunt, it's me! Think, Hunt! Think!" There were tears traversing her cheeks. Despite all that had happened she had feelings for the man. Love, actually. As much as it rankled him, Thorpe had to admit that it was love she felt. Such a scene as this would certainly torture her already emotionally fragile state.

The maniac emitted another piercing shriek as he, in one fluid motion, scrambled to his feet and charged Dana. Four of the prisoners, three men and a woman, rushed between them in an attempt to give Dana an oppor-tunity to flee. Hunt bit and clawed his way through them like a rabid animal, raking one face with his nails as he bit another man on the bicep, flaying his arms, and screeching that earsplitting howl. Dana struck him again, and again, and again, but he kept moving forward. It appeared as if at least one of the prisoners was severely injured, with a long jagged gash in her left forearm that bled profusely. Two of her companions pulled her toward the safety of the cell they'd just recently escaped.

Thorpe had intended to join the fray even as it began, but was struck with the same weird sensation he'd felt when Nishati Azibo mesmerized Dana, that peculiar tingle on his right thigh. But this time the sensation was much more intense, nearly debilitating, warm at first, but becoming all but searing within seconds.

Distracted from his purpose, Thorpe stopped, batting at his leg as if at invisible flames. Dana was holding her own, but even with the help of the prisoners, it was clear to Thorpe that it was a losing battle. Huntington was a frenzy of movement: slashing, jabbing, kicking, biting. But, Thorpe was incapacitated. His leg was on fire. Surely there were invisible flames, or possibly some sort of electrical charge, maybe something akin to a Taser.

He felt the first stutters of panic as his heart raced and his limbs began to jerk with heightened adrenaline.

What was happening? Within a span of seconds the pain had become unbearable.

He batted at his leg as he danced about in agony. It seemed there was no means to escape the phantom sensation. Dropping to the stone surface, he rolled one direction and then another in a frantic attempt to douse the unseen flames. But the pain continued to accelerate. Nothing he had done diminished it in the least.

And now he heard an almost deafening buzz, this also originating at his leg.

He batted his leg again, smacking at it with his palms, but felt no burning on his hands as he touched the fabric. If there were indeed flames, how could his leg burn but not his hands? Thorpe was just about to pull his pants off to inspect his leg when his hand struck something hard and uneven.

Jamming his hand into his right front pocket, he withdrew the amber-encased locust necklace.

Immediately, the sensations subsided.

Thorpe had carried this trinket with him since the day Dana had relinquished it. It had been nearly a robotic act. He'd never consciously decided to possess the thing, but had mechanically moved it from pocket to pocket each day as he dressed, never separating from it, always keeping it within reach. Only now did he realize any of this.

He held it before him and all became clear.

For, impossibly so, the locust was in motion, the centuries-old wings fluttering at an incredible rate within the amber cocoon. But not just within. For the wingspan was greater than the diameter of the stone and the wings reached beyond the boundaries as if there was no barrier at all. Thorpe could not feel the wings as such, not as flesh, but he saw them nonetheless. And though this object had burned him terribly while secreted away in his pocket, the only sensation now was that of an electric-like vibration and comforting warmth.

The opaque eyes moved; a leg twitched. The locust was watching him. But not just watching, communicating. Not in language, certainly not. But, Thorpe supposed, sensation. Yes, communication through sensation. Impossible, yet here it was.

Rising, Thorpe saw that though Dana was holding her own against Huntington, she was wearing down. Sweat now mingled with tears. Her blouse was torn, her bottom lip swollen. She kicked and jabbed, keeping the screeching maniac at bay, but only just. It seemed her legs quivered and her movements were becoming sloppy. As to the prisoners, most had fled. The few that remained were either injured or too terrified to be of much use.

Without another thought, Thorpe sprinted at Huntington, a war howl on his lips, diving on him just as he snatched Dana's arm. Dana was wrenched to the floor with the two men, Huntington hissing and howling, a nasty smelling orange bile dripping from his elongated lips.

Thorpe couldn't believe the man's strength. After weeks of torture and near starvation, Huntington couldn't weigh much more than one hundred pounds, but still he fought with the strength and vigor of a UFC champion fighter.

Thorpe punched him in the belly with every bit of strength he possessed, but Huntington seemed not to register the pain and immediately clawed Thorpe across the cheek. The man's nails had not been clipped recently and were long and sharp. Blood dripped onto Huntington from the fresh wound in Thorpe's face.

"Jonathan, don't hurt him!" ordered Dana as, jerking free of Huntington's grip, she pressed his arm to the floor in an attempt to subdue him.

Lying across Huntington's body, Thorpe responded. "There's no time to be gentle, dear. Just help me to hold him down."

With Dana holding Huntington's left arm against the floor, Thorpe pressed the right down while using his torso and legs to restrain the man's legs and trunk. With his right hand he brought the amber-encased locust forward.

"Jonathan, what are you doing?"

He couldn't answer just then. Every ounce of energy was spent in subduing the maniac. Huntington was snapping at Thorpe like a rabid dog, screeching and grunting, bucking and twisting. Some of the vocalizations seemed they might contain language, but if so, it was some dark tongue born in the recesses of hell.

"Jonathan!"

"Not now, Dana."

As the amber was brought closer to Huntington's face, he began shaking his head wildly, the screeching soared into earsplitting falsetto, the jaws snapped frantically.

"Jonathan, stop!"

Chapter Thirty-Nine

Botma Africa

What was Jonathan doing? Dana struggled to hold Hunt's arm in place amazed at his near-superhuman strength as he thrashed about howling like some mythical banshee. His eyes registered no recognition, his face was tortured, his mouth stretched to inhuman proportions. Everything about him was of some other being. There was no aspect that Dana would recognize as Hunt. And yet it was Hunt. Most certainly, it was Hunt. There was no mistaking the battle-scarred features and steel blue eyes. It was just that the mind behind those features could in no way belong to the man she knew and loved.

The words of the prisoner echoed about her head.

Possessed. Was it really possible? Dana had such difficulty believing, and yet...

Dana glared at Jonathan who was holding the amber amulet, attempting to hold it against Hunt's thrashing face. "Jonathan, what are you doing?"

"What I must. Please, Dana, help to steady his head." Jonathan's voice was strained, his words nearly barked. It was obvious he was struggling simply to maintain his position.

"Will it hurt him?"

"I don't know!" shouted Jonathan. "Please, Dana! I can't hold him much longer."

Before Dana could decide a course of action, the elderly prisoner slipped to beside her, clasping Hunt's flaying head. "Go ahead, son. Be quick about it."

"Will it hurt him?" screamed Dana for a second time.

No one answered her, but Jonathan brought the amulet to Hunt's forehead, pressing it against the pulsating scorpion-shaped image just above and between the eyes.

The scorpion actually tried to scamper away—to run! The thing Dana had supposed to be a mere tattoo ran! But Jonathan trapped it with the stone, bearing down with his full weight.

Hunt screamed and thrashed.

"Jonathan, stop! You're hurting him!"

But, he didn't stop and Hunt continued to scream as Dana had never heard a human being scream before.

"Jonathan!"

Dana reached out to pull Jonathan's hand away, but the prisoner grasped her wrist, disallowing the movement. His grip was firm, his intent clear. "Miss, please."

Hunt's face began to ripple like water disturbed by a tremor. It seemed his flesh was nearly liquid as rivulets moved about in each direction, it almost seemed his skin boiled, bubbling, drifting, seeking an escape. His back arched, his mouth opened in a cavernous yowl, and tiny scorpions scampered out of every orifice on his head: nostrils, eyes, ears, mouth, hundreds, maybe thousands of deep blue scorpions fleeing Hunt's form, pouring out like a waterfall after a downpour.

Dana fell back with a screech, batting the foul-smelling things from her hands and clothing. The sound was like that of ten thousand dominos tumbling one upon the other as the things scampered in all directions. Somehow, still, Jonathan pressed the amber against Hunt's forehead, never releasing it for even an instant.

Chapter Forty

Botma Africa

Scorpions crawled up Thorpe's arms, into his clothing, down his legs, but he couldn't release the amulet or lessen the pressure on Huntington's forehead for fear that whatever he'd accomplished would be undone. Dana and the elderly prisoner both fell aside, batting at the things, shaking them away. Dana rolled about the ground and then scrambled to her feet where she then began to stomp on the creatures, accentuating each jab with a scream or a curse. The prisoner was no less fervent, though tended to the task in solemn silence.

To Thorpe's surprise and horror, the scorpions were actual physical creatures, not some phantom fiends or immaterial images. How had they come from Huntington? How had they been within the man? How could he have remained alive with these hideous creatures inhabiting his body?

Thorpe wasn't sure about Dana or the prisoner, but he was fairly certain that he had not been stung and wondered if the amber amulet somehow sheltered him. The thing had done nothing to protect Dana during her captivity in Louisiana, but had come to life here. He wondered if that had somehow been the intent all along. Had this anonymous Mexican witch woman passed the mystical talisman to the town sheriff with instructions to give it to a woman from afar so that he would then hand it to Dana who would in turn relinquish it to Thorpe? Had all of this occurred for his use in this specific instance? The chain of events was unlikely, even impossible, and yet seemed to be the absolute truth of the thing.

Thorpe came to the slow realization that Huntington was no longer thrashing about. Nor was he screeching. The scorpions had fled. True, there were still some visible within the room, but even these were finding tiny cracks in the masonry to slip within and then scurry away in the darkness.

He could no longer feel them moving about his limbs or within his clothing. It seemed the storm had passed.

The amulet was no longer warm to the touch. It did not vibrate. There seemed nothing beyond the ordinary about it. Cautiously lifting it off of Huntington's forehead, he saw that the locust within was still. There was no sign of movement or life. The eyes were again vacant and dark, the wings folded neatly against the insect's body. Thorpe stared down at Huntington wondering if he was yet alive. The image of the scorpion on his forehead was still there, but faint, very faint, nothing more than the dirty gray hint of a shadow. One could look at him and think it merely a smudge of dirt.

Thorpe slipped the amber amulet into his pocket still staring down at the silent form, but unwilling to move away for fear that the maniac within might somehow still exist.

"Jonathan, is he breathing?"

It was Dana. She'd knelt beside him.

"I don't know, dear. I haven't had an opportunity to examine him. But, he seems awfully still."

"Jonathan, tell me he's alive."

Chapter Forty-One

Botma Africa

Swirls of red and black undulated before his eyes. But, the voices were gone.

They had been voices, hadn't they? Maybe not physical voices exactly. It hadn't been actual conversation. Anything resembling language had been bizarre and incomprehensible. But still, he supposed they had been voices. At the very least they had been presences.

It took Hunt several moments to come to the realization that he existed. This may seem a strange thought, but he was certain that he'd been torn apart, that his soul had been separated and then devoured, that he had ceased to be. Not only had he died, but he'd been disassembled, divided, split into so many shreds as to almost never have existed.

This was true in its entirely. And yet he did exist. He was here, now, thinking, breathing, living. He was a cognizant being. Whatever had come before had been undone.

He blinked.

He blinked again.

Yes. He did inhabit the physical world. He had eyes. He could see. And taste. There was the rancid taste of bile on his tongue and a fetid smell in his nostrils. On his belly, a pressure, a weight.

Another blink.

A face stared down on him.

"Thorpe?"

How was it that Thorpe was here?

And then it was as if a second wave of consciousness surged over him. Whatever murk and mire inhabited his brain was washed away. His head was suddenly and completely clear. He knew where he was, who he was, what had transpired. It seemed insane, but it was true. He was fully in his right mind for perhaps the first time in well over a year. Whatever drugs had traversed his veins had been purged; whatever strange spirits had taken up residence had fled. And somehow, the torn remnants of his being had been reassembled.

"Marc, are you alright?"

It was Dana. She was stroking his head, fear and concern in her voice. Her touch felt both wonderful and entirely alien.

"Get off of me, Thorpe. And go on a diet. It feels like you weigh three hundred pounds." He didn't, of course. He was as fit and trim as ever. The man had likely never worn a pair of pants with more than a size thirty waste.

Thorpe shuffled to Hunt's left and then rose. "Yes, well, you're welcome. It isn't as if I just saved your life or anything."

Hunt glared up at him. "Sorry to scuff your ego. It's been a rough day. What are you two doing here, anyway? And more specifically, what are you two doing here together?" He waved his hand dismissively before either could think to respond. "Never mind. It doesn't matter. Help me up, Thorpe. My mind is clear, but physically I feel like barbequed road kill on a skewer."

"Well, that's a cheery little simile." Thorpe bent at the knees, offering Hunt a hand and then hoisting him to a standing position.

"Marc, are you sure you're up to standing? You've been through a terrible strain."

Dana moved toward Hunt arms spread to embrace him.

"Nope. Not up to it in the least." He turned away from Dana, escaping the hug as he addressed the elderly prisoner. "Hello, President Azibo."

The man nodded. "It seems, young man, you've come back from the dead."

"Wait. Excuse me," said Thorp. "President Azibo?"

Hunt nodded. "Nishati's father." Hunt wasn't sure how he now remembered this. He'd been close to grasping it when he'd first met the man;

he'd seen pictures of the former president in the Azibo file. He'd been younger, true, but the same man still. And yet like so many memory-related issues, the recall had been illusive. How was it now so fresh, so certain in his mind? It was the renewed clarity of thought, he supposed. Whatever the Egyptian amulet had done to his mind had freed his memories, had made all clear.

The Egyptian amulet.

The locust, it had originated in the biblical plague.

This was knowledge he'd never possessed, something he couldn't have known. It was impossible for him to have identified the origin of that golden blob Thorpe had pressed against his head. He had no basis for that knowledge, no means to have gained even a hint.

"Badrani Azibo? The world believes you to be dead," said Dana to the former president.

"That's right, young lady," said Badrani Azibo. "Nishati believed me to be weak and ineffective and so drove me from power. But when the time came, she could not kill her own father and so hid me away."

"Though apparently, she had no issue with forcing you into slavery," said Dana. "Quite the daughter."

Badrani leveled his gaze at Dana. "That woman ceased to be my daughter the day she slew my grandchild."

Hunt shook his head. Images cascaded through his mind. Piece upon piece fell into place. Grandchild. "Tahir," he said.

"What?" asked Dana.

"Tahir. He's in danger. Azibo knows I'm not under her control any more. She's going to sacrifice the boy."

"How do you know that?" asked Dana.

"He just does," said Badrani. "Trust his instinct."

"Excuse me," said Thorpe. "But, we came here to rescue you. This, well, diversion, it might send the whole thing astray."

Hunt stared at him. "You rescued me. Thank you. Go home now if you want. But, I came here to rescue the kid and I'm not leaving."

With that, he raced from the room and into the darkened corridor.

Chapter Forty-Two

Botma Africa

They followed Hunt through the winding corridors. It seemed he knew exactly where to go and Dana had trouble keeping his pace on the uneven stone floor. He'd said barely a word to anyone, had hardly even glanced at Dana. She wasn't sure if this was out of anger at her, out of concern for the boy, or if there was some other cause. He was himself again. Dana was certain of this. His movements, his speech patterns, even the tiny twist at the lips, it was all the man she had known for years. But, there was something different as well. A singularity of purpose, a drive, and a bitter calm.

Dana had attempted to contact Corky Meeks but heard only faint sounds and garbled echoes in response. It was Corky's voice in her ear. Dana could tell that much. But there was no communication, at least none that headed in Dana's direction.

The room they entered was large but not massive, round in shape, with walls of rich rust and tan stones, jagged and of varying size and shapes. These were mostly draped in flowing burgundy wall hangings that wafted as if in a gentle breeze. Two stories high, the ceiling bore tentacle-like rafters that were more or less S-shaped. Light filtered down from arched openings far above. Two side-by-side fireplaces, each nearly ten feet in height and six feet in width, blazed at the far end of the room. The convergence of light from above and from the dancing flames conspired to create shifting shadows upon the walls which appeared unsettlingly like thousands of insects scurrying in and out of the gaps between stones. Golden images of serpents circumvented the space just inches below the lofty ceiling. There were several stone statues, all of Azibo's scorpion god, Anascoreth. Each of these made Dana shudder as they brought to mind the hundreds of scorpions which had flooded from her husband's form.

At the center of the room was a crude wooden altar, bloodstained and notched in numerous places as if by hatchets and knives. Upon it lay a young boy of perhaps seven. He was bound to the structure with crimson fabric and cried uncontrollably as he sought freedom from the unyielding restraints. His mother, Nishati Azibo, stood before the altar, a long curved dagger in hand. She wore a flowing silk robe of rich purple and gold that trailed behind her like a bridal train. The woman appeared solemn, nearly that she might come to tears, her lips downturned, her eyes narrow and moist and it surprised Dana to realize that the woman was saddened by what she planned to do.

Flanking the altar on either side were lions, actual living lions, full-manes, rippling musculature beneath sleek sable coats, just sitting there like centennials awaiting an order. Dana had to force herself to remain calm. The beasts easily weighed seven hundred pounds each and certainly could be upon her in three easy bounds. But, they seemed docile for the time being, and Dana determined to follow Hunt's lead on this. Besides, sudden movement would likely draw the predator's attention, while currently they seemed nearly asleep.

There had been an appalling lack of security leading to the room, but Hunt had assured Dana that it was Azibo's intent that they be there to witness the sacrifice. How Hunt knew this, she could not say, but this thought did not hearten Dana. If Azibo wanted them there, then she'd be prepared for them. They were unarmed with no plan of attack or clear way of escape. But, not once did Dana consider turning away from Hunt. She would follow this through regardless of what might transpire in their relationship after. That was, assuming, they exited the room alive.

"We're here," said Hunt as he marched toward the center of the room, Dana, Thorpe, and Badrani Azibo, trailing ten steps behind. "I know you don't want to do this."

Nishati Azibo offered a hint of a grin. "And you know, Huntington, that I must."

"Nah. I know you've convinced yourself that you must. Or maybe Anascoreth convinced you. But you don't have to do this."

Azibo took one step forward, her eyes locked on Hunt. There was no surprise, no indication that she was shocked that he'd been freed from the possession. "The boy was conceived specifically for this purpose. It is through the blood of my offspring that I will be granted the power needed to guide Botma from poverty and instability."

"At what cost, Nishati? You've already lost one child. Isn't that too much already?"

"At any cost, Huntington. That's something I doubt an American would understand."

Hunt actually chuckled. "Obviously, you have a twisted impression of America. Let me give you a clue, I'm here right now, willing to risk everything to save your child. Your child, Nishati, not mine. It's a shame you can't say the same."

Azibo exploded in fury. "How dare you accuse me of indifference! How dare you stand there smug and arrogant condemning me for my heart-wrenching sacrifice! You've never born the responsibility of a nation. You've never known a burden such as this!"

"And what of that nation?" asked Badrani as he stepped to beside Hunt. "In the time since you sacrificed your daughter has Botma prospered? Have your raids on villages brought you prosperity? Do the people of this land praise the name of Nishati Azibo?"

To Dana's surprise, Azibo's eyes went momentarily wide. Somehow, it seemed she hadn't realized she was in the presence of her father. Their eyes locked on one another. Palpable hate flowed in both directions. "The land, father, is poised for greatness. My military is strong. Monies I have raised through unconventional endeavors have allowed me to seed foreign pockets and purchase international support."

"Unconventional endeavors? Selling our little girls into the sex trade? Using our banking system to launder money from drug cartels? Oh, I may have been locked away, but I know of your unconventional endeavors and find you despicable."

"Enough!" shouted Azibo. "Enough!" She paused, surveying the tiny group, eyes meeting each person in the room. And when she spoke again, it was as if a calming cloud had settled over her, for her voice was even and unemotional, though still there was sentiment in the words. "I accept that none of you understand the greater good. None of you can fully conceive of the many worlds that exist behind this world. Each so called atrocity has its purpose. Each act is one of greater design. And though, yes, these grieve me as a woman and as a mother, I rejoice as a leader. For I know that soon little Botma will stand secure and formidable on the world stage no longer subject to the whims of its neighbors. And for that, I am willing to risk all."

She paused, glancing back at her struggling child. A single tear escaped her left eye, zigzagging down her cheek to then moisten her fine silk robe. "You each will take part in the ceremony, in the form of witnesses." Again, turning to stare directly at the foursome, she then spoke in some long forgotten tongue, her eyes burrowing into each person as if she stared at that individual alone. Her voice was melodic, mesmerizing, and seemed to surround them as if projected from numerous points about the room. No. That was wrong. The voice wasn't coming from without, but from within Dana's own skull. She felt something akin to a gentle but frigid breeze brush past her face, after which she tried to turn and flee, but found that she'd been completely immobilized. She could move nothing, not even the tiniest twitch of a finger.

Chapter Forty-Three

Botma Africa

Nanji didn't feel good about this day. He'd been relieved of duty, told to retreat to his barracks as a more senior man would guard Tahir Azibo during his shift. Things had not been the same with Tahir since the boy's failed escape attempt. Tahir had been very sullen and quiet, refusing to talk with Nanji. At random times, additional guards had been stationed about his room. And Tahir could not brave to look directly onto his mother's face without weeping uncontrollably. As to Nishati Azibo, she behaved alternately tender and distant, angry and nurturing, toward her son. Tahir responded to none of these, but only pouted, arms crossed, head down, in his mother's presence.

To Nanji, Azibo was warm, almost motherly, in a way he'd never seen her behave with Tahir. She would whisper little tales in his ear, pat him on the head, sometimes she'd even offer candy. And though Nanji would always accept this, he never ate any of it. This was the devil's treat. He wanted none of it.

Nanji was terrified of the repercussions should he be found outside of the barracks when he'd been ordered to remain, but he had to find out what was happening with Tahir. He just had a sense that something was wrong, that Tahir needed him. They were friends now, or, as close to a friend that Nanji could know. Tahir had even been kind enough to ask his mother where Nanji's brother was being held. Surprisingly, she'd asked a man to look into it and so Nanji learned that Diallo was housed in a center just outside of Mirembe where he would remain until he was old enough to join the armed forces. He was safe and relatively well cared for. Nanji planned to take him from the place before they turned him into a killer.

Nanji walked through the winding corridor toward Tahir's room as if he belonged there: back straight, rifle resting on his right shoulder, full uniform. At least if he was seen while acting natural, he could claim that he thought he was supposed to return to post. If he snuck about like a criminal there would be no denying that he was disobeying orders.

His heart beat quickened with every turn along the way. He was certain that he'd encounter a superior officer and that he'd be executed. Several times, he paused, nearly turning back. He was such a coward. Tahir deserved a better friend than Nanji. If ever confronted with true resistance, certainly Nanji would run weeping from the room. Likely, he'd pee his pants. He was a poor soldier indeed.

Nanji encountered no guards along the way.

This was unsettling. He could think of no time since arriving at this locale that he'd walked the corridors without encountering someone. True, the contingent was small, just a handful of soldiers. Nishati Azibo didn't like to draw attention to her location by heightening the military presence when she was in residence. But still, Nanji should have seen someone by this point.

Glancing through a narrow arched window, Nanji peered out onto the grounds. Yes. The grounds were patrolled. In fact, it seemed extra personnel had been added to the exterior detail. From this single vantage, he could see three men patrolling the grounds. Certainly there were others beyond his view. This explained the lack of traffic within the corridors.

But, why?

Something had changed. There was some reason for the reconfiguration.

And Nanji. Why was he confined to barracks? He'd done nothing wrong. Until now.

And on the night of Tahir's attempted escape.

Did they know that he'd been aware of Tahir's flight? Was it possible that they'd known all along but had withheld punishment till a better time?

Again, Nanji nearly turned to run back to the safety of the barracks, but he was nearly to Tahir's room. He should at least check on the boy, make sure he was alright. He'd pretend to have left something in the room. Maybe his shift rotation. He'd claim he'd left his shift rotation in the room and had come back to find it.

But, there was no need for lies or excuses. No guard stood before the door. And upon entry Nanji found the room to be empty. Tahir was gone and Nanji had a terrible feeling building in the base of his gut.

Chapter Forty-Four

Botma Africa

Nishati Azibo had cast some sort of hypnotic spell over Hunt's companions, that much was evident. All three stood motionless, eyes blank and unblinking, jaws slack. Hunt didn't know how he'd been spared just like he didn't know how he'd known that Azibo was at that specific time preparing Tahir for sacrifice, or the most direct route through the winding corridors to this chamber. He just knew. Some residual effect of the locust, he supposed.

Azibo either didn't realize or didn't care that Hunt was unaffected as she turned toward the altar, chanting in that ancient tongue he'd heard so frequently of late. Her voice rose in volume in an attempt to speak over her son's frantic cries. There was a quiver in her tone as she raised the dagger above her head.

"Nishati, there are other ways to help your country," said Hunt, stepping forward.

"No, Huntington. It would take decades to bring Botma into the modern world. With the help of Anascoreth, we can achieve it in months." She did not seem surprised that he'd been unaffected by her spell.

"Nishati, he's your own kid!"

"Stop! Just, will you please stop!" she cried, and then added something in another tongue.

At this, both lions rose, walking casually to before Hunt, their vacant eyes set in his direction. They were possessed, he knew. Just as he had been. The mark of Anascoreth was upon their brows. The blue scorpions pulsed and bubbled, like grotesque tumors on the regal best's foreheads. He stopped walking, eying them warily. Neither seemed poised to attack, but Hunt knew that if he tried to intervene, they'd be upon him in a second's time.

"Think, Nishati! Just think before you do this!"

"Do you not understand that I've thought of this every day of his life, Huntington? Do you not understand how I've agonized? Now, enough! Please! Enough!"

One of the lions stepped closer, now standing less than five feet before Hunt, staring up at him, awaiting a command. The thing's head was nearly as large as Hunt's torso, the paws the size of a dinner plate. Those claws could shred him in two with one fierce swipe. Hunt remained silent. He'd pushed the woman as far as he could. Tears streamed down her face, the dagger wavered in her upraised hands. Azibo was a beast, a sorceress, a ruthless dictator, the murderer of thousands of her own people, but she was also a mother, and though she was guilty of so many hideous atrocities, still she hesitated. Hunt could do no more. The lion would attack if he said another word. He could only hope that something he'd already said, or even plain old motherly instinct, would prevent her from taking the boy's life.

"Mommy," cried Tahir, for what had to be the hundredth time. "Mommy, please don't. I'll be good, Mommy. I'll be good!"

The boy's cries had become a constant backdrop to the scene, nearly fading into background noise due to their unending persistency, but now it was clear that Nishati Azibo heard every syllable, was affected by every utterance. Again, her hand wavered and shook. It seemed the dagger nearly slipped from her grasp. Her voice cracked as she chanted her dreadful litany.

The boy screamed.

Azibo chanted.

The blade wavered but did not descend.

Nishati glanced toward Hunt, her eyes wide with, what? Regret? Uncertainty? Fright? Slowly, as not to alert the lions, Hunt moved his head first left and then right as he mouthed the words, "No, Nishati. No."

Still the blade wavered. Still the boy screamed. Still Azibo's eyes were locked on Hunt. "No, Nishati."

She offered the slightest nod. Hunt wasn't sure if this was her assent to him that she would forgo the sacrifice or her final confirmation that she would proceed. Her arms bent at the elbows, it seemed she might lower the blade. Still, her intent was unclear. A fresh flood of tears washed over her cheeks. She said something, but Hunt couldn't distinguish the words. He wasn't even sure if it had been English or the other, more ancient, tongue.

And then there was a blast of gunfire.

Chapter Forty-Five

Botma Africa

Nanji was terrified as he stood in the doorway trying not to hyperventilate. Not only was the she-devil in the room, but there were two lions as well. Nanji had seen these before. Often they accompanied Nishati Azibo on what he assumed were her most delicate tasks. She had done something to them, transfixed them as she had Rafiki, the young guard she'd coaxed into suicide when Nanji had first met the woman. There were other people as well, strangers to Nanji, of whom he knew nothing. One of them wore a Botmain military uniform just like Nanji's. It did not fit him well and Nanji deduced by the man's bruised and battered state that he was likely a prisoner and not a soldier. Besides, the uniform did not fit him well. Clearly, the man did not belong.

Tahir was tied to the altar and wrestled against his binds, likely tightening the knots all the more through his struggles. Nanji had been able to hear his terrified cries even as he made his way up the corridor and toward this devil's room.

No one saw Nanji at the doorway. All human eyes were fixed on the altar. As to the lions, they were positioned in front of the uniformed man. Nanji assumed the she-devil feared this man might try to prevent the murder of her child and so ordered the beasts to guard him.

There was an exchange of words, but Nanji could make out little of it as Tahir's frantic cries echoed about the space. The she-devil turned, chanting, a dagger raised high as she prepared to thrust it into Tahir's heart.

Nanji hefted his weapon. Why did it feel so heavy? It was as if twenty pounds had been added to the weight of the thing. Nanji struggled to aim. His nervous jerks and shudders caused the gun to slip from its position at his shoulder. Twice, he nearly dropped the thing. It seemed his hands did not wish to obey the commands from his brain.

Finally, he had settled the weapon in place. The she-devil was in his sights. All he needed to do was to squeeze the trigger. Even if his aim was less than true, a spray of automatic gunfire would make up for his short-comings. Certainly at least one bullet would find the demoness. All it would take was one bullet.

But, what if he missed?

What if all of the bullets went astray? What if the gun jammed? What if Azibo moved, or worse, what if one of the others moved into the line of fire?

Coward!

He was a coward!

Was this not the moment he'd dreamt of? Was this not the moment he'd awaited since that day so many months—so many lifetimes—ago when he'd arrived home to find Azibo's men in his home?

But, Nanji was a coward. He would always be a coward.

They'd made him kill his parents.

His, father. They'd made him kill his father.

They'd made him kill his mother.

No. Not they.

She.

Azibo.

The she-devil.

She made Nanji kill his own blood.

And still he was too cowardly to kill Azibo.

Too cowardly to deserve even the simple breath of life.

But, then, he wasn't was he?

How was it that he only now realized that he was, even now, in the process of firing the weapon?

Chapter Forty-Six

Botma Africa

Dana was abruptly free of the mind fog and was thrust immediately into chaos. Nishati Azibo pitched forward, landing on her son's bound and prone form before spilling onto the cold stone floor limp and unmoving. One of the lions bounded toward the young soldier at the doorway—he couldn't be any more than ten years-old—while the other moved in the direction of the altar.

The child soldier stood, eyes wide, and terrified, the automatic weapon held loose, not even lifted to aim or shoot.

Dana acted instinctively, lunging toward the beast with a howling scream, catching its tail, but only just barely. The lion turned, teeth bared, now charging at Dana who could not maintain her hold. It was then that Jonathan struck the beast with a roundhouse kick, connecting in the midst of the heavy mane just behind the left ear.

The beast turned toward this new attacker with a frustrated howl. Lions don't howl, but this was no ordinary lion. It was possessed as had been Hunt and its movements and sounds were more similar to what she had witnessed in her husband than in any lion she'd ever seen. The beast hissed now as it lunged toward Jonathan.

Regaining her footing, Dana kicked it in its underbelly.

The thing turned, now rearing up on its hind legs as it swiped at Dana. She danced away screaming, "Shoot it! Shoot it!"

But still the boy soldier stood transfixed. He'd raised his gun to a firing position but seemed too terrified to fire. Perhaps he was afraid of hitting either she or Jonathan. But, they couldn't continue to avoid the fangs and claws for long. The more agitated the beast became, the more dangerous it would be.

Jonathan kicked, sharp and quick at the left rear knee joint. The beast howled in fury.

Dana followed up with a jab to the right flank.

Jonathan kicked it in the groin.

Dana noted movement. It was Badrani Azibo. He'd made his way to the boy soldier.

The lion turned toward Dana, sudden and fierce. She was too close. The thing was upon her. There was the *rat-a-tat-tat* of automatic gunfire. The lion struck Dana full on sending her to the floor.

Chapter Forty-Seven

Botma Africa

Hunt sprinted toward the altar in pursuit of the lion. It had turned, bounding away the instant Nishati Azibo was shot. Hunt was unarmed and had no means of battling the beast. Maybe he could try to distract it, perhaps lead it from the room. Something. The one thing he knew was that he would do anything to keep it away from the still-bound Tahir. The boy was defenseless.

Tahir was the target. That was a definite. The beast ignored Nishati Azibo's prone form moving directly for the altar.

Hunt leaped, landing on the lion's back. The thing was solid, its musculature like steel coils beneath the sleek sable coat. The beast reared with a near-human screech attempting to throw Hunt to the floor as he clasped the dark brown mane with both fists, clinging for his life. The lion reared again, emitting a strange warbling call, and then, failing to loose the troublesome Hunt, bucked like a rodeo bull.

Still, Hunt clung to the mane. It was coarse and stiff, almost prickly. He wrapped the long hairs once around his fingers in an effort to secure his grip as the beast pitched and reared. It was a desperate maneuver. He would not be able to maintain this position for more than a few seconds, but saw no other options. He squeezed his legs tight against the lion's torso, attempting to stabilize his position, but the rearing twisting form was too volatile, and he couldn't maintain one posture for more than an instant.

The beast bounced and shook its great head with a vicious cackle unlike any Hunt had heard on earth. Hunt was bounced free of the lion's back and managed to land on his feet and to the creature's right. Now, unseated, he still clasped the mane, but was standing alongside the frantic creature.

The lion twisted and snarled, snapping at Hunt, but Hunt's hold on the mane restricted its range of motion. He slipped his left leg under and behind the lion's right rear leg while simultaneously yanking right with all his might. The tangled legs caused the lion to lose its footing. Both man and beast tumbled to the floor. The lion landed on Hunt nearly crushing him with its massive weight, but Hunt used his leverage to maintain the momentum causing the screeching, thrashing beast to roll over him and onto the floor.

Once again he was astride the animal, though the lion had yet to regain its footing and so was in an awkward position, legs splayed on the floor as it shifted and adjusted in an attempt to rise. Hunt saw his opportunity and decided to take the gamble. Leaping away from the beast, he scrambled toward the form of Nishati Azibo.

The lion nearly bounded to all fours, shaking its great main, and emitting a great rumble from within its throat. Hunt had only just reached the inert form when the beast lunged. Snatching the fallen dagger from Nishati's side, Hunt rolled left and jabbed upward. The blade struck the lion at the base of the jaw. Hunt pulled back and jabbed again even as one of the great claws raked his left arm.

The second stab bit deep into the lion's throat. Despite the searing pain in his arm, Hunt twisted the blade, pulling from right to left, severing arteries. Blood sprayed across his face, but still he wrenched the blade further yet.

The beast reared up with a mighty roar, took three wobbling steps, and then fell before the altar. It shuttered, raised its massive head, the golden eyes locking on Hunt, not in anger or insanity, but something much more subtle, possibly understanding if such could be the case in such a creature. It was then that the thin thread of life snapped and the creature went limp, spilling to the floor in a graceless tumble.

Hunt shifted into a sitting position, still panting from the exertion. His arm screamed in pain. There was plenty of blood. But, he was able to lift it—with difficulty. This was a good sign, he supposed. Apparently his muscles and tendons were intact. Likely there was only superficial damage.

There was a commotion at the opposite end of the room, a spray of gunfire. Instinctively, Hunt ducked. Turning toward the sound, Hunt almost missed seeing the lion's mouth jiggle. Just a bit of a shake. Then a little more of a twitch. A long bony leg extended from within, and then another. Hunt gaped in horror as a great scorpion, roughly the size of a football, deep blue and covered in thick streaming slime and blood scrambled from the dead lion's mouth, racing toward him with malignant purpose.

Chapter Forty-Eight

Botma Africa

Nanji had done it. He had slain the she-devil. His aim had been true. She had danced a death's dance as the bullets ripped through her form and then she'd spilled forward, first across the altar and then to the floor. He had done it. He had really done it!

And now he thought he might be sick to his stomach.

But it was then he saw the lion and all aftereffects were cast aside as survival instinct kicked in. Where seconds before the two beasts had sat as still as statues, now one bounded toward the altar while its companion raced toward Nanji with a Satan's sneer on its massive face.

The people were in motion as well. One chasing the altar-bound beast, two others moving to distract the one intent on Nanji. They actually engaged the beast, kicking it, jabbing at it, though neither was armed. What could they be thinking? Did they wish for death?

"Shoot, son. Shoot!" came a voice from Nanji's left. "They can't keep that up for long. Shoot."

It was one of the slaves. Nanji had seen him amongst the others. He was old, and, somehow Nanji suspected, wise. "But I might hit one of the people!"

"If you don't take down that lion they're both dead anyway. Raise your gun, son. Fire!"

With quivering hands, Nanji raised his gun. The lion was crouching to pounce, the woman the obvious target.

Nanji aimed.

"Now, son!"

And squeezed the trigger.

Chapter Forty-Nine

Botma Africa

Hunt scooted back in a frantic scramble as the scorpion scurried forward with amazing speed. The tail was identical to the images of Azibo's god, Anascoreth, in that a serpent's head capped the tail instead of a barb.

The serpent head shot forward, snapping as it did so, the fangs dripping thick golden venom that sizzled and popped, the red-orange eyes ablaze with the fires of hell.

Hunt pulled back a foot just in time to avoid the strike.

Another thrust.

Another near miss.

Hunt twisted, found his footing, rose, sprinted. The snapping hissing impossibility followed in pursuit. Hunt heard multiple voices. It seemed they originated from within the creature, bouncing around from within, hollering, screeching, taunting.

The beast was much faster than Hunt.

He leaped, avoiding a strike and then zigzagged right, left, right. Still he heard the tumbling voices, one upon another upon another. None that he could understand, but still he knew that there was madness in each. He'd hosted such voices within his own skull until less than an hour ago.

Spinning, he kicked the scorpion-thing like a football. Though his effort failed to move the creature any great distance. It had grown in these few moments of chase, now being the size of a microwave oven and nearly twice as heavy. His punt was a feeble effort at best.

Hunt sprinted toward the large double fireplace. A part of him cried that this creature was some sort of spiritual being that the laws of physics and nature wouldn't apply to it. But another part of him argued that even so, it currently inhabited this physical world and had clothed itself in flesh. Perhaps the thing could be killed. Or, if not killed, at least stopped.

He skipped sideways, avoiding another thrust as the still-growing demon was once again upon him. The voices shouted overlapping insanities from within.

Again, he tried to kick it, but this time it was prepared and wrapped its six limbs about his shin and calf, hugging him in a vice-like clamp. Hunt snatched the tail, just below the snapping, hissing viper-head, as it thrust forward to strike.

It was cold to the touch.

That same searing cold he'd felt in his own body as the scorpion spirit invaded him. He could feel his flesh freeze, the beginnings of frostbite already moving through his palm. Still, he hobbled forward, battling the thrashing tail. The thing's strength was amazing and Hunt knew that in a prolonged battle the demon would be victorious.

Hunt tumbled forward, just short of the fireplaces, and crawled the last few feet in an awkward shuffle, fighting the snapping drooling tail, pushing the spindly legs back as they sought to break his bones with the thing's amazing strength.

Reaching into the blaze with his free hand, heedless of the flames, he withdrew a burning log about two inches in diameter and half the length of a baseball bat. He jammed it into the thing's scorpion head.

And pressed.

And twisted.

Digging deeper. Deeper.

The scorpion's tough outer shell began to sizzle, the legs jittered, the voices screeched and sang. Abruptly, he pulled the flaming log away and jammed it into the serpent head's open mouth.

There was a piercing screech and then the head melted away like ice cream on a summer sidewalk. Some of the liquid splashed onto Hunt's wrist before he could pull away and immediately his skin blistered and popped.

The scorpion's legs released their hold with a reluctant jitter and Hunt kicked the foul beast into the roaring flames of the fireplace where the remains burst and sizzled.

Turning, Hunt finally had an opportunity to survey the room. Badrani Azibo and a young guard were by the door. The boy soldier had his weapon trained on the second lion which was bloodied and still. Dana was trapped beneath the apparently lifeless beast and Thorpe was attempting to roll the creature off of her.

Snatching a burning log from the second fireplace, Hunt marched toward the scene. He didn't know if the scorpions were manifestations of Anascoreth himself or simply servants of a like kind, but he knew the danger they presented. "Dana, get away from that thing."

"Well, that is the plan, Hunt," said Dana with an exasperated sigh.

Both Dana and Thorpe gave a final heave and the lion rolled over. Dana scrambled to her feet.

"You okay, there?" asked Thorpe of Hunt. "Seems you had a bit of a tiff over there."

"Physically, yeah. Dana. Stand clear of that thing." He waved his arm indicating she should move away from the lion. There was no time for explanations.

"It's dead, Hunt." She met his gaze, her expression revealing that she hoped for something from him, likely an emotional response.

Hunt nodded. "The lion's dead. Not the thing inside of it. Move."

It seemed Dana was about to say something further when the dead beast's mouth jerked open and a football-sized scorpion scrambled out.

"Dear, God," gasped Thorpe as Hunt jabbed the thing with the flames, twisting, pressing. The scorpion sizzled and squirmed, emitting a piercing cry before finally disintegrating into a puddle of blue-red goo.

All was silent for several seconds until Hunt noticed the boy soldier. He had walked past them unseen as Hunt dealt with the beast and now stood before Nishati Azibo's inert form, his gun aimed at her head.

Hunt turned, dropping the flaming wood and moving toward the boy. Tahir Azibo was still strapped to the altar. He simply stared silently at the kid. It almost seemed he was afraid that the boy wouldn't go through with it if Tahir broke his concentration.

"Hey," said Hunt. "You don't need to do that."

But, the boy ignored him. He was speaking to Azibo. "You turned me into a killer. You made me kill my parents. You turned me into a killer. You made me kill my parents." Over and over, he repeated the mantra.

"Kid," said Hunt once he was within reach of the boy. "Really, you don't have to do this."

"She's still alive," he said, his gaze never leaving Azibo.

Hunt glanced down at the prone form. The boy was right. Her breathing was shallow, she'd lost a lot of blood, but at least for the moment she was alive.

Hunt glanced up at Tahir. Their eyes met. The boy was crying, his emotions confused and unyielding. Who could imagine what this poor child felt in this moment? "You've done a good job here today. You saved us all. Leave it at that."

"But, she's still alive. She's a devil and she's still alive."

"And she's in no shape to do anyone any harm. Put down the gun, son." It was Badrani Azibo. He'd stepped up to beside the boy, though his gaze was fixed on his bleeding daughter. He made no move to give her aid.

"She made me kill my parents."

"I know," said Badrani. "The woman's a monster."

"I can do it. I'm not a coward. I can do it."

Hunt placed his palm on the boy's shoulder. "You've already proven your bravery today. Now it's time to show wisdom and compassion. Sometimes it takes more guts to step away than it does to fire the gun."

The soldier boy looked as though he might protest but Badrani interjected, "He's right, son. Sometimes remaining still and allowing events to unfold naturally is the bravest thing a person can do."

The boy looked back toward Hunt who nodded his agreement. Hunt then turned toward the altar, forcing a smile as his gaze settled on Tahir. He bent to hug the frantic child, leaving the child-soldier to his decision.

Epilogue

Washington DC

"Where's the boy?" asked Colonel James "Lucky" Lindell.

"With his father," said Hunt from his seat on Lindell's plush leather couch. The office was both lavish and utilitarian, upscale in furniture and tone, functional and ordered in every aspect.

"With Tahir Ubora. You were sent there to retrieve the boy from Ubora and return him to Nishati Azibo."

Hunt shook his head as he eyed his former mentor. In truth, the situation wasn't ideal, Hunt would rather the boy be put in the care of his grandfather, but Ubora was the legitimate parent and, Hunt believed, actually showed a genuine love for the boy. "Not going down that road, Colonel. You know the circumstances. Don't try to twist this thing into something it's not."

Lindell rose from behind his mahogany desk and strolled around it to square himself before Hunt. "Our goal was to stabilize Azibo's position and to undermine Ubora's. Instead, Ubora has now assumed leadership in Botma and Azibo is comatose, shot by one of her own men, and hidden away by Ubora."

Hunt rose, meeting Lindell's gaze. For the first time in Hunt's memory the colonel looked his fifty-one years. His steel gray eyes were clear but wary, his nostrils flared like those of a cornered beast. "Let's get this straight," said Hunt. "My only goal in going to Botma was to get that kid to safety. Period. I wasn't concerned with the U.S. position, I could give a damn about those diamonds, and for the record, Ubora is far from ideal, but at least he has a conscience. Nishati Azibo, God help us if she ever regains power. And, FYI, the elder Azibo is advising. The man's been through a lot, but he has a sharp mind. He'll be an asset."

"I'm not concerned with the state of his mind, or what you think he has to offer. You don't know the backroom politics, Sergeant."

"I'm not a sergeant anymore and you're not my commanding officer. You got that?" Hunt's tone was harsh, his tone final.

"All I was saying is that there are other factors beyond those of which you're aware."

Hunt began to pace, rubbing his forehead where the scorpion image resided. "Yeah. Factors. Let me tell you about factors. Let's talk Iraq. They did things to me in Botma, Colonel, things you would never believe even if I showed you footage of it. But, the end result is that I have my memory back." Here, Hunt paused, glaring into Lindell's cold gray eyes. They betrayed nothing. "Yeah. My complete memory. Everything. Clear as a crystal ball. You ordered the Iraq mission, Colonel. But, you had no authorization. You would have faced charges if word got out about what you were trying to pull off. Political assassinations are a dicey business, after all. But, you convinced me of the need. Like an idiot I trusted you. My men knew nothing of our true mission. I kept them in the dark—again, on your orders. But, you didn't want loose ends. And so you ordered Rodriguez to pull the men back as I entered the target area, leaving me no back-up. You wanted me dead, Colonel. You wanted me to do your dirty work and then you wanted me dead. Thing is, everything went sideways. You didn't know about that child suicide bomber. She'd been sent there to eliminate the same man. I was forced to shoot her before she detonated in a public area, killing not only the target, but possibly dozens of others. As it was, I was severely injured and two of my men died. The two that, once they realized what Rodriguez was doing, came back. The two that refused to abandon me."

Here, Hunt paused, turning, and then continued to pace. "Some of the rest is guesswork, but my take is that you fed my surviving men a cover story. They were to testify that it was an unauthorized mission, that I was drunk, acting with no authority, and so got a child and two of my men killed. You put pressure on them, telling them that they'd be deep sixed if they revealed the truth. It turns out I survived, but had amnesia, no memory of those events at all. So, you let things ride. You kept tabs on me to make sure my memory wasn't coming back. I wouldn't doubt that you even encouraged the doc to give me a high dose of Oxycontin. I'm sure my addiction, in addition to my muddled brain, helped you sleep at night. As to Botma, I'm guessing that once again, you hoped I'd be killed. Here I was, depressed about my failed marriage, addicted to painkillers, in no shape to be of any good to anyone, and you coerce me into going into a no-win scenario. My memory was starting to return. Not a lot, but fragments. You were probably sweating it. And so you used a child to lure me in. You knew the guilt I carried over the death of that little girl in Iraq. You knew I couldn't stand by if I thought I could save a child."

Lindell remained silent as Hunt stepped to within inches of him. "It took me a little while to figure Corky out, though. Why would you send her? She was a wrench in your plan. But, you didn't want her there, did you? She figured it all out and forced you to send her to Botma as back-up. I saw her computer, Colonel. She's got enough to sink you. And I'm sure she has it backed up somewhere safe where you'll never get to it."

With this, Hunt turned, moving across the spacious office and toward the doorway.

"What now?" asked Lindell.

Hunt paused, his hand on the door handle. "Now nothing," he said. "I have no desire to take you down. I don't have it in me for a prolonged battle, a trial, press coverage. Nah. I walk away, Colonel. I've got a lot to think about. Some crazy stuff happened in Botma. Stuff I can't explain. My marriage is a train wreck. I don't even know who I am any more. I just want all of this behind me."

"So, that's it. No retribution? That hardly makes sense."

Hunt smiled. "Yeah, to you it wouldn't make sense. Let me put it this way, you leave me alone, I leave you alone. I've got evidence that I've collected and I've got a copy of Corky's files. I don't want to ever use them. I keep them only for insurance. Now, get out of my life, Colonel."

Hunt exited the office and walked directly across the hall to Corky's, much smaller, office space. He did not knock before entering. "One question," he said without preamble. "How long did you know?"

Corky looked up from her computer, meeting Hunt's gaze. "What?"

"You know what I'm talking about, Cork? How long did you know and when were you planning on telling me?"

Corky swallowed, but made no move to respond.

"Okay," said Hunt. "That's what I thought."

He turned, exiting without another word.

***

Dana stared across the table at Hunt. He'd regained some of his weight, though he still seemed worn and weary. She wasn't sure if he'd ever achieve his former physique. His time in confinement had played horrors on his system. There was still a gray smudge on his forehead, the remnants of Anascoreth. If one would look closely it would be obvious as the shape of a scorpion. It was still bitter cold to the touch, though Hunt claimed he didn't notice this unless he touched it with his fingers. It had not moved, had shown no signs of life. Hunt claimed that he was convinced the thing was gone from him, that this was only a footprint left behind. But then, she wasn't quite sure he believed his own claims.

The waiter, a balding man with a broad grin and an Italian accent, brought Hunt a cola and refilled Dana's wineglass. He then left the two alone. "I understand the boy soldier, the one that shot Nishati Azibo has been reunited with his brother."

Hunt nodded, though his gaze was far and away. "The two boys are living with relatives."

Dana attempted to meet his elusive gaze. "We really haven't talked much about what happened in Botma. I'm speaking of the supernatural aspects."

Hunt nodded, but remained silent, remote, unemotional, showing no signs of affection or desire. Dana was reminded of Nishati Azibo. She'd said there was a savage distance between Dana and Hunt. Maybe so. Dana wondered if it was a gap that could ever be bridged.

"Jonathan believes that the locust amulet really does originate with the biblical plague. He said it's the only thing that makes sense, considering its rather fantastic properties."

"Hooray for Jonathan," said Hunt. He then sipped his cola.

"He said it's lifeless now. It's almost as if it was meant for the single purpose of freeing you from whatever it was that infected you."

Here, Hunt sighed, meeting her gaze. "Dana, you know I've never given this mumbo-jumbo stuff much stock. And I don't know exactly what happened to me in Botma, but I'd be an idiot if I didn't admit that there are things in this world beyond our grasp." He took another sip of cola and then offered a weak and pretending smile. "Thorpe's probably right. The locust performed whatever duty it was supposed to perform and now it's gone inert. He could probably sell it on the black market for a nice profit."

"Hunt, he won't do that. Not after what happened." Dana dipped a hand into her purse, withdrawing the amulet and setting it before Hunt. "In fact, we both agree that you should have it. The thing, whatever it truly is, was obviously meant for you."

Hunt grunted, but did not reach for the necklace. "What happened in Botma, Dana? Was I truly possessed by crazed spirits? In some insane way I hope I was. Because then at least I don't have to live with the fact that I tried to kill you."

She reached across the table, taking his left hand in her right. "Hunt, you're not to blame. There was nothing of you left when the attack occurred. Not one thing I recognized as the man I love. My God, Hunt, you barely appeared human."

Using his free hand, Hunt lightly rubbed his forehead, directly on the scorpion image. It seemed an unconscious move. "If there was nothing left of the real me, then how am I here now?"

Dana shook her head. "I don't know. The locust, I suppose. It somehow brought you back. Maybe you were buried in there somewhere, maybe, like you've told me, the spirits tore your soul apart. Perhaps the locust knitted it back together. I have no answers, Hunt. This is all far beyond me."

"I have no answers either, Dana. Not a one. Demon possession aside, I'm finally clearheaded enough to realize that I haven't been the guy I try to believe myself to be for quite awhile." Here, he paused, gazing at the amulet, or, more importantly, avoiding Dana's gaze. "I was hiding my addiction from you. And that means I wasn't being loyal to you. If a man is a man at all, he should be loyal to those he loves."

Dana squeezed his hand. "You're too hard on yourself. Everyone occasionally strays from the person they seek to be. That's why life is called a journey. Sometimes we veer away from the main thoroughfare. The true test is whether we find our way back to our intended course. Besides, there are other types of answers as well, other types of questions." She attempted a grin, with only marginal success.

"Yeah? Meaning what?"

"Questions about us. About our relationship going forward." Dana wasn't entirely sure she was ready to resume an intimate relationship but also realized that perhaps the only way to prepare was to put herself in that position.

Hunt withdrew her hand from his and reached for his cola, lifting it to his lips and drinking deep before speaking. "I'm a mess, Dana. A complete basket case. I don't know if it would be healthy for you to resume a relationship with me. You're dealing with issues of your own."

Dana opened her mouth to assure him that this wasn't the case, but he waved her off.

"No. Let me say this. I'm a whole person for the first time since you've known me. I have all of my memories. I'm not addicted to anything. I'm clean. But with those memories come a hell of a lot of baggage. Lucky Lindell was like a father and a brother combined. I loved him like family. I trusted him to my very core. And he betrayed me with barely a thought. Corky was my close friend. At one point she'd been my lover. There was a time when we shared everything. She knew about this, Dana. She knew what Lucky had done and she didn't tell me. Yeah, she helped me in the end. And maybe she was just gathering evidence before telling me what she'd learned, but maybe not. And the surviving members of my unit, they testified against me. They lied, Dana, caved to Lucky's pressure to save their own skins. Pile all of that on top of the fact that I went to Africa and ended up possessed by demons. And now you, my wife, who sent me packing when all I wanted to do was be there for you, wants to talk about our relationship going forward."

"Hunt, if now is not a good time…"

"When would be a good time? Tomorrow? A year from now? When will I have this sorted out? When will I ever be able to trust again? Don't you understand? The people closest to me in this world have all betrayed me at some level. And that includes you."

They stared at each other for several moments before Dana finally spoke. It was an effort to do so. Her voice felt small and distant. Her mind was spinning, trying to think of something soothing to say to Hunt, but all she came up with was, "So, where does that leave us?"

Hunt stared at her for several moments, studying her, seemingly memorizing her every contour. Finally, he leaned forward on his elbows, offering as much intimacy as the table separating them would allow. "I love you, Dana. Always will."

"And?" she asked.

Hunt shrugged. "And, I don't know. I guess we try to make whatever sense we can of all that's happened and go from there."

Dana took his hand, squeezed, nodded, and then wiped a tear from her cheek.

www.ingramcontent.com/pod-product-compliance
Lightning Source LLC
Chambersburg PA
CBHW050550260626
47157CB00002B/501